Praise for

ACROSS THE
ENDLESS RIVER

Thad Carhart

Across the Endless River

A dual citizen of the United States and Ireland, Thad Carhart lives in Paris with his wife, the photographer Simo Neri, and their two children.

www.thadcarhart.com

ACROSS THE ENDLESS RIVER

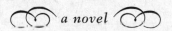

a novel

Thad Carhart

Anchor Books
A Division of Random House, Inc.
New York

FIRST ANCHOR BOOKS EDITION, OCTOBER 2010

Copyright © 2009 by T. E. Carhart

All rights reserved. Published in the United States by Anchor Books,
a division of Random House, Inc., New York. Originally published in hardcover in
the United States by Doubleday, a division of Random House, Inc.,
New York, in 2009.

Anchor Books and colophon are registered trademarks of Random House, Inc.

The Library of Congress has cataloged the Doubleday edition as follows:
Carhart, Thaddeus.
Across the endless river / Thad Carhart.—1st ed.
p. cm.
1. Charbonneau, Jean-Baptiste, 1805–1866—Fiction. I. Title.
PS3603.A7456A65 2009
813'.6—dc22   2008054443

Anchor ISBN: 978-0-7679-3173-1

Map by Mapping Specialists

www.anchorbooks.com

Printed in the United States of America
10 9 8 7 6 5 4 3 2 1

For my children, Sara and Nicolas

CONTENTS

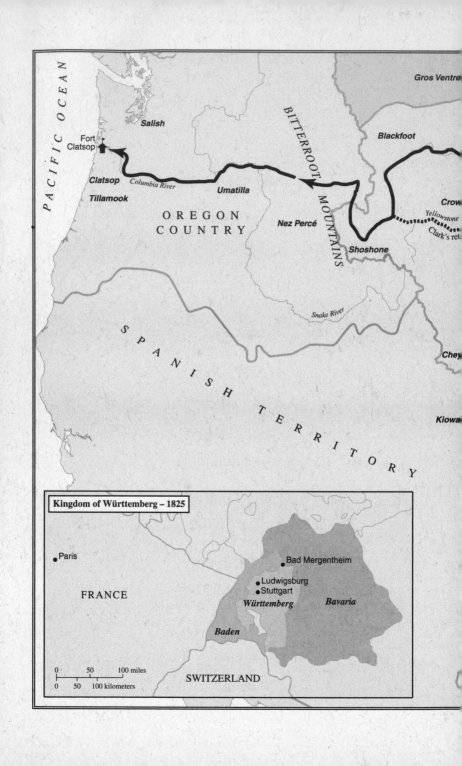

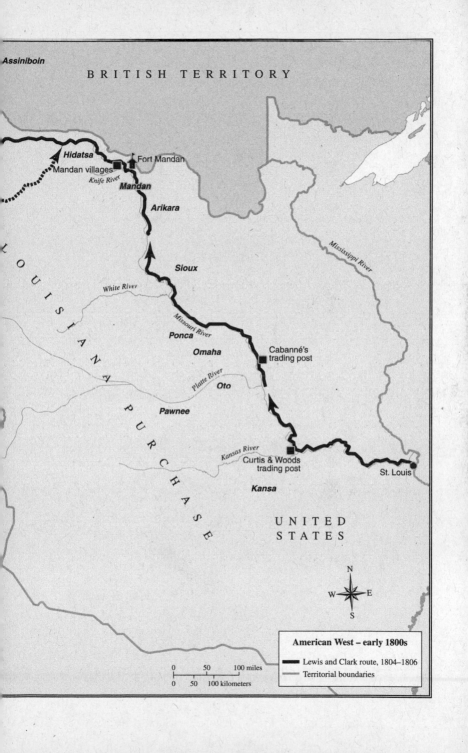

Assiniboin

BRITISH TERRITORY

Hidatsa
Mandan villages
Fort Mandan
Knife River
Mandan
Arikara
Sioux

Mississippi River

White River
Ponca
Missouri River
Omaha
Cabanné's
trading post
Platte River
Oto
Pawnee

Kansas River
Curtis & Woods
trading post
St. Louis

Kansa

UNITED
STATES

L O U I S I A N A   P U R C H A S E

N
W   E
S

American West – early 1800s

━━━ Lewis and Clark route, 1804–1806
──── Territorial boundaries

| 0 | 50 | 100 miles |
| 0 | 50 | 100 kilometers |

PART ONE

TWO PATHS

ONE

All afternoon her cries could be heard throughout the small wooden enclosure they called Fort Mandan, winter quarters for the expedition across the river from one of the tribe's villages. Two rows of huts faced each other at an oblique angle within the stockade, and from one of these the guttural shrieks emerged with a grim regularity. In and around the other huts the men kept to their business— skinning game, cutting wood, cleaning guns—but each flinched inwardly when the next cry reached his ears.

"It's her first," René Jesseaume said as he ground an ax blade on a whetstone inside his hut. "She can't be more than fifteen; it's no wonder she has been at it for so long."

"All you can do is wait," said the young soldier across from him, shaking his head. He continued to dress the elk meat they had hunted two days before.

"Maybe," Jesseaume said. He put down the ax, oiled the stone, and let himself out into the biting cold.

He crossed the central space enclosed by the palisade. On the river side the American flag snapped fiercely on its pole above the rough-hewn gatehouse, its edges already frayed. Hunched against the bitter cold wind, he approached the door to the captains' quarters opposite his hut. As he prepared to knock, the door opened and Charbonneau, the squaw's husband, emerged in a daze. His eyes were rheumy, his look distracted; he passed Jesseaume without appearing to see him. Jesseaume knocked lightly on the half-open door and let himself in to the close confines of the room.

Captain Lewis looked up from where he sat by a low pallet covered with a buffalo robe. His features were worn. The young woman lay beneath a woven blanket, her face turned away from the candle at Lewis's side. Lewis began to say something but the woman cried out suddenly, a long howl that paralyzed both men before it tapered off in a whimper. Jesseaume approached and knelt by Lewis's side.

"Captain, my wife's tribe has a potion in such cases where the labor is long and difficult." Lewis nodded for him to continue. "They crush the tail of a rattler, mix it with water, and have the woman drink it. I have never seen it fail."

At length Lewis said, "I have given her as much tincture of laudanum as I dare. I don't suppose the Mandan remedy you propose can keep nature from taking its course."

He rose and walked to the other side of the hut, its interior dank with the smell of sweat, blood, and wood smoke. On one wall a profusion of pelts, tails, snakeskins, and bones hung on the rough timber. He produced a knife from his pocket and snipped the rattles from the tip of a snakeskin. Then, setting his cup on an adjacent plank, he ladled out a quarter measure of water and returned to where Jesseaume crouched beside the woman.

"Will this serve?"

"Very well, Captain. I thank you."

Jesseaume neatly snapped two of the rattles from the tail, dropped them into the water, and broke them into tiny pieces, using his thumbnail as a pestle to the tin cup's mortar. Kneeling low to the pallet, he raised the young woman's sweat-drenched head in one hand and whispered in her ear in Mandan, "New Mother, the power of the snake will tell your body how to work. Drink this, and let the snake show your baby the way out." He held the cup to her lips then, and she raised her head to drink it, her matted hair stretched across her mouth. Gently, he pulled the strands clear and she drank the cloudy liquid, slowly at first, then in one long swallow. She lay down as if the effort of drinking was a new source of exhaustion. A short while later her body contracted, her knees rose to her chest, and she let out a shriek.

Lewis said, "I am going out for a short while. I fear our vigil may yet be long."

"It may, Captain," Jesseaume whispered. "But in case it is not, could you ask my wife to attend? She is at the gatehouse with Black Moccasin and his squaws."

A quarter of an hour later the girl they called the Bird Woman, Sacagawea, brought forth a fine and healthy boy. Charbonneau was found dozing in one of the soldiers' huts. He returned, tearful and smiling, and cradled the infant, wrapped in a blanket of fox fur, as he announced proudly to all, "We will name him Jean-Baptiste, like my grandfather."

His father called him Baptiste, but his mother called him Pompy, "Little Chief," the Shoshone name she chose to honor the tribe into which she had been born. Her knowledge of the Shoshone language was the reason Charbonneau had been hired as an interpreter for the expedition, after all. He didn't speak it, but her girlhood had been spent with the Shoshone, the Snake tribe, at the foot of the Great Stony Mountains to the west. They were the only tribe in the area with horses to trade, and the captains and their men would need horses to cross the mountains on their way west. She would be the go-between when they left the river and started to climb.

As she lay with her newborn and suckled him in those first few days, she thought of the new paths that lay ahead for her and her baby, one of which might lead to the place where she had been born. Four summers earlier she and three other Shoshone girls had been carried off during the seasonal buffalo hunt by a Hidatsa raiding party. They were after horses and young women, in that order of importance, and after killing several hunters and their squaws, including her parents, they galloped off with Sacagawea and the others tied to their mounts. They rode eastward for many days, through land that was different from anything Sacagawea had seen, broad and open, with swift rivers cut into the ground and tall grasslands in every direction. When they reached the Hidatsa and Mandan villages on the river they called the Knife, she had not seen mountains for a long time. She knew that her kinsmen could never rescue her from this powerful tribe so far away from their lands. She wondered if she could live the life that had now become hers.

In a dream her bird spirit came to her and pecked at her tongue, sharp and insistent, and she woke with the taste of blood on her teeth. Sacagawea must speak with a new tongue, the bird told her. She clutched the small obsidian figure her mother had placed in her medicine bundle, a tiny bird, all that was left to her from her first life. "I must do this," she said, over and over, in those first months of captivity. "I must do this."

Gradually she met other girls who had been stolen from their tribes in that summer when all followed the herds: a pair of Assiniboin sisters, several Crow and Gros Ventre, even a Nez Percé girl from across the Stony Mountains who wept for weeks until the brave who had captured her beat her into a watchful silence. Each of the Mandan and Hidatsa villages was far bigger than any Shoshone encampment she had known, with thirty or forty large earth-and-timber lodges grouped around a central clearing. Both tribes kept extensive fields of corn, squash, and beans. It was a dark time, a time of silences when Sacagawea understood almost nothing of the new language she would have to learn, but she noticed right away something that set these people apart from the Shoshone: no one went hungry. As large as the villages were, there was food for all.

She held Pompy close and looked in his eyes, gray-blue like his father's, and thought, *You are the only thing I can truly call my own, little one. Soon we will leave this place and you will have neither tribe nor village. You and I will be part of this band of wanderers, headed to the far edge of the land, to the place the Shoshone call The Big Lake That Smells Bad. The Pacific, the captains name it. So begins your first life, on rivers and trails. Will it always be so?*

Two months after she gave birth, Sacagawea set off up the river as part of the Corps of Discovery together with Charbonneau and her infant, strapped to her back on the cradleboard she had fashioned at Fort Mandan. Its cedar slats gave forth an aroma that pleased her with its sweetness. She felt like a mother.

There were better men than Charbonneau, she knew, but far more who were worse. A year after they were taken, he had bought Sacagawea and another Shoshone girl from the Hidatsa warrior who had captured them. They became Charbonneau's squaws, maintaining a lodge for him in the Mandan village and sharing in the women's work of the tribe. He took his pleasure with them by turns, sometimes for long hours, but never roughly like the warrior from whom she had learned what it was to lose one's body. Over time she came to accept his ways, but she was often glad that Otter Woman was there, too, when it suited Charbonneau.

She was jealously protective of her right to accompany Charbonneau on some of his trading trips along the river. He didn't often take her, but when he did she felt more alive than at any other time, delighting in the departure from her routine chores in the village and keen to see what the world looked like elsewhere. She worked doubly hard to be sure he knew her worth, gathering firewood, cleaning the trade goods, brushing the pelts, cooking his food. The presence of a woman, she knew, was by itself a message that men of all tribes understood: no fighting was intended. She took pride in her role as the companion of the white trader, a free agent who could pass from tribe to tribe without causing alarm.

In this, she realized that Charbonneau possessed a quality that the French *voyageurs* often showed but that was rare among the American and British traders: he was persistent, and infinitely patient. When, in the heat of negotiations over furs or beads, horses or guns, the chiefs would use hard language and refuse to be moved, more often than not Charbonneau knew what words to use to veer away from an ending, to hear "maybe" when the chiefs had said "no." He was like water in a stream, finding its way around a boulder, and then another and another, mindful that suppleness was more useful than speed, keeping the talk going until everyone had something he wanted. He was sometimes criticized for it by other whites, usually the English. Even the captains had called him "unreliable" or "unprincipled" at times because he would not confront an adversary directly. But his ways were more like Indian ways, and the proof of his effectiveness was that he continued to be welcome where the path had been closed to other whites by many tribes. He was three times Sacagawea's age when Pompy was born, a man who had seen more than forty-five winters. She knew that despite his faults he was far more likely to see many more than some of his rash counterparts, who believed that confrontation and strength were the best way of dealing with the tribes.

JUNE 16, 1805
BELOW THE GREAT FALLS OF THE MISSOURI

"If we lose her, the baby dies, too."

"I know it," Lewis said grimly. "He is not even close to being weaned, and he would not last a day on what we eat." He looked at Clark and gave voice to the thought that passed between them. "So we must do all we can to make sure she lives." What was foremost in their minds remained unsaid: if Sacagawea died, the negotiations with the Shoshone for horses would be impossible. The Shoshone had had almost no contact with white men. No one else spoke a word of their language, and without horses the party would not be able to cross the mountains. The expedition would fail.

Lewis continued his examination. Sacagawea lay on a deer skin in the tepee under a light blanket, her breathing labored and irregular, her skin hot to the touch. One of her arms twitched convulsively. She grimaced as a wave of pain passed through her belly, an unfocused stare in her half-open eyes.

"She won't bear being bled again," Lewis murmured, "but if we can cause her to perspire, I think the fever may yet subside. I propose to continue the bark poultice you commenced. I should also like her to take some water from the sulfur springs we passed on the opposite bank. Drouillard can fetch some this afternoon." His face was drawn, his mounting concern apparent. "Perhaps you could tell Charbonneau to occupy himself with the child while I change the poultice."

"I can watch the boy," Clark answered quickly, moving to lift the baby from where he lay in the crook of his mother's arm. The infant started to fuss as Clark lifted him gently, and the captain held him close to his chest, looking down into the clear eyes that were inquisitive and somber.

"Come now, Pomp, come to Captain Clark and be a good boy. Captain Lewis will help your mama feel better," he cooed, swaying lightly as he stepped away from Sacagawea's prostrate body, his hair the color of a fox pelt standing up from his forehead.

Sacagawea's menstrual flow seemed to be blocked, causing pain throughout her pelvic region. While Clark talked to the infant in soothing tones, Lewis set to work assembling his meager supplies on a piece of elk hide spread open on the ground. He poured warm water from the kettle into a shallow tin basin and tore several strips from a length of clean linen. He then removed the blanket and cautiously raised her knees, spreading her legs as he did so. Lifting away the darkened mass that lay at the opening of her vulva, he wetted a strip of cloth and carefully bathed the entire area with a steady hand. He fashioned the new poultice as he knelt at her side, placing three small pieces of Peruvian bark on a clean strip of linen and rolling it into a soft cylinder. Onto its surface he sprinkled twenty drops of laudanum, the tincture of opium whose small bottle was counted among the most precious medicines in the rudimentary apothecary he had assembled for the expedition. Satisfied that her inner thighs had dried sufficiently after his cleansing, he inserted the poultice and slowly lowered her knees, covering her body once again with the blanket. When Drouillard returned with a canteen of sulfur water, Lewis urged her to take small sips until she had downed two cupfuls.

That evening when he felt for her pulse as she slept, at her wrist and again at her neck, it beat strong and regular to his touch. Her face was covered with tiny beads of perspiration and her skin was not as hot as before. The tremors in her arm had stopped, and her face no longer bore the mask of pain that had covered it for days. When he withdrew his hand she opened her eyes and looked into his, and put her hand on his fingers. Neither spoke the other's language but all was understood in that long moment. *I will live and Pompy will live,* she told him with her eyes, *and it is your doing. Your spirit is strong.*

AUGUST 17, 1805
AT THE HEAD OF THE JEFFERSON RIVER

Four months after they left the Mandan villages, the party of thirty-one men, one woman, and a baby boy reached the land of the Shoshone, among the first hills of the great mountain range that stood between them and the western ocean. To cross those mountains—the Great Stonies, the Rockies, the Bitterroots—they would need to trade for this tribe's horses.

"You talk to your people in Shoshone, then tell me in Mandan," Charbonneau said to Sacagawea as they approached the Three Forks area early in the morning with Captain Clark's group of men. They hoped to rendezvous with Lewis, who had gone ahead to join the Shoshone. "Then I'll tell Labiche in French and he can speak English to the captains." She agreed. Even compared to the parleys among several tribes, this was a complicated arrangement, but it was the only one they had. She was in a dream, she felt, seeing on this voyage, as if for the first time, lands that she recognized, places she had known as a girl. Who would be left from that time? What would they make of her? What if they could not find her tribe?

They had not walked more than a mile when they saw several Indians on horseback coming in their direction. Sacagawea and Charbonneau walked slightly ahead of the others, and suddenly Sacagawea threw up her arms and let out a wail of joy, circling Charbonneau with little dancing steps as she looked from the mounted Indians back to Clark and the rest of the party. *These are my people!* she signed again and again to Clark, and he understood at once. She ran to the approaching group and addressed one of the braves in Shoshone, and he confirmed that he was a member of her childhood clan. Accompanying them was one of Lewis's men, who explained that the others were less than a mile distant. The Indians sang all the way to the nearby camp, joined at times by Sacagawea whose red-painted cheeks glistened with tears.

That afternoon Lewis had the men stretch one of the large sails overhead as a shield from the sun, and robes were spread out beneath it so that he, Clark, and the principal Shoshone chief, Cameahwait, could confer and negotiate for horses. By now they had parleyed with the chiefs of several tribes and they prepared the setting for these talks with care. It was important that a sense of hierarchy prevail, that they be seen as chiefs from the great nation whose distant father had set them on their path. The three men smoked a pipe and made the formal statements of respect and good will necessary before any bargaining could begin. The chain of languages took time—Shoshone to Mandan to French to English, and back again—but all was going well, both captains agreed, in the first part of this negotiation that had to be successful.

Suddenly Sacagawea rose up from her place, ran to where Cameahwait was seated between Clark and Lewis, and threw her blanket over his shoulders, wailing his name repeatedly as she embraced him. Although his formal mien and the chief's ceremonial headdress of otter fur and eagle feathers had masked his features, she had finally recognized him. It was like the way one of the small mirrors the captains offered as gifts—things like solid water—dazzled the eye with sunlight, and in the next instant showed you your face. He was her brother.

The captains offered coats, leggings, ax heads, knives, tobacco, and the usual mix of minor trade goods that often sealed the bargain: beads, flints, handkerchiefs, and the like. Cameahwait was presented with a medal bearing the likeness of President Jefferson who, he was told, was now the Great Father to him and his people. On its reverse, Clark pointed out as he placed it around the chief's neck, the clasped hands of an Indian and a white man stood out in relief beneath a crossed pipe and tomahawk. Around these symbols were inscribed the words "Peace and Friendship." In return the Shoshone provided twenty-nine horses, all they would need.

During the several days of preparation for the trek across the mountains, Sacagawea discovered that she was a curiosity to her tribe, a go-between whom they asked to explain the white man to them. Why did they have fur on their faces? Was the one they called York from the spirit world, with his curling hair and skin the color of a beaver? They wondered if Lewis's huge black dog was a kind of bear cub, they wondered how the rifles and the air gun threw their power to any far place. And they asked about Pompy: why did he have his mother's hair and skin, but eyes the color of the evening sky?

When she was alone in the tepee with her baby, she thought about all their questions and her attempts to explain. *They have not seen what I have seen. How can I tell them?* The joy of her return to the people she had grown up with was tempered by a new awareness. *These are my people, but this is not my home anymore.* Charbonneau was French, she told herself, but he lived with the tribes and on the river more than he did with his people. So did René Jesseaume and Georges Drouillard. They were whites who didn't live like other whites. It was a path they had chosen or, rather, two paths that made them something else. *I have two paths also,* she thought. *I am Shoshone and not-Shoshone, Mandan and not-Mandan. And I travel with a voyageur. This is my life.*

The day before the departure, when all was ready, Clark took her and Charbonneau aside in the camp. He looked into her eyes and said, "Cameahwait wants you to spend the winter with your people while we cross the mountains to the Pacific. It would be safer for you and your baby."

She waited for Charbonneau to interpret Clark's statement into Mandan, but she had understood its sense. Without hesitating she said in English, "We go." She held Pompy in her arms and said the words in Mandan that came without thinking. "We will go across the mountains and back. Our path is with you."

JANUARY 8, 1806
FORT CLATSOP

In November the Corps of Discovery descended the Columbia River and reached the Pacific Ocean, completing the outward-bound leg of Jefferson's enterprise. They spent some weeks along the river's estuary, battered in their makeshift camps by perpetual winter storms. In early December they chose a sheltered cove and built a winter camp, Fort Clatsop, where they would wait for spring before beginning the return journey. Most of the men visited the coastal beaches on hunting parties or to collect salt, but by January Sacagawea had not yet been to the ocean's edge. One evening in that first week of the new year, Captain Clark entered the hut where Charbonneau, Sacagawea, and Pompy were quartered.

"A group of Tillamook report a whale has washed up onto the beach south of our salt camp," he told Charbonneau. "Tomorrow I want you to go with me and ten other men to see what meat and oil we might take from the carcass." Understanding part of what was said, Sacagawea pressed Charbonneau for details. Clark turned to leave but she put her hand on his elbow and spoke rapidly, her eyes wide with anger and impatience.

"She says she has traveled very far to see the Great Waters; she has walked as swiftly as the others and carried her baby without complaint," Charbonneau told Clark, surprised at the forcefulness of her words. "Now there is a huge fish lying on the very edge of the ocean. It is unlike you, Captain, to keep her from seeing either. She would take it hard."

Clark met Sacagawea's imploring gaze, which was full of indignant dismay. "Very well," he said. "Tell her to be ready to go with us at dawn."

When they reached the low sand flat where the whale had been beached, they found not a carcass but a skeleton. The whale had been stripped bare by the Tillamook, the structure of its bones intact on the muddy inlet, but all the blubber, skin, and oil already taken away. Clark overcame his initial disappointment and set to measuring the animal's remains. "One hundred and five feet in length," he announced with awe. He wrote all the numbers in his book, as he always did. "It is so that the animals and plants we see can tell their story to others," he explained to Sacagawea through Charbonneau. Then he set out on foot to the nearby village to see if he could buy some blubber or oil.

Sacagawea stayed on the wide beach with Pompy and looked out upon the water, constantly rolling toward her in blue and black waves streaked with white, like an endless storm on the river. Some called it The Big Lake That Smells Bad, others The Great Waters or the River Without Banks, but to Sacagawea it was more like the sky: you could stand at its edge and look at it, but you could never cross it. Before the others returned she held Pompy in her arms and stood upright between the whale's ribs, as one might stand in a sizeable room. She talked to her child as she nuzzled and kissed him, turning this way and that so his wide eyes could see what surprising creatures sometimes emerged from the belly of the earth.

JUNE 30, 1806

They were over the mountains. The Bitterroots had still been covered with snow, but on the return they had Nez Percé guides and never lost their way. Their horses had grass on every day but one of the six it took to get across. Now they were camped at the place the captains called Traveler's Rest, a valley on the eastern slope that afforded the party plentiful game in a series of grass-covered meadows along the mountain stream.

We will live, Sacagawea allowed herself to think. *I have not been the cause of my baby's death. After this voyage we will return to the Mandan and make our lives on the river with Charbonneau.* She knew that perils still lay ahead—dangerous rapids, unseasonable storms, hostile Indian raiding parties—but the mountains had threatened them more than anything else, and the fear had been lifted from their shoulders like a heavy burden that had fallen away. Even the captains allowed themselves to smile and walked with a light step.

The evening of their second day there, the warmth of the sun stayed in the valley until dusk, and the men made a fire by the stream. They sat along the banks and lay on the grass, talking and arguing in an easygoing way. Captain Clark stood with Pompy at the water's edge, a shallow stretch of back current with a gravel bottom. He was a robust baby, almost seventeen months old, despite all the ordeals of the expedition. He stood facing the small river, holding each of Clark's massive thumbs for support, and ventured into the water, where he stamped his feet in delight.

Cruzatte had begun to play his fiddle, one of the old Breton tunes the men favored, and Pomp stamped half-rhythmically to the music. He gave forth little squeals, surprised and pleased at the explosions of wetness that his feet made upon the captain's leggings. It turned into a dance as Clark lifted his feet and turned the boy back and forth. Seaman, Clark's good-natured Newfoundland, barked and wagged his tail, striding into the water to join in the fun. Everyone laughed, Clark most heartily of all, and Sacagawea saw that more than one man had to turn away to hide moist eyes. The winter had been wet, cold, and cheerless, and they were still far away from home, but for the first time they could taste the end of the voyage. This vision of the child's joy in the surrounding warmth of others made each man conjure a memory of his family. They needed to be among their own: sweethearts and siblings, parents and elders. Each one missed his home most sharply that night.

AUGUST 14, 1806

They reached the Mandan villages in the late afternoon, coming down the river like boatloads of visitors appearing from the spirit world. It seemed impossible to the Indians that all those who had set off sixteen months before in search of a route to the Great Waters had reached their goal and returned safely, including the squaw and her newborn. It gave her and her *voyageur* husband a new status in the eyes of the Mandan, and everyone agreed that the boy was destined to lead. "In his first year he has been where none of us has been," the Mandan chief Black Cat announced when the captains smoked a pipe to mark the reunion. "His spirit has breathed in the trail to the west, and we will learn from it."

The news from the tribes was not good. While they had been gone, the Arikara had attacked white traders as well as Mandan and Hidatsa canoes below the villages, making any travel south along the river extremely hazardous. The Sioux, too, were acting warlike, and several bands had raided the Mandan and Hidatsa lodges. Anxious to return to St. Louis and to get news of the expedition's successful conclusion to President Jefferson, the captains assured the Mandan of their support. They convinced the Mandan chief Sheheke to accompany them downriver and then continue to Washington to visit the Great Father, the better to make known his people's grievances against the Arikara and the Sioux.

Two days later the captains said their goodbyes and prepared to leave. Charbonneau and Sacagawea had decided to remain with Pompy in the Mandan villages, promising to journey to St. Louis when river travel was safer. Lewis was ailing and gave a feeble handshake from the makeshift litter on which he lay. As the last of the canoes was being loaded, Clark drew the couple and their son to one side at the river's edge.

"Do not forget, Toussaint Charbonneau, my pledge to you: bring your darling boy to me in St. Louis and I will raise him as my own and see to his proper education." He shook Charbonneau's hand and turned to Sacagawea, who held Pompy close. During their sixteen months together on the trail, Clark had formed a strong attachment to the baby. "Let him learn the white man's ways," he said to her, pleading with his eyes. His hand reached out and stroked the boy's hair lightly, then he strode away quickly and the boats shoved off.

TWO

In the following months Clark sent several letters to Charbonneau in which he repeated his offer to look after Pompy in St. Louis, entrusting his mail to fur traders headed north to the Mandan villages. Soon, however, the Sioux and Arikara closed the river, attacking any who dared to cross their territory. Even Sheheke could not return to his people for many months after his arrival in St. Louis on the way back from Washington. Only after several armed expeditions and extended negotiations did a relative peace return, and the Mandan chief was escorted to his village in September of 1809.

Finally, three years after their voyage with the Corps of Discovery, the little family headed to St. Louis in the fall, before the river froze. Just after Christmas Charbonneau had his son baptized by a French priest. Lewis had died in October of that year, and Clark was in Washington on government business, but Auguste Chouteau, cofounder of St. Louis and its preeminent citizen, served as godfather. The boy's Christian name was Jean-Baptiste. He was almost five, and of the ceremony he would remember nothing but the clean smell of the priest's starched white vestment as he splashed water on his head, and the vision of his godfather, patient and encouraging, kneeling at his side and holding his right hand as he showed him how to make the sign of the cross.

SPRING 1810

When the ice broke up the following spring Charbonneau prepared to head north with Sacagawea, leaving Pompy in Clark's care. The captain had married two years before, and he and his young wife now had a one-year-old son, Meriwether Lewis Clark. Charbonneau promised to return soon so that Pompy could spend some part of each year with his Mandan cousins, but meanwhile he was to attend school in St. Louis and live as Clark's ward.

Before they went down to the landing where the keelboat was being loaded, Sacagawea took the boy into the small garden behind the boarding house where they had lived for the winter months. The apple trees were beginning to leaf and a bright green mantle of grass surrounded the newly turned rows where kitchen vegetables would soon be planted. Together they stood looking at the simple plot, silent and watchful, until a small gray bird appeared and hopped about the clumps of upturned soil. Sacagawea lowered herself fluidly so that she was crouching at Pompy's side. She placed in his hand a small figure of a bird made of polished black stone and closed his fist upon it. Still holding his hand in her own, she looked in his eyes and motioned to the bird, which continued to search for grubs and worms. "My spirit will be your spirit," she told him in Mandan. "Always keep the bird with you and I will be with you." He opened his hand and they both looked at the tiny figure, worked in obsidian, with the outline of wings etched into the stone and two dots of white shell for eyes. When they looked up the bird had flown away.

Although he showed no fear and adopted the solemn countenance that his Mandan uncle, Limping Bear, counseled for what he called Pompy's new path in life, a feeling of bottomless dread took hold of his belly when his parents set off up the river and left him behind. His young body vibrated with a resistance to everything that surrounded him, all of it strange and new.

St. Louis was an awful place to stay. Captain Clark's wooden house creaked and whistled at night. In the Mandan village, his parents' lodge had been like every other, adorned with clothes, blankets, weapons, and utensils. Captain Clark's house was bigger and fancier than all but a few of the other houses in town, filled with shiny wood furniture that was rubbed and polished daily so that it resembled brown glass. Everyone he met told him how lucky he was to be living there, but he didn't feel lucky. He felt confused and alone. The people looked different to him, yet soon he discovered that he was the one who stood out. He was a mixed-blood. Clark's housekeeper, Alberta, a short, fat old Negro woman who kept a kindly eye out for him, used to tell him periodically in those first months, "You look down the road before trouble finds you, honey, 'cause there's people would love to see you run into some." Young as he was, he understood: he had to keep his eyes and ears open and never forget he was different.

Pompy became Baptiste, his Indian name used only by Clark as a term of endearment when the two of them were alone. Clark's slave, York, took him to the dry goods store and watched while Mr. Kennerly fitted him out according to the captain's instructions with corduroy pants, a flannel shirt, socks, shoes, a woolen coat, and a brimmed hat. The shoes, especially, troubled him. Baptiste had never had anything but moccasins on his feet, and now he did not like to wear these strange pieces of footgear with their rigid soles, stiff leather uppers, and a complication of holes and laces. When he complained, Captain Clark was understanding but firm. "Save your moccasins and deerskin shirt for the river, Pomp. If you are going to live with white people, that means dressing like them, right down to your toes."

So he dressed like them and talked like them. His French was much stronger than his English, but that soon changed. At first he stayed with the Clarks, but before long he moved into the home of a Baptist minister and schoolteacher who boarded Indian and mixed-blood boys whose parents had gone up the river in the fur trade. The Reverend Welch was a stern disciplinarian, but he was a patient schoolmaster and Baptiste enjoyed his lessons. Baptiste's sundry supplies for school were the first things he owned aside from his clothes and the few objects in his medicine bundle, and he doted on them as if they were living creatures that could receive his affection.

The small slate and sticks of chalk intrigued him. He had seen slate outcroppings along the river, but he had never imagined its use for this purpose. Sums tired him, though, and soon the association of arithmetic with his slate was inevitable; he used it only when obliged. But his sheets of paper and quill pens were another matter. From the outset, the deliberate precision required for writing captivated him. He loved the way the continuously changing pressure of his hand on the quill moved slender lines of ink across the page, magically blossoming into words and then sentences. Like languages, writing—"the art of penmanship," Reverend Welch called it—was something that came to him easily, its satisfactions inherent in the act itself.

After they wrote out the alphabet many times, each boy was told to cover a sheet of paper with his own name. "Jean-Baptiste" appeared five times in his tenuous hand before Reverend Welch, walking among the benches, covered Baptiste's hand with his own and stopped him. "You are named after John the Baptist," he intoned, "a very great honor since he was so close to our Lord. In English we write only 'John.'" But the name never stuck, and beyond that one exercise, he continued to be Baptiste to all in St. Louis.

The domestic arrangements were simple, but there was always activity and companionship: daily chores and lessons, Sunday church, meals together at the big table of rough-hewn planks that took up half the kitchen. Boys came and went for extended periods when their parents reappeared, but there were usually six or eight at any one time. The only part of the routine that was disagreeable to Baptiste was the weekly bath. Every Saturday evening a long zinc tub of hot water stood in the wash house at the back of the main structure, and the boys took turns. As the youngest, Baptiste went last. The water was invariably tepid and dirty, a week's worth of sweat and grime forming a thin gray scum that covered the surface. Mrs. Welch stood guard outside the door, and after they had put on their trousers, she made each bare-chested boy hold up his arm for her to sniff so she could be sure he had used the thick yellow block of soap. "I will not have you smelling like a herd of buffalo," she announced with a shrewish look. "Not under *this* roof!" In later years, whenever Baptiste thought of Mrs. Welch, that was the image that came to mind: a bony-faced woman in a plain long-sleeved dress waiting expectantly to thrust her nose in the armpit of the next boy.

Captain Clark's household was different, and Baptiste was often invited for meals. "You are always welcome here," Clark told him, and he understood that the captain's special bond with his parents extended to him. But "No Indians in the house" was Mrs. Clark's rule, as she did her best to make the family's quarters as close an approximation of southern refinement as memories of her plantation girlhood in the Virginia Piedmont could conjure. Baptiste felt she admitted him there upon sufferance, but fortunately her domain, and the genteel rules that went with it, extended no farther than the main house.

Captain Clark was the Superintendent of Indian Affairs for the entire territory, and anyone who had business up the river had first to secure his say-so. Indians from various tribes, government agents, slaves, French *voyageurs*, Negro freedmen, soldiers, adventurers—all could regularly be found around the large wing of Clark's house that was his office. Its walls were covered with Indian objects from the many tribes along the upper river. Baptiste often sat against the wall in the big council room and watched them come and go as they consulted Clark for advice, examined his hand-drawn maps, petitioned for assistance, or argued among themselves. Unless a private meeting required Clark to close the door to his inner office, Baptiste was never excluded. The Superintendent often introduced him to his visitors, but Baptiste discovered that he most enjoyed watching and listening. When you weren't noticed, he found, you could learn a lot.

The sound of the different languages entranced him. He understood the chiefs who spoke Mandan and Hidatsa, and he understood some of the related tongues of the Omaha, the Osage, and the Dakota Sioux. The occasional groups of Pawnee or Arikara, however, spoke a different language, whose inflections were unknown to Baptiste. The same was true for the Arapaho and the Cree. All of the Indians were obliged to use an interpreter to converse with Clark. Among themselves, the tribes whose languages were dissimilar relied on sign language.

French in its many variations was frequently heard. The *voyageurs* from the Great Lakes and Hudson Bay region spoke with flat, nasal intonations, while the Creole merchants and traders from New Orleans had a lilting, singsong openness to their words that sounded like music to Baptiste. Travelers newly arrived from France spoke in an entirely different way, and they often had trouble understanding the *voyageurs*. *"Monsieur, parlez français!"* Baptiste overheard a Frenchman say to an old trapper whose pronunciation he could not comprehend. The *voyageur* spoke French with the same inflection as Baptiste's father, and to a recent arrival from Paris the sounds were impenetrable.

English, too, resonated in tones that could have been different languages until you knew the speaker's origins. Captain Clark's speech was soft-toned and even, with a gentle cadence that commanded attention, while his wife had a Virginia drawl. Factors and tradesmen often spoke English with the strong accents of their native tongue—French, German, Spanish—but they always made themselves understood. The household slaves, Baptiste noticed, spoke English clearly and well when they addressed their masters, but among themselves the sound of their talk changed altogether, a barrier of inflections, rhythms, and meanings that kept others from understanding.

The clothes of the visitors were as varied as their ways of speaking. The fur traders usually wore fringed buckskin leggings and shirts, fur hats, and colorful sashes at the waist. Indian chiefs displayed their full tribal regalia: massive bear-claw necklaces, beads and shell loops dangling from their ears, stiff roaches of vermilion-tinged hair standing up from shaved scalps, elaborately painted robes of buffalo or elk hide about their shoulders, and often a silver peace medal from the Great Father gleaming on their painted chests. As the government's representative, Clark was careful to create a sense of occasion with his clothes also. He wore a deep blue uniform with gold piping and epaulets, a black silk neck scarf over a starched white shirt, and highly polished black boots. Government officials and judges sometimes appeared wearing clean white shirts, fancy cravats, broadcloth coats, and carefully creased trousers, dress that was as exotic in its way as the tribal costumes from throughout the territory. No one wore formal clothes above St. Louis.

His parents returned in the summer of that first year and took Baptiste to the faraway Mandan villages, where he remained with them for the warm months. He knew the other children in the tribe, and Limping Bear, the head of their clan, made sure he was included in the Kit Fox Society, the "young foxes" who together prepared for their initiation as men. Their activities, supervised by elders, developed the skills young boys would need in adulthood: the use of a knife to remove the skin of an animal with fluid and precise movements; how to wait noiselessly in the places where animals passed along their trails and at favored points for crossing streams and rivers; where to find the best wood for a bow and how to fashion its grain into an arc that had strength and suppleness. These and a hundred other things they learned in organized groups that often erupted in play against the ceaseless flow of the river. There was an openness to life with the tribe that felt very different from the rhythms he had known in St. Louis.

One evening during that first summer, he had finished playing with his companions on the sandbank along the river's edge. Tired, hungry, and dripping water from his soaked leggings, he ran to the tepee his mother had put up at the edge of the camp. He burst through the flap to the hot and close interior. Directly in front of him he saw his father astride his mother, who lay uncovered on a deer skin, her knees drawn up to her chin. Her eyes were shut tight, a kind of grimace playing across her features as high, piercing sounds issued from her half-open mouth. His father looked up in breathless surprise and with one arm gestured furiously toward the outside as he continued to move his hips rapidly across Sacagawea's prone body.

Baptiste turned and ran, stumbling outside. As he picked himself up, he saw Otter Woman, his father's second squaw, sitting to one side of the tent as if she were waiting. He looked at her and she looked back, her gaze passing through him. She offered no word of reproach, explanation, or comfort, just her strange and disquieting presence on the other side of the taut animal hide that provided no barrier at all to the sounds within. Baptiste walked away quickly; the mix of shock and wonder he felt was amplified by Otter Woman's silent presence.

For the next few years Baptiste followed this seasonal rhythm, traveling up the river with his parents when the ice broke up and returning to St. Louis before the current froze again. In the Mandan village he fit in, though the other boys wondered why he disappeared to the white man's world for months at a time. In St. Louis, too, he found his place, and his periodic absences seemed normal to the other boys. But at first his two homes made him feel like two different people: he had different names, languages, food, clothes, lodgings. Nothing was the same in his two worlds. Gradually, though, and with the encouragement of his parents, he came to see that he was one of the few who, like them, could go back and forth. Sometimes he felt as if he lived in between the two places, but eventually he accepted that he lived in both places alternately. As he grew, passing from one to the other came to seem natural.

As Baptiste got older, Auguste Chouteau, the patriarch of a rich and influential clan of fur traders, often included him in family gatherings. In the French manner, Chouteau took seriously his role as Baptiste's *parrain,* his godfather, and liked to tell him stories from the old days on the river. The French-speaking Chouteau household was unlike the Clarks' or the Welches'. The big house was always alive with Indian visitors, various white and mixed-blood traders, *voyageurs* just off the river with boatloads of furs, strong women who were actively involved in the business, an occasional priest, and children of all ages who were members of the extended family.

Everyone talked incessantly: business, politics, family matters—it didn't matter what the topic was. What counted, Baptiste saw, was to be part of the conversation, and to speak well when someone asked a question. The other constant in daily life among the Chouteau clan was good and plentiful food, sumptuous dishes prepared with rich sauces and savory spices that Baptiste had never eaten anywhere else. The bounty of the frontier was not simply consumed, but transformed into feasts that lingered in his memory when he returned to the plain dishes at the Reverend Welch's or Captain Clark's. Baptiste learned the delight the French took in the occasion of a meal. "Food is just fuel for the body," Captain Clark told him once when he enthused about a dinner he had shared with his godfather. "It need not be fancy."

Chouteau had several mixed-blood children and grandchildren by what he called his "country wives," Indian squaws who lived among the tribes he visited when he bartered for pelts. Baptiste made a number of friends among the Chouteau cousins of his generation; under their roof he never felt different or excluded. Though often lonely, Baptiste knew that his situation was one of privilege compared to most of the other boys at the boarding house. Chouteau and Clark were two of the most important men in St. Louis, and both looked out for his welfare.

FEBRUARY 1813

One snowy evening when he was eight years old, his father appeared at Reverend Welch's house. There were shouts followed by whispers, then his father took him for a walk along the river. Reeking of whiskey, Charbonneau told him that his mother had died, breaking down several times and swearing in his sentimental way that he would have a Mass said for her every month.

"She caught the belly fever," his father told him in a choked voice. "She took sick, and within ten days the fever burned her up until she was gone."

It was important for Baptiste not to cry in front of his father; he felt that if he could keep the tears back, he could keep the ground beneath his feet from spinning and hurtling him down.

When his father went back north two days later, he cried many times, always alone. Captain Clark was away in Washington when the news came, and he didn't return for several months. Soon after Clark came back, Baptiste saw a light in his office late one evening; he knocked and let himself in. He found the captain, red-eyed and distracted, at his enormous desk in the big cluttered room. They looked at one another and both of them began to cry, and neither cared to hide it. Clark hugged him and tried to dry his tears, but Clark's own sobs would not stop. They gave in to their sadness then and wept together.

When Baptiste thought of his mother, he thought of his spirit bird. The summer before she died she took him aside, down to the stream where they gathered willow branches in the Mandan villages. She had him show her the small black bird she had given him. He knew that it wasn't a Mandan or Hidatsa piece; it was one of the small fetish objects—all of them birds—that she kept in a medicine bundle that was always with her, whether among the Mandan, along the river, or visiting him in St. Louis. She sat him in front of her and declared in a kind of solemn song, "I am the Bird Woman, and the spirit bird will always protect you, no matter what path I have taken."

Now she was gone someplace he could not follow. Everyone claimed to be his father: Charbonneau, Clark, Chouteau, Limping Bear, President Jefferson, Jesus himself. But he missed his mother. When he attended Mass with the Chouteaus, the priest often reminded him that the Virgin Mary was everyone's mother, but Sacagawea was *his* mother, and the sound of her voice, her smell, her touch came to him in dreams. When he woke he was pained by the endless distance that lay between them, and he gripped the bird as if it were life itself, his fingers bloodless and trembling. Opening his palm, he saw the stone's faint imprint on his skin, slowly fading in the pale light of morning.

THREE

1813–1815

For the next two years Baptiste remained in St. Louis. The United States was at war with England, and the Missouri and Mississippi river basins were disputed territory in their conflict, with many Indian tribes siding with the British. Word drifted down the river that Charbonneau was missing after a battle on the upper Missouri—perhaps killed, perhaps captured—and more than ever Baptiste felt cut off from his life among the Mandan.

He thought often of his mother, the Bird Woman. Not every bird he saw made him think of her. The great flocks of blackbirds over the prairie, the eagles and vultures soaring above rocky outcroppings, the owls and nighthawks that flitted along the roads in the dusk: none of these brought Sacagawea to mind. But when he sat along the riverbank, immobile and watchful, and a single bird landed nearby to search the ground for food, his thoughts were full of her. As when she prepared to leave him that first time, the bird would hop about, then stand unmoving with its head tipped to one side, waiting for something unseen. At these moments he felt her presence, and he sensed that she still watched him.

It was during this time that he discovered the miracle of letters. He saw Captain Clark write down his thoughts, send them far away, and the person who received the folded paper with his name on it would be able to read what was on his mind. He knew that Captain Clark sent such pieces of paper to family members in Kentucky and Virginia, with traders and merchants along the river, and with government officials in Washington. The Mandan said that this was one of the white man's mysterious powers, that he could make known orders, plans, and wishes by sending paper along this great system, but only now did it come to mean something to him.

Baptiste asked Captain Clark if he could send a letter to his mother so that he could share his thoughts with her. Clark looked up from the map he was working on at the long table.

"You can write out what you have been thinking, Pomp. But it would be wrong to tell you that I can deliver it to her, or that she can reply. Do you understand that?"

He did and he didn't, but he said yes anyway.

Clark put down his pen and laid his hand on Baptiste's shoulder. "Pomp, I am sure that wherever she is, your mother can read your thoughts. But if you want to write them down and keep the letters for yourself, we call that a journal."

The next day Clark gave him a small cloth-bound book with blank pages and taught him to write the date at the beginning of each entry. He also cautioned him to keep his book in a secret place where others would not be tempted to read what he had written.

Baptiste got into the habit of writing in his book once a week. It became a time that he looked forward to. At first he wrote only a line or two of what was on his mind, but gradually he included events and news that others talked about. And he always started as if it were a letter to his mother, since she was the farthest away.

OCTOBER 1813

Dear Mother,

I think of you in the spirit world and hope you are content there. Sometimes I am sad here but I know it is my path and I will walk it. Your bird is always in my pocket.

Your loving son,
Jean-Baptiste

JANUARY 1814

Dear Mother,

Captain Clark is now the Governor of the Missouri Territory and also the Superintendent of Indian Affairs. He wears a sword sometimes, and says we will beat the English.

Mrs. Clark had a baby girl on the first day of the year. She wants to take her away to Kentucky before the tribes fighting on the side of the English kill us all. Many people are afraid.

Reverend Welch preached last Sunday that we are evil and must be washed in the blood of the lamb to be pure. I do not want to be evil or pure. Lamb is something we eat sometimes at the Chouteaus'. I do not understand what he says in church.

Your loving son,
Jean-Baptiste

AUGUST 1814

Dear Mother,

Papa has come back to St. Louis! He escaped to the Mandan villages after fighting at Fort Manuel. He is often drunk, but I am still glad to see him.

Soldiers came back last week from a fight on the Mississippi.

Many were hurt, two have died here. The war is getting worse, the river is still closed. I want to see my Mandan cousins but I must wait.

Mr. Chouteau explained why some tribes fight with the British and others with the Americans. I do not understand it.

There are more water birds on the river this year than anyone can remember. No one knows why. I think of your spirit.

> Your loving son,
> Baptiste

AUGUST 1815

Peace was negotiated among the various tribes in the summer of 1815, and Baptiste was again able to go up the river with his father. It felt strange to be returning to the Mandan without Sacagawea, but the tribe's village still felt like home.

Baptiste stayed in Limping Bear's lodge for two months rather than with Charbonneau and Otter Woman. The boys in the Kit Fox Society had learned much in the two years he had been away and were preparing for the ceremony in which the young men would become braves. His closest friend in the village, Jumping Fox, taught him some of the new skills, especially riding bareback and taking care of the horses. But the time passed too quickly and soon Baptiste was heading downriver in a canoe to continue his schooling. Now that the war was over, Baptiste wondered how he would choose between St. Louis and the Mandan.

JULY 1816

Prancing Wolf had allowed him to remain in the lodge that day to see the initiation of the boys his age. "Since your path is with your father's people, you cannot be a Mandan warrior," Prancing Wolf told him. "But you can stay and watch, and send your friends your good medicine." The pronouncement was harsh but true: since Baptiste would not be living with the tribe, he did not have to be excluded like all tribal members except the elders, the shaman, and the initiates. He sat to one side of the lodge, between the elders in their eagle-feather war bonnets and the drummers who chanted rhythmically over their ceaseless pounding, watching as the young men were led to the center of the lodge in groups of two and three. Each one submitted to the offices of a pair of experienced braves, who prepared them with grim efficiency for the ceremony's climax.

Each young man was allowed to choose whether to lie facedown or on his back for the trial that would make him a man. The initiate stayed still as an elder grabbed the skin and muscle of his chest or upper back, pulled the handful of flesh away from his torso, and pierced the taut skin between his fingers with a hunting knife, once on each side. Another brave then passed a sharpened foot-long length of wood through the slit until it protruded from both sides. Then he fastened the skewer with a length of cord lowered through a hole in the roof and over the lodge's main roof timber by braves waiting outside. The same was done with smaller pieces of wood through the skin on both arms and legs, and to these were fastened the initiate's bow and shield and a horned buffalo skull. When the brave wielding the hunting knife was satisfied, he signaled to those outside by pulling on the two cords. Immediately the young man was raised up by the skewers until he swung above the heads of those in the lodge. His body was distorted in a terrifying way, its full weight bearing upon the skewers and cords and stretching the flesh on his chest or his back until it seemed as if it must give way under the strain.

They were pulled up to the lodge's roof timbers two or three at a time, blood dripping from the cuts and their bodies shivering with the effort at self-control. The drumming and chanting continued their hypnotic cadence in the quivering light cast by a fire that was constantly stoked. After a lull, one of the elders approached the hanging bodies and gently touched their shoulders with a long pole, turning them as they dangled from their cords. They twisted slowly at first, then faster and faster as the pole repeatedly struck them, until their obdurate silence gave way to cries of agony that soon turned to entreaties to the Great Spirit for protection and strength. The screams grew louder and resonated for what seemed like an endless time until they overpowered the drumming and chanting. Then one by one the initiates fainted and grew silent, their bodies still as they twirled slowly overhead. The elders examined them closely for any sign of movement. When they were satisfied that the young men's spirits had temporarily left their bodies, they tapped lightly on the cords, the signal for them to be lowered gently to the ground. Each boy had to die completely in this way before he could be born anew as a man, and experience the transformations that awaited him in the rest of the ceremony.

Baptiste had watched as close friends, cousins, and childhood playmates from the Kit Fox Society filed in to undergo the rite of full membership in the tribe. He had been jealous of their new status, but as he watched the ceremony unfold he felt apart from his kinsmen. Partly he feared the violence that was being visited upon his friends, but he knew that fear was normal—many times they had talked about it as boys. The principal undertaking was to appear fearless. Beyond that visceral response, though, a voice spoke clearly in his head: *This is not your world.* That he could witness their change was the ultimate expression of his difference: in strengthening their bonds through a shared ordeal, his friends were also excluding him from their number.

When Jumping Fox entered the lodge and submitted to the elders' knives, Baptiste saw the chasm widen before his eyes. He hardly recognized his sinewy playmate standing before him in the dancing light. As Jumping Fox lay on his back, he turned his head and sought out Baptiste's gaze. His eyes burned fiercely, and Baptiste wanted to look away as the knife flashed, yet he was unable to avert his eyes, so strong was Jumping Fox's hold on him. His friend's face was bathed in sweat, his jaw muscles were clenched, and when the knife pierced his chest, an involuntary shudder coursed across his face. But in the seconds before the knife was again forced through his skin and muscle, Jumping Fox smiled at Baptiste and his quivering lips appeared to be saying with fierce pride, *I will undergo this and you will not.* When the braves pulled on the cords and raised him up, his mouth opened in pain, and with a horrifying intake of breath he closed his eyes and threw back his head as his body was drawn upward.

Baptiste held his breath as he looked up at his friend dangling like the flayed body of an animal. Even though he knew it was what Jumping Fox and his companions wanted most in this world, it was like watching them die. Their acquiescence added to the atmosphere of sacrifice, resolution, and courage. The smell of their blood and sweat mixed with the smoke that rose around them to exit through the hole in the center of the lodge's roof. The drumming and chanting cast a feverish spell, and the firelight flickering across the feathered headdresses and buffalo skulls threw lurid shadows on the hide-covered walls. As an elder began to turn Jumping Fox's hanging form, Baptiste was overcome with concern for his friend. His body turned faster and faster and Jumping Fox cried out to the Great Spirit in a voice that Baptiste had never before heard. "Help me!" he yelled desperately. "Help me!"

Baptiste wanted to help his friend, he wanted to run from the lodge and have nothing more to do with their trials, he wanted to cry for being different from them. Suddenly Jumping Fox's cries ceased, and his body turned slowly overhead, its spirit departed. Baptiste closed his eyes and clutched his spirit bird tightly, repeating inwardly to himself over and over, *Their path is not my path*.

FOUR

He noticed the horses first. Even from a mile away he could see that they weren't the usual half-broken Indian ponies that scouts rode with a mule or two strung behind to pack supplies and that walked a plodding, even gait. These two were tall, broad-chested bays with black manes and tails; they held their heads high, alert to every scent as they advanced along the river's grassy shore. They had the shiny coat and the bearing that Baptiste remembered from Auguste Chouteau's carriage team in St. Louis, yet they didn't seem troubled by the unusual terrain or the sights or the smells. These were no ordinary frontier saddle mounts. *I'll be damned*, Baptiste thought, *those are purebreds*.

The two riders sat their horses differently, too. Rather than the slouch so common on the frontier, which a man could sustain for days at a time if he had to, these two held their backs straight and their shoulders squared as they advanced at a rapid pace, one ahead of the other. In a quarter of an hour they reached the small storehouse at the front of the camp, where Baptiste was counting pelts on the porch

34

with Henri, the old Creole who had been with Cyrus Curtis since the beginning.

The two men rode up to the small clearing, drew up their horses, and raised their arms in an awkward salute. The one in front, considerably younger and heavier than his companion, addressed Baptiste in a formal and accented English.

"Good day, sir! We are looking to find Mr. Andrew Woods and Mr. Cyrus Curtis. Do you know of their whereabouts?"

Baptiste took them in as he straightened up and acknowledged their presence with a nod. The newcomers wore broad-brimmed felt hats and tailored broadcloth coats, clothing not only too fine for where they were but far too heavy for midsummer. Their boots and tack were of beautifully worked leather. *Two greenhorns,* he thought.

"Mr. Curtis is up the river for several days on business, but you can find Mr. Woods in the main storehouse." Baptiste gestured to his left, where the stream curved through the woods a few hundred yards distant. "I will take you to him."

Henri helped the newcomers hitch their mounts to one side of the clearing and let their horses drink from the water trough as he attended to their needs. These two intrigued Baptiste. They were new to the frontier—that much was clear—but they didn't resemble the fur traders who sometimes came up the river from New Orleans, nor did they look like anyone he'd ever seen in St. Louis. They were reserved and had an air of quiet authority, particularly the younger one. They were used to having their way without a fuss and clearly had money. Baptiste was reminded of Père Raynaud, the Jesuit priest who had tutored him in Latin and encouraged his fascination for music by introducing him to the mysteries of the keyboard on the church's pump organ. Not only did they show some of the same measured reserve in their movements but they displayed a similar attentiveness, like schoolboys listening carefully to everything around them. Their eyes were alert, taking in their surroundings as if committing every detail to memory.

The older man removed a leather satchel from the pommel of his saddle and slung it diagonally over his shoulder. Then he took a briar walking stick lashed to the outside of the rifle sling and handed it to the younger man, who took it from his companion, rubbed the ivory handle and brandished the stick before him, as if feeling its weight in his hand gave him great pleasure. It was clear now that the older man, if not exactly a servant, was some kind of retainer. He anticipated the younger man's needs before any word was spoken.

Baptiste introduced himself, rolling out his full name with a fastidious French accent. "I am Jean-Baptiste Charbonneau."

"Yes, of course. General Clark talked about you when we were in St. Louis." The younger man extended his hand. "Forgive me, I should have introduced myself. I am Paul Wilhelm of Württemberg. This is my traveling companion, Mr. Schlape."

With the mention of General Clark, they now talked easily. The two were from Europe, from a German-speaking kingdom to the east of France. They were visiting the still-wild parts of North America to learn about the plants and animals that could only be found there. Paul Wilhelm called himself "a student of natural history," a term Baptiste had never heard before, and said he was very interested in learning about the Indian tribes in the region.

They set off toward the storehouse at a brisk walk, and the younger man—Baptiste guessed he was about thirty years old to the other's fifty—breathed deeply and smiled as he exhaled, planting his walking stick firmly in the flattened grass at the edge of the prairie. He said, "General Clark suggested that we engage the services of your father as interpreter and guide when we visit the Indian villages."

"He would be the right man to have along," Baptiste said.

He was starting to understand, and yet there was still something that puzzled him. His father was often paid to accompany the typical fur company hangers-on to the Mandan and Hidatsa encampments because he spoke the languages. Such men occasionally arrived from St. Louis, restless men with impatient looks who wanted to "visit the Injuns" or "see the operation," and who coaxed shoddy new trade goods—beads and blankets and tools—on the trading post factors. These two were far more polished than those jobbers and clerks, yet Paul Wilhelm had the same eager look in his eyes that Baptiste always saw when "the Indian villages" were the topic of conversation. *What are they hungry for?* he wondered. *What besides money gives a man that look?*

They talked with Andrew Woods for a quarter of an hour outside the main storehouse. Woods seemed bemused by the unexpected presence of rich Europeans. The letter from Pierre Chouteau, Auguste's nephew, presented by the one who called himself Paul Wilhelm made Woods take them more seriously than he would have otherwise.

"These gentlemen most particularly want to see some Indians," Woods said to Baptiste, raising his eyebrows. "A band of Kansa hunters were down from Wakanzere's village last week," he said, motioning toward the river with his head. "You might find them if they want to be found."

That afternoon, Baptiste took the two up the Kansas River in a canoe. At first they made awkward progress. Paul Wilhelm settled himself in the center of the canoe and passed forward to his companion the paddle that Baptiste had handed him. Schlape was worse than useless, though, and dropped the paddle twice before Baptiste told him to quit and propelled them from the rear of the canoe. The back current from the Missouri calmed the Kansas considerably and, together with the heat, lent the placid waters upon which they advanced the air of a lake.

Paul Wilhelm concerned himself with writing in a small notebook, several times asking Baptiste about the river's seasonal flow or the types of parrots they saw perched in noisy profusion in the trees along the riverbanks. Once when a group of large white cranes flew directly overhead, the older man produced a telescope from his bag, extended it, and handed it to Paul Wilhelm, who tracked the birds' passage with utter concentration.

"They are larger than our cranes," he announced as he lowered the glass. "An exceedingly pretty bird." He turned at once to his notebook and made an entry. Then he looked around at Baptiste and asked, "Can you tell me what tribes may be seen in this area?"

"Well, it would depend on the season," Baptiste told him. "These are the lands of the Kansa, and the Oto and Pawnee lands are nearby. This time of year, though, when hunting parties wander far from their homes, you might come across Cheyenne or Arapaho, even Omaha or Ponca."

"And Sioux?" The younger man's voice conveyed anxious anticipation, even in his heavily accented English.

"No," Baptiste replied, "it would be unusual to come across Sioux in these parts. They live much farther north, along the river."

After an hour of slow progress they approached a large, heavily wooded island. Easing the canoe toward the right-hand channel, Baptiste noticed movement in the underbrush that covered the island's point, still a hundred yards distant. A sizeable animal would not normally be moving in the midday heat. His senses quickened, alert now to every noise or motion that could tell him what lay beneath the thick cover of summer foliage. Something hung in the air, and Baptiste paid close attention.

The two men seemed unaware of the change in atmosphere until Schlape noticed a movement among the trees on the island, just beyond the water's edge. Soundlessly the older man handed the telescope back to his companion, but before he could extend it, Baptiste hissed, "Put that away!"

Paul Wilhelm started to protest. "But I merely—" But Baptiste cut him off.

"It might look like a gun," he whispered. Baptiste focused more intently on the island, and as if in response to his piercing gaze, the heads and shoulders of half a dozen Indian men rose above the underbrush. "Don't make any sudden movements," Baptiste said in a low voice.

The canoe had entered the river's right-hand channel, and the overgrown bank where the Indians stood half-concealed lay twenty yards ahead. They followed the canoe's lazy progress as it glided slowly along, the heavy back current making for almost slack water. One of the men came out of the brush to a small clearing at the water's edge and glowered at them. He wore a breechcloth and held a bow in his left hand. Around his neck hung a strand of glass beads, and they were close enough to see the pattern on the loops of shell pieces that hung from his ears. His head was shaved except for a tall, stiff roach of hair that ran down the middle of his scalp and from which two eagle feathers dangled.

Paul Wilhelm turned to Baptiste excitedly. "Can we meet him and his band of warriors?"

Without taking his eyes from the man standing in the open, Baptiste replied quietly, "We will see if he wants to meet us."

Baptiste back-paddled and stopped the canoe in front of the Indian. Raising his hand in a greeting, he addressed him in a variant of Mandan. These were Omahas, he knew, and he could usually make himself understood to them. The two exchanged words, and the two visitors from Württemberg could sense the tension rise palpably as each man made his declarations. It seemed to them that it was not a conversation, but a series of rhetorical flourishes. The Indian had quickly become agitated and narrowed his features into a scowl as he made jabbing movements with his right arm. Once he held high his left arm and brandished the bow as his voice rose in what sounded like anger, while his fellow warriors raised their bows, too, in menacing uniformity.

When the weapons were raised in silent threat, Baptiste slowly raised his right arm and lowered it, then spoke in the clear, soothing tones one might use to calm an injured animal. Gradually the Indian's threatening tone subsided and the two talked in what seemed to Paul Wilhelm a calmer register for another few minutes, apparently exchanging information. Baptiste then waved his arm slowly in acknowledgment, nodded, and turned the canoe back from where they had come.

After they had moved well away from the island he said, "Something bad has happened up the river." To their questioning faces he merely shook his head. He did not know the details. The Omaha brave had spoken darkly of "big trouble" and "many dead" and ominously mentioned "blue jackets," soldiers, but Baptiste guessed that he did not yet know exactly what had happened. He was upset because another Omaha hunting party had gone up the river some weeks before and should have already returned. "We have to go back," he told the newcomers as he leaned into his paddle strokes. Hearing the urgency in his voice, neither questioned his judgment.

It might be anything, Baptiste knew: a hunting party attacked by another tribe; a dispute between white trappers and their Indian suppliers; a confrontation at one of the trading posts or forts along the river involving women, whiskey, or guns. Until he learned the details, though, and what the Omahas' stake in it might be, it was best to withdraw. He was familiar enough with the shapeless dangers that came down the river in the form of rumors, as if the current itself carried news of violence.

Over the next few days the facts became known as groups of *voyageurs*, traders, and Indians made their way down the Missouri with the news. In the first days of June, a large party of fur traders led by William Ashley had clashed with some six hundred Arikara outside their villages in the far northern reaches of the Missouri. A dozen or more white men had been killed and the Arikara vowed war on any others who came up the river into their lands. The survivors of Ashley's party had arrived with their wounded at Fort Atkinson and demanded that the army mount a campaign of reprisal. Bands of the Lakota Sioux, ancestral enemies of the Arikara, were reportedly being recruited for an attack in force. The situation was explosive, and the jittery menace of the Omahas had, in fact, been dangerous. Ashley, the new lieutenant governor, had occasionally appeared at William Clark's door in years past astride a prancing white stallion, a pack of baying hounds in tow, bellowing that it was a good day for a hunt. Such arrogance, Baptiste knew, could well have led to misunderstandings with the Arikara.

"Word is that Colonel Leavenworth is taking more than two hundred troops up the river, along with a couple of six-pound cannon," Andrew Woods told him a few days later as they tied pelts into bundles in the main warehouse. "And Pilcher is riling up the Oglala, the Sans Arcs, the Brulés, and any other Sioux he lays eyes on. Mark my words," he said with an air of resignation, "this will be a dirty season." He reached across the table for one of the cigars he favored, a signal that they would take a pause in their work. Baptiste sat down, and Woods continued as he lighted his cigar.

"You sure impressed those two Germans the other day. The one that calls himself Paul Wilhelm thinks you walk on water. He couldn't stop talking about how you handled that band of Omaha, asked me how many languages you spoke, and wanted to know about what you do here."

Baptiste laughed. He knew the old trapper had guided a fair number of rich visitors from the East bent on seeing real Indians, and these two were as ignorant of the ways of the frontier as the rest.

"You know why he's got two first names, that Paul Wilhelm?" Woods drew on his cigar, aware that Baptiste was curious to know but unwilling to acknowledge his interest. He raised his chin and blew out the smoke in a thin trail, then contemplated the cloud above his head as if it held the secret to a mystery. "He's a duke, that's why," he said in a near whisper. "His brother or uncle is the king of a place between France and Russia called Wittenberg or Wootenburg or some such." Woods added, "Mr. Chouteau sent word to keep him happy."

"That explains why he doesn't know a paddle from a pitchfork," Baptiste commented. "On the other hand, I've never seen a better shot at a hundred yards, or a fancier rifle."

"He wants you to take him after buffalo next month," Woods said; "then he's going with Schlape to visit the Arikara. He may not be coming down the river again in one piece."

The two Europeans had spent three days as guests of Wakanzere, chief of the Kansa, at his encampment to the north along the river, then returned to the trading post later that afternoon. They arrived with three heavily laden canoes, filled with goods they had bought in the Kansa villages. The duke, as Baptiste now thought of him, called the goods his "Indian treasures," and Baptiste saw that weapons, tools, ornaments, and articles of clothing had been acquired in quantity. Paul Wilhelm immediately set about having the goods unloaded by their boatmen. Shields, leggings, awls, headdresses, blankets, and parfleches were piled near the river's edge. He prevailed upon Woods to have it all boxed and carried down the river to New Orleans, where it could be loaded on a boat to Europe. Schlape was made to produce several gold coins to show good faith, and the process of crating began at once.

Paul Wilhelm was full of enthusiasm for the sights and sounds of his previous three days. He said that Wakanzere was what he called "a natural aristocrat" who led his people with "subtlety, intelligence, and dignity." Woods and Baptiste exchanged a look but remained silent as they organized the goods that the young duke had assembled. This acquisition of so many tribal goods was new to Baptiste and Woods. William Clark had a large collection of Indian objects that he displayed in the Council Room in St. Louis, but each one had been the fruit of long years of contact with the tribes and had most often been presented to Clark as a gift. Others who visited the tribes along the river, whether they were merchants, confidence men, government agents, or *voyageurs,* sought pelts, not tribal objects—principally beaver, the standard of a tribe's wealth throughout the region. This newcomer was not interested in furs. But he asked incessant questions about plants, animals, the river, weather patterns, and tribal relations as they packed his prizes. Woods soon tired of the questions and feigned ignorance, but Paul Wilhelm's insatiable curiosity sparked Baptiste's interest. *He wants to see, know, and study everything,* Baptiste thought.

The visitor was extremely attentive to what Baptiste had to say and often stopped to write in his notebooks as they worked. Paul Wilhelm was also interested in Baptiste's mixed blood. The fact that he was the son of a French *voyageur* and an Indian, far from being a liability, seemed to increase his stature in the eyes of this observer from Europe.

After dinner at Woods's house that night, they sat around the fire and drank whiskey, talking over the rumors that continued to filter down the Missouri about the extent of the fight. Cyrus Curtis had returned in the late afternoon, and the two fur traders dominated the conversation. Baptiste took the opportunity to observe the European visitor closely. From where he sat on a low stool by the hearth, Baptiste could see the finely etched lips normally hidden under the full moustache, and the muttonchop whiskers extending in russet profusion from the darker brown of his curly hair. Paul parted his hair well to one side, which had the effect of exaggerating his already-wide forehead; together with his full cheeks, rounded nose, and muscular neck, it gave his whole head, not only his face, a look of great strength and dignity. His eyes were much lighter than Baptiste's, and Baptiste knew their extraordinary hue would fascinate the Indians along the Missouri, who were unused to the gray-blue pearlescence that nearly matched the shell fragments they highly prized. The silvery irises gave his regard, when attentive or concentrated, the steely focus of a bird of prey.

Paul Wilhelm's upper body was like a barrel, considerable girth in the shoulders extending to a broad belly. His bulging stomach and ample chin, so visible in repose, suggested that fat might eventually prevail, though now the overall impression was one of strength and stature.

The following day a keelboat belonging to Pierre Chouteau arrived in the early morning. It was fitted out with a crew and supplies to facilitate the upriver voyage of the two visitors. As their belongings were being loaded, Paul Wilhelm said to Baptiste, "I trust that we shall see each other again in the next few months if the buffalo hunt Mr. Chouteau is organizing for me comes to pass."

"It will depend on the location of the herds," Baptiste responded. Chouteau's men had brought a message that he was to accompany the duke if the herds were nearby.

"Of course," Paul Wilhelm replied, inclining his head. He had something else on his mind, Baptiste could see; he leaned in close as he continued, and fixed Baptiste with a penetrating stare. "If we can find common ground on such an expedition, as I suspect we will, I have a proposal to make. I should like you to consider accompanying me back to Württemberg this fall. Your services would be priceless in helping me to organize my collection and prepare my notes for publication. You know the flora and fauna of this entire region as only a natural hunter can, which will be of inestimable value in helping me to make sense of everything that is being sent back to my homeland for study. Your guardian, General Clark, tells me that you converse fluently in French and Spanish, as well as in three different Indian languages."

Baptiste was dumbfounded. Before he could respond, Paul Wilhelm continued, his voice full of the will to persuade. "I can assure you that you will have all your material needs taken care of as a full member of my household. In addition, I am prepared to pay you one hundred pieces of gold per annum for the time you spend in Württemberg, and I shall undertake to secure safe passage for you and your goods back to St. Louis once our work is completed."

The duke added with a reassuring smile, "Your uncle is a chief, from what your father told me. You are almost a duke yourself!" Paul Wilhelm noticed the look of surprise that crossed Baptiste's features and said, "You will be accorded all the rights of a gentleman at court, and we will work as equals."

Some response was called for, Baptiste knew, and he murmured the formula he had heard William Clark use countless times in negotiations with tribes or traders when he wanted to buy time. "Thank you for your offer. I shall consider it very carefully."

"I can ask for nothing more," the duke responded. With that, he shook Baptiste's hand firmly, then turned and boarded the keelboat.

Within a short while the boat was lost to sight around a bend in the river, and Baptiste was left to make sense of the offer. The likeliest prospect, he told himself, was that nothing would come of it. The duke might be just another fast-talking visitor with big ideas, or he might change his mind and never think of Baptiste again. It was even possible, as Woods thought, that the Arikara would hack him to pieces, yet another white intruder on their sacred lands. But his fervor was genuine.

Baptiste wrote to his guardian that night, out of courtesy and to see what his reaction to such a plan would be. He entrusted his letter to traders going downriver, and within three weeks he had a detailed, reasoned, and encouraging reply. Clark had a high opinion of Paul Wilhelm, who had been present at a grand council at which Clark received the chiefs of the Potawatomi and the Osage. He had impressed the Indians. Baptiste had much to gain and little to lose by going to Europe as the duke's protégé, Clark assured him. "You will have nothing to regret for the experience so long as the terms you agree to are clear and honorable."

His father would have heard by now, and would likely make some noise about it when next they met on the river. But his chronic drunkenness lessened the import of anything he said, and Baptiste had felt independent of him for many years. At eighteen, the decision was his.

FIVE

The herds had descended to the Platte River earlier that summer, then headed northeast. Word came down the river in early August that Baptiste should join the Europeans at Cabanné's trading post on the Missouri for the buffalo hunt. Two weeks later, they rode out together in the company of two Pawnee scouts the duke had paid to lead them to their band, which was following the herd. Now he was "Paul" to Baptiste, having insisted on the single name. They joined the herd on their fourth day out. Baptiste was impressed with Paul's respect for Indian ways. He was infinitely adaptable: he slept in the open, ate what the others ate, never complained about the withering heat or the plagues of insects. He had an air of authority and dignity, which counted for much among the braves: his great height was an advantage, as was the rumor of his stature as a chief among his own people. Nor did Schlape's constant presence go unnoticed. But the duke was principally respected for his own considerable qualities. He never made himself ridiculous by acting like an Indian or by drawing back when faced with the unknown. For a newcomer on the frontier, that was truly unusual.

The duke mentioned his offer to travel to Württemberg only once during their time together, and Baptiste acknowledged that the prospect interested him.

"Splendid! Then I shall count on it. You should plan to join us when we descend the Missouri this autumn. Please organize your affairs so that you can leave with us. We will continue to St. Louis and then go on to New Orleans."

Baptiste was surprised that his expression of interest was taken as an acceptance, but he quickly found that he was excited. The voyage to Europe now assumed an air of reality where before he had dismissed it as a daydream. He had not dared to allow himself to believe that such changes could come to pass overnight. He knew that his future was about to change in ways he could not imagine. Instead of making his way up the river as a trapper and trader in Mr. Chouteau's empire, as he had always figured it, he would be crossing the ocean.

Europe was too great an abstraction for him to consider, and Württemberg itself was entirely unknown to him, so he focused on the voyage. He tried to imagine what he would see on the passage and returned again and again to something Paul had said. Standing together on a rise and looking across a limitless expanse of undulating hills covered with head-high grass, Paul told him that the prairie looked like the ocean. *What does that mean?* Baptiste asked himself. He had been on huge lakes where the water stretched to a distant horizon, but the duke had said that on the ocean, the hills, too, were made of water. *What did that look like?*

This year the herd had come close to the Pawnee villages and the tribe's hunters had been taking animals for three days. Baptiste and the four others crossed the high plain in the early morning, riding in single file on sturdy hunting ponies. They had passed returning groups, their packhorses heavily laden with meat from their hunt. One large band of hunters remained with the herd, they were told, and were preparing a final assault that very day, before turning back.

One of the Pawnees suddenly slid from the back of his mount, his right arm raised in a silent halt. With infinite grace he crouched on one knee, his forearm in the fine dust of the plain, then slowly lowered his head to the ground until his ear touched the powdery red dirt. The horses stiffened, eyes wide and muscles shuddering. The fierce alertness of the crouching warrior descended upon them like the stillness before a storm. He rose slowly. "Buffalo."

They rode north at a brisk pace for another hour, the wind rising from the west, not quite full in their faces. The warrior dismounted several times to confirm what he already knew. By now the horses had picked up the scent and felt the vibrations in their hooves, and they stamped and pranced, straining against the reins, as they made their way to the river. Paul was a seasoned horseman, but this was unlike any riding he had done before. The Indian ponies were half-wild now that they sensed the presence of the herd, and he was grateful for the bridles and thin cavalry saddles that Baptiste had procured.

The land ahead changed gradually from a limitless expanse of dried grassland to a stretch of rolling hills with brush and low pine defining the edges of a valley. The river made a deep cut in the high, flat plain. It lay half a mile distant, below limestone bluffs and long stretches of rocky outcroppings. Stands of trees along the rim of the valley hid from their view the broad expanse of water and most of the opposite bank. The bluffs descended to the water's edge a mile or so upstream, but in that direction, too, brush and trees blocked their view of the river. The Pawnees headed for the high ground to reconnoiter the herd from a vantage point that gave the best chance of remaining undetected. As they approached the trees, the strong smell of the animals reached them on the wind, different entirely from the scent of sage and sun-baked grasses that lightly perfumed the air.

They dismounted at the edge of the trees, hobbled all five horses with leather thongs, and went forward on foot, eager to see what lay below and beyond. They made their way deliberately through the remaining hundred yards of undergrowth to the edge of the escarpment. Now they heard the constant lowing of buffalo and felt the ground vibrate. Pushing through a final thicket of scrub oak, they stood side by side on a small rocky ledge at the top of a sheer cliff that descended a hundred feet to the water.

The opposite bank was covered with buffalo to the far horizon. The animals trailed down to the river through a wide break in the cliffs that followed a stream; the small valley broadened and flattened as it neared the water's edge. The landscape was alive with the shaggy brown bodies of bison. Several hundred stood in the water drinking while hundreds more rolled in the shallows of mud and reeds that flanked the tributary stream.

Up the valley and on the heights above, the terrain was dark with their forms; the contours of the land a mile away undulated with their movements. They looked like bees swarming on the distant hillside. Only the steepest hills and the sheer faces of distant buttes were not covered by the thousands of buffalo, and the trees that flanked the stream and parts of the river's edge looked like islands floating above the churning sea of dusty fur. On a sand bar upstream on the other side of the river, a small herd of elk, mostly cows, with a mammoth stag standing alongside, watched the buffalo as the hunters watched from above.

For the Indians there was game and, soon enough, there would be food. But for Paul the immense herd was an awesome spectacle. High, thin clouds brushed the deep blue overhead with white streaks, and on the far horizon fat, hazy columns of white, gray, and black presaged a storm.

They moved back slowly from the ledge to a small clearing. The two Pawnees and Baptiste conversed in sign language and Paul talked excitedly to Schlape in German, unaware of the mystical code of silence that descended when a herd had been sighted. Paul's chatter stood out against the utter quiet, and he realized that something was amiss. Schlape sensed the ire of the others and signaled to Paul with his eyes. Paul confronted the steely gaze of the older Pawnee, whose look held contempt, disbelief, and a magisterial authority that cut off Paul's talk like a bolt of lightning. He held Paul's stare for a soundless second, then turned and continued his exchange in signs, the three of them making occasional soft grunts of agreement that sounded more animal than human.

Baptiste explained in a voiceless whisper that they planned to ford the river a mile downwind of the buffalo, then join the hunters on that side of the herd. An hour later they were riding into a makeshift camp where twenty Pawnees were listening to a warrior who said only a few words and filled in the rest with gestures and grunts. Baptiste drew close to whisper an explanation. "The scouts have just come in. Their hunters are about to drive the herd toward us."

The Pawnees jumped on their horses, bareback or with a flimsy hide girthed well forward, and seized the reins. Paul noticed that instead of bridles, cords of braided hair were lashed around the horses' lower jaws. Eagle feathers tied to their manes and tails fluttered in the light breeze. The hunters wore only loincloths and moccasins. Each held a bow in one hand and had a whip lashed to the other wrist and a quiver of arrows slung across his shoulders. Their excitement was growing. The first riders began to leave, heading up a nearby hill that separated them from the herd.

Schlape hissed at Baptiste, half in request, half in alarm. "I have no weapon. I had best wait here until you return."

"You will come with us!" Baptiste replied. He was astonished at how completely Schlape misunderstood what was about to happen. "This draw may be full of stampeding buffalo in another ten minutes. Just stay close, hang on, and, no matter what happens, don't get off your horse!" Then he turned, waited for Paul and Schlape to follow the Indians, and fell in at the rear as the band set off at an easy run to the top of the rise.

They sat their horses side by side along the ridgeline, no longer concealing themselves. Paul beheld the beginning of a classic pincer movement, as pure as the map exercises he had studied in military school. From a range of hills directly opposite, about a mile distant, a dozen riders could be seen descending on the left flank of the herd. To the right, another group of hunters was riding toward the buffalo at a full gallop; the animals on that side of the herd had begun to turn and run toward the river to the left. As the herd turned and gained speed, some of the bulls began to gallop up the hill toward the line of motionless horsemen. The Pawnee warrior at the far end of the line raised his bow high, gave a piercing yell, and the riders descended at a full run into the immense basin filled with stampeding buffalo.

They forced the approaching bulls back down the hill and into the headlong race toward the river. In less than a minute, all was chaos. Paul was surrounded by running buffalo and the riders were lost to view in the walls of dust thrown up by their pounding hooves. The din was like a long explosion, the thunder of thousands of hooves punctuated by the bellowing of the bulls as they took flight. Several times Paul's horse shied away from buffalo that came too close, but it never faltered on the uneven terrain. The basin floor, which had looked smooth from above, was in fact pitted by an endless network of dry cracks and fissures that sometimes opened into larger holes, and Paul's mount instinctively avoided the dangers. As the herd thinned out and less dust hung in the air, Paul saw that most of the buffalo had run through ravines or breaks in the hills away from the river.

All around him lay the carcasses of freshly killed animals as whooping Pawnees continued to pursue smaller groups of buffalo, drawing close alongside and shooting arrows into their furry hides. Paul caught sight of Schlape, an indifferent rider, who grasped the leading edge of his small saddle with both hands as his piebald horse bounded forward. In an instant he was gone in a flurry of thick dust. The exhilaration of the first clash with the herd throbbed in Paul's veins and the impulse to continue the chase took over. Ahead he saw a Pawnee close in amid a band of buffalo that had veered down a dry wash, and he reined his horse sharply in pursuit.

The Pawnee hunter disappeared over the edge of a shallow ravine, and Paul galloped directly behind a dozen buffalo. His horse drew close to the trailing bull and dodged a jerk of its head and its dangerous curved horn. The buffalo's repeated attempts to gore the horse slowed it. Trusting the horse to maintain a safe distance, Paul grasped the reins in two fingers of his left hand, raised his twin-barreled rifle with his right, and sighted behind the point of the shoulder. He fired and saw the animal flinch as a trickle of blood appeared along its hump of muscle, but the beast continued to run at full speed. He pulled the trigger again, and this time the buffalo abruptly slowed and soon stopped.

Paul reined in his horse and stood off from where the wounded bull faced him, its tongue lolling out heavily, dripping saliva and blood onto its matted beard. From the frenzy of the chase the atmosphere was transformed into an eerie quiet, an intimacy between hunter and prey. Paul could hear the bull's labored breathing, their isolation accentuated by the distant cries of the others. Two or three times the buffalo turned its head, its glassy eyes staring dully, as if waiting for something. Paul felt for his belt and found his small revolver. He removed it as he started to coax his horse toward the bull. A close-range shot to the head would surely be an adequate *coup de grâce*.

"Stop!" he heard Baptiste cry. He was descending the nearby rise at a gentle gallop. As he drew close, he explained. "Pistol shot won't do a thing to that animal except rile him up." He walked his horse carefully to the other side of the bull. "Yearling bulls usually have a lot more fight left in them than you would think." He loaded his rifle with a tamping iron that was slung around his neck, raised the barrel, and drew a bead behind the bull's shoulder blade, aiming to pierce its heart. He fired, and the bull shuddered, fell on its knees, then rolled heavily onto its side as blood poured from its mouth. Its outstretched legs shivered violently, and it was still.

In the excitement of the breakneck pursuit Paul had lost all notion of time or distance. As they made their way back to the river, he took in how much ground he had covered in the chase. They had traveled several miles. He and Baptiste came upon small groups of Indians skinning and butchering the dead animals. The air was thick with the drone of flies and yellow jackets as the hunters stacked pieces of bloody raw meat next to the carcasses. Paul watched the Indians work their knives quickly to separate flesh from bone, occasionally stopping to eat a choice morsel sliced from the innards.

They passed three Pawnees gathered around a massive bull in a small hollow. One of the hunters was a boy Paul judged to be no more than twelve years old. As he and Baptiste drew near, the boy shouted and laughed to his companions and reached into the gut of the buffalo with his knife. He withdrew a steaming mass of dark brown jellylike flesh and held it high above his head and twirled around in a little dance. Then the boy took a bite of the dripping viscera and his friends shouted their approval. Paul was astonished, but curiosity quickly overcame his surprise. Baptiste turned in his saddle to explain.

"It's his first buffalo. He's eating the liver to celebrate."

The boy saw them watching and ran to where their horses stood, holding the liver up to Paul and nodding exuberantly as he offered his trophy. Baptiste said, "It's a great honor to taste his first kill." Seeing Paul's eyes widen in disbelief at what was expected, he added, "Even a very small bite is enough to save him from insult." Paul nodded slowly, breathed deeply, then leaned down to taste the boy's prize. He felt the warm ooze of liquid on his moustache and chin as he bit off a piece of liver and closed his mouth. He swallowed without breathing, tasting the bitterness of the buffalo's gut and his own bile rising. Baptiste also took a bite of the liver, bestowing signs of congratulation on the boy, who had become a man that day.

Vultures wheeled thickly above them as they continued toward the river. They encountered others collecting the spoils of the hunt. Women had appeared with packhorses and dogs fitted with travois poles to carry the meat back to camp. The groups laughed and shouted as they butchered the dead buffalo that lay all around.

Not far from the river, they found Schlape in the company of three Pawnee women. He was lying on a buffalo hide watching them remove the tendons of a cow, his face, hands, and shirtfront covered with blood. Paul leaped from his saddle and approached him anxiously, fearing a serious wound, but Schlape, guessing Paul's concern, shook his head and smiled wanly. The two men conversed briefly in German.

"He fell from his horse several miles from here," Paul told Baptiste, "and these women found him and carried him here on their litter. He has only bruised his shoulder, but since he was very thirsty and far from water, they gave him the buffalo's blood to drink." Baptiste nodded as if this were normal. Paul's hand, too, was stained with blood and his moustache soaked in it. In fact, everyone they passed bore the same markings. *We look like a pack of wolves,* he thought, *our muzzles and paws soaked with the blood of our prey.*

PART TWO

A NEW WORLD

SIX

DECEMBER 1823

Baptiste gazed out over the gray expanse of the Mississippi Delta in the early-morning light and thought back to the beginning of the voyage. From his youngest days, he had been in and out of canoes on the Missouri and the Mississippi and on most of their tributary streams. Long river voyages were nothing new to him. Even the trip he and Paul made from St. Louis to New Orleans had not been so very different from what he had expected, though he had never before traveled by steamboat. The river was the river, and while it grew ever wider and more powerful as they headed south, its essential nature didn't change. Its waters roiled constantly in muddy turmoil, snags of bushes and branches sometimes blocked the entire width of the channel, sand bars could ground a boat suddenly in a place where deep water had flowed only days before, but the fundamental proposition was always the same: the current wanted to carry you downstream, and your efforts and calculations had to take into account the simple fact of the river's southward flow. He had been impressed by the way a river pilot could read its currents and moods in a glance, as if he were a hunter looking at a trail and assessing the recent passage of animals.

Living on board the small steamboat had taken some getting used

57

to. Its engine ran constantly and the paddle wheels churned to keep them in the channel and added to the downstream momentum. The lack of effort was the hardest part to accept, and the absence of contact with the water. In a canoe, the steady rhythm of one's paddling became as automatic as breathing. He felt cut off, idly watching the banks roll by and sleeping on the boat, rather than making camp on the shore.

At first the countryside was familiar, and boyhood memories returned as they steamed past places that held meaning: the broad sandy island in a bend of the river where he had shot and dressed his first buck; the flat shoals along which he and his father had camped twelve years earlier and been roused from their sleep by a tremendous shaking of the ground that turned the river into rapids wherever they looked; the fast-moving channel where a friend had drowned with his entire family when their flatboat smashed against submerged rocks.

In those first days, too, they had passed the tiny group of wooden buildings on a sheltered inlet—a two-story tavern and three low shacks—where men stopped for an hour or two of pleasure with one of the women who lived there. Baptiste had visited a number of times in the last year with his earnings from Curtis & Woods, and he shrugged as he recalled the peculiar mix of longing, relief, and sadness that stayed with him after these encounters. Young women in the Mandan villages had encouraged his first awkward advances years ago, but since then he had understood that, in the white man's world, marriage or payment were the only sure ways to be with a woman. The last time, it had been a Creole girl from downriver no older than him. When they had finished, she bit his ear as he sat up, then rubbed herself down with a cloth like an animal that has been exercised.

Gradually he had watched the banks of the river change, and two days after they had passed the place where the Ohio joined the Mississippi, he became aware that he had never been so far downstream. He would not see any of these places for a long time, Baptiste realized, but the thought did not make him unhappy. He only wondered when he would return, and what sort of person he would have become. These and a thousand other thoughts filled his mind as they made their steady way toward the mouth of this river that was longer than he had imagined.

Something set New Orleans apart from all the towns he had ever visited. In St. Louis, the men talked about setting off for the upper Missouri, loading up with supplies for their trips to the trading posts. Leaving with traps and guns and ammunition, they wouldn't be seen for a couple of seasons or a whole year at a time. When you left St. Louis and headed upriver, you left behind the white man's ways and entered the world of Indians. In New Orleans, there was no sense of being on a frontier. The long stretch between St. Louis and New Orleans was no longer wild and separate. The towns and settlements they stopped at along the route confirmed his impression that the white man was in possession of the river and the surrounding land.

From Baptiste's earliest years, he had known that other tribes were sometimes to be feared, and this sense of menace had always been a part of the landscape. For the first time in his life, he now came across a long stretch of the river where Indians not only were not feared—as they sometimes still were even in St. Louis—but thought of as shiftless louts or, at best, godless heathens, to be pitied and converted to Christianity. This was at odds with everything he had known before. In St. Louis, Indians were often vilified, but they were never dismissed as insignificant.

The Indians in St. Louis were generally trading parties of Pawnee or Omaha, occasionally a group of Mandan or Crow that had made the trip downriver from the far north. They kept to themselves, doing business with one of the agents in town in the daytime and camping in the clearings across the river at night. Only a few Indians lived in town by themselves, cut off from their tribes for one reason or another. They were sad cases who helped at the livery stables or the blacksmiths and lived in shacks or haylofts behind the main buildings. Most often you would see them in a drunken stupor down by the water, but everyone understood that they were exceptions, and even the Indians who passed through scorned them pitilessly.

In New Orleans, what he saw shocked him. Rather than a handful of individuals with a vacant look and a liking for whiskey, there were dozens of exhausted Indians wandering the streets or slumped in the shadows, sometimes in the company of similarly wretched Negroes or Mexicans who also seemed lost. Men, women, and whole families sat on the boardwalks or along the levee, begging handouts from passersby. No vestige of tribal clothing remained; rags and cast-off garments covered them. The look of despair in their eyes was like the look of frightened animals. Only the color of their skin showed that they were Indians.

The memory of a chance encounter in New Orleans still troubled Baptiste. He had been walking along one of the arcaded streets near the cathedral in the company of Schlape when he was startled by a Mandan cry. A woman leaning against one of the arcade's pillars yelled, "Young one!"

The sound of Mandan so surprised him that he looked up at once, and as their eyes met there was no doubt she had been calling to him. She repeated the words more softly, and the familiar sounds resonated deep within. The woman stared as if she were looking through him to a place that only she could see. Her tone was so personal that at first he wondered if he knew her. Was she from the villages he had lived in as a young boy, a friend of his mother, perhaps, come to grief on the streets of this city? But he saw nothing familiar in her features, nor she in his, other than the sight of another Indian, incongruously dressed in a suit of clothes and conversing with a white man in a foreign tongue. Her eyes showed dismay.

Schlape had broken the spell by producing a coin from his pocket and laying it at the squaw's feet. She did not acknowledge the gesture, and Baptiste felt her eyes follow him as they passed by. He could at least have responded with a few words of Mandan, but words failed him, in any language. *What had she wanted? Was it in his power to give it to her?* Baptiste shook his head and tried to banish her memory. Here at the end of the Mississippi, the longest part of their voyage was about to begin.

SEVEN

Dear Captain Clark,

I write to you near the end of our sea voyage. I have in mind your advice to commit my new experiences to paper and to send them your way when I can. These two sheets do not permit a full account of all that has happened since the Duke and I left St. Louis, but I will mention some of the things I have seen during my seven weeks aboard ship.

Our ocean passage got off to a slow start. The day before Christmas, we boarded the *Smyrna* in New Orleans, twenty passengers all together, with all the Duke's "specimens" in the hold. Then we set sail for the mouth of the Mississippi, but after a day the winds gave out and the current wasn't strong enough to carry us on its own since the tide comes up the river so strongly. It wasn't until the 7th of January that the wind shifted and we could leave the pilothouse at Balize and set out to sea. It was strange to leave the land behind, but pretty soon it seemed normal. I even got used to eating my meals at a table that rolled back and forth like a canoe in bad rapids.

We saw the coast of Cuba and then some islands off Florida, but that was the last land we set eyes on. It was warm for the first couple of weeks, with a steady wind to keep us going. The water was so clear we could see fish every day, large bonitos and dorados, little ones with wings that sometimes flew right up onto the deck, and groups of dolphins that swam and jumped close to the ship. Duke Paul told me that dolphins are actually mammals and have to come up to breathe, like whales. We saw many whales the second week, not more than a hundred yards from the ship. Of course I thought of the story you told me about my mother holding me inside the whale skeleton. They make a loud snort, like a dozen buffalo bulls in rut, then they shoot a fountain of water from the nose hole on their backs.

South of Newfoundland in Canada (I noted the latitude and longitude: 40° 36′ north, 54° 21′ west) the wind came up from the west and the sea turned as nasty as the clouds in a twister. The temperature dropped like a stone. We got hail, snow, and sleet, and even lightning and thunder. We lost gear overboard, some of the rigging blew away, and we all got wet, even inside with the doors closed. The waves were like mountains that moved, and all we did was go up one side of the mountain and down the other for ten days. The *Smyrna* is three times the size of your house, yet in that sea it felt small and flimsy. But, as you would say, we proceeded on—what else could we do? There were a couple of times when it seemed like we'd be headed straight to the bottom of the Atlantic Ocean—even the other passengers felt so—but somehow we came through the storms in one piece and no one overboard.

The crew race around the masts and rigging like squirrels. I learned how to climb up to a platform called the maintop, way up the mainmast, where the crew let me sit and watch as long as the weather was clear and the wind steady. It was like being in the tallest tree you can think of, with no branches to block the view, planted right in the middle of the ocean. It was a relief to get away from the others when I could; a ship gets mighty close when you're on top of each other all day and night, too.

Other than the weather, the only big run-in we had was when Duke Paul went down into the hold to see how his specimens had come through the storms. He found that the crew had broken into two of the crates and drunk the preserving alcohol out of the jars. The animals (mostly birds) had rotted and had to be dumped overboard. The Duke has a temper—I've learned that—and it built into a white fury. He and the captain had words. The next morning three of the men were whipped. They were tied down the way the Blackfoot do it, and flogged until their blood covered the deck. It seemed harsh. When we were in the tropics, these same men had gone out in small boats and collected the carcasses of the birds Duke Paul shot from the deck.

We entered the English Channel today (my birthday) in a fog as thick as any I've seen, worse than the Missouri in August. In two or three days we are to land in Havre-de-Grâce, hopefully on a clear, calm afternoon. I'll post this as soon as we arrive so you'll know we made it across.

Please remember me kindly to Mrs. Clark and the children, and to those associates of Mr. Pratte and Mr. Chouteau who may be in St. Louis. As ever, your affectionate,

Pomp

P.S. We spoke English on the ship, and some Spanish (two of the other passengers were from Veracruz), and Duke Paul and Mr. Schlape started me on German lessons. Soon it will be nothing but French.

Eight

A shrill cry echoed from overhead. Baptiste shifted in his hammock and pulled the thin pillow over his ears. The cry was repeated, and this time unclear words played upon his torpor. To the shouting was soon added the commotion of feet on the deck above, and more voices. It was not crew members changing the watch—he was sure there had been no bell—so it must be other passengers making their way onto the brig's foredeck at an uncommonly early hour. He lay in the lightly swaying hammock, suspended between wakefulness and sleep, until one of the words being called by the top watch suddenly separated itself from the others, swooped down, and spoke clearly in his ear: "Land!"

The simple word, so long anticipated, galvanized his spirit and body and propelled him from his berth. For days the passengers had speculated about how long it would be before they sighted land, and only yesterday the captain had told them that he expected to raise a landfall within a day. He threw on his clothes, wrestled his feet into his soft boots, and splashed a tumbler of water onto his face before he hurriedly made his way to the upper deck, dabbing his features with a handkerchief as he ran a damp hand through his hair. Outside it was only slightly less dark than in the ship's close and dank interior, but when he scrambled up the companionway to the foredeck, he saw the faint lightening to the east that signaled dawn.

About half the ship's passengers—ten or twelve in all—were gathered at the front of the vessel, peering off to the left and pointing at what looked to Baptiste like another bank of gray clouds low on the horizon, the same endless vista that had surrounded the ship much of the last several weeks. As he approached the rail, though, and gazed intently where the others pointed, he saw a thin line of white along the horizon. The narrow band stretched to the north and tapered off into the haze, bracketed by the rolling sea below and scudding clouds above. Baptiste felt a giddy sense of joy rise up within him.

He could smell the land now, a distinct heaviness in his nostrils different from the previous seven weeks of sea air, and he was reminded of the awful moment of departure from the mouth of the Mississippi, when another odor had overwhelmed him. A slave ship had dropped anchor two hundred yards from where they were moored at Balize; the putrid stench that emanated from it smelled like the buffalo carcasses that lay rotting at the bottom of cliffs after the Indians ran a herd off the edge, butchering all they needed but leaving a mound of bodies to the wolves and vultures. As his ship prepared to make sail, curses and shouts arose from the slave ship, distinctly audible in the morning calm. They were followed by thumps and resonant splashes. When the wind rose and they began to make way, Baptiste's hunter's eye saw the V-shaped waves of crocodiles circling the slaver in the flat water near shore. Now he breathed deeply of this new, earthy smell to clear the image from his head.

"That's England!" one of the woman passengers cried, her relief and delight apparent in her broad smile. *So it is,* Baptiste thought. To the left rather than to the right, where France, their destination, lay. His disappointment was intense, but his spirits were lifted when he asked a bosun's mate for particulars.

"We're well into the Channel, sir. We'll make the entrance to Le Havre by this evening. Then we can dock and unload tomorrow morning if she doesn't come on to blow." He hurried to the bow as he offered this last piece of news, then scrambled up the rigging like a treed raccoon and was gone. Baptiste marveled at how these youngsters, five or six years younger than him, climbed up, down, and around the constantly moving masts and sails with no more concern than if they were walking up a flight of stairs.

The knowledge that they were now so close made it worse to have to remain on board another night, and the idea that a storm might keep them on the ship even longer was unbearable. He moved to the opposite rail and, gripping one of the lengths of taught hemp rigging, stared at the clouds and the sea, willing the coast of France to appear on the steadily brightening horizon. He desperately wanted to leave this ship and stand on land again.

He had imagined the voyage would be like a long canoe trip on the widest part of the Mississippi, but it was nothing like that. When the river had threatened and shouted danger, as it often did, his reaction had been direct and immediate: he had paddled furiously to avoid swirling tree trunks, he had leaned and pushed and back-paddled to make his way through rapids and boils, he had peered anxiously into the roiling water to discern rocks and sand and sunken logs that could tear the bottom out of a canoe.

On the ship, though, the water was a great abstraction from which you took refuge when a tempest howled. Unlike any river he knew, there loomed no distant bank to make for if lightning suddenly lit the sky, no sheltering inlet or quiet cove where canoes could be hurriedly beached and protection sought in the rocky overhang of the shore. No, in those times the ocean became a wild horse that had to be ridden for hours or days at a time, and the only ones who could do anything to affect the outcome were the captain and his crew. Occasionally manning the pumps with the crew when water flooded the hold at a furious rate proved an unsatisfying way to help, removed from sight of the immediate danger. Baptiste could not even glimpse the battle.

He had seen them come in from the deck, wild-eyed, gasping for air, and streaming with seawater, as if they had been wrestling a band of watery demons. Sometimes he saw in the eyes of a crew member a look that hovered between pity and contempt. *We're out in it,* it seemed to say, *and all you can do is hole up in here and wait.* Baptiste had found this arrangement profoundly disquieting. He was not used to being helpless.

A Pawnee chief who had been to England and back in earlier years described the ocean to William Clark when Baptiste had been in the Council Room. A sense of awe and wonder lit his features as he summed it up for his listeners as "the endless river." It was, Baptiste now understood, an apt description.

"Good day to you, Baptiste. Have you turned your back on England so soon?"

"Good morning, sir. I am not facing away from England, but toward France."

Paul laughed and approached the rail to stand beside him. He wore one of his gray broadcloth coats with a black velvet collar, a dark green wool waistcoat, and a broad black silk tie. His spotless white dress shirt must have been one of the last of the stock Schlape had had laundered before they set out from New Orleans. The effect was regal. By the shirt alone, Paul could lay claim to a higher station than everyone else on board. Even the captain, the uncontested master of the ship and every crew member and passenger, could not produce a perfectly clean shirt. People were impressed or intimidated by him, but they were seldom surprised to discover that he was Duke Paul of Württemberg, a member of a reigning royal family. Everything about him said *nobleman*.

"You shall soon enough lay eyes on the Continent."

"I want to lay my feet on the Continent," Baptiste responded. Paul smiled; he was as excited as Baptiste to be showing him a new world. Their anticipation was palpable, and added to their companionship a new level of understanding, one for the other.

NINE

DUKE PAUL, FROM HIS PRIVATE JOURNAL
FEBRUARY 13, 1824
ABOARD THE SMYRNA

The pilot is on board, and we shall enter Le Havre harbor tomorrow morning. It occurs to me that I should keep a record of Baptiste's progress—for progress I assume there will be—during his time in Europe. I am wary of treating him as an experiment for he is no animal any more than I am a gamekeeper. But the improbability of his circumstances continues to fascinate me, as it has since the day I first met him. Now that we are about to arrive, I find myself wondering what he will see in a world that is so familiar to me and so utterly new to him. We will talk about his impressions, of course, and he can be quite forthcoming and original in his observations, as when he told me that what he calls his "spirit bird" had brought him a vision of the ship as a fallen branch with its leaves still attached, blown before the wind on a limitless river. When I asked about the spirit bird, though, he simply told me that it was his spirit but refused to explain or describe how he acquired it (or it him?), under what circumstances it brings him visions, or any of the other questions that to me seemed pressing.

There is a part of him that is like any young man embarked on an adventure. When Baptiste saw his first whale close by the ship, blowing a spout fully thirty feet into the air, he jumped about like a demon possessed: delight and excitement brimmed out of him with such abandon that I thought he would fall into the sea for his wonder. When we talked about it later, he said with a voice full of awe, "I've been in a whale before, but this is the first time I've seen one alive." What to make of such enigmatic pronouncements? Perhaps it is his "spirit bird" business, or a nuance of English usage that has escaped me. Fortunately, Baptiste has made the acquaintance of several of the crew members, young men of his age, who can answer his many questions and explain the workings of a sailing ship, and this occupies much of his time.

But there is another, more reserved side to his person that is without the exuberance of youth. He does not enjoy the company of strangers, I have noticed, especially when he is expected to engage in the general conversation. Coming down the Mississippi, and in New Orleans itself, our dealings were very rarely with more than one or two others at a time, and then only for limited periods. This suited him. It occurs to me that New Orleans was surely his first contact with the frenzy of commerce typical of a port city. Everywhere it was apparent that slavery makes the wheels turn, and I wonder if Baptiste saw a vision of what St. Louis might soon become. For a while yet, the upper river is protected by its wildness, its danger, and its inaccessibility, but that can only change. In the face of so much that was new, it is small wonder that Baptiste was quiet and aloof as we made our preparations to embark.

Aboard ship, however, there is no escaping one's fellow passengers, and when the twelve of us gathered for meals with the captain and his two officers, the effect on Baptiste was noticeable. He can be civil, even quite talkative, when the matter is between him and his neighbor and involves a subject of interest to him, such as the way in which various animals manage to fool the eye and disappear in their surroundings, or the clothing and adornments of the several Indian tribes he has come to know. However, when the talk becomes purely social and the entire table is attentive, he withdraws altogether from the discussion.

At the beginning of our passage, he was pressed by a foolish lady missionary from England with a commanding manner that masquerades as concern. "How have you come to be traveling in the company of Duke Paul, young man?" she asked in a tone that made the cabin quiet. Baptiste looked at her evenly and replied, "It is a complicated set of circumstances. You would have to ask the Duke, I suppose, if the specifics matter to you." A neat dodge, and an effective one, too. The chirpy Christian lady was left with her mouth hanging open. She looked at me hesitantly, ready to begin her investigation again, I think, when I assured her most jovially that the details were unremarkable, merely that Baptiste and I had many friends in common. She didn't dare pursue. There are, most certainly, advantages to being a duke in such situations.

Baptiste, by contrast, was defenseless or, rather, unwilling to attempt any defense other than evasion or downright flight. He has taken to climbing the masts with some of his friends from the crew, planting himself in the crosstrees and gazing upon the wide ocean for hours at a time, safe from the probing questions and relentless small talk he so despises. When I mentioned it to him as a necessary evil of social life among most peoples, he protested that such "busy talk," as he calls it, is an affliction he cannot countenance. "It's only when people don't really want to know you that they ask about your circumstances." He has a point, and the demands of a garrulous society are also burdensome to me.

But what will Baptiste make of the salons of Paris or—far more taxing—court life in Württemberg? If I am to avoid regarding him as an experiment, I must give what advice I can and then step back and allow him to act for himself.

TEN

They docked at Le Havre early the next afternoon. After the French customs officials came aboard to collect documents, the passengers were directed to the low limestone building marked DOUANES at the center of the wide basin where several of the extended piers converged. Paul stayed behind at the *Smyrna*, concerned for the unloading of his boxes, and promised to catch up with Baptiste during the customs formalities. As Baptiste followed the others, he felt as if had swallowed several measures of Captain Clark's best brandy: his knees were unsteady and his head spun.

The ship that had seemed so substantial when first he went aboard in New Orleans now looked small compared to the other ships that filled the basin. Some were tied up two and three deep at the piers, while the largest ones lay moored in the placid open water, protected by stone jetties, their bows and sterns secured by anchor lines. Most were sailing vessels—schooners, brigs, ketches, even two French ships-of-the-line. Baptiste also noticed a number of steam-powered vessels; several crisscrossed the wide part of the enclosed port between the anchorages, towing barges and ferrying crews from one side to the other. The low reports of their engines echoed over the water like a hammer-

71

ing while their narrow funnels spewed forth gray and black smoke in profusion. One of the *Smyrna*'s crew members told him that such ships were beginning to cross the Atlantic and were the likely mode of future conveyance. The musky smell of burned coal reached him as it wafted across the harbor in the light breeze and mingled with the strange odor of the city that lay before him.

The light streaming through the clerestory of the customs house was a relief. For two months he had known only the cramped interior when he was not on deck, but here was a spacious and light-filled structure whose proportions were majestic after the ship's narrow cabins and companionways. The floor was made of huge slabs of dark stone, and the bustle at the far end of the hall echoed against the high ceiling, fully thirty feet above.

He found two lines of people waiting for the inspectors, one for the passengers from the *Smyrna* and the other, he learned, for passengers who had just disembarked from a large sloop from Cork. An air of agitation surrounded the others as they talked animatedly among themselves. At first he did not recognize the language in which they were conversing, but as he drew closer he picked out words and phrases that told him it was indeed English, in an accent he initially found hard to understand.

"Jesus, Mary, and Joseph, too! The waves as high as a church steeple, and none of God's mercy shining down from the black!" a florid-faced man said as he gesticulated wildly to his neighbors, his face a study in mock horror that called for agreement, or at least understanding, from anyone standing nearby. Several nodded their assent and voiced their own disbelief and indignation at the ordeal they had been through.

"God and Mary in heaven, you can say what you like, but I'd sooner hurl myself from the mountaintop than set foot in anything that floats! Never, by St. Brigid's wimple, I say, *never* again!"

The woman who spoke had a piercing voice and a commanding presence. Her voice rose and fell in dramatic inflections, as if her rich contralto might break into a song of lamentation. She was swathed in layers of black, a complication of rich draped cloth, topped by an enormous bonnet lined in white tulle and encased in the hood of her volu-

minous cape. The lack of color in her clothing was relieved by the bil-
lowy red hair that filled the hood and by her lively blue eyes, clear as
cornflowers, which shone in a face that was very white. Her massive
headgear obliged her to move her entire head and shoulders in fluid
sweeps from side to side in order to convey the relief and amusement
that animated her performance. For it was indeed a performance, a ritual cleansing of her fear now that the danger had passed and she stood
upon land once again. She reminded Baptiste of the Mandan shaman
in his towering buffalo headdress.

She was attended by a short old woman servant in less ample folds
of black, and by her daughter. The young woman had the same entrancing eyes and skin of her mother, but her hair was black and shiny
and pulled back from her face tightly. She wore a gray-blue jacket and
long skirt and a less dramatic version of the older woman's bonnet and
cape that, together with her high cheekbones and strong chin, kept
her from being overly pretty and gave her a serious air.

He overheard her say softly, "It's all over now, Mother. Try not to ex-
cite yourself." She moved closer and took her mother's elbow. "We'll
soon have our baggage and be on our way." Her reassuring words
brought a gradual calming of her mother's agitation, in the same way
one might soothe a horse's skittishness with even tones and a sure
touch.

His line advanced and he drew even with the three women. The
daughter swung her head around as if she were looking for someone,
and when she turned back her eyes caught Baptiste's for an instant.
She noticed him—of that he had no doubt. He saw a look of puzzlement on her face, perhaps at seeing a dark-skinned foreigner. A nudge
from the man behind told him that their line had advanced while he
daydreamed, and he stepped forward.

Baptiste continued to watch her as they moved up the line. Suddenly several documents dropped from the young woman's hands and
fell at his feet. He stooped down to gather them and found himself
face-to-face with the blue eyes that had so startled him.

"How foolish of me!" she exclaimed, and then, more softly, "How
very kind of you."

Baptiste gathered the papers and gently brushed away the dust with a handkerchief. He rose and handed the papers to the young woman. She extended her gloved hand and smiled. The scent of her hair mingled with the starch of her blouse drew him closer. "Thank you so much. I'm Maura Hennesy." She turned to her left. "And this is my mother, Mrs. Hennesy."

Her mother, too, extended her hand, but with a doubtful look. Baptiste realized he was still wearing his hat. He grabbed at it quickly with his left hand as he took hers.

"Very pleased to make your acquaintance, ladies." This was Captain Clark's invariable formula. He was about to introduce himself, when Paul appeared at his side in the company of a uniformed customs official. Paul said, *"Voici Monsieur Charbonneau, mon compagnon de voyage."* The official made a small bow in Paul's direction and murmured deferentially, *"Oui, Monsieur le Duc,"* then addressed Baptiste directly. *"Venez, Monsieur. Venez, s'il vous plaît."* In the buttonhole of one of his lapels Paul wore a small width of silk ribbon—crimson, with narrow black and yellow stripes along one edge. Baptiste had noticed the custom inspector's gaze drawn to this tiny swatch of cloth. Before stepping away Baptiste said, "Jean-Baptiste Charbonneau, at your service, Mrs. Hennesy." He exchanged a fleeting smile with her daughter as he put on his hat and hurried after Paul.

They walked along the pier back toward the *Smyrna* where Schlape was busily supervising the removal of the baggage from the hold of the ship. Paul's two large trunks, a neat mahogany folding desk with brass fittings, and a soft valise of thickly grained leather sat on the pier. A dozen large reinforced boxes of rough-hewn pine were adjacent to them, no two of precisely the same dimensions. Six crew members were removing the freight from the hold, and they struggled mightily with each box that joined the growing stack of Paul's treasures.

The smell of alcohol and of decaying flesh rose from some of the boxes and hung heavily in the air; others made muffled tinklings and rattlings as they were hefted from below. Baptiste had not seen the baggage being loaded in New Orleans and had not imagined the volume of containers Paul had assembled.

Paul engaged in small talk with a French customs official, assuring him that all the specimens in his collection would transit France in their sealed containers, *"en compagnie de Monsieur Schlape."* Occasionally he warned one of the American crew members in his heavily accented English about the fragility of the contents: "Please to be careful!"

Finally the shout "Clear below!" echoed up from the hatch as the last two boxes were placed near what was now a small mountain of containers. Paul summoned Schlape to his side. He spoke to him in German, clearly giving instructions, though Baptiste understood only one or two of the words they exchanged. After counting the boxes, Schlape turned his back to Paul and extended a bulging white envelope to the customs inspector. In halting French he stammered, *"Voici pour vos efforts, Monsieur. Merci de votre compréhension."* The official pocketed it quickly, then shook hands with Schlape. *"Je vous en prie, Monsieur."* He bowed his head, then turned on his heel.

The hotel Paul took Baptiste to was sumptuously decorated. It had lamps with shiny brass fittings, upholstered chairs, fine wooden furniture, large mirrors on the walls, even a pianoforte in the main salon. Captain Clark's house in St. Louis had many of these features, as did a few of the big new houses built by merchants who had grown rich from the fur trade, but they were the exception. Almost all the buildings in Le Havre were made of stone, whereas in St. Louis most had been constructed of rough-hewn or painted wood, or of brick. But that was only the beginning of the new things Baptiste was to see. In St. Louis, entering one of the grand houses was like entering a richly appointed church from a plain and unremarkable street. Here, this level of comfort appeared to be commonplace. More remarkable yet, it was available to everyone. A steady stream of people walked in and out of the hotel as if they belonged there and took meals together in the room reserved for that purpose. What surprised Baptiste the most about his first experience of a French city was how public it all was, as if the fine houses of the rich shared the openness of the bars he had known in St. Louis or New Orleans.

But soon a profound exhaustion overcame him. Only with difficulty did he manage to stay awake for a light supper before falling into a deep sleep in the hotel. The solid bed was an unimaginable luxury after the ship, and Baptiste slept for more than twelve hours. He took a short walk in the early morning before they left Le Havre, trying to fix in his mind this city that was so different from the few towns and cities he had known in America. *Everything* was different: the low gray light; the earthy scent of coal smoke in the air; the feel of stone paving underfoot; the sounds of the port echoing across the water.

As they made their way out of Le Havre on the two-day journey to Paris, he counted half a dozen churches before they left the city limits, several of which were larger than the cathedral in New Orleans. Every village they passed through had a sizeable church on the main square, its stone walls and steeple covered with lichen, as if it had sprouted from the ground ages ago and grown slowly.

A strong wind blustered from the sea, sending clouds speeding across the sky that cast shadows on the varied landscape. But the sun appeared frequently enough for Baptiste to see at its most radiant the region Paul called Normandy. The rolling hills that began outside Le Havre were given over to farming. Small fields separated by hedgerows covered the hills and dipped down into the valleys, following the softened contours of the land. The road, too, rose and fell and rose again, within sight of a river for the first hour or so. Pastures filled with sheep and cattle alternated with the fallow fields. Occasionally they drove through a forest, short interludes before they reentered the world of low stone walls, half-frozen fields, and leafless trees planted in neat rows as boundary markers.

The coachman had placed a portable stove containing hot coals on the floor of the carriage to warm the interior against the biting February wind; periodically, Baptiste found that he had to lower the window to breathe fresh air. The sea air had been replaced by a pungent mixture of rotting leaves and of animals kept in enclosed pastures for a long period. He saw extensive orchards outside several of the villages they passed through, and a distinctive kind of house, sometimes quite large, with a thatched roof and visible timbers embedded in the outside walls.

Baptiste and Paul talked little. Baptiste was transfixed by the views out the coach window, and Paul was distracted and tired after making the arrangements for transporting and protecting his countless specimens. At breakfast he had talked of little else, and checked the details with Schlape repeatedly. The several wagons would follow them to Paris at a slower pace, two men having been engaged through the customs inspector to ride along with Schlape as guards.

That evening they found lodging and food in a comfortable inn on the outskirts of a small city, where they changed horses. When they left the next morning on the last leg of their journey, they talked of Paris. Baptiste could not conjure up anything in his mind to match what he would soon see. Paul told him they would be staying with his uncle, a prince of Württemberg.

Paul explained that Prince Franz was a skilled and valued diplomat who had been an early admirer of Bonaparte. He had fought in Napoleon's victorious battles at Wagram, Eylau, and Austerlitz. Paul's uncle King Friedrich, Franz's brother, had switched sides after Napoleon's defeat in Russia years later, but Franz remained a true believer, though he had had to keep his sentiments to himself after Waterloo and the restoration of the Bourbons to the throne of France. "He thinks for himself. That, you will see, is not always welcome in this part of the world."

He retained influential friends in Prussia, Austria, Russia, France, and even England, and represented the kingdom's interests in France. "He must hide his distaste for Louis the Eighteenth and the *ancien régime*. Still, he prefers Paris to all other cities and lives there in luxury."

Paul sounded weary, and it occurred to Baptiste that he wasn't happy about returning home after his North American adventure. Fatigue from the voyage was surely catching up to both of them as they entered the outlying districts to the northwest of the capital. Tired as he was, though, Baptiste could hardly contain the excitement he felt at the prospect of reaching Paris, the place whose name meant in St. Louis a kind of earthly heaven.

ELEVEN

Baptiste's first few days in Paris were like a waking dream. Antici-pation, excitement, doubt, and wonder flooded his mind as he looked around him. He had felt this way only once before, when his parents left him in St. Louis with Captain Clark, but his surroundings there had been understandable, if not entirely familiar. Here, nothing in his life prepared him for what he found in this vast city.

This time, though, he felt no dread and no fear. He was an adult, not a child, and he had chosen to leave. An insatiable urge to see and experience for himself what he had only heard of, usually in tones of deference and respect, now took the place of his childhood timidity. He remembered the reverence with which Captain Clark handled the cut-crystal decanter that reigned in honey-hued splendor at the center of the mantel. "Mr. Jefferson made me a gift of this for my wedding," he announced to visitors as he poured out glasses of sherry. "He brought it from Paris." *From Paris:* those two words conferred magic. No higher provenance could be imagined.

They arrived in the evening and found that Paul's uncle was in Württemberg, expected back in three days. Prince Franz's house was in an open part of the city north of the river and about a mile west of the center. It was an imposing stone structure, three stories tall, set back from the street behind an elaborate wrought-iron fence. The paved forecourt was large enough for a carriage to turn with ease; at the back of the main house, gardens and flower beds, gray in the February chill, extended to a small orchard. Similar properties flanked the grounds behind stone walls, and each had its own gatehouse staffed by a liveried servant.

The interior was sumptuous, like nothing Baptiste had ever seen—even Mr. Chouteau's big house seemed plain by comparison. The floors were worked in complicated patterns of oak; the walls and ceilings were richly carved and painted; the banisters and doorknobs and window pulls were shaped in fancy brass curves, with gold and black detailing. Everywhere he looked Baptiste saw gold-framed portraits, all of them royal relatives, Paul told him.

The luxury of the rooms was a new experience, but the number of servants in Prince Franz's household was even more surprising. They were everywhere, uniformed and waiting, and Baptiste found their presence unsettling. Doors were opened, food served, boots shined—everything was done without any request or suggestion. Paul paid no attention to those who waited on them. Baptiste followed his example, but at first he stole glances at the servants, curious to know what they were thinking. *They aren't slaves,* he reminded himself.

The following day they set out just after breakfast, the two of them in a shining black carriage with tall glass windows that was pulled by a pair of perfectly groomed grays. After they had driven for a short while, Paul motioned down a very wide and long boulevard that descended gradually toward buildings and trees in the distance. "The Champs-Elysées," he said with a flourish, enjoying his role as Baptiste's guide. They headed down the long sweep of road, its edges lined with double rows of elms and stately houses that overlooked the intermittent parade of carriages. Baptiste could not understand why so much space had been made for a road; the passing traffic seemed puny against the boulevard's grand proportions. Even stranger, the perfectly spaced tree trunks looked as if they had been built rather than having grown from the earth.

With the horses trotting, it took ten minutes to reach a broad square at the bottom. When they turned away from the river, Paul pointed out the Jardin des Tuileries on their right. "These are the royal gardens," Paul explained in response to Baptiste's bewildered look. "This part is now open to the public," he added, but Baptiste's confusion was profound and he scarcely heard the words. It seemed impossible that men had shaped everything he was looking at—not just the numberless buildings but the trees, too, like a forest that had been planted. The bare branches and symmetrical rows of trunks were stark in the low February light, and the relentless patterning of their forms took his breath away. *Who thought of this? How did they do it?*

As they drove along the north side of the gardens, Baptiste saw narrow streets and crowded alleys. There were far more vehicles now, many of them wagons pulled by mules, and their coachman cried out continually for the right-of-way, cracking his whip and reining the paired horses smartly. Soon they came to an immense structure that rose above them on the right—fully fifty feet tall, Baptiste guessed— its vast stone expanse worked in carvings of larger-than-life scenes that appeared to move even when the carriage was stopped. "That's the Louvre," Paul told him, "the royal palace." Half-nude women smiled coyly from above, warriors brandished swords and spears, horses reared, old men glowered from niches, richly carved chimneys towered over several domes. It seemed as long as the Champs-Elysées. When finally they turned toward the river and looked back on one entire side, Baptiste turned to Paul. "That roof is bigger than all of St. Louis," he said excitedly. Paul laughed as he took in the truth of Baptiste's words.

Paul left him opposite an island in the Seine covered with buildings. Before he disappeared into a nearby building for his first appointment, he pointed out the two towers of Notre-Dame, almost hidden behind the jumble of buildings covering the Ile de la Cité. Giddy with wonder, Baptiste stood against the low stone wall and watched the activity on all sides.

Twenty feet below, at the water's edge, men were unloading wine casks from several boats and stacking them like firewood on the muddy shore. Just upstream was moored an enormous barge, a hundred feet long, with a sign above the gangplank, BATEAU LAVOIR, a laundry boat. The length of the barge adjacent to the bank was covered with laundry hung overhead to dry from a wooden lattice structure. Looking beyond the lightly flapping sheets, Baptiste saw dozens of women bending low, each in an open compartment facing the river, a washboard and stacks of linen at her side. *Women wash laundry in the Missouri, too,* he thought, *but this beats all.*

Small boats passed constantly, most of them propelled by a pair of oarsmen. Occasionally larger craft powered by steam engines, like the ones he had seen in Le Havre, made their way upstream laden with sand or wood. Ribbons of black smoke issued from their stovepipe stacks, and their low chuffing resonated from the embankments.

To his right, two hundred yards downstream, a pedestrian bridge crossed the river, its arches a delicate tracery of black struts on solid piers. Baptiste realized the structure must be iron, and he marveled at how the light showed through the underside, as if it were no more substantial than the branches of a sapling. It led to a formal building topped by a tall and graceful dome. On each side a pair of two-story wings extended back toward the Seine in a gentle arc, as if they were embracing all who walked across the strangely pretty bridge.

The number of vehicles increased rapidly as the morning progressed, and their clatter filled the air. Baptiste could not fathom the number and variety of horses: huge draft animals with hooves the size of a man's head, sleek matched geldings harnessed to carriages, prancing Arabians ridden by dandies, docile nags pulling ramshackle carts, high-stepping mares in front of brightly painted gigs. He thought of old Limping Bear, who loved horses more than anyone he knew. *What would he make of all this?*

People walked by on all sides, some striding purposefully, others strolling in small groups. Gentlemen wore tailored suits and matching high-crowned hats; ladies had fine shawls and elaborate bonnets. The working people all wore head scarves or caps. Soldiers passed in twos and threes, their uniforms like dazzling finery: navy tunics set off by polished brass buttons, red trousers with black side stripes, white canvas belts drawn diagonally across their chests, and tall feathered helmets.

Many of the passersby were headed to the cafés that abounded. CAFÉ DEUX BILLARDS, CAFÉ GARNIER, CAFÉ DU PONT, Baptiste read above their big striped awnings. When Paul emerged after half an hour, he suggested they have a drink in one of them. What most impressed Baptiste was the size of the interior—there were thirty tables or more on the ground floor alone—and the constant bustle of activity. Waiters raced about with laden trays, people came and left, and everyone talked as if conversation were an entertainment that could never be exhausted.

That evening Paul took him to the Palais Royal, across from the Palais du Louvre, for what he called a *divertissement,* an entertainment. Organized around the extensive planted courtyard of a palace owned by the king's cousin, it was the center of nightlife for the rich and well connected. The horde of carriages as they approached was another shock to Baptiste; never had he seen a crowd like this. They jostled one another beneath arcades that opened onto the rectangular formal garden, with shops, cafés, and restaurants on the inside. Baptiste saw money changers, boot makers, barbers, tailors, gun sellers, clothiers. Paul told him there were gambling parlors in the upstairs rooms.

It seemed to Baptiste that everyone in Paris was there at the same time, all of them promenading as they inspected one another and bought things. When he and Paul tried to make their way across one of the large interior rooms, the press became so great that they were slowly being carried backward by all the bodies. For an instant Baptiste felt powerless, unable to understand what was happening or why others would seek out such a crowd. A rouged woman with blond ringlets and a low-cut dress caught his eye and smiled broadly. *Did she nod at me?* Paul grasped his elbow firmly and pulled him to the side, whispering in his ear over the din, "Come, Baptiste, not tonight."

They returned to Prince Franz's well past midnight, after eating at the best restaurant at the Palais Royal. But Baptiste was too excited to sleep, and for a long while he sat in his room and thought about all he had seen in a single day.

He considered the buildings that Paul had shown him on their drive—the Ecole Militaire, the church of Val-de-Grâce, the Chapelle de la Sorbonne, and many more—all of them calling attention to themselves with carvings and fine tracery. Baptiste had not known that stone could be quarried in such huge pieces, or that it could be worked as if it were river clay into shapes that looked lifelike and supple. He was puzzled when he considered the bulk of all that stone they had driven past, like an endless wall with infinite variations on one basic idea: to make something heavy look light.

He thought, too, of the odd glow from all the gaslight lamps at the Palais Royal, brighter than the afternoon sun, and of how it painted people's faces with seductive shadows. He opened the window and listened for something he knew he would hear, a dim background noise that subsided at night but did not go away. It was strange, and yet exciting in a way he had never before imagined.

Baptiste spent the first few days walking around the city on his own. Paul was immersed in the paperwork that had accumulated at his uncle's household during his eighteen-month absence: correspondence, acquisitions, family affairs, and, as he growled several times when he left the library table piled high with documents, "Bills! Nothing but God-blessed bills from my accursed creditors," as if they were there only to persecute him. But Baptiste had passed enough time with Paul to see how he spent money: he never calculated the cost of a purchase. In the flurry of nervous activity before they left New Orleans, Paul had bought everything he saw, so it seemed, and left Schlape to deal with payment. Baptiste couldn't square this appetite for acquisition with the surliness that now attended the resulting requests for money. Paul was rich. What was the problem in paying for the things he had so eagerly bought?

Baptiste's wanderings took him away from Prince Franz's house for hours at a time in ever-widening circles of discovery. The tailor had visited the day after their arrival to measure them both for new clothes, but in the meantime Baptiste wore the dark gray suit he had bought in New Orleans for the voyage. Freshly cleaned and pressed, and set off by a white shirt and loose black necktie, his suit passed Paul's muster as "respectable," though a gray felt hat with a narrow brim was forced upon him with a categorical pronouncement: "A gentleman always wears a hat in town." He had been offered the use of a horse, but he declined. After the sea voyage, he felt the urgent need to keep his feet on the ground. He also bore in mind one of Captain Clark's favorite pronouncements to his many visitors: "If you want to get to know a place for yourself, your own two legs are the surest conveyance."

Everything was interesting, every street, alley, window, doorway, courtyard. All his senses were sharpened and attentive to what lay ahead, as if he were hunting back in the Missouri forest. But instead of stalking game, his eyes fed on Paris. He surprised a coachman and servants by staring at the carriage they polished and the paving stones they swept. Instead of the dismissive gestures that he half-expected from his years in St. Louis, however, they reacted with embarrassment, a half bow, and a murmured *"Monsieur"* to acknowledge him. So here on the streets of Paris he was assumed to be a gentleman because he was dressed like one! That was a new and heady feeling, especially since the reaction of others was not the result of Paul's commanding presence. A new Baptiste had been fashioned without his realizing it, and he discovered that he liked it.

On his second day in Paris he walked a good distance east beyond the Hôtel de Ville, City Hall, to a section of the city where neither the streets nor the courtyards were paved. This area was much busier than any of the others he had walked through, with horses and vehicles filling the roadway while pedestrians jostled for room on both sides. The street ended in a substantial irregular square filled with awnings held up by poles. They covered an expanse of wagons whose open beds were laden with more kinds of foodstuffs than Baptiste knew existed: huge brown bread loaves stacked like flattened cannonballs; tables of cheeses in great wheels, triangles, and pyramids; sugar beets piled high in wine-colored mounds; bulky open bags of beans, lentils, and peas in warm hues of green, orange, and burgundy. He had happened upon a market, and its pungent smells and the high, piercing cries from the sellers hawking their goods caught him by surprise. *"Venez, venez! Approchez-vous, Mesdames, Messieurs!"* He plunged into the noisy crowd.

He was surrounded by strangers, many of them shrill and insistent, yet no one seemed bothered by the closeness or the din. But this was very different from the Palais Royal. Rows of carts on either side made little alleys, and the intersections and crossings were even more crowded. It felt like a festival. Every vendor had his own cry, many in accents and dialects he didn't understand, and their voices rose and fell with urgency. They singled out passersby and harangued them with loud pleas to look, to consider the quality, to buy. *"Regardez, Madame! Regardez mes jolies pommes!"* The reaction of those who passed was one of nonchalance, as if they had not heard the entreaties directed at them. When they continued on, the litany ceased and the vendor turned and found another mark.

The sellers all had double-pan scales on their carts, and they counterbalanced their merchandise with varied iron weights, calibrating the balance with dazzling speed as they cried out the cost. Watching their deft gestures, Baptiste thought of the card dealers in St. Louis saloons whose mastery had the same mix of insouciance and skill.

He eventually came to the far side of the square, which was flanked by a wall of buildings. Fish and creatures of the deep were spread out in the last several carts he passed. He looked in wonder at their staring eyes, shiny scales, and menacing teeth. The bed of snow on which they were arrayed astonished him, too—snow on a sunny day in the middle of the city! Yet the market-goers walked by as if it were usual. As he ventured out into the sunlight again, he felt in his coat's inner pocket for the coins Paul had cautioned him to hide. The heat of the covered marketplace had made him thirsty.

He walked past several piles of refuse that rose to his own height and from which emerged the fetid odor of spoiled vegetables. At first he thought the creatures sniffing through the market's leavings were dogs, but as he drew close he saw that they were human beings covered in filthy rags, rooting in the garbage for whatever they could find to eat. Torn cabbage leaves, shriveled carrots, half-rotten fruit—their haul was meager, but they clutched their findings close and looked around them with an air of distrust. Baptiste saw two tiny children crawling amid the garbage, their bodies covered with a layer of dirt that looked as if it had been baked into their skin. Only their eyelids, their mouths, and the palms of their hands revealed pink flesh. Baptiste looked around to see if anyone was with the two, but they seemed to be on their own. One of them—it appeared to be a little girl, though it was impossible to be sure—raised her arms toward him and began to cry. He crouched down at once and tried to calm her. But she only closed her eyes and sent more tears rolling down her grimy cheeks. Baptiste fished in his coat for a coin, thinking that the glint of metal would capture the child's attention.

Suddenly a hand brusquely swept up the child and snatched the coin from his fingers in one fluid movement. A young woman stood before him in the same rags as the others, her features scrawny and drawn where they could be made out beneath the grime. The child stopped bawling.

"Merci, Monsieur," she said, then asked if he had another, so that they might eat a bit of meat that night.

The stench that emanated from this creature was sickening. She gave him a semblance of a smile, and Baptiste saw that she had few teeth, and those were badly discolored. Her breath smelled of wine. He took another coin from his pocket, handed it to her, and walked on quickly.

The exchange had not gone unnoticed. Others materialized along his path and begged for coins. He hurried along, escaping their entreaties by darting down an alleyway. Leaning against a building for a moment, he found that he was breathing heavily. Across the street, a tavern's sign—a jug of wine and a cluster of grapes—swung lightly in the morning breeze. He would have a glass of wine to soothe his nerves.

It was dark inside the tavern. A few candles guttered in their wall holders on either side of the broad planks that served as a bar, and a bed of coals glowed brightly in the facing hearth. Rough-hewn tables and benches filled a plain room, and a few posters and handbills adorned the smoke-blackened walls. The atmosphere differed entirely from the cafés Paul had taken him to.

He removed his hat, ordered a pitcher of wine, and sat near one of the narrow windows that looked out onto the alley. Boisterous conversation and laughter came from a room in the back, but only half a dozen people occupied the front room. Baptiste greedily drank a glass of wine, then relaxed and sipped a second. Three men wandered in from the back and sat at the table next to his, loudly talking about politics. They reeked of alcohol.

"Taxes, and then more taxes! Tell me, how is this better than Bonaparte?" The man who slouched at Baptiste's side was tall and burly, and he slurred his words.

"Bonaparte, Bourbons, it's all the same shit!" his companion cried, and was immediately shushed by the third, who looked around nervously.

"Shut up, you imbecile," he hissed. "The police have informers everywhere."

Baptiste's attention was riveted on his neighbors, though he pretended to be uninterested. They looked at him, and he felt menace in the air.

"So they do," the big one said slowly; then, looking directly at Baptiste, he continued with an unctuous grin. "Perhaps you are one, Monsieur." He picked up the hat Baptiste had laid on the table and held it appraisingly, as if it were a piece of evidence. "Such a fine hat in such a poor neighborhood."

Baptiste put his glass aside, returned the man's stare, and said evenly, "Put the hat down." The husky man's friends watched in excited anticipation, as if they had seen this before.

"And if I don't?" The big man rose unsteadily from his seat and straightened up to his full height. He lifted the hat to put it on his greasy head, and as it passed in front of his eyes, Baptiste jumped to his feet, grabbed the man's shirt with his left hand, and pulled him forward. His right hand emerged from his vest grasping a hunting knife whose eight-inch blade flashed in the candlelight as he thrust it against the troublemaker's throat. All was still in the room. The two friends leaned back from the confrontation; laughter continued to drift in from the back.

Baptiste said softly, "You will put the hat down."

The other man didn't dare take his eyes from Baptiste's. Beads of sweat covered his brow and spittle caught in his scraggly mustache and beard as he silently mouthed his assent. He reached out and opened his palm, and the hat fell to the table, where it hit with a muffled thump.

"Stand up, all three of you!" Baptiste demanded. He released the burly man and pushed him toward the others. Still holding the knife in the direction of the three cowering together, he picked up his hat, put it on, and pulled several coins from his pocket and threw them on the table. "Monsieur, this is for the wine," he said to the owner, who was still behind the bar. He drew his knife in close to his face, looked at the three men across its tip, and said, "Good day, gentlemen." Then he was through the door.

He knew enough not to linger. The knife had surprised them, but it wouldn't be possible again. Baptiste hurried down the street and turned the corner, then headed down the first alley he came to. Once he had made sure he wasn't being followed, he relaxed. Then he recalled the initial exchange, so like boyhood quarrels, but with the strange addition of politics that were unknown to him. He reached up and touched the brim of his hat. *So this makes me look like a police informer,* he mused. *What else don't I know that could get me into trouble?*

His route back to Prince Franz's house took Baptiste along the Seine in the heart of the city. He sat on a stone wall at the water's edge. *It's not much of a river,* he thought, *but at least it has a current you can see.* As he watched workmen loading barges, his mind drifted to the life he had known before. *What would my mother think if she could see where I am?* he wondered.

When Baptiste thought of his mother, he thought of his spirit bird and the day she had said goodbye. Many more times in subsequent years she had told him to have strength, and he heard her voice now. *The spirit bird will always protect you, no matter what path I have taken.*

He felt in his pocket and found the little obsidian bird that meant strength. Since her death the stone figure had never left him, wrapped in a square of elk hide that fit neatly in his closed fist. It represented his tribal ties in a way that meant more to him than the Kit Fox Society, to which he could never fully belong. He thought of his mother's broken childhood and why a guardian spirit would have been important to her. She had fashioned the idea of this protective companion from her own mixed experience among the Shoshone, the Mandan, and the white *voyageurs,* and this, he thought, approximated his own destiny. The spirit bird seemed right for someone living in two different but overlapping worlds.

TWELVE

MARCH 1824

Prince Franz had decided to give a ball. Officially it was to be in honor of Paul before he and Baptiste left for Stuttgart, their next stop, but the reason mattered less than the gathering itself to this lover of the good life. *"Tout prétexte est bon!"* Paul said good-naturedly. "Any pretext will do."

Paul and Baptiste sat in the dark green leather-covered armchairs in the room Paul's uncle called his library, a long formal space on the second floor with five full-length windows that looked down onto the garden. Although shelves of books lined the walls, the owner's principal activity in this chamber was not reading, but the examination of his extensive collection of maps. Three or four large maps lay unrolled on a long trestle table in the center of the room, their corners held down by magnifying lenses, rocks, and fossils. Nearby, a huge globe nestled in a floor stand; its upper hemisphere turned so that North America faced the adjacent chair.

Paul and Baptiste had gotten into the habit of spending at least part of their mornings together in this long, cluttered room. It was the one place in Prince Franz's vast house where they could step out of the constant round of his activities: the frequent visits, official and unofficial, of diplomats with business to conduct with Württemberg; the comings and goings of mistresses; the dinners and card games that sometimes didn't wind down until after the sun had risen. The prince was not only an ambassador from a small but strategically important state and an aristocrat with ties of blood or marriage to most of the princely families of northern Europe; he was also a *bon vivant* with a prodigious appetite for women, gambling, hunting, and good food. An army of servants maintained the life of his household. The library was his refuge, the only room where servants were forbidden when the prince was in residence.

"We'll have to visit a number of suppliers before leaving Paris next week," Paul said. He mentioned half a dozen scientific instruments he was anxious to acquire.

"We are also to meet with Professor Picard," Paul went on. "He is an old friend of Professor Lebert, my teacher at the Stuttgart Gymnasium. Both of them worked with Bonpland and von Humboldt, and together they have educated an entire generation in the importance of the natural sciences. He's keen to examine some of the tribal objects I brought back."

Paul picked up one of the magnifiers and turned it slowly by its handle. "Now, it occurs to me, my friend, that before we travel to Württemberg I owe you a bit of background if you are to understand my family. Other than the bits and snatches you may have picked up on our passage from America, you really know next to nothing about my country and my family's place in it. Let me tell you about where I come from."

Paul pulled his chair close to the table and riffled through the maps until he found the one he wanted and laid it on top of the others. "Europe—1820" was printed in large gothic letters across the top.

"Here we are in France," Paul began, gesturing toward the large, roughly hexagonal shape colored in light blue. Close by, to the east, he indicated a much smaller territory in yellow. "This," he said as he pointed to it, "is the Kingdom of Württemberg; Stuttgart is its capital. My cousin Wilhelm is the king; that much you know. His father—my uncle Friedrich—was a duke. Then Napoleon came along and started making alliances with everyone but the devil, and all of a sudden, in return for fighting the Austrians, Friedrich woke up with a crown on his head." Paul shook his head at the image he had conjured. "It goes without saying that whatever I mention here today remains strictly between us."

Baptiste nodded.

"My uncle Friedrich was extremely clever and, let us say, original. His middle name could have been 'Excess,' starting with food. Napoleon said of him when they first met to conclude their alliance, 'King Friedrich is God's laboratory for testing the ability of the human skin to stretch!' He was far taller than me, and fully two hundred pounds heavier. You can imagine." He shook his head at the memory. "For whatever reason, my uncle took a particular interest in my education and made sure that I was part of his official entourage. Some of the older courtiers said I was his twin as a boy. When I was nine, I was named a captain in the King's Guard. Not even my older brother was given that honor. When I finally resigned my army commission at nineteen, I held the rank of major general."

"Why did you leave the army?"

"I never wanted to be a soldier in the first place!" Paul responded. "Of course, it's a bit more complicated than that, but that's the essential point," he added quietly. "There simply aren't other avenues available to a lesser member of the royal family. A young duke can't be a diplomat, he can't be a government functionary, and he certainly can't be involved in commerce. That leaves the clergy"—Paul grimaced— "but that has always seemed other than a real life to me. And so it was the army, whose ideals of chivalry, honor, and duty align perfectly with those of a small state whose very existence has been assured by feats of arms. My father and uncle were soldiers, my brother is a soldier, my sister married a soldier. Soldiers, soldiers, soldiers! It must seem unusual to someone from the wilds of the Missouri, where you do as you please, but this is what happens in the little world of the Württemberg aristocracy." He was laughing now, though halfheartedly. "They manage these things better in England. There a nobleman can have his enthusiasms as well as his passions, and learning is respected for its own sake. And here in France not even the Bourbons have been able to corrupt the idea of scientific exploration as an honorable pursuit. There's a reason von Humboldt has spent decades in Paris. Alas, things are different on the other side of the Rhine."

He saw the question in Baptiste's eyes. "The essential point is that I've chosen to devote myself to natural history, and it has set my family against me. That is what I am returning to."

"So your family disapproves of your trip," Baptiste said, trying to understand Paul's agitation. "Will I meet them all in Stuttgart?"

Paul shook his head slowly. "No, actually. But my cousin the king is in Stuttgart, and where the king goes, the court must follow."

"So we must go there," Baptiste said.

"Think of it this way, Baptiste. A royal family is like a grand version of Chouteau's fur traders on the Missouri, a family business where trust, loyalty, and control are everything, even over a difficult cousin like me."

Paul rose from the table and added, "With the difference, of course, that fur traders are actually expected to *do* something." He walked to one of the windows and gazed down into the garden, his hands clasped behind him.

The massive door to the library burst open. "So here you are!" Prince Franz cried, a tumbler of red wine in one hand, a lit cigar in the other. "Cooped up with my maps again, up to God knows what sort of mischief."

Paul and Baptiste both smiled as Prince Franz strode into the room and settled into one of the armchairs. He placed his glass carefully on a side table and drew deeply on his cigar.

"I was just telling Baptiste a bit about Württemberg, Uncle."

Prince Franz turned to Baptiste. "Then let me tell you a bit about the landscape you're about to enter, young man. Take a seat, both of you, and listen to an old diplomat talk about something he actually knows."

Prince Franz was remarkably frank in assessing his family and its future prospects. "My brother Friedrich had his quirks and excesses, God knows. Still, he had intelligence, audacity, and a sense of humor, which is far more than can be said of most rulers in Europe. It's little wonder that he and Bonaparte managed to come to terms so quickly."

His nephew, Wilhelm, the current king, had none of his father's qualities, according to Prince Franz, just an earnest blandness that commanded the attention, if not the respect, of his subjects. "He'll be on the throne until the day he dies," Prince Franz muttered, "when, for better or worse, his eldest son will succeed him. What a peculiar system, this business of families installed forever. It can't possibly go on."

He leaned forward to extinguish his cigar in a marble pestle on the table beside him, then immediately produced another from his vest pocket and lit it.

"Every family *I* know has a dullard uncle, an idiot cousin, a simple brother. Now imagine if your country were ruled by one of *them*. Your sons would serve in his army, your daughters would dream of his castle, your taxes would fill his coffers. And every time you were confronted with his portrait—on every coin, in every public building, on every monument—a little voice would whisper in your ear, *The man who rules my country is stupid.* The public knows about his true capacities. That's the secret no one will tell these kings."

"The French Revolution didn't change France very much?" Baptiste asked.

"Why it changed everything, everything!" Prince Franz shot back, then added, "Though I can well imagine that it appears that nothing at all had changed with these fool Bourbons back on top. It's simply that the overturning of the *ancien régime* hasn't filtered down for good. It will take time, but it will happen."

"What did change?" Baptiste inquired.

"For one thing, the whole business of the divine monarch and his ruling family. In one of history's better jokes, Napoleon's ascendancy to the throne of France was possible only because of the French Revolution," Prince Franz told him. "No Revolution, no Bonaparte: it's as simple as that. Within ten years the greatest defender of the Revolution's ideals had crowned himself Emperor of the French." Prince Franz took a long drink of wine and then continued, warming to his topic. "Once Napoleon came along, the whole system of rule by inheritance was turned on its head. That's why those of the *ancien régime* loathe him so and rail against him as a usurper. On top of that, the power, skill, and ambition of the man made every crowned head of Europe look mediocre, and everyone saw it. Everyone! Because whatever else you can say about him—and there is much to turn the heart sour—by God, he was *smart!*" He spat out the last word like a challenge, this trait that had lifted Bonaparte above the dreary stream of monarchs, princes, and hangers-on he had known, whose lack of intelligence hid behind divine right.

"My dear uncle, if Bonaparte was so smart, how do you explain his pathetic attempt to found his own dynasty?" Paul asked.

"This was surely one of his blind spots. If ever there were a man to whom there could be no logical successor, it was he. But never under-estimate the attraction of a family to serve as one's natural allies and protectors. In this the Bonapartes would have been no different from the Hohenzollerns, the Hapsburgs, the Bourbons, or the Romanovs." Prince Franz turned to address Baptiste.

"Tell me, how does a man become chief of one of your Indian tribes?"

"It's mostly by his courage and his accomplishments in battle, in de-feating the tribe's enemies. It also has to do with his wisdom in the Council of Elders. A man has to speak clearly and show that his deci-sions about things like choosing hunting grounds, making alliances, or settling disputes have been good ones."

"In other words, they are a pure warrior class," Prince Franz said. "Does a chief's son automatically become chief after his father?"

"Oh, no, sir. He has to prove himself, too. It's far more common that another young brave—perhaps his cousin or even a friend—will be recognized as chief by the Council of Elders."

Prince Franz drew deeply on his cigar and then said, "After Napoleon, Europe's warrior class is done for. They can prance about in their uniforms for as long as they like, but the man-at-arms as leader is a relic of the past. The future lies in commerce; the English have seen to that. Bonaparte wasn't infallible after all. He called the English a nation of shopkeepers. Perhaps it's just as well he hasn't lived to see the shopkeepers rule the earth." He settled back into the well-worn leather of his armchair. "I expect this is all new to you, young man. In your United States of America, you *elect* your leader; you don't in-herit him."

Baptiste sensed that Prince Franz was asking a question more than making a statement. "The details are new to me, sir, but my school-teacher in St. Louis made a particular point of the importance of what he called the two revolutions that changed the world, the American and the French." Prince Franz seemed interested, so Baptiste continued. "And Captain Clark often talked to me about Napoleon and how Mr. Jefferson's purchase of Louisiana would someday make the United States a great nation."

Prince Franz pulled his chair closer to the table and gestured to Baptiste and Paul to look at the map laid out before him. "Just imagine! Half a continent for sixty million francs!" He placed his hands on the center of the North American landmass and shook his head in disbelief. "But it did give Bonaparte the money he needed to equip his armies and secure his control of Europe. One continent for another."

"Baptiste was born in the far reaches of the territory that Bonaparte sold," Paul said. He placed his finger on the map and traced the Missouri northward until Baptiste nodded his assent, indicating the location of the Mandan villages. The three men peered at the map and the broad expanse surrounding Paul's finger, an area that bore no place names or geographic markers save the river.

"You're just another of Napoleon's lost children," Prince Franz exclaimed, "wandering the earth in search of an adventure whose time has passed!" He rose and strode to the window. "Ah, don't mind an old man's musings," he said in a soft voice as he looked up at the broken clouds. "That's the Old World talking, and you're from the New."

THIRTEEN

MARCH 1824

The mild weather on the night of Prince Franz's ball delighted everyone. While not warm, neither was it harsh and damp, a common circumstance in late March. The sun had shone brightly all day, leaving a breath of spring in the evening air that promised milder weather. When Baptiste and Paul returned at six o'clock, they found the entire household had been in a fury of preparation for the festivities: windows had been washed, floors stripped bare and polished, whole rooms of furniture moved to make way for the expected crowd. A few hours still remained before the first guests arrived, but Baptiste found it hard to see how the house could be made ready in such a short time with so much activity on every side.

They stood at the open doors of the cavernous ballroom on the second floor and watched the enormous chandelier being lowered from the ceiling to hang just above the floor. Half a dozen servants stood on chairs and reached into its branches, cleaning each of the faceted crystals with damp cloths. Others placed fresh candles among the gleaming clusters. The sparkling cascade of prisms made Baptiste think of laughter turned into glass. He had been fascinated with glass windowpanes when he first visited St. Louis as a young boy, and he remembered thinking as he watched Alberta clean the Clarks' oil-lamp chimneys that nothing could be more beautiful than curved glass. It was like a ripple in the creek transformed into a clear and brittle stone. A touch on his elbow woke him from his revery. Paul indicated the far end of the room.

"There's something you won't see on the frontier: *les frotteurs.*"

Baptiste watched three old men moving in circles as if they were skating on ice. They wore large felt pads on their feet, and they moved their legs back and forth vigorously as they turned around one another. Baptiste looked at Paul.

"They're polishing the parquet, don't you see?" Paul declared. "It wouldn't do to have a dance floor that didn't shine."

Paul continued up the main staircase, but Baptiste lingered.

A group of men carried in gilt chairs and music stands for the orchestra; they were followed by the musicians themselves in the most colorful clothes he had ever seen. Each wore a suit cut in the same style as those worn by the liveried servants, with a long coat and knee breeches, but fashioned of a brilliant purple brocade set off by black velvet touches at the cuffs, collar, and button closures. White silk stockings, shiny black shoes with buckles, and pure white wigs completed the antique effect. Baptiste thought of the portrait of General Washington in Captain Clark's study, an image when he was a boy of everything that was old and formal. The musicians removed their resplendent coats and placed them on the backs of the chairs, then took off their wigs and placed them on top of the music stands.

The men who had all looked so perfectly similar moments ago were, in fact, of different ages and countenances, some balding and grizzled, others with full heads of hair framing boyish faces. As the members of the orchestra found their places, a young man about his own age put a clarinet to his mouth and, miming the ardor of a snake charmer, addressed a slow glissando to his wig as if it were a sacred effigy. The musicians on either side laughed, and he was about to begin another passage when he glanced up and caught Baptiste's eye. He stiffened and lowered his instrument, smiling awkwardly. Baptiste saw that the music director had just entered the room. He wore no wig, and he did not remove his coat as he called the orchestra to order.

The musicians sat down, took up their instruments, and, at the conductor's downbeat, sounded a long full chord that thrilled Baptiste. Lost in the pure pleasure of the dance rhythms that filled the ballroom, he listened to them play several pieces. Eventually Schlape appeared at his side, a look of concern on his face. "Sir, wouldn't it be wise to take your bath and dress for the evening?"

"Yes, Schlape, of course. I just want to listen for a while." Baptiste gestured toward the orchestra.

Schlape leaned in closer and added in a more insistent tone, "If you don't mind my saying so, sir, your presence makes them uncomfortable."

Baptiste was surprised. "Why, Schlape?"

The older man raised his voice a little. "These musicians are preparing a prince's ball in honor of Duke Paul. You are one of Duke Paul's friends and cannot properly be seen to consort with the servants. Your proper place is among the guests tonight."

The conductor gave them both a long glance before taking up his baton and calling the ensemble to order.

"And you?" Baptiste asked.

"I am in service, sir, and you"—he raised his eyes to indicate the floor above where both Baptiste and Paul were housed—"are not."

Baptiste thought of the young clarinet player's diffidence. He saw that there was no use arguing, so he left the room, shadowed by Schlape, who waited on the landing while he walked up, as if to assure himself of the compliant behavior of a schoolboy.

Paul greeted him through the open door of his apartments. "There you are, my friend. Time to put on that new suit of clothes and prepare to meet Paris society."

He was standing in front of a cheval glass set diagonally in the corner of the room, adjusting his white tie and pulling his shirt cuffs down from his coat sleeves. To Baptiste, there were two Pauls, the real one seen from behind and his reflection, which nodded and talked to Baptiste as he primped before the mirror. A gold medal suspended from a broad scarlet ribbon hung around Paul's neck, and on his left breast pocket was pinned a smaller medal with the same striped ribbon Baptiste had first noticed in Le Havre. His face was ruddy from its recent scrubbing, his hair still damp and freshly combed; his eyes sparkled and his teeth gleamed. *I've never seen him look like this,* Baptiste thought.

"Quite impressive!" Baptiste said, and Paul turned around.

"It's time to clean up the uniform and"—he flicked an imaginary speck from his forearm—"brighten the armor."

"The ladies will notice; that's for certain."

"They can notice all they like, but nothing will come of it. Tonight is strictly about wives, untouchable daughters, and elderly aunts and, as the guest of honor, I have to be on my best behavior." Paul grimaced with pretended affliction.

"What does the big medal signify?" Baptiste asked.

"It's a decoration given to members of the Württemberg royal family."

"It is like the peace medals Indian chiefs wear around their necks, with the likeness of the Great Father in Washington," Baptiste said. Some of the old chiefs still wore profiles of Jefferson, given to them by Captain Clark or Captain Lewis many years ago. *Like Paul's decoration,* he reflected, *they conferred importance on the wearer.*

"Yes, I suppose it is"—Paul laughed—"but in this case the Great Father is the founder of our dynasty."

"And the one on your coat?"

Paul fingered the ribbon lightly. "That one is special. It's for valor and was conferred by my uncle when I served in his guard." He turned back to the mirror and changed the subject abruptly. "I asked Schlape to help you dress." Paul's face spoke to him from the frame. "You'll find that it takes a bit of getting used to."

Not long afterward, Baptiste descended the staircase looking elegant, or at least formal. Schlape had been indispensable in attaching the studs down the shirt's starched front and the links at its cuffs. There was nothing he could do about the stiff collar, however, and Baptiste strained against its chafing like a young horse fighting the bridle.

Downstairs he found a thorough transformation. The *frotteurs* had disappeared and the broad expanse of wood gleamed. The smell of wax was replaced by the perfume of flowers, which adorned every surface.

The musicians were all seated, wigs on their heads and jackets in place, a double arc of premature grandfathers, it looked to Baptiste. Tables bearing food and wine lined the salons and wide hallways, and countless candles augmented the gas lamps to cast a glittering light throughout the rooms. There was an expectant hush, like a drawing in of breath before the change that was about to occur.

A liveried footman whispered in Prince Franz's ear and hurried back down the main staircase. The prince drew Paul to stand with him just inside the entrance to the main salon. Another uniformed servant stood at attention at the top of the stairs, and when the first guests arrived and gave their names, he struck the floor with a long wooden rod and shouted out to the empty rooms, "His Highness Prince Philippe de Savoie and Her Highness the Princess Elisabeth!" Baptiste stood on the broad landing, keeping well off to the side, where he could lean on the balustrade and watch the parade of arrivals. Within ten minutes the quiet atrium was awash in the din of social chatter: greetings, laughter, the tread of feet, and the constant braying of the *maître d'hôtel* as he presented the guests to Prince Franz and to Paul. The clatter of horses in the courtyard welled up from below, met by the swells of music that issued from the ballroom and gave those waiting to be announced a sense of urgent gaiety. Baptiste felt a thrill of excitement and let the sensations roll over him like a wave: whiffs of perfume, flashing jewels, uniforms covered with gold braid and medals, gowns that shimmered like liquid.

The pace of arrivals didn't slacken, and the broad staircase was crowded with those waiting to greet their host. Baptiste decided it was time to go in to the ballroom. He passed slowly through each of the salons being used, observing the groups of guests gathered together drinking, eating, and talking with determined good humor. They all seemed to know one another and greeted each other easily as they walked about. *I am clearly not one of them,* he reflected as he returned their occasional looks of curiosity with an even gaze, *and they don't know what to make of me.*

He entered the main salon and took a glass of champagne offered by a servant. Above the din he heard, *"Monsieur Jean-François Hennesy et Mademoiselle Maura Hennesy!"* Baptiste was surprised and curious for a moment as he strained to see the receiving line, but he told himself he was mistaken. Then, through the mingling guests, he caught a glimpse of the porcelain white skin of her neck and shoulders as she curtsied to Prince Franz. Her hair was up, and a dark blue silk dress set off her light complexion dramatically. Beside her, a tall man with craggy features and gray temples greeted the prince warmly and shared a private joke that made them both laugh.

Following at a discreet distance, Baptiste watched Maura and her father make their way through the crowd and stop several times to talk with others. He maneuvered so that he could see her from the side and, convinced he was unnoticed, watched her over the shoulders of the couple who had joined her and her father. When she turned to address them, her face was even more astonishing than he remembered. Her dark hair, eyebrows, and eyelashes set off her perfect skin, which tonight was touched by a blush of pink. Her square, strong jaw was apparent in profile. She wore a necklace and earrings of clear blue stones that amplified the deep blue of her eyes, as if they, too, were jewels in the set. *How can I talk to her?* A thousand doubts raced through his mind and heightened his frustration and his desire. *Will she remember me?* The little group broke up, and before he could withdraw, he saw her coming toward him.

"Monsieur Charbonneau, that *is* you, isn't it? I was hoping you would be here." She greeted him in English, and the familiar cadence mixed with her lilting accent was like music. "Come meet my father, won't you?" He shook her hand and smiled awkwardly, pleased and surprised, and she led him across the room, striding ahead with a forthright step.

"Papa, I'd like you to meet Monsieur Jean-Baptiste Charbonneau, Duke Paul's friend from St. Louis in America," she said as they reached her father.

"Delighted to meet you, Monsieur Charbonneau," Mr. Hennesy said with a smile. His face exuded warmth and curiosity, and his grip was strong. "Maura tells me that she and my wife met you in Le Havre."

"Yes, sir. We met in the customs shed. Our ships arrived at the same time."

"I'll wager you are glad to have your legs on solid ground once again," Maura's father said. "My wife was still talking about the storm at sea when she left for Bordeaux last week." He paused. "Overland." He gestured to Maura. "But my daughter has the sea legs of a sailor: never seasick a day in her life."

Maura laughed and put her arm on her father's shoulder. "I got that from you, Papa. It is very useful to feel at ease in a ship." She turned to Baptiste. "Don't you agree, Mr. Charbonneau?"

"It was my first time on the ocean," Baptiste said. "Duke Paul and I will travel to Stuttgart by coach in a few days. I expect it will be easier to bear."

Baptiste tried hard to focus on the pleasantries, but he was distracted by the beauty of the woman who stood before him, swathed in silk and animated with good humor. Mr. Hennesy signaled with a wave and a nod to someone across the room, then turned to Baptiste. "Sir, may I leave my daughter in your care? There are some gentlemen waiting to talk to me."

"Yes, of course, sir. It would be my pleasure," Baptiste responded, suppressing a smile at the quick turn of events.

Hennesy turned and disappeared into the crowd.

Maura spoke first. "He'll be a while, I'm afraid, Mr. Charbonneau. It's business he's talking."

"That is my gain. Is he a diplomat?"

She looked at him appraisingly. "Not exactly. He's a wine merchant. He supplies Prince Franz's household and many of the other embassies. But the wine business, to borrow a phrase from the nuns, covers a multitude of sins."

Baptiste decided not to ask about the specifics. "How did you know I might be here tonight?"

"The prince is one of Papa's better clients. My father learned that the two of you were staying here. You didn't expect to see me, though, did you?" she said as if she were teasing him.

"No, I didn't. I was surprised." He felt himself blush. "And very glad!" he added quickly.

Maura laughed happily. "Then why did you follow me about like a schoolboy and not come and say hello?" she gently chided him.

Baptiste began to stammer an explanation, but she cut him off. "You have not been to many balls. A woman is constantly aware of who is looking at her. She has to be."

"And why is that?" Baptiste asked.

Maura paused, as if considering a riddle. "Let me put it this way: the prey is wise to observe the hunter."

"Is this a hunt?"

"Oh, yes, certainly. Come, let's find someplace to sit and you can tell me what you think of Paris."

Maura led him to a small room opposite the ballroom where chairs and small tables had been set in clusters along the walls. Several small groups of guests, most of them elderly, had installed themselves there to talk. She found two chairs that faced the darkened garden through a window and set her champagne flute on the adjacent table. "We'll be fine here," she said as she sat. "No one can accuse us of running off into the night, and we won't be bothered by the dreary visiting in the main rooms."

Baptiste was impressed by Maura's decisiveness, and glad to be in the company of someone familiar. "Do you know most of these people?" he began hesitantly.

"Let us say I have met many of them, and been to many of these affairs in their company," Maura responded. "But that isn't the same as knowing someone. I'm sure you would agree."

Baptiste nodded. "I've met a few of them in the last few weeks, but I don't recognize a soul tonight."

"You recognized me!" Maura exclaimed, then added quietly, "Now we can get to know each other better, if you like."

They talked intently for a long time. Maura told him about her family. The Hennesys had been in France for many generations but still thought of themselves as Irish. They had been expelled from Ireland by the English at the end of the seventeenth century, and had served as mercenary officers in the armies of France and Spain. Her great-grandfather returned victorious and rich from one of the many campaigns and had established the family as wine producers in the Gironde region outside of Bordeaux. The business flourished with the extensive contacts he maintained throughout Europe. Fortunately, she told him, the age-old mistrust of France for England allowed for a special relationship with certain elements in Ireland, on the basis of religion and politics, and her family was at the center of that connection. "My father is a passionate republican for both Ireland and France," she told him, and alluded to the delicate nature of his position under the restored Bourbons. He was convinced that France would be better off without a monarchy, and his ideas set him at odds with French rulers at a time when opposition to the regime was mounting. Baptiste knew little of the specifics of the history and politics she talked about, and he asked many questions. Her passion for justice was clear.

Baptiste watched Maura's lively eyes and the way the skin of her throat grew taut and then slackened, and he realized that he was listening to every word she had to say while at the same time being lost in her features, the sound of her voice, the imagined velvet of her skin beneath the crisp folds of silk. The awareness of the contradictory impulses that crossed his mind was both disquieting and pleasurable.

Her mother was Irish, and Maura had been born in County Cork. Her mother and she were on a trip to France when Maura was seven, and they had been barred from returning to Ireland. She had lived for much of her life in Paris.

"Why couldn't you go home?" Baptiste asked.

"It was during the Napoleonic wars," Maura explained, "and the British blockade of France became impassable, even for my father. So my mother set up house in Paris for the duration, before moving to our vineyards in the Gironde when peace came." Now Maura was a student, determined to study medicine, though it was unheard-of for a woman to be accepted at the medical faculty of the Sorbonne.

Her account of sudden departures, new beginnings, and endless travels comforted him and made it easier for Baptiste to talk about himself. He told her about his parents and she seemed interested as he described his youthful wanderings. He explained how he came to be in Paris with Duke Paul.

"What do you think of the French?" she asked.

He hesitated, trying to find the right words. "The French certainly value their opinions. I've met people who know about the history of America and others who know nothing of my country, people who love the king and others who hate him, people who want change and others who fear it, but I am never in doubt about what they think."

"Yes, the French will always state their point of view forcefully. But that is not necessarily a bad thing. Don't you agree?"

She asked what he thought of the Palace of the Louvre; she wondered if he had visited any of the *quartiers populaires,* the poor sections of Paris; she wanted to know what he thought of Prince Franz's ball. None of her questions were frivolous. *Here is someone,* he thought, *who would always be worth talking to.*

"Do you think you will stay in Europe for a long time?"

"Duke Paul talked about a year or two when he proposed that I come here to help with his collection," Baptiste told her. "I'm seeing wonders every day, meeting his acquaintances, and learning about things I never imagined. Even though I expect that will change once we settle down in Württemberg, I'm in no hurry to turn around. The frontier will still be there when I go home."

They both paused, sipping champagne and sharing glances. Then Maura continued. "Are you enjoying your travels?"

"Yes, I am," he responded without hesitating, "but it is taking some getting used to. In America, I was the one with experience and useful contacts. While we were on the river, Duke Paul depended upon me to handle the officials, the Indians, the riverboat men and traders. That changed when we arrived in New Orleans, and here in Europe I might as well be a newborn. It's peculiar to be on the other side of the fence."

When he whispered that Paul had been intent on shooting anything that moved in North America, "for the collection," Maura laughed and looked around hurriedly to make sure that no one could hear them.

"Heavens above, the German collectors! Papa says they'll shoot your cow if she's not on a lead, all in the name of science." Baptiste found her charming.

"I will say this for them, though," Maura continued. "They are interested in our fellow human beings. Some of them are prepared to regard servants and foreigners as something other than animals, and are not blinded by the curse of class. Why, right here in Paris, Mr. von Humboldt has been very outspoken on the subject of slavery." She added in a more reflective tone, "My father says the dignity of man might actually amount to something if these new travelers continue with their questions about the human race, but meanwhile"—she looked about her—"very little changes."

She inclined her head to the side, signaling Baptiste to listen to the group of four seated nearby. He heard the patter of frivolous commentary on clothes, houses, hunting, and the other guests. She met his eyes with her own and shook her head very slightly.

"There you are, the two of you, hiding like a pair of bandits! I've been through half this house to ferret you out." Maura's father winked at his daughter as he sat down. His face was flushed and he seemed in high good spirits.

"I've been hearing about Monsieur Charbonneau's first experiences in Europe, Papa, and trying to help him understand the French."

"Good luck to you on that!" her father shot back. "We can't understand ourselves, we French." He shrugged. "Though we'll talk you under the table while we try." He looked around as if searching for something; his features brightened as a uniformed servant entered the room with a tray of glasses. "Splendid! Let us drink a wee dram, the three of us together. What do you say?"

Baptiste and Maura nodded their assent. As they waited for the servant to reach them, a woman's voice rose shrilly. "Now they want half the day Sunday free. 'To go to Mass, Madame.'" The woman parodied a peasant's accent, then sailed on in a tone of injury. "Have you ever heard the like?"

The three were riveted by the woman's pronouncement, silenced by the pitiless message in her words. Mr. Hennesy coughed to cover his discomfiture. As the servant leaned forward to offer the glasses, Baptiste saw that his eyes glistened and his jaw muscle was clenched in a mask of control beneath his powdered wig. *Underneath that ridiculous costume,* Baptiste said to himself, *there's a man who could break that woman's neck with his bare hands.* The servant withdrew, the moment passed.

Maura's father raised his glass and said in a loud voice, "To the rights of man."

They drank and then Mr. Hennesy said, "Come, what do you say to a breath of fresh air?"

Clearly familiar with the layout of the rooms, he led them along a crowded corridor to the end of the wing opposite the ballroom. He opened a door hidden in the painted woodwork and they stepped out onto a wide terrace that capped the wing. To their left, across the central courtyard, was the house's other side and the ballroom. To their right, they could look down to where the stables and the servants' quarters were set around a roughly cobbled square, one floor below. Hennesy inhaled the night air deeply and said, "Prince Franz calls this his 'secret terrace,' where no one can find him. We often come here to smoke a cigar and talk business."

Baptiste looked across to the dancers and the immense chandelier glittering through the row of tall windows, the orchestra resonant but muffled. The ballroom looked like a colossal music box with figures turning and bowing in time to the melody. He imagined the floor flexing and creaking under the weight of the dancers.

"This is *much* better! Thank you, Papa." Maura looked over the stone banister to the stable courtyard at ground level. "I'm not sure I would call it secret, however," she said in a quiet voice. "There are plenty of others to keep us company." Dozens of servants and grooms were drinking and chatting in small groups, their forms lit by lanterns hung from the stable bays or placed directly on the cobblestones where they were gathered. Baptiste saw two Negro servants sitting apart from the others on stone steps, dressed in a green-and-gold livery whose splendor outshone even the lavender silk worn by the musicians. Maura saw Baptiste take notice and volunteered, "They're the Duchesse de Chaumont's grooms. They come from her sugar plantations in the West Indies. She's very proud of what she calls her *free* Negroes and their fancy suit of clothes." Baptiste saw a hardness in her blue eyes. "They'll sit by themselves all night, two tigers in a zoo, until Madame la Duchesse is ready to return to her palace."

Hennesy lit a cigar and gestured to the servants' courtyard. "These are two separate worlds."

"Why is there such hatred for those who serve?" Baptiste ventured. "That woman inside talked as if the servant were invisible."

"In the minds of their masters, they don't exist, certainly not as equals. Yet thirty years ago a king was put to death to prove that they *did* exist, that they drew breath and dreamed and laughed and suffered just like their betters."

"Then why does this go on?"

"Do you know what Talleyrand said of the Bourbons?" Hennesy asked him. " 'They have learned nothing, and they have forgotten nothing.' But if I may make so bold, history has not forgotten. Some say that Louis the Eighteenth is sitting on a powder keg. It only remains for someone to light the fuse"—he lowered his cigar as if doing so— "and *boom*! No more Bourbons."

The three of them stood for a long moment in the stillness of the evening, the sound of the orchestra filtering across the courtyard and overlying darkness while occasional laughter and exclamations, close by and immediate, rose from below.

"Shall we go back in?" Hennesy turned slowly, then threw his unfinished cigar in the direction of the ballroom. Its glowing tip described a lazy arc, then disappeared when it landed on the gravel. "I've got to find that duke of yours before the evening wears thin."

Hennesy arranged to meet Maura in the ballroom in a quarter of an hour, then hurried ahead. As Baptiste and Maura made their way down the long hallway, he turned to her, unsure of what he wanted to say. "Maura . . . That is, Miss Hennesy . . ."

She shook her head. "No, Maura, please. I like the way you say my name."

He said it again, then struggled through a question. "I'll be going to Stuttgart in a few days. I'm wondering if we'll see each other another time."

"Not before the two of you leave, that is certain. And I won't be going to Württemberg." She considered her words. "But you may well return to Paris. Isn't that so? I am here more often than not."

What she said was so vague that it confused him. He did not know if she wanted to see him again or not. But he pictured her descending the stairs with her father, stepping out of his life, and he was unwilling to accept it. She saw this in his eyes. He was about to speak again when she said, "You can write to me if you would like to."

"Yes, I would." Baptiste trembled inwardly with relief.

"You'll have to commit the address to memory. Are you ready?"

He tried to pay attention to what she was saying but was unable to focus on anything but her face, so close to him, full of animation and urgency: dark lashes against the palest skin, the finely turned edge of her nostrils, the delicate curve of her lips where the shiny red paint gave way to the pink flesh within as she whispered. Then she had finished, and he had heard nothing.

When he was unable to repeat it to her, she looked at him, exasperated. "Did you not hear me?"

"No, I . . . I . . ."

"Collège des Irlandais, rue du Cheval Vert, Paris. Just think of an Irishman riding a green horse in Paris, and you won't forget it."

As they continued toward the ballroom, she said, "One thing more: you're my cousin," as if they were any couple trading pleasantries at a ball.

Baptiste looked at her questioningly. Other guests were nearby now, so she whispered. "Your letters will be read," she told him. "You are my American cousin on my father's side. One of his brothers moved to America years ago. Don't write anything you're not prepared to have a stranger read."

Just then her father appeared with Paul outside the ballroom and called them over. "The duke and I have concluded our business, my dear." He turned to Baptiste. "Thank you, young man, for keeping my daughter company. I trust her curiosity did not wear you out."

"On the contrary, sir. I think I asked more questions than she." He turned to Maura. "It was a pleasure I hope to have again."

"We'll have to convince them to visit us in Württemberg," Paul said jovially. "Knowing how much my cousin favors your wine, Mr. Hennesy, you would be foolish not to make an appearance at court."

"So I would, my good duke. Let us hope our paths will cross there before long. But now we must say our goodbyes."

The four of them shook hands, and in the next moment Maura and her father were descending the staircase while Baptiste watched from above. His pulse quickened as he repeated Maura's strange formula for her address.

FOURTEEN

The next afternoon, Paul and Baptiste took Prince Franz's barouche to Professor Picard's. Paul was unhappy to be in such a showy vehicle. It was lacquered and highly polished, the Württemberg coat of arms on the doors, a liveried coachman up on the box. But none of his uncle's closed carriages could accommodate the bulky mahogany case packed with the curiosities from North America that Paul was eager to discuss with Picard. He had spent the morning carefully packing the crate with relics from his voyage up the Missouri: rocks and crystal formations, dried plants, several whole animals in sealed bottles of preserving alcohol, and many of the objects that he had bartered for or bought from the Indians. The box sat opposite them on the rearward-facing seat, firmly braced with wooden struts against the tufted leather. Its sheer bulk and fancy silver fittings made it seem as if the two men were in the company of a third passenger.

They drove for half an hour across the city, threading through neighborhoods Baptiste had not yet seen. At first most of the streets were narrow and lined with high stone walls, behind which, Paul told him, lay gardens, courtyards, and fine houses. The sharp-edged clatter of the horses and carriage echoed from the walls and the elegant wooden doors set into them at irregular intervals. Baptiste noted again that many of the streets were paved in stone, unlike the roads in St. Louis.

It must have taken armies of laborers, kneeling in the dirt and mud, countless years to place, replace, and repair each chiseled block of granite so that they formed the fanlike patterns over which they now rode. It amazed him: solid, extensive, and perfectly measured, the stone streets of Paris seemed as if they had always been there and would long outlast all those who trod on them.

Paul told the driver that he wanted to pass in front of the cathedral when they crossed the river. The coachman said *"Oui, Monsieur!"* over his shoulder. They had already seen several impressive churches whose domes and bell towers rose high above the surrounding structures. "Saint-Paul," "Saint-Gervais," Paul announced in turn as each came into view, enjoying his role as guide to someone so impressed with what he was seeing. Then, as the carriage turned onto a bridge, the ponderous profile of a mammoth twin-towered church rose on an island directly in front of them: "Notre-Dame." They drew up before it and Baptiste strained to take in every detail of the facade, which vibrated with statues of countless figures.

"Who built this?" he asked at last, his question a mixture of awe and curiosity.

"Thousands of people, thousands of the faithful. It took them over two hundred years. It's one of the masterpieces of the Gothic style," Paul told him. "There are cathedrals more or less like this all across Europe. You must return to see the interior before we leave Paris. But now I'm afraid we mustn't keep Professor Picard waiting." He told the coachman to drive on.

In a quarter of an hour they pulled in to the forecourt of a small palace that was even grander than Prince Franz's stately house. As the gates closed behind them, they surveyed the sober expanse of stone, which extended forward on both sides in curved wings of a single story. In answer to Baptiste's wide-eyed stare, Paul said, "Picard is from minor nobility in Burgundy. But his wife"—he inclined his head to take in the entire *hôtel particulier*—"is part of the de La Rochefoucauld family, one of France's noblest and richest."

A small door opened in one of the flanking wings and a short, grizzled man made his way briskly across the gravel. He cried out, "Here you are at last, back from across the sea to show me your wonders!" as he wiped his hands on a coarse brown tunic that covered his clothes.

They descended and the man greeted Paul warmly, then turned to Baptiste.

"I am Marc-Antoine Picard, and you are most certainly the young man Duke Paul told me about. Welcome!" The professor turned back to the house, talking excitedly as he led them across the forecourt. "If you don't mind, we'll go directly to my studio." He told a servant, "Have Monsieur le Duc's trunk brought to us in the atelier at once."

They followed him down a long, light-filled gallery whose floor was worked in large squares of black and white marble set diagonally. On both sides, busts and vases stood on classical pedestals between window bays that gave on to a side garden. "My wife's family collected antiquities in Italy under Napoleon," he told Baptiste, who looked with curiosity at the statues, "but despite my given name, Mark Antony, I do not share their passion for long-dead emperors." He turned to Paul and added, "Nor, now that I come to think of it, for recently dead emperors, either." The rounded ceiling was covered with paintings, and Baptiste caught glimpses of what looked like processions and battle scenes, richly tinted against a sky that varied from the palest blue to the ominous gray clouds of a thunderstorm, as if damnation were arriving from on high.

They stepped out into a garden bathed in sunlight. It was warmer there, as the high walls protected it from the March wind. In the center lay a formal array of flower beds around a large fountain of carved dolphins. Beyond the round basin, the paths led into a tree-filled park. The fountain was dry, the flower beds unturned, but Baptiste could envision the luxuriance of spring in this hidden place south of the Seine, so near the heart of the city. Picard led them through an iron gate recessed in a tall evergreen hedge to a long, low stone pavilion that looked out onto the park. Picard pushed wide the oak door and beckoned them in with a flourish.

"Gentlemen, my *sanctum sanctorum!*"

Baptiste's eyes adjusted slowly to the dark interior, and out of the gloom materialized a very large room filled with long oak tables covered with objects. He saw rocks and mineral specimens; two tables along a wall held bones and partial skeletons; at the far end of the room, he noticed, were several stuffed birds. Along the bank of windows that looked out on the park, several tables supported numerous tall jars containing specimens in fluid. Baptiste approached and saw that the smaller bottles contained large scorpions and spiders suspended in blue liquid, and the larger ones held small mammals— mice, squirrels, a pair of raccoons—in a yellowish solution, their legs extended and feet splayed as if they had been frozen while swimming. On an adjacent table, the partially dissected body of an animal lay in a pool of blood at the center of a marble slab, next to several scalpels and probes and a flickering gas lamp. The professor had no doubt been summoned from this operation; the air was heavy with the odor of preserving alcohol.

"Felis pardalis," Picard said with evident pride, "a nocturnal wildcat recently collected by a colleague in Mexico. It much resembles a miniature leopard." He opened a small cupboard and produced the skin. "Have you ever felt more luxuriant fur? Of course Monsieur Villandry skinned it *in situ* so the viscera could be preserved, but one can imagine the heavenly grace of this"—he brandished the pelt—"in motion."

Paul and Baptiste ran their hands through the fur, whose mottled bands and black-ringed spots of orange made a vivid pattern against its tawny background. Paul peered at the cat's organs. "A mature male, is it?"

"That's right. Quite a bit smaller than his cousin *Panthera onca,* what the Spanish call 'jaguar.' This species we call 'ocelot,' from the Nahuatl word *ocelotl.* I'm sure we're far from done with the cat family in Central and South America." He replaced the fur in the cupboard carefully. "How I would love to observe this fellow in the wild! But an old man must content himself with pleasures closer to hand." He motioned them to the back of the long atelier.

They eased between the laden tables and shelves. Baptiste corrected his first impression of impenetrable clutter; as they threaded their way through the room, he saw that although every surface was crowded, each object was carefully arranged. Octagonal paperboard labels bearing the scientific details of its subject in a precise hand were attached to every specimen. The atelier was meticulously clean.

At the back of the room, the professor's broad desk sat diagonally across a corner, facing his collection. It was covered by an intricately patterned Turkish carpet whose deep reds and blues overhung the sides of the desk. A blotter pad was flanked by a crystal inkstand and penholder. The only other object was a large round wooden platter; its dark center was incised with asymmetric carvings, and its rim decorated with eight white triangles evenly spaced around the circumference. On the blotter lay a sheet of paper with what looked like a tracing of the platter's central design. When Picard saw Baptiste's inquisitive look, he picked up the platter and said, "Haida, from the northwest coast of your continent. A colleague in Saint Petersburg collected it from a fur trader." He set it down carefully and motioned them to several chairs drawn up nearby in front of a small tile-covered stove; its faint heat made the corner of the cool room comfortable.

"I allow just one of my servants in here, and that infrequently," Picard said, "so I can only offer you the Armagnac I pour myself." As he sat down, Baptiste looked at Picard closely. His sparse hair was black on top and gray at the temples, cut short and brushed forward without much care. The deep lines on his face amplified an impression of age and authority. Picard poured three glasses and sat back. "Here's to the unknown, gentlemen."

As they drank, two men arrived with Paul's trunk. Picard carefully guided them to the back of the atelier with their unwieldy burden, and they deposited their load in the open space before the stove. He rubbed his hands with anticipation.

For the rest of the afternoon they sat together, enthralling Picard as Paul showed him woven blankets, embroidered buckskin shirts and leggings, weapons, tools, jewelry, handicrafts, and what he called "fetish pieces," which Baptiste knew as sacred objects that bound their owner to a specific clan or ceremonial society. Paul savored the role of benefactor and collector, removing each piece in turn and, as he unwrapped the folds of cloth, telling the story of its provenance and how he had bought or traded for it. His surprise and delight were as evident as Picard's at the appearance of certain pieces, as if he, too, were seeing them for the first time. Baptiste thought he had quite likely forgotten about many of the things he had brought home.

"This is from the Sioux," Paul said as he lifted a painted round shield of stretched buffalo hide two feet in diameter. "Every Indian brave has his own."

Picard rose up from his chair, not waiting for it to be handed over for examination. "Oh, what an extraordinary piece!" he exclaimed, running his fingers across its surface. "I wonder how effective it would be in battle."

Picard's spontaneous eagerness to know about each object intrigued Baptiste, and made him feel knowledgeable. He explained that it was an essential part of a warrior's weapons. "The designs aren't just decoration; they are sacred. Once the rawhide has been stiffened with lye, it can withstand the impact of an arrow."

"I would never have known," Picard murmured.

Paul next produced a pair of elk-hide moccasins richly embroidered with porcupine quills worked in a circular pattern. "I collected these from a Pawnee when we stopped at Cabanné's Post," he said.

Again, Picard was taken with the beauty and strangeness of the objects. "Have you ever seen such beadwork on a moccasin?" His eyes, his voice, his whole body expressed joy at seeing wonderful things whose existence he had not imagined.

Baptiste had never seen anyone take such pleasure in holding ordinary things used by all the tribes, and Picard's curiosity puzzled him. *Why did he trace the designs of the Haida platter, or turn quivers and shields and knives this way and that against the light?* Even Paul seldom examined so closely the things he bought and traded for.

When Paul held up a bow that he identified as Arikara, Baptiste gently corrected him. "That's a Cheyenne design on the handle," he said. "They can look very similar." Paul shrugged and handed the piece to Picard, who turned its arc slowly in his hands and felt the bone and hide inlays. "Gervais brought me one not unlike it from the Crow tribe three years ago," Picard told them.

As he expounded on the origin or function of a piece, Paul often turned to Baptiste for confirmation, and Baptiste supplied the asked-for information as plainly as possible. "No, that is a warrior's necklace.

A squaw would never wear grizzly claws," or "Those are not Blackfoot leggings; they are Lakota Sioux. The quill work shows the warrior was a member of the Bear Clan." His lucid elaborations brought a courteous assent from Paul.

Paul gently lifted a bundle from deep within the box. "These are toys from the Mandan tribe," he said as he unfolded a brown cloth wrapper. He picked up a sphere and held it in the palm of his hand. It was six inches in diameter and minutely embroidered with colored porcupine quills in geometric patterns of green, red, and yellow. Its bright colors caught the light and glistened as Paul turned it in his fingers. "It is used in the women's ball games," he said, placing it on the table. Next he picked up an eight-inch hoop of light-colored wood, across which rawhide strips had been fastened to divide it into quadrants, with several large openings spaced along the inner circumference. He held it high as he reached in the box with his other hand for a three-foot length of slender blond wood, one of its ends sharpened to a point. He jabbed at the crisscross circle with this improvised spear and said, "Many such hoops and poles are used by the boys of the tribe in a fast-moving game in which they run about the entire village."

Paul smiled as he reached for the next piece. He lifted out two foot-long cylinders bound together, put them to his lips, and produced a raucous discord as he blew into their slender chambers. They were whistles made of goose bone, each one wrapped in bright beadwork bands of green, black, and red, hanging together from a long loop of rawhide. They looked like tiny snakes, exotic and mysterious, in the atelier's dim light. "A child's toy, I suppose," Picard volunteered, and Paul nodded.

Baptiste was unable to contain his uneasiness. The ball, the hoop, and the pole were, in fact, used in Mandan games; many times he had raced about the village with his friends as they battled for control of the fast-rolling hoop. But the double whistle was sacred. Only a member of the Ravens, the men's secret society, would be allowed to blow in it, and then only during their ceremonies. He wondered how Paul had convinced its owner to part with it.

Baptiste's emotions danced around in his chest. Pride, surprise, nostaligia, regret, anger—all came to the surface, triggered by these familiar objects. He knew almost every one from his own experience, having encountered them among the tribes who had fashioned them and used them daily or bartered them as trade objects along the Missouri. How lifeless they were here as Paul and Picard examined them with admiration. Seeing them away from that long stretch of river and endless plain that had been his entire world until recently, he felt sad. He missed the world of his childhood, and he didn't like seeing these things handled this way.

When Baptiste described the function of a bone scraper used to clean hides, Paul said, "My dear Picard, you see how lucky I am to have brought back with me such a knowledgeable informant."

A moment of pure silence descended upon the room, punctuated only by the faint hissing of the stove.

"Come, come Paul," Picard said. "You are very fortunate to have this young man in your company, but you mustn't talk as if he, too, comes out of your box of treasures." He smiled at Baptiste. "I should like to know something about your background and how you came to know so many languages. But it is my understanding that it is the practice of many of the peoples of North America to offer information about themselves before making inquiries into the background of their guests. Much the same courtesy is expected here in Europe. Allow me to tell you about my family and my origins, and how I have come to be preoccupied with natural history."

FIFTEEN

Picard had been raised in Burgundy on his family's lands, the third son among many children. He described a childhood of privilege as the son of a marquis, but his story differed greatly from what Baptiste would have imagined. It was filled with family misfortune, political intrigue, and the social convulsions that racked France in the years before the Revolution. His mother died in childbirth, his father turned to drink and gambling, and the children were left to fend for themselves, with the help of in-laws, servants, and friends. Picard told a tale of hurt and loneliness assuaged by the solace of nature. Baptiste thought of his own early years and how the open plains had been a refuge from the solitude he often felt in St. Louis.

"My mother was a d'Andelot," he said, "one of the oldest Huguenot families in Burgundy, and my father was a rigorous Catholic who thought that Jesuits made the best schoolmasters. Whenever I could, I took refuge from both creeds in the woods." A cousin owned a château renowned for its forests and streams, and there the young Picard had discovered a love of nature and science. "At Courances, I understood that the simple act of observation, however pleasing, was not enough. I learned to analyze, then to observe again, then to compare my findings with those of others. It was an escape that became a fascination and eventually"—he gestured broadly to include the pavilion and all its contents—"an obsession." His father had refused to emigrate when the Revolution came, he explained, but since his mother had always treated the peasants with dignity, the family and their château were saved from the upheavals. "That's one thing you can say for the Protestants in France—they took seriously their notion of responsibility toward others."

Picard rose and added wood to the stove, making a small commotion of sparks and cinders, which suspended the spell of his story without breaking it. Then he settled himself again in his chair, glass in hand, and went on. His way of talking inspired confidence; his unhurried cadence and low-pitched voice made Baptiste curious about the details.

Burgundy was one of the bloodiest regions of the Revolution, he told them. Although his family was spared the fate of so many others, the constant spectacle of accusations, violence, looting, and fear changed him profoundly. "I was raised always to consider both sides of a problem, to weigh the arguments for and against, and then to decide by force of reason. I can thank the Jesuits for that particular way of analyzing the world and its ills. But I was also taught that in human dealings pure reason was always to be tempered by a consideration of what is just. By that standard, it was clear to us all that France had to be changed from top to bottom."

Even in the villages of a region as prosperous as Burgundy, he explained, poverty and misery were commonplace. The Revolution hardly came as a surprise, but the form it took very quickly left reason and justice far behind. On both sides he saw rage, passion, and a vengeful fury he had never before witnessed in man or in nature. He stayed in the country and concentrated on his correspondence with his friend Georges Cuvier, who was just beginning his groundbreaking work in studying fossils.

"We were almost the same age, but even before he had reached the age of twenty, his genius at organizing the natural world was apparent. He encouraged me to collect all manner of specimens. Now Cuvier is known as the father of comparative anatomy, and is revered for those powers of classification he taught me so long ago. We remain good friends, but I can match him only in my ability to preserve specimens."

Baptiste realized that Picard must have been close to his own age—nineteen—when this had all happened, and he tried to imagine himself in similar circumstances as he listened. In the moment, Picard seemed far younger than Paul, and Baptiste found both his irreverence and his moral code attractive.

Picard sipped his Armagnac. "My skill at embalming had happy consequences for some of my relatives. My great-aunt was the *chatelaine* of one of Burgundy's noblest and grandest châteaux, a country seat whose family was targeted for arrest early on by the revolutionary committee. My aunt was in her eighties and sickly at the time of the committee's first visit, and the family pleaded her infirmity to sue for time, even inviting them to see the invalid in her sickbed to judge for themselves. For many months there were surprise visits in the night and desperate pleadings, always ending in my great-aunt's bedchamber where, the committee was assured, the old lady was at death's door. When she actually died in late 1793, my cousins were beside themselves: on their next summons the committee would surely arrest them all, ransack the house, plunder the stores, and reduce everything to ruin.

"I was called to the house and asked in the greatest secrecy if it would be possible to preserve my aunt's body so that with bedclothes and a nightcap her face could retain the appearance of someone near death. I filled a *baignoire* with preserving alcohol straightaway and set to work." He lowered his eyebrows in mock disapproval and went on. "The results were remarkably satisfactory—good enough, at least, to fool the committee three times more. The chief difficulty was in keeping her skin from shriveling, though generous applications of *pommades* just before the bedchamber was opened kept a convincing tonus on her features. But I don't think we could have managed another visit. She had shrunk, poor woman, almost to nothing."

Paul was uneasy with the images Picard's story conjured, and he shifted nervously in his chair as he listened. "Did you have to change the preserving liquid frequently in an open tub?" he asked. Picard exploded with laughter.

"Come, Paul, you needn't be clinical. You'll never be faced with such a situation. I've told you a most grotesque tale, gentlemen, one whose telling I can justify only by an appeal to that all-forgiving goddess, the truth. It is as fair a memory of the Revolution as any I can conjure from my own experience. But if truth is to be served, then I must add that that branch of my family were reprehensibly cruel to those who lived on their land, dreadful examples of all that the *ancien régime* was reviled for. But they went free, while others who were far more just were led to ruin and death. That, too, was an education for me."

Picard pulled a handkerchief from his pocket and wiped his brow. "These embers still have the power to burn. The Revolution was a catastrophe for us—all of us. But its aftermath opened a door for me." He went on to describe how Cuvier had enlisted his help in forming the nascent collection of the Muséum d'Histoire naturelle.

"We were all too young to be intimidated by the prospect of classifying the entire natural world!" They were a strange and improbable group of teachers, craftsmen, artists, doctors, and collectors, he explained, with one shared trait: a passion to know and name the constituent parts of the world. Buffon's writings guided them and his dictum was their creed: "Let us gather facts in order to have ideas."

Picard nodded approvingly, then continued. "Increasingly there is specialization—anatomy, the science of forms and structures, the study of fossils, botany, languages, and human societies—but there is still so very much that is entirely unknown, especially from the New World, that the days of the dedicated generalist are hardly over." He leaned toward Baptiste. "Now it is regarded as desirable to leave the books and the theories behind and go to the far ends of the earth to bring back whatever new and unthought-of mysteries may be hidden there. Beyond a certain intelligence and curiosity, the chief qualifications for such work are a probing mind, a grasping hand, and an unquiet spirit."

Paul added, "You've left only one thing out of your list of necessities: a very full purse."

"Of course. Nothing happens without money! But what price knowledge, my dear Paul?"

A delicate chime sounded from Picard's waistcoat and he removed a gold watch with a rosy patina from his pocket. As he opened the top, it sounded its fourth and final chime.

"Gentlemen, I had no idea I had been so long-winded. Forgive me. My wife has begged the pleasure of our company after four so that she can give us coffee." Baptiste stood up and stretched his arms above his head, delighting in the luxury of movement after remaining immobile so long. "Let us stretch our legs in the garden and get some fresh air on the way to her," Picard added.

"Is that a pocket repeater? Why didn't we hear it until now?" Paul asked.

Picard handed over the elegant instrument. "This one is rather special. It sounds the hours you choose. Breguet made it up for me."

Paul looked at it admiringly and handed it back. "My favorite watch is at the bottom of the Missouri River. Do you think he would have another before we leave for Württemberg?"

"You must take this one," Picard said without hesitation. "Breguet will make me another," and he placed the watch in Paul's hand again. "It is a feeble gesture of thanks for the bounty you have showered on me today."

Paul's protests were fruitless. He finally put the watch in his vest pocket.

Picard opened a box behind his desk and offered his guests each a small cigar, then took one for himself. Bending low in front of the stove, he fired a taper from the coals and deftly lit them, drawing the smoke with an air of deep satisfaction. As they made their way to the garden, the pungent smoke trailed in the air behind and settled slowly on the bones, rocks, plants, and other objects that sat on their tables in the twilight, awaiting Picard's attention before they could have names and a place in his order of things.

The sun had sunk below the walls and the air was chill when they emerged from the pavilion, though light still brightened the sky and sent long shadows across the garden. Picard led them back through the hidden gate in the hedge and then along graveled paths toward the far edge of the property. Baptiste was surprised at how much land was enclosed by the stone walls here—there were several acres within the tree-flanked walk that meandered around the perimeter.

They walked in silence for a while, enjoying their cigars and the deepening blue of the twilight. Between the brandy and the cigars, Baptiste was feeling a bit light-headed. He was being treated like a man of the world, an adult, someone who had his own voice and his own story to tell. Picard turned to Baptiste and said, "Which Indian languages do you speak?"

"I am strongest in Mandan," Baptiste told him. "That was the language of my mother's tribe on the northern plains. I can generally understand and make myself understood in Hidatsa, Crow, Dakota—any of the Sioux tribal languages—though there is much I miss because of local variations. I also speak some Blackfoot because of my contacts with them in the fur trade, but it is limited to business on the river— fur, money, barter goods. Blackfoot is not related to the Sioux languages. I also have a few words of Shoshone from my mother; it is the tribe she was born into. But I couldn't speak with a Shoshone."

Picard asked, "How do the different tribes like the Sioux and Blackfoot converse? Are there many polyglots? Or designated translators?"

Baptiste wanted to laugh out loud. The idea of designated translators suggested how little Picard grasped of life on the plains, but Baptiste liked him and decided to explain.

"For important occasions like war councils or signing treaties, there are translators. But in everyday life when different tribes come together, they use sign language."

"I have read accounts of that but have never witnessed an exchange. Could you possibly show me?"

Baptiste clenched both hands into fists and, with a trembling motion, crossed his arms in front of his chest.

"You're cold!"

Baptiste couldn't help smiling at Picard's exuberance. Baptiste next bent his arms and raised his hands to shoulder level, fingers hanging down, then pushed his palms up and down slightly, wagging the fingers almost imperceptibly. Picard looked at him expectantly, straining to understand. Baptiste continued the motion, then looked up to the sky and moved his chin toward the clouds overhead.

"It's raining! Or, that is, it may rain."

Baptiste nodded, then raised his right forefinger and pointed upward, then in a fluid motion pointed the same finger downward. He repeated the motion several times, but Picard's face showed puzzlement. "Up, then down. Is it a mountain? Or perhaps a law?" He paused, then cried, "A lightning bolt?"

Baptiste lowered his hand and shook his head.

"Ah, my dear Picard," Paul said, "that sign is one of the most important." Paul made the gesture, too. "It means chief."

Awareness dawned on Picard's features. "I see. The chief on top and his people below, is that it?"

They reached the far end of the park and Picard stopped short at the high stone wall. "The dog has reached the end of his leash," he said with mock resignation and slowly turned back toward the house. "Were you raised among the Mandan?" he asked Baptiste. "You seem to know many Indian tribes firsthand."

"My father worked the Mississippi for years as a trapper," Baptiste said, "before he headed up the Missouri and set his traps on the streams along Mandan country. That is where he met my mother, just before they set off with Captain Clark and Captain Lewis on their Voyage of Discovery. Indeed, sir, I was born on that journey. I spent four years in a Mandan village; then my parents left me in the care of Captain Clark in St. Louis so that I could have proper schooling. He has been my guardian ever since."

"The same Captain William Clark whose map of western North America is so talked about by my colleagues in London?" Picard asked.

"The same man, sir."

Picard shook his head slowly. "Your life has taken a most singular path. Did you go to a school in St. Louis?"

"I had several years with Jesuit teachers—at my father's insistence—and I perfected my French and learned Church Latin. There were still many Spaniards left in St. Louis, and I picked up Spanish from my friends at school."

The aroma of wood smoke from the chimneys reached them as they approached the rear of the house.

"Forgive me," Picard said. "I'm afraid I've worn you out with my questions. Allow me to lay the blame on the Jesuits, will you? We have that much in common." Picard tossed the spent butt of his cigar into the empty fountain and led them inside. Baptiste was relieved that the memories Picard had conjured, and the longings they stirred, could be put aside for now.

SIXTEEN

MARCH 23, 1824
PARIS

Dear Captain Clark,

I have finally got some time to myself and wanted to let you know of the many things that have happened since I last wrote. Where to start?

I have managed to see a good part of Paris, and you will be glad to know I get around on my own two legs. Duke Paul wanted me to take a horse, but, as you know better than anyone, it changes everything when you are in a saddle looking down on the world in the streets. It is far easier to pass unnoticed, I have found, in a crowd of passersby in a big city. Duke Paul told me, "In town a gentleman rides or takes a carriage," so I suppose I am not a gentleman. He also told me, "A gentleman does not carry a concealed weapon," after he saw the skinning knife strapped to my belt. I told him it was because I was interested in keeping my face in one piece. It has already come in handy more than once. There is sometimes a bad side to being on foot in a place like Paris; you don't want to be empty-handed in parts of that city, day or night. He didn't like it, but he looked the other way.

On one of my walks in Paris I came across a building on fire in a crowded section of the city. Black smoke was pouring out of the windows and there were flames on the roof. Suddenly I heard bells and horns and the fire brigade came around the corner. Over here they're called *"sapeurs-pompiers."* There were a dozen men in fancy blue uniforms with red stripes, shiny buttons, and big brass helmets. Four of them pulled a huge oak cask on a caisson mount. It looked like a delivery of Augie Schmitt's tavern brew, on the double, but this one was filled with water.

The crowd cheered and they went to work. Two of them pumped until they got a spray of water going onto the flames. Half a dozen others went at the door with axes, then barreled in and up the stairs with the hose. They can't waste any time; otherwise, the whole city would burn to the ground, since everything is built so close together. When it was all over, one of the *sapeurs* had burns on his arm and shoulder, though they were not too serious. Everyone got out of the building. It turns out it was a shop that makes wigs, and (you will appreciate this) it smelled just like singeing the fur off a dog before a Mandan feast. They don't eat dog here, though when I told him about it, Duke Paul remembered the smell from his time in the Pawnee villages. I would say it was not one of his better memories.

There is one other thing I want to tell you about Paris. Duke Paul took me to something called Le Diorama. It's a big round room, at least thirty feet tall and sixty across, *"la rotonde,"* with three long rooms that stick out from the side like the spokes of a wheel. The public sits on a platform in the middle of the *rotonde* and looks down one of the rooms done up with big paintings of the outdoors, like a long theater. Then the whole platform rotates with some complicated machinery on pivots and rails, and you're looking down the next room at a different set of paintings. The day we went, it was a representation of "A Storm in Nature." The big paintings were of trees and mountains and clouds with changing lights, and in front of it they had running water, like a creek, and sheep and rabbits and ducks on real grass. The lights on the sky changed and—that was it! Then they all came out and told each other that it was just like a day in the country. Someone actually said that to the Duke. Strange to think that people can sit in a dark room and have nature presented to them in a paint-

ing and think it's real! If you could put a frame around the Mississippi, you could sell tickets to these Parisians.

I have met some people who have traveled a lot and tell interesting
stories, though. Recently, a friend of Prince Franz, who is half French
and half Irish, and who sells wine, described how the English took
him from an American ship in 1812 and accused him of being a
French spy. They were about to hang him, but he was traded for some
English prisoners at the last minute.

You can probably guess that I miss the Missouri sky, and the river,
but I know I will miss Paris, too. There is always something going on
in the street, even at night, with gas lamps and crowds in the the-
aters. But you have to be rich so that you can enjoy it. Most people
are very poor. I can't think of a harder life than being trapped in a city
with nothing to live on.

I'll write to tell you my news when I can. We are supposed to leave
for Württemberg soon. Please remember me kindly to Mrs. Clark. As
ever, your affectionate,

Pomp

SEVENTEEN

Two days after their visit to Professor Picard, Baptiste found Paul in a state of rare excitement. He had just received a note from Picard, replying to his request to visit Georges Cuvier at the Muséum d'Histoire naturelle. Cuvier would receive them on the following day and show them his renowned collection.

Baptiste knew that this museum in Paris was revered as the most important center for the study of the natural world, and he had learned that its scholarly papers were hotly debated among those who collected, observed, and classified plants and animals. Paul regularly mentioned the great names of the museum's faculty—Lamarck, Lacépède, Jussieu, Saint-Hilaire, Cuvier. Professor Picard explained Cuvier's importance the next day as they sat together in the carriage on their way to Cuvier's apartment.

" 'Form follows function' is Monsieur Cuvier's guiding principle," Picard told Baptiste, "and that credo informs his display of specimens. He has set himself no less a task than classifying the whole animal world, and the number, diversity, and condition of his specimens is unparalleled. The placement and development of the internal organs is his special concern, and he is uniquely attentive to the interplay of physiology, structure, and natural conditions in determining an animal's form. For people like Paul and me, who concern ourselves with comparative anatomy, Monsieur Cuvier's findings have made possible a whole new approach to classifying species."

"No one comes close to his overview," Paul added. "He was born a subject of Württemberg in Montbéliard and speaks flawless German. His initial studies were at the Karlsschule in Stuttgart!"

Baptiste thought they looked like two excited schoolboys anticipating a special treat.

Cuvier received them cordially. Framed by a shock of white hair, his features were finely drawn; deep-set eyes, a prominent arching nose, and delicately etched lips gave him a dignified air. He looked to Baptiste far older than Picard, though Picard had said they were about the same age. But the wrinkles disappeared when he talked of his work. "Alas, my responsibilities as permanent secretary have me permanently tied to Paris. I must rely on such intrepid adventurers as you, *Monsieur le Duc*"—he bowed to Paul—"to provide me with the raw material that fuels my studies."

After some small talk, Cuvier offered to show them what he called his *"cabinet,"* and he led them outside, down a small staircase, and around the walls of a long building to the main entrance of the galleries. They began their visit with a tour of three rooms, each of which contained the fully intact skeletons of related animals: cows, sheep, goats, and antelope in the first; deer in the second; camels and llamas in the third. Baptiste's hunter's eye was drawn to the bones, which differed from those of the buffalo and elk that he knew. Cuvier explained some details that he found significant, responded to questions from Picard and Paul, and led the small party into a very long room with a high ceiling.

Nothing prepared Baptiste for what stood before them. The skeleton of a whale was propped on a series of metal stands that extended from one end of the room to the other. It was more than twenty yards long, Baptiste guessed. Shafts of sunlight streamed through a series of high windows set in the side wall, bathing the top of the whale in a soft light.

Cuvier led them to the head, pointing out how the structure was adapted for a marine mammal, but Baptiste was mute with awe at the fantastic proportions. When Paul spoke to him and indicated that they were continuing to the next gallery, Baptiste said, "I prefer to stay here for a moment, if you don't mind."

Cuvier nodded his assent. "Very well, Monsieur, as you wish. We shall return this way." They filed out and Baptiste was left alone with a creature that seemed more like a spirit than an animal. He sat on a bench against the wall and contemplated it.

The head rose high to one side, the upper jaw bone like the beak of an enormous bird, long and pointed, with two massive curved bones forming the mandible of the lower jaw. The ribs enclosed a huge space; each bone was as thick around as a supporting timber in a Mandan lodge. Above the ribs, the long voluptuous arc of the spine stretched away to the other end of the room, each vertebra topped with a bony spur that gave the shoulder the look of a castle battlement. The fluid line tapered and descended, then rose again to end in the triangular forms of the tailbone.

Baptiste remembered his excitement when he had first seen a whale close by the ship in the North Atlantic: the creature's sleek blue-black skin; the huge, watchful eye; the jet of watery spray that was its breath; and the long, smooth arc of the body as it descended, the flukes towering high for a split second as if in farewell. The majesty of the animal's skeleton that stood before him revived that sense of wonder.

Captain Clark had told him many times of how a dozen members of the Corps of Discovery had set out to find the beached whale near the mouth of the Columbia, and how his mother had insisted on being included in this group, since she had not yet been to the ocean. Sacagawea, Clark told him, had never been so satisfied as on that sunny, blustery day in January when she stood in the tidal shallows of the Great Waters and played with Baptiste in the sand, the stones, and the white foam. *I have stood inside a whale before,* Baptiste thought.

He began to comprehend, in a way he had not before considered, the fascination that Paul, Picard, Cuvier, and their like all felt at seeing the structure of animals revealed. A strange beauty spoke to you when the bones were reassembled, and comparing different kinds revealed unsuspected truths. *How much can you learn from such things?*

Eighteen

Duke Paul, from his private journal
March 27, 1824
Paris

We have been in Paris for over a month and the time has passed rapidly. I look back at last summer on the far reaches of the North American frontier and I am amazed at how entire is the contrast with Paris. Yesterday I took delivery of a splendid matched thermometer, barometer, and hygrometer to replace those that were destroyed when a buffalo stampede sent my pack animals into a desperate gallop. That particular eventuality illustrates the contrast eloquently.

Along the Missouri, I walked and hunted incessantly, collecting and describing plant and animal specimens. My sole activities were moving up the river, choosing a campsite, and finding food enough for meals in the evening and again the next morning. Many of our days were devoted entirely to overcoming obstacles that arose unexpectedly: clearing impassable jams of driftwood across the river's channel, taking shelter from storms of a rare violence, contending with the river's endless propensity to rise above its banks and find a new path across the surrounding lowlands. How can I forget taking refuge on an island when grizzly bears prowled the river's banks? Or the merciless attack of huge mosquitoes?

Every day we had to ask ourselves whether the Indians we might encounter would be heartless savages bent on our destruction or members of a tribe whose contact with the white man had left them open to accommodation, if not real friendship. These concerns were constant, but to catalog the dangers is to lose sight of the context that made them not just challenging but enjoyable.

All these pitfalls had elements in common: each had to be overcome to ensure the eventual success of our expedition, and each required all the strength, intelligence, wiliness, and good instincts I possessed. I had never before felt my being so concentrated in a single purpose. I had never felt so wholly alive.

Here I am surrounded with the accomplishments of civilization and all the comfort and pleasure they afford, yet my life feels empty, as if the undertakings the city offers are displacing something more vital. This morning, Uncle Franz went for an early-morning ride along the boulevards, then, upon his return, concluded a delicate negotiation with the finance minister on the assessing of import duties on goods from Württemberg. He gave us a sumptuous private lunch with delicacies only Paris can provide and wines that have no equal, while regaling us with stories of the increasingly delicate position of the Bourbons: a catalog of industrious activity for half a day. Six thousand miles to the west, we would have considered ourselves fortunate to have advanced five miles up the river in the same amount of time, with nothing but the flesh of the previous night's kill to fuel our efforts. Uncle Franz's abiding concern when I met him in the morning, and again during our noonday meal, was whether the five new pairs of boots his boot maker is preparing for him will be as comfortable as those he had made last year in Milan. I had to laugh—inwardly, of course—when I considered that our new shoes on the frontier were always a matter of strict necessity, never of vanity, and were fashioned like Indian moccasins, in rough-hewn strips of hide from whatever deerskin or buffalo leather was available.

Nor is it simply a matter of the city and its inevitable comforts. When we rode in the forest of Royaumont last week, I felt myself contained and protected, even though we traversed the deepest parts of the woods. No grizzly bears lurked among the oak trees, nor any animal that presented a real danger. Nor was there a possibility that any plant or animal life I came upon would be unknown or unexamined. Every beetle and lichen and bird and fern and squirrel on this continent has been collected, studied, and cataloged for generations. The newcomer will find no *terra incognita* to fire his imagination.

As I write, I recall how exciting it was to wake each day along the river and to know—to know for certain!—that we would happen upon plants, animals, geographic features, native tribes, and entire ways of life that had never before been observed systematically by a European. This awareness that so much was unknown, that so few had been there before me, that so vast an area remained to be discovered, gripped me each morning, as if von Humboldt and Cuvier were themselves laying encouraging hands upon my shoulder and whispering in my ear, "Go forward, for all of us, and find what is unknown to science!"

Baptiste provides another kind of window on Europe, though his enthusiasm for the city does not mirror mine for the frontier. Still, he seems fascinated by what he discovers, and very often he observes aspects of life here that I would have imagined least worthy of notice. Nor is his experience always one of unalloyed joy. On first seeing the Seine, he was dismissive, proclaiming it a good-sized creek. Neither did the noble stone bridges impress him; rather, they seemed tangible proof of the river's puny size and its predictability. When I drew his attention to the carved forms that embellish the bridges, he pronounced them "Nice, for bridges," and changed the subject. His standard of comparison is the Missouri River in all its unadorned and unspanned wildness, and on that score, I must admit, the comparison is ludicrous. What will he see in the Rhine?

Otherwise, Baptiste fits in easily and is quietly accommodating when introduced to friends and acquaintances. Many of my friends have commented upon the effortless nobility of his bearing. He seems to have a special understanding with Uncle Franz. He likes Uncle Franz's straightforward way of talking, and his opinions and anecdotes. Apparently, it reminds him of his General Clark. What Baptiste lacks, naturally enough, is a frame of reference for evaluating my uncle's categorical pronouncements. Napoleon was a genius, the Pope is a despotic temporal ruler, to cite but two of his themes. The other day, he railed against the Vatican's oppression in the Papal States. He could equally well have made a case for the tyranny felt under Bonaparte in Romagna twenty years ago, but that would sub-vert the standing of his hero, and so the Church was the target. Even an accomplished diplomat abandons nuance when it suits him. I wonder if Baptiste senses that.

This morning I asked Baptiste why he always refers to his guardian in St. Louis as *Captain* Clark, when I had been told he was properly *General* Clark, a rank he had held for years as head of the Missouri Territory's militia. Baptiste explained that, among a handful of men, Clark preferred "Captain." It was the rank he had held as one of the leaders of the Corps of Discovery, and the accomplishments of that small band gave the name Captain a higher place in his esteem than any of the other titles—General, Governor, Superintendent—to which he could justly lay claim. Baptiste said that there existed among the survivors of the Corps of Discovery a sacred trust, and those who had been on the expedition still called him "Captain."

In the short time I have known him, I have come to understand more of Baptiste's position in St. Louis as Clark's mixed-blood ward, and I understand, too, why it is important to him to be regarded as a full member of the Corps. Even though Baptiste was a baby, he told me, Clark always talked about the expedition as if Baptiste had par-ticipated fully. Clark welcomed the intimacy that "Captain" implied, and corrected those who had not made the voyage. It was also Clark's way of honoring the memory of Baptiste's mother, who served with her husband, Toussaint Charbonneau, as a translator. I see that Bap-tiste has a sense of this birthright, a tradition of discovery, adventure, and no small amount of glory. It remains to be seen whether he will fulfill that destiny when he returns to North America.

Here in Europe, Baptiste is something of a chameleon, effortlessly absorbing European culture and assuming the superficial characteris-tics of the group in which he finds himself. With languages, this qual-ity is nothing short of a phenomenon: His French has become entirely fluent, even Parisian, in expression and accent, while his German, nonexistent when we met, has benefited from Schlape's daily hour of exercises. Already I sense that Baptiste understands most of what Schlape and I say between ourselves, though he is careful to give nothing away, answering me haltingly when I query him in German. Uncle Franz is convinced that Baptiste possesses uncommon skills of social discernment that are masked by his exotic appearance and improbable origins. He would make the perfect spy, Uncle Franz said to me, since most Europeans are incapable of ascribing intelligence to those whose skin is not white; hence, Baptiste fits in everywhere without posing a threat. An interesting theory, one whose soundness I shall have occasion to judge, no doubt, in the months ahead.

PART THREE

THE LIFE THAT LAY AHEAD

NINETEEN

The trip from Paris to Stuttgart was long: almost two weeks of slow going because they had a wagon train of wine along, a gift for the king of Wurttemberg from Prince Franz. An armed guard accompanied them. The amount of protection puzzled Baptiste, as they met only a few border guards and some friendly soldiers at the different towns along the way where they left parts of their load. It occurred to him that not all the covered boxes they dropped off carried wine.

Baptiste was increasingly uncomfortable with the passive role he assumed in Paul's company, as if all that was expected of him was to go from one place to another and take in what he found. In the Mandan villages and even in St. Louis, intense physical activity and harsh conditions were a daily commonplace, but here they seemed distant: he saw others working, but he didn't have to do much himself. It was a strange and new feeling that left him ill at ease.

The inside of the coach was upholstered in dark blue velvet with tufted seats. The symmetrical array of dimples reminded Baptiste of the lining of Mrs. Clark's jewelry box, glimpsed once when he took it for her to the blacksmith in St. Louis to have the latch repaired. Now he sometimes felt they were locked inside an enormous jewelry box that was rolling its languid way across Europe. He didn't like riding in the coach—he knew that—but he realized that he was getting used to Paul's life of comfort and riches, as if his privileges were common-place, and the idea caught him by surprise. This was an adventure, he reminded himself, and sooner or later it would end.

Early in their voyage, Baptiste asked Paul about the nature of Mr. Hennesy's business. He had been thinking about Maura and whether he would hear from her, trying to imagine what her life was like in Paris. She resembled no one else he had met, and he reasoned that it was because of the mix of Irish and French in her family and the travels she had mentioned, and something intriguing in her family's business. He knew that Paul could likely shed light on her father's mysterious undertakings.

"You know perfectly well he's a wine merchant," Paul responded. It was late morning, and Baptiste was already tired of sitting in the coach.

"I also know there's more there than meets the eye. He has contacts all over Europe; people raise their eyebrows when his name comes up; these mounted soldiers"—he gestured outside the coach—"who never leave our sight: surely that is not all because of wine!"

Paul extended his hand and, as Baptiste shook it, he said, "Family secret." Paul knew that Baptiste could be trusted absolutely, and this had become their ritual for signaling a bond of silence. Paul told him that Hennesy was a wine merchant, and a very good one. Over several generations, his family had built a renowned vineyard and a network of contacts second to none. A passionate believer in the ideals of the French Revolution, he had supported Bonaparte until he declared himself emperor, but had sought to make common cause with republicans since then. Using his wine business as a cover, Hennesy also regularly dealt in guns, often providing arms to those fighting what he regarded as oppression. Ireland had received many shipments over the years, and some of the guns they were delivering along their way to Stuttgart were destined for partisans in Greece fighting for independence. His dealings were secret, delicate, and highly lucrative.

"Uncle Franz buys large quantities of wine, and sufficient numbers of the latest weapons to keep the garrisons of Württemberg well stocked," Paul said. "He turns a blind eye to Hennesy's other activities, but he finds him indispensable in the matter of intelligence regarding enemies, actual or potential. No one has better information."

"It sounds dangerous," Baptiste said.

"That is putting it mildly, my friend! But there are people in this world who have a gift for danger, and for always coming out on the side that prevails. Hennesy is one of that number. As a young man, he was caught up in the Irish Rising of 1798, and ever since he has been at odds with the English. Of course I do not pretend to understand his scheme of values, necessarily filled with contradictions and *louche* characters, but he always seems serene. I think one can rightly call him an idealist."

After a brief stop in Stuttgart—King Wilhelm was in Vienna—they left for Ludwigsburg, the king's country palace. They set out in the early morning in a large, black closed carriage, followed by a smaller carriage carrying servants and an open wagon for the luggage. They were joined by Paul's cousin Princess Theresa, who was a few years older than Paul and whom Baptiste had not met. At the *porte cochère* of the palace in Stuttgart, the princess didn't wait for the footman to hand her up, but climbed in on her own.

She was attractive, but not in a conventional way—not, certainly, like the profusion of young women at Prince Franz's ball in Paris. She wore a dress and cloak of light brown silk, and her chestnut hair was pulled back from her face. She used little of the heavy powder and rouge much favored by the ladies Baptiste had met so far. Her face was fair, her cheeks a healthy pink, and her full lips plum-hued. The sharp line of her nose and the piercing gaze of her amber eyes gave her face a solemn look that Baptiste found intriguing. She wore a single oval brooch where her lace collar closed, a cameo of a woman's head in pale white on a field of dusky rose, a reiteration of her own coloring, which Baptiste felt had not been worn by chance. She wore small coral earrings as well, but none of the pearls, rings, gemstones, or gold that Baptiste had by now come to expect. Neither did she use the cloying perfumes that enveloped so many French women in a cloud of nauseating sweetness.

They spoke French, the *lingua franca* for the three, and the language in which everyone at court was fluent. He enjoyed hearing

Theresa speak since her accent differed significantly from his. Baptiste learned that the princess was Paul's favorite among his many cousins. She told him she had been raised in Stuttgart and shared Paul's fascination for geography and the natural sciences, though her curiosity had been discouraged by tutors and nannies who thought it improper for a young lady to be interested in such matters.

"I would see Paul at the palace on Sundays, along with the rest of the family, and after church and lunch I would force him to tell me about what he had read during the week. We'd spend hours in the library looking at the globe, imagining what manner of people and animals lived on all the territories marked 'Unexplored.'"

They talked of many things: news of family, different political systems, the new means of transportation. As the morning wore on and they rolled through the sun-bathed countryside, a shared understanding formed among the three.

Baptiste saw a side of Paul that he hadn't seen since their time together on the Missouri. In the carriage, he was not addressed as "Duke"; there were no servants or underlings, no public before whom an image had to be maintained or a role played. Paul enthused about his experiences on the Missouri, about meeting Cuvier, and about the work of organizing his collection.

"Paul, you are happy when you talk about serving science, just as you did in America when you were collecting specimens," Baptiste observed. "Couldn't you have continued with your studies in botany and zoology and become a professor at the university?"

Paul shook his head. "The choice was not mine. The army was unavoidable."

The princess took his arm gently in hers and said to Baptiste, "Wilhelm, the king, would not understand taking any other path. It is what a nobleman in Europe does. He serves his prince in the army, just as surely as a woman finds a husband and produces babies."

"The warriors among the Hidatsa and the Mandan are the same," Baptiste said. "It would be impossible for them to be anything else." He had never imagined Paul as something other than totally free, a rich and influential nobleman with the world at his fingertips. Now he saw his host in a different light.

They stopped at midmorning to water the horses in a small town, and descended briefly from the carriage to stretch their legs. The other vehicles were covered with a layer of gray dust from following behind; they looked like a ghostly escort from a different world, both men and horses wearing a mantle of fine powder. Gradually they left behind the smells of undried hay that rose from the newly cut fields and Baptiste saw that the forest was now unbroken, its understory open and awash with the golden green infusion of light that filtered through the new growth above.

"It won't be long now!" Paul exclaimed. It was evident that he was delighted to be returning to this landscape. He had not been here since he set out on his adventure to the Missouri River two years earlier.

As the mass of trees began to thin out, the small party of carriages entered the outskirts of a town. Stone buildings and substantial houses lined the streets, including an elaborate twin-towered church whose facade dominated a very large square filled with tented market stalls. They turned onto a wide tree-lined avenue, on one side of which sat more fine houses and on the other what looked like a garden of trees. Baptiste could see beneath the branches of ordered plane trees an immense facade stretching across the entire park. Its roof was alive with statuary. As they came closer, he saw that the front of the palace was given over to symmetrical flower gardens. Spring had arrived here, like an apparition through the haze of tender green that sprouted from the trees.

They continued beyond the garden, turning in at an ornate wrought-iron gate. The carriage stopped as guards in scarlet tunics and gold braid saluted Paul respectfully, then continued into an immense white gravel courtyard. The carriage swung around a central fountain and came to a stop beneath a stone porch that jutted out from the flag-draped Palace of Ludwigsburg. The vehicles carrying the servants and the luggage had been directed elsewhere.

Theresa said to Paul, "Before I do anything, I must have a walk in the gardens. I'll take our guest along while his things are being settled this afternoon, before we lose the sun."

"Very well," Paul responded, "but don't try to show him everything on his first afternoon here."

As they entered the vestibule of the palace, courtiers bowed low and opened doors, footmen carried what little baggage they had kept with them, and older servants curtsied and bowed, greeting Paul and Theresa with special warmth. They proceeded into a monumental columned hall, and Paul turned to an old retainer who appeared to be in charge.

"Suber, this is my good friend Monsieur Charbonneau. See that he has everything he needs to feel at home." He spoke in German, and Baptiste was happy to discover he understood what was being said.

"Of course, Your Grace. It shall be done." He inclined his head toward Baptiste and, when he raised it, Baptiste could not help feeling that a steely eye of appraisal flashed upon him as the old servant opened his mouth in a servile smile.

After they had washed and had a light lunch, they strolled along the wide paths of the sprawling gardens. Theresa led Baptiste around the first of the big circular pools that lay spaced at intervals along a central axis, then chose a path that brought them to the double *allées* of plane trees flanking the gardens. Under the canopy of leaves and branches she turned to Baptiste and let out a sigh of relief.

"That's better. We can no longer see the palace. Here I can talk," Theresa said.

Only a small corner of the facade was visible from where they stood; the rest was shielded from view by the low-hanging branches, trimmed severely along their outer edges and shaped into a high vault on the inside. She continued walking, and Baptiste fell in step alongside her. He felt curious, unsettled, shy, and jubilant, all his senses sharpened now that he was alone with Theresa.

The perfectly spaced columns of trees stretched before them for hundreds of yards, the barrel roof moving slightly in the breeze. An occasional bird flitted overhead and twittered among the boughs, punctuating the perfect quiet that otherwise prevailed.

"This is like another palace corridor," Baptiste ventured.

"Monsieur Dupin would love to hear you say that. He has been the chief gardener here since the time of King Friedrich, and has spent his life applying the ideals of French landscaping to the grounds of Ludwigsburg. The French have long made their gardens an extension of architecture." Theresa became more animated with each step separating them from the palace.

At the end of the tree tunnel, they walked through the sunlight to a tall evergreen hedge set at right angles to the line of trees. Theresa hurried ahead, continued along the perfectly regular edge of the bushes, and turned a corner abruptly. Baptiste followed but found only a recess in the hedge. He entered the small passage and discovered a narrow pathway that threaded through the evergreens, turning twice to conceal the entrance. He finally emerged on the other side of the hedge, which was over ten feet deep, in the corner of a perfect square whose boundaries were marked by tall evergreens. Their seamless planes and razor-edge joints mimicked the finest carpentry. Statues stood in alcoves cut into the four sides, stone benches formed a pattern around flower beds and symmetrical paths, and at the center stood Theresa, striking a pose. With her shawl draped over one outstretched arm, she was a Greek goddess presiding over her temple. When she saw Baptiste's startled face she broke the motionless pantomime.

"Do you see? It's a room with walls, furniture, and the sky for a roof."

Baptiste relaxed. "What an idea," he said slowly, turning to inspect the dimensions as if to find a flaw.

"Every palace in Europe has one," Theresa told him, "or a maze fashioned from shrubs, or a life-sized chessboard worked into the lawns. They're *de rigueur*. Monsieur Dupin is very proud of it."

"I don't understand this place," Baptiste said softly.

"It is a very convenient refuge from the prying eyes at court, which was the original idea. But trimming and shaping plants for years so that they resemble stone and plaster reminds me of what my grandmother used to say: 'If God had intended for trees to grow in straight lines, he'd have made them square.' "

They sat on one of the stone benches, and a feeling of intimacy enveloped them. Theresa said, "I can only imagine how strange this must seem to you. But where you come from seems strange to me, too. Can you imagine that? The few people I have met who have been to your part of the world say that it is like no other place on earth."

"Many things are different where I come from," Baptiste said, unsure how to respond.

"Perhaps I can help you understand our ways," Theresa said gently. "Let us describe our worlds to one another."

Baptiste hesitated for a moment, then nodded. "In my country when you conclude an agreement, you always shake on it." He extended his hand.

Theresa laughed as she took his hand in hers.

TWENTY

Dear Cousin,

I write to you from Württemberg. Duke Paul and I came up from Stuttgart some days ago, but I am now here on my own while he visits relatives in Baden. There is plenty for me to do, however. I am being introduced to court life, having German lessons, and venturing into the town to see how the local people live. I am also taking piano lessons! I learned to play the pump organ a little in St. Louis, but this is more difficult.

As I mentioned to you, I did not have the opportunity to get to know France other than by my solitary walks in Paris. I cannot say I met or talked to anyone outside the Duke's circle of friends. Here things are different. The town is much smaller than Paris (still very large compared to St. Louis) and it is an easy matter to walk among the people. Market days are best, I have found. There are many outsiders in town and I blend in more readily, easily mingling with the crowds filling the taverns around the main square. I have acquired some simple clothes that allow me to pass unnoticed, and the color of my skin is taken as proof of Mediterranean parentage.

When I open my mouth, of course, I do not pass for a local. My German is coming along—I am told my accent is good—but I don't yet have enough words to allow me to say anything of substance. My teacher would prefer that I learn every rule and exception of grammar. Very few people outside the palace speak French and almost no one speaks any English or Spanish, so I stick to German and try my best. Everyone drinks beer in the taverns, and one or two mugs help untie my tongue.

Two days ago a woman in the marketplace recognized me as a friend of Duke Paul, and as soon as she said the words, the atmosphere changed. She and her friends drew back, suddenly cool and reserved, and acted as if I were a wild animal that might bite. When I mentioned it later to Duke Paul, he cautioned me about such "adventures," as he called them, among the local population. He told me he won't walk into town on his own. I asked him why, and he said that for a member of the royal family to wander at will was "unthinkable." That was the end of the discussion. Here there is a reverence for the king and his relations that borders on fear, an attitude Americans don't feel toward their leaders. Nevertheless, I have decided to continue my walks as discreetly as I can.

I will be traveling again soon. Duke Paul plans to visit his family's lands in Silesia, where his brother lives. According to him, it is the wild edge of Europe. Then we will go to Berlin and possibly to Saint Petersburg to meet with his fellow natural historians. We might go to Paris again, too, though probably not until much later in the fall. I hope to have the pleasure of finding you there.

You can write to me here at Ludwigsburg if you like. We won't leave before late August, and any mail that arrives after that will follow me with Duke Paul's own correspondence.

I realize that I have hardly asked about you. I trust that you are well. It seems like years rather than weeks since we last met at Prince

Franz's ball. Your father's words about the Bourbons are still vivid in my mind, as is the vision of your blue dress. Remember me a little when you think of your father's family in America.

Your affectionate cousin,
Jean-Baptiste

TWENTY-ONE

Paul left the countless boxes in Stuttgart, "in safe warehouses," he told Baptiste, "until the collection finds its home." A few items were sent to Ludwigsburg, packed in fine trunks and presented to Paul's friends and family as exotic gifts that showed he had been to the far ends of the earth. In the ensuing weeks, Baptiste saw some of the pieces in the family salons: a pair of moccasins on a mantel, or a powder horn with a beaded lanyard on a table lying amid precious baubles and porcelain vases. They looked sadly out of place on a polished wood sideboard or a marble hearth.

The week after they arrived, Paul planned to return to Stuttgart for two or three days and then visit friends in nearby parts of Württemberg. Baptiste was content to remain at Ludwigsburg, exploring. His daily German lessons with Schlape continued, and as his speaking improved, the older servant taught Baptiste court protocol, the arcane rules of conduct that prevailed in the sovereign's presence.

Theresa accompanied him around the palace and its grounds. As a member of the royal family, she could go where she pleased, and her knowledge of the domain was intimate and extensive. She taught him the names and uses of the royal apartments that ringed the vast courtyard: the state dining room, the family dining room, the ambassadors' waiting room, the map room, the music room, and the throne room. The column-lined hallways connecting the rooms seemed to go on forever. Only a few of the rooms had open hearths; the others were warmed by huge gray metal cylinders set against the wall, sometimes decorated with pieces of porcelain, which Theresa explained were heating stoves, stoked in winter by servants who passed through a network of invisible passageways behind the walls. Baptiste wanted to see the servants' side of the wall, but Theresa told him it was not possible.

She showed him the royal theater, an elaborately decorated hall with four tiers of seating and the royal box at the center of the first level, richly draped in red velvet and gold braid. The royal chapel looked much like the theater—there was even a royal box in the balcony that was accessible from the king's apartments—but in place of a stage stood a marble altar flanked by huge paintings whose crowded tableaux Baptiste recognized from his study of the Bible. Intricate carvings of foliage and broad bas-relief medallions covered the walls and ceiling; overhead, angels were stringing garlands and laughing down at him. The shimmering expanse of organ pipes looked like a frozen waterfall, and he wondered how you could talk to God amid such clutter.

Theresa took him to the far side of the palace, whose facade was fronted by a wide stone terrace that looked out on gardens and fountains well below. When they arrived, two soldiers stood at attention in front of little stone guardhouses at opposite ends of the terrace. They looked down to the boxwood parterres and perfectly manicured flower beds worked into a large design that he recognized as the royal coat of arms. Mrs. Clark's kitchen garden came to mind. She was so proud of its patch of verbena and hollyhocks, which gave color around the vegetable beds, its flagstone walk, and the bench beneath the rose arbor. *What would she make of all this fuss?* he wondered.

"What is that structure?" he asked, indicating a towered building visible in the middle distance, crowning a rise in the forest.

"La Favorite, the hunting lodge. Our grandfather used to keep the surrounding woods stocked with pheasant, but it's used very little now, only for an occasional celebration."

"I'd like to see it," Baptiste said.

"Some day when the weather is fine," Theresa responded, and turned away.

As he and Theresa stepped back inside, he looked over his shoulder and saw the sentry at the near end relax his stance and exhale in relief.

In those first days, they walked together in the mornings under the pretext that Theresa was helping Baptiste improve his German, but once they were alone they spoke French, and told each other about their different ways of life. Baptiste looked forward to these meetings, and to the new companionship that came with Theresa's easy manner. She was unlikely ever to visit North America, she told him, and was hungry to know everything about it. How long was a canoe? What was it made of? What did they eat in the morning? How did they hunt? She felt an engaging attraction to the particulars as she tried to visualize what was so distant and so unknown.

One morning in that first week a persistent drizzle soaked the grounds of Ludwigsburg, so they couldn't talk in the outdoor room, as they had on previous days. They sat instead in one of the small salons in a distant wing of the palace. The room was a study in green, yellow, and brown: the walls were covered in light green watered silk to match the drapery, and the couches and side chairs were upholstered in a deeper emerald shade. Dark brown walnut tables, chairs, and desks swam on a lake of blond parquet, their surfaces laden with crystal bibelots that picked up the floor's fiery sheen. An elaborate gilt clock sat on a ponderous side table, two swooning female figures flanking the large white enameled face that told the passing seconds with a sharp-edged tick. Theresa stood at one of the long windows looking out on the gardens, their green a suffused luminescence that held the wet and reflected it into the room.

After he had described how *voyageurs* set their line of traps, Baptiste asked about Theresa. "Is all of your family from Württemberg?"

"My father was King Friedrich's brother—that is how Paul and I are cousins—but my mother was a French countess. She left Balleroy in 1787, just before the Revolution, and was lucky to be out of France when it erupted. I was born here three years later. Her parents and brothers all went to the guillotine." Baptiste thought of Picard's strange stories about the Revolution. *Everyone in this closed world of privilege seems to have been directly affected,* he thought.

"And have you lived here all your life?"

"Heavens no!" Theresa exclaimed, turning from the window. "I married when I was sixteen. I thought you knew."

"I knew you were a widow," Baptiste murmured, "but I thought your husband was from here."

"That's something else for you to learn about our tribe, Monsieur Charbonneau," Theresa said. "The job of a titled woman is to take her dowry and marry elsewhere, cementing bonds of blood and treasure with another royal household."

"It's not so different among the Indian tribes," he told her.

Theresa nodded, then continued in a softer voice. "My husband was a Russian prince, a cousin of the czar. We lived in Saint Petersburg. He died at the Battle of Borodino, and I returned to Württemberg." She paused and ran her fingers across the drapes. "Suppose you tell me how you came to live in St. Louis. Are your parents there?"

Baptiste sat on one of the long couches that flanked the interior walls of the room, and Theresa saw a vacant look in his eyes. When she said his name softly, he gave a start, as if he had just been awakened. "My parents aren't in St. Louis," he said, and then added, "My story is very different from yours."

"Yes, of course it is. No one chooses his parents, or his family, or where he'll be born, or any of it, really. We each have our circumstances; my cousins would call it God's choice for us, though I prefer the idea of destiny."

Baptiste didn't respond. He stood abruptly, walked over to the clock, and grabbed its exposed pendulum. The ticking stopped and only the sound of the rain on the trees could be heard in the room. He turned to Theresa. "Why must there be so many clocks? I've counted thirty-four in this place. The sun tells you the hours without making noise. Even in the gardens, the bell tower in the courtyard makes sure you know the time."

Theresa laughed. "My mother hated the clocks, too. Everywhere she went in the German states, she railed against them." She crossed to the couch where he had been sitting, sat on the far end, and continued. "Thank you for stopping this one at least. Now we can enjoy the quiet. Come sit with me." She motioned for him to join her. "Tell me about your family," she said.

Once he was beside her, Baptiste felt less guarded. "My mother died when I was eight. Before that, I lived with her until my parents sent me to stay with Captain Clark's family in St. Louis. We were together every summer in the Mandan villages, and sometimes I made a trip there in the spring. It was her idea for me to live in St. Louis, so that I could go to a proper school and live like the white man."

Theresa wasn't sure whether bitterness or plain regret colored Baptiste's words. "That is an extraordinary sacrifice for a mother to make. Not every woman would be capable of it."

"Her name was Sacagawea. It means Bird Woman in Shoshone."

"How did she come to have a name from a different tribe?" Theresa asked.

"A Hidatsa raiding party stole her from the Shoshone when she was twelve, along with several other young women and a dozen horses. They took them to their tribal lands on the Missouri, where she was traded to the Mandan."

"Was she a slave?"

Baptiste flinched. "No! She was raised as a Mandan. Indians don't have slaves the way the white man does. If they let their captives live, they are usually well treated. You're not really an outsider, but you're not like everyone else in the tribe, either. You're always between two tribes."

Theresa looked at him intently, captivated by what he was telling her, then asked, "Did she ever go back to her own family or tribe?"

"No," he continued, "but when I was a baby, she and my father crossed the Rocky Mountains with Captain Clark and Captain Lewis. They bought horses from the Shoshone and my mother was their translator. Captain Clark told me he had never seen a person happier than when she was with her tribe again and found that her brother was the chief. Captain Clark asked her why she didn't return to her tribe after the expedition. She told him, 'The path of my life has turned forever.' "

"You went with her when she accompanied these explorers?" Theresa asked.

"Yes," he told her. "I was born at the beginning of that expedition, and she carried me on a cradleboard for eighteen months."

Theresa was astounded. "You mean to say that your mother carried a newborn baby across the wilds of North America and back again?"

"Yes."

"What an extraordinary destiny for you, Jean-Baptiste Charbonneau!"

They sat together quietly for a long moment. For the first time since he had arrived in Europe, he felt close to someone. With Maura, he had been excited, elated, and intrigued. With Theresa, he felt understood. Finally she asked, "Did your mother give you a Shoshone name?"

"It's Pompy. It means firstborn, or Little Chief."

TWENTY–TWO

"Why is it called La Favorite?" Baptiste held the reins of the surrey lightly in one hand and let the chestnut mare find her own pace. The sunlight streamed through the trees and dappled their faces as they rolled along the forest path.

"That depends entirely upon whom you ask." Theresa laughed. "The official version is that this was the sovereign's favorite retreat from the cares of state. The more popular version is that our grandfather came out here for more than pheasant."

Baptiste met Theresa's gaze. "You mean he kept a mistress right here?"

"Heavens no. She couldn't actually live here. But as a place for safe liaisons, a hunting chalet possesses every advantage that a palace does not."

"But everyone at the palace would know." Baptiste thought about the servants perpetually watching as they waited on him. "They're aware of every time I sneeze or go out the side gate or don't come down for breakfast."

Theresa twirled the ribbon of her sunbonnet in her fingers as she spoke. "Everyone did know, but as long as it happened out of sight, they could pretend not to know. The fiction of the perfect king and the perfect father was maintained, and life went on as usual."

"And nothing could change that?" Baptiste asked.

"Within boundaries. King Friedrich, my uncle and Paul's, was an effective king. In a time of terrible peril and almost constant war, he strengthened the duchy's finances, built a respected army, forged alliances to secure his borders, and even made common cause with Napoleon when it suited his interests. The result was a prosperous, secure, and respected domain. The grand duchy was transformed into a small but important kingdom when Bonaparte reorganized the German states. Friedrich made a brilliant marriage to a German princess, produced an heir, and saw him married to a daughter of the czar of Russia. He gave his daughter in marriage to Jerome Bonaparte, king of Westphalia. After his first wife died, he married one of the daughters of the king of England. He was an astute ruler and a respected head of his family."

"Prince Franz told me he was eccentric and intelligent," Baptiste said.

"That is true," Theresa responded, "but he had another side, which would have been unacceptable to his subjects had it been known. He had a passionate attraction to men, and throughout his adult life he had a series of male lovers." The surrey rolled along soundlessly now, as if they were swimming through green-gold water. "Everyone at court knew of Uncle Friedrich's secret arrangements, but it never went beyond his closed circle. It was regarded as strictly private and it never caused a scandal."

"So the king can do as he likes in his private life. Is that the basic rule?"

"As long as the monarch marries and produces an heir, builds a strong army, and makes his domain prosperous, no one cares who he invites into his bed."

"So why does Paul feel constrained by this arrangement?" Baptiste asked.

"Because the court has expectations," Theresa said. "All members of the family are expected to do their duty and fulfill their role. And Paul? No marriage, nor any prospect of one. He resigned his commission; he squanders the money he has inherited; he spends more on his travels and collections than his family is willing to pay. He doesn't abide by the rules. They call him 'the gypsy duke.' Believe me, that is no compliment."

The carriage emerged from the woods into a grass-covered clearing. A cobbled road led up a gradual rise to a symmetrical three-story structure. Its dark orange stucco was startling, set off with bright yellow detailing and bone white statuary. Broad staircases led to both sides of a terrace that ran the width of the second floor, whose facade was entirely made up of tall glass doors. Four squat towers loomed overhead, statues and scrollwork adorned the windows, and elaborate carved vases and finials made the structure look to Baptiste like a toy. It was as if someone had carved off a piece of the palace, added whimsical details and riotous colors, and set it down in the forest. He reined in the mare at the top of the drive.

"It looks like that dollhouse you showed me in the royal nursery," Baptiste said.

Theresa narrowed her eyes doubtfully, inclined her head to the side, and pursed her lips for an instant. "It does, rather, doesn't it? My ancestor who built it had spent time at the court in Naples and couldn't bear to leave the colors of Italy behind. This is the result. Come, let me show you the inside."

Baptiste tethered the horse to a bench flanking one of the staircases and they went in to the ground floor. The main hall was devoted to hunting and its paraphernalia. Two walls and parts of the ceiling were covered with racks of antlers, each mounted on an identical plaque with an engraved silver medallion listing the particulars of the hunt. Baptiste followed Theresa up a broad staircase to the main floor. The rooms here were grander, like those in the palace, intended for entertainment, with dining tables, a piano and a harp, and several gaming tables arrayed about an airy expanse. Baptiste passed over the familiar opulence of the chandeliers, the statuary, and the wall paintings to look across the dining room to a bank of windows. They gave an unparalleled view across the top of the forest, as if the room floated above the tops of trees.

Theresa motioned for him to follow. "Come," she said over her shoulder as she disappeared through an adjacent doorway, "I'll show you something truly special." He followed her up another staircase, which grew narrower as they climbed. He could hear the rustling of her skirts above him, but she managed to stay just out of sight until he emerged, bathed in light, into a small room that rose above the roof. They were at the top of one of the towers: the walls were made of glass, and the forest looked like a carpet you could tread upon, luxuriant and inviting.

Theresa stood at one of the windows, facing the trees. Baptiste crossed the room and stood behind her. Without thinking he put his hand on her shoulder, and it rose and fell imperceptibly with the rhythm of her breathing. His heart raced with fear and longing. *Will she allow this? Will she turn and laugh at me?* He opened his mouth to speak, when Theresa put her hand on his and slowly turned. She raised her fingers to his cheek and drew him near. They breathed together, face to face, then their lips met. Lost in her scent, he held Theresa gently, trembling a little. She kissed his fingers, one by one, then turned to the window where they stood side by side, as if they were looking at the forest.

Later, they drove into the woods on the far side of La Favorite. The air was warm, even in the shade of the overarching branches. Twenty yards ahead a small herd of pure white deer crossed in front of them, untroubled by the presence of the horse and carriage. Baptiste reined in the mare and stopped short. Theresa saw Baptiste's astonishment.

"Those are called Duke Eugene's deer. He started the herd ages ago with a gift from the czar," she told him.

"Where I come from, a single white deer is a great rarity and is respected by the tribes as a messenger from the spirit world."

"They are exceedingly rare here, too, which is why only the king has such animals."

Baptiste couldn't understand why the deer didn't run away. "Why aren't they afraid of us?"

"They may as well be a flock of sheep, they are so protected and doted upon here in the Ludwigsburg grounds."

They soon came to a widening in the path. To one side stood a moss-covered fountain, three cherubs holding a single broad basin above their heads. At its center a single jet projected straight up and collapsed upon its own thin column, overflowing the basin with a muffled splash. A narrow stone-lined channel led down a slight incline to a pool on the opposite side of a small clearing. After he and Theresa drank from a spigot on the side of the fountain, Baptiste led the mare to the other side and let her drink from the pool.

"There is a natural spring," Theresa explained. "We shall have lunch here."

Baptiste lifted the hamper out of the surrey. Theresa unfolded a spotless linen cloth and spread it on a broad stone bench, as if it were a dining table. She asked Baptiste to remove a rosewood box from the hamper. It held a set of porcelain dishes, silver utensils, and crystal glasses cushioned in its plush interior. Theresa arrayed them upon the cloth. There was even a tiny Limoges vase, which she dipped in the fountain and filled with wildflowers. The food came last: cuts of cold meat, cheeses, bread and butter, and a bottle of still-cool white wine.

"I do so love eating out of doors," Theresa said, looking at her handiwork with satisfaction. Baptiste laughed, softly at first, and then louder, until his frame shook. Theresa was perplexed, and she waited for Baptiste's laughter to subside.

"I am very sorry—" he began, but she cut him off with a dismissive wave of her hand.

"You needn't explain," she said.

"I'm not used to this," he told her, shaking his head. "For me, eating out of doors means living on what you shoot: a deer's hindquarters, or a turkey stuck on a branch and quick-roasted over the campfire, or, when game is scarce, the buffalo strips you've dried and carried along in your pack roll with a little johnnycake, if you're lucky." His voice had grown softer as he recited the details. "This is nicer than anything I ever saw *indoors* in St. Louis or even New Orleans!"

Theresa's features relented, and she laughed. "Come, sit with me and tell me of the hardships you endure in the wilds."

They feasted on what the Ludwigsburg kitchens served up for a princess's outing: quail's eggs in aspic, duck liver pâté, slices of lean beef dressed in herbs, even a small jar of caviar with its own special spoon made of horn. They drank a light white wine with a sweet after-taste that Theresa explained came from a cousin's vineyards along the Rhine. She replenished Baptiste's glass, sipping from her own infrequently. The midday sun shone fiercely through the green canopy above, raising the temperature noticeably. Even the insects ceased their hum, so the fountain's gentle splashing was all they heard in the heavy air beneath the trees. Baptiste asked Theresa's permission to remove his coat—he had seen Paul do the same once—and when she nodded her assent, he rose and put it aside, then stretched his arms high overhead as he yawned.

Her look seemed to draw him to her, but he hesitated until she extended her hand to him. He caught her arm and drew her into his arms and kissed her. When at last they separated, she was smiling, and her eyes said yes, and he repeated what he had just done, this time holding her tight, as if she were a deer that could escape and disappear into the forest. When he let her go, Theresa kept her hand on Baptiste's neck.

"Let us save the rest for later, shall we?" she said in a languorous tone. To his searching eyes, she responded, "They will have ideas about us at the palace. It wouldn't do to prove it to them."

That night they made love in Theresa's rooms. During dinner, Theresa had managed to join Baptiste alone at the buffet table and slipped a note into his hand while she offered him more soup. He opened the small envelope in his room afterward and unfolded a half sheet of vellum. She had written in a bold hand, "Come to the small music room at ten and wait. Leave your boots outside your door. Bring your lovely smile." No one had ever addressed him that way, and as he heard Theresa's voice say the words in his head, he felt a thrill of anticipation.

He stood before the small oval mirror that hung between the windows, composing his face in the reflection and analyzing its parts. What did Theresa see when she looked at him? His blue-gray eyes were set wide, beneath a prominent brow, like his father's. From his mother came his dark and finely shaped eyebrows, his high cheek-bones, and his olive skin, which had caused one woman at court to ask if he was a Sicilian, another to assume he was Spanish. Both were compliments, Theresa had assured him. For the first time he considered that his copper-hued skin and chiseled features might make him attractive to a woman. The idea surprised him.

Theresa's beauty was less pronounced than that of many of the other women at court. Her fine features appeared almost sharp in certain lights, but her curious eyes gave her face its power. She was fifteen years older than his nineteen, and yet she didn't seem old at all. Unlike so many of the unmarried women he had met at Ludwigsburg, many of them younger than Theresa, she wasn't sad or forlorn or frivolous or lonely. Was it because she had been widowed so young and found herself rich and independent? Or was it just who she was, someone who was determined to draw from life everything it could offer?

In the music room, he found a single oil lamp lit and the heavy drapes on both windows pulled shut to ensure that the light would not be visible. The piano that stood against one wall looked like an oblong table, its keyboard inset in one side; it differed from the far larger piano, with its voluptuous curved top, that they called a *Flügel,* a wing, that reigned in the palace's larger music room where concerts were often held. The scale here was more intimate. Only a small harp and a cello laid on its back on a narrow table suggested that this room was given over to music. Baptiste stopped at the piano and lifted its fall board to examine the keys. The door from the hallway opened suddenly, and he let the cover drop with a slam. He looked up in horror, suddenly aware of how anxious he felt, and saw Theresa's maid, Marie-Claire, swooping down upon him with a reproving hiss.

"Shhh! Monsieur, you must be *very* quiet!" Her sharp look softened, as if she were addressing a child. "We must be silent if our passage is to remain undetected." She picked up the lamp and motioned him to a door in the room's paneling. Baptiste understood that they were to negotiate the hidden world of the servants' interior corridors. Before opening the door, Marie-Claire turned to him and said, "If we come across anyone, conceal yourself at my signal."

Baptiste walked behind Marie-Claire down a plain, unadorned passageway that apparently continued along the entire inner perimeter of the palace's rooms, providing access to each by one or more service doorways. Racks of keys, piles of fresh linen, serving trays and flower vases, brooms and mops were neatly arrayed at periodic widenings of the corridor alongside small staircases that led to the upper floors. Baptiste saw the backs of each room's heating stove, which servants could stoke without entering the rooms.

His musings were cut short by the sound of voices approaching from a side hallway. Marie-Claire stopped and motioned furiously with one hand behind her back for Baptiste to enter a small alcove on the right. This he did, hiding behind long aprons hung from hooks in overlapping profusion. Two men's voices came closer, their tones strained as they apparently carried a great weight down the passageway.

"Who'd have thought the old lady would call for firewood so late in the season?"

"Ah, she's a hundred if she's a day. At that age, the cold is in your bones for good."

Both of them grunted and wheezed as they grappled with their load. Baptiste understood most of what they said, though a few words were beyond him. He knew from Schlape that the "old lady" was the dowager queen, the king's stepmother, who lived in semiseclusion in the far reaches of the palace.

"If you ask me, she should— Why, good evening, Madame. A late-night errand for your good mistress?" Marie-Claire bantered with the two of them, telling them she had to fetch some correspondence that Theresa had left somewhere and commiserating with them about the caprices of the royal family. They continued down the hallway with their lantern and, Baptiste saw, two large canvas bags of firewood. Marie-Claire proceeded, obliged to make it seem as if she were walking purposefully, leaving Baptiste in utter darkness. A few minutes later she returned and retrieved Baptiste from his hiding place. They turned down another corridor and took a staircase to the next floor. Marie-Claire then led him down a narrower service corridor to a door, knocked lightly three times, then twice, and opened the door. She hurried Baptiste in as if he had been standing out in the rain, then closed the door quietly and set down her lamp.

"Please wait here. Madame will be along presently." Marie-Claire disappeared into an adjacent room and Baptiste contemplated his surroundings. It was as if he had surfaced from subterranean murk into a world of sunlight and splendor, so great was the contrast between the servants' passageway and this room. The walls were painted the palest yellow, with light blue detailing on the paneling, a scheme that was echoed in the drapery, the embroidered upholstery, even the carpet. A dozen candles flickered in wall sconces and candlesticks, casting a soft glow and pervading the air with the aroma of a spice unknown to him.

Baptiste caught sight of himself in a mirror that hung above a small inlaid chest of drawers, and he was stunned by the transformation of the face that had stared out from the mirror in his own room. The light here was strange, captivating and golden, suffusing his skin with a radiance that seemed to come from within. *How different I look,* he thought.

He heard muffled voices, then the door to the next room opened and Theresa was framed in the doorway. The robe she wore was light-colored and the room behind her darker, so that she stood out like an apparition before she took a step forward and broke the spell. She wore a long dressing gown embroidered with shimmering metallic threads, and her hair was worked with golden ribbons. Baptiste struggled to find words. He had never seen her look so beautiful. *Is it possible this apparition has chosen me?*

Transfixed by Theresa's radiance, Baptiste was acutely aware that he had done nothing special to prepare for this moment, and he regretted it intensely. His shirt was clean at least, but his trousers were rumpled and his coat had seen long wear since its last cleaning.

Theresa crossed to where he stood, held his hand in both of hers, and said, "Come, Baptiste, you look as if you've seen a ghost. You've reached your safe haven and now you must relax. Sit down here and I'll pour us something cool to drink." She led him to the couch and kissed him full on the lips, a long, lingering kiss that made him forget everything that had come before it. Then she withdrew from his embrace, poured two glasses of champagne from a bottle that stood on a nearby table, and sat beside him. He was struck by her ease, as though this rendezvous was natural. He wondered if he would know how to play his part.

"To life, and all its myriad surprises." They touched glasses and Baptiste was about to drink when Theresa caught his arm. "No, Baptiste. Lovers must look in each other's eyes when they toast. Otherwise Cupid's curse will descend upon them."

He did as she said, looking long into her eyes. He knew then that he had only to follow his instincts and she would do the rest. After they had drunk together he asked, "What is Cupid's curse?"

"It is taking each other for granted."

Later he remembered that Theresa's dressing gown was covered with tiny embroidered butterflies, and it had seemed important, beautiful, and true to who she was. When she led him into the dark bedroom, she kept two candles burning, and he learned that a dim, flickering light was more inviting than the total dark that had prevailed with the girls he had known. He would remember, always, how she had asked him to remove the golden ribbons from her hair, and how humbled he had felt. When she removed his shirt, she took one of the ribbons and draped it loosely around his neck so that it hung down on his chest, and it had felt like tiny tongues of fire upon his skin. Beneath her dressing gown Theresa wore a sheath of white silk, and in his excitement he had pulled hard at the straps. Without a hint of reproof or dismay she said, "There is no need for haste, my love. We have all the time we need," as if she wanted him to enjoy with her this great gift of forgetting time. She helped him with the clasp, and then there was the softness of her skin on his, and the expanse of linen and pillows upon which they sailed, and the golden steady light of two candles, like an undying sunset upon the river.

TWENTY-THREE

After that first night, Baptiste went to Theresa's rooms two or three times a week as spring turned into summer. After their lovemaking she would sometimes kneel by his side as he lay on his back and run her finger lightly across each of his four scars and bend forward and kiss each one, finishing the ritual with a whispered prayer: "Neither knife nor ball shall pierce the flesh of him I hold dear." Her incantation gave her a feeling she could protect him against the things she could not control. Her husband had died in battle, he reminded himself. Baptiste's scars, though, had only been the result of childhood games and foolish accidents. He tried to tell Theresa this, but she hushed him.

Just below his left eye he had a small triangular indentation from a stubby arrow shot in haste by a fellow member of the Kit Fox Society as they played at war. An inch higher and he would have lost his eye, but the cheekbone had protected him. On his left breast, just below the nipple, he bore a diagonal scar six inches long and one inch wide, an impressive mark of other roughhousing with his Mandan cousins, when the head of a war club, brandished in glee, came loose and struck him to the ground. He had bled spectacularly, his chest and stomach latticed with red, but the wound was superficial and had soon healed. Another puncture wound on the right side of his stomach had been far more serious. He had fallen onto the blunt end of a lance when his horse shied at a rattlesnake. The fever had lasted for over a week. When Baptiste recovered, the shaman told him that he had left to visit the Great Spirit and had only reluctantly returned when they called to him through the big pipe.

The last scar caused him pain. He had jumped into the river from a high bank, responding to the cries of his father, whose overloaded canoe had upended. As strong a paddle as he was in a canoe, his father had never learned to swim; though he was only thirty feet from the bank, his terror was real. Baptiste leaped and hit a submerged rock, which peeled off a flap of skin on his right hip as cleanly as if it were a strip of hide flensed after the hunt. Once he got his father and his load of pelts safely to shore, he had looked in awe at the flesh hanging from the bone and had come near to fainting. But the shaman bound up the skin and muscle with a poultice and changed the herbs frequently. The wound had taken a long time to heal, and still, five years later, he felt a deep ache in his hip when the weather was damp. It sometimes frightened Baptiste to look at the mottled patch of skin with its thick, ragged edge. He realized that these must seem like savage wounds to one not used to life on the frontier.

Theresa was contemptuous of the cult of war, which she derisively called "men and their endless games." Her husband's death surely played a part in her attitude. She was dismissive about the practice of dueling over points of honor. The dramatic scars on the faces of fashionable young men she referred to as "self-inflicted." He wondered what she would make of the life he had known as a boy among the Mandan if she could see it for herself. If these marks from boyhood pranks made such a strong impression on her, what would she think of the ones borne by his kinsmen and friends when they became full members of the tribe?

One night, shortly before midsummer, he felt Theresa's soft and pliant shoulder against his in the warm air, and he closed his eyes. He dreamed that night of the Mandan initiation. Once again he heard the chants and felt the throb of the drums in his bones, once again he watched as the young men cried out for strength. He saw Jumping Fox hanging overhead, twirling vividly in the firelight, and this time he sprang up to help him. He grabbed for his legs, and heard a piercing scream. Instead of holding the body spinning above him, his arms grasped something cold and brittle that seemed to disintegrate in his hands. Then a crash resounded below him and there was another scream, and he was awake. He was standing on the bed, and he heard Theresa urgently say, "Don't move. There is glass all over. Let me light a candle."

When the light flared up, he saw what he had done. In his right hand he grasped one of the branches of the Venetian chandelier that hung above the bed; on the floor at the foot of the bed lay the shattered pieces of another. She lit two oil lamps on the dresser. There came a knock at the outer door and Marie-Claire's worried voice: "Madame, is there some trouble? Madame?" Theresa put on her dressing gown, went out, and reassured Marie-Claire in low tones.

Baptiste's body shone with sweat in the faint light. "Let me move some of these sharp pieces from the bedclothes." Theresa picked up several jagged shards of blue glass and placed them on a bedside tray. "Now you can get down safely." He crossed to the opposite side of the bed and jumped to the floor.

"You're bleeding," Theresa said.

Rivulets of blood traced a scarlet net from his hands to his elbows. She sat him in a chair, gently uncoiled his fingers from the curved piece of Murano glass, and sat on a footstool with a basin of water and a small towel and washed his cuts. He was still captivated by the reality of his dream. Now, with just the two of them enclosed within the lamp's gentle nimbus, the world seemed diminished, and he felt a stab of loneliness as he considered how far behind he had left his other world. He sat wordless before her and watched her movements with a distant interest.

"What did you dream of?" Theresa asked gently.

"I saw a friend very clearly."

"Ah," she said as she wrapped strips of linen around his palm. "Was your friend in danger?"

"No. Not exactly. He just seemed . . . he seemed to need me."

She tied off the last strip and touched his forearm with her fingertips. "Come, let me give you some cognac." Her eyes were sad as she rose.

The brandy spread a warm flush from his gut to his head and then slowly to his limbs. The pulsing in his hands eased, and the stinging of the cuts. Theresa stoked the fire's embers and added a log, and together they sat before it in facing chairs and watched the flames take life. Then he told her about the initiation ceremony.

"I didn't grab for Jumping Fox when I watched in the lodge. He became a Mandan brave that day, like all the others."

"And you?"

"To the Mandan, I was part of the white man's world. I took another path, and it has brought me here. But I sometimes think that there is no more place for me in this world than there was among the Mandan."

The silence was almost entire save for the fire's gentle hissing, and they sat together for a long time before Theresa spoke. "Suppose I tell you a dream I sometimes have." Baptiste inclined his head, and she went on. "I am flying, looking down on a carriage in which I am traveling. My body is in the carriage, but the *real* me, my essence, is flying high above. It is taking me to my parents' house in Silesia on a trip I must have made a dozen times in the years before I was first married. It was a road I knew well, a comfortable voyage, a homecoming. Yet as I fly above, I imagine the coach turning off the road that leads home and taking another one, a turning at a crossroads. Sometimes the carriage turns left, sometimes right, but it always turns off the usual path. I don't know where it is going, and that seems to be the important part. My destination is unknown, new, mysterious. As the coach turns, my being is filled with anticipation at the adventure ahead. I wake up excited, hopeful, and full of happiness at having set off for somewhere unfamiliar." She looked at him full of enthusiasm and asked, "Can you imagine how the unknown can actually give us hope?"

Baptiste was puzzled, and he shook his head.

"In many ways that dream is curious," she told him, "and yet it comforts me when I consider the turns my life has taken. I was sixteen when I married and moved to Russia. I had visited my grandmother in

France every year, and I'd been to Vienna once or twice, but otherwise I knew only Württemberg. Saint Petersburg seemed familiar, but when we spent time on my husband's estates in the country, I quickly realized how completely different Russia was from anything I had ever known."

She gazed into the fire.

"The people were very nice. They had to be, of course, but some were genuinely welcoming. Still, I was an outsider—they called me *'la petite française'*—and I knew that if I stayed for a thousand years, I would never truly be one of them."

She had felt different and alone, she told him, and it had made her unbearably sad. She had longed for everything she had known as a girl. But soon she had decided to make the best of it, and learn about her husband's country, rather than thinking constantly of her own.

"What made you change?" Baptiste asked.

"I realized there was no going back. That is always the lot of women, but men often have a choice. Your own mother chose to stay with your father rather than return to her tribe. That was the only way forward for her in the world."

Baptiste nodded, sensing the truth of her words as he considered the direction his mother's life had taken.

"You, too, can choose how to use your time in this strange place. You could return to America, of course, and I expect that someday you will."

"Someday." He repeated the word without inflection.

"While you are here, though, absorb everything that is new to you. Me, Paul, Ludwigsburg, Europe—all of it! Someday it will help you fashion your life. Live in the present, but take in all you can for what lies ahead."

"It is hard for me to imagine the future," Baptiste said.

Theresa took his uninjured hand in her own. "There is not much in this world I am sure of, but that is one thing I know. It is like the manhood ritual you described, Baptiste, except that you are not surrounded by friends and cousins who are going through the same ordeal. There is only one you, and you must make it up as you go along, here in the present. My friend, that is one of the most difficult tasks we face."

Later, he would remember "my friend"—she had called him *"mon ami."* Of all the guileless things a woman could say in the quietness of intimacy, this was surely the most satisfying.

TWENTY-FOUR

FALL 1824

After one of Paul's trips to Stuttgart to see to the details of his collection, he worried aloud about the need to find a permanent home for his treasures. Baptiste had often heard this before. "How can I study what I've collected if the pieces can't be suitably housed?" Paul complained, but Baptiste didn't understand the problem. "Paul needs to find a very rich wife," Theresa told him.

It was an evening in late August when Baptiste and Theresa lay in bed, talking in unhurried tones as they traced arabesques with their fingertips on each other's arms. Baptiste had come to savor their lovemaking, learning the luxury of taking his time. Nor was there any concern about Theresa's becoming pregnant; she had told him that, after two miscarriages in Russia, she was no longer able to conceive. The prospect of Paul's and Baptiste's departure arose. "Paul seems finally to be serious about leaving Ludwigsburg," Theresa said.

"We were supposed to have left for Silesia by now," Baptiste replied, "but Paul always has just one more detail that needs to be taken care of."

Theresa rolled onto her side and traced her fingers lightly across

Baptiste's chest. "But this time there are things that will hasten his departure."

"What things?"

"Money. The court chamberlain has received several demands for payment from Paul's creditors in America. Apparently, it is quite an extensive list, starting in St. Louis and continuing down the"—she paused, letting Baptiste provide the word—"yes, the *Mississippi* River to New Orleans. When Wilhelm returns in two weeks, he'll be furious to discover that his gypsy cousin has engaged the kingdom's finances to cover the debts incurred on his expedition. If I know Paul, it is only the beginning of the bills that will come due."

"How is leaving going to help?" he asked.

Theresa shrugged. "It won't. But Wilhelm has a fearsome temper, so it is best if Paul is far away when the wave breaks."

"What will Paul live on now?" Baptiste asked her. "I am part of what he likes to call his 'household.' I'm just another bill to pay, isn't that so?"

Theresa put her arm around Baptiste's shoulder. "No, no, *mon ami.* You misunderstand. What it costs for you to be attached to Paul's household is not significant, because it is not really about money. It is about a choice in life. Either Paul settles down and acts the part of a royal duke of Württemberg as Wilhelm understands it or his access to the royal funds will always be severely limited. Money is just the weapon. Do you see? If Paul wants to retain his independence, as I know he does, he would do well to marry and start a family."

"How does he find the right kind of wife?"

"The halls are filled with candidates, if he would choose to notice them. The trick will be finding one rich enough to meet his needs and tolerant enough to indulge his travels. Young women in our world generally think very little about science and exploration. Being married to a man whose life is ruled by them is hardly the dream of most princesses."

"Does he have to marry a princess?"

"A duchess might do," Theresa told him, "even a countess if she were very rich and from an ancient, noble family."

Baptiste laughed. "This is the way horse breeders talk."

"But that is exactly what it is like! You couldn't have put it better! The importance given to ancestry, bloodlines, relatives near and distant, and the ability to produce an heir is just another form of animal husbandry."

She explained for Baptiste which considerations of lineage would be weighed, and how political and geographical alliances would also be taken into account. Then negotiations could begin between two households about the money, land, and treasure that would seal the union. All such royal marriages were arranged; marrying for sentimental reasons was regarded as a form of madness.

"I was unusually lucky. My dowry was not very great, but my family was illustrious. My husband was a very decent man who loved me in his way, and he was exceedingly rich and generous. Despite our lack of children, he arranged for a sizeable part of his fortune to be controlled by me in the event of his death. My independence is in the form of gold bullion in the bank vaults of Saint Petersburg, Berlin, and Vienna."

"I take it Paul doesn't want to marry who his family tells him to?"

Theresa rose and put on the dressing gown that hung nearby, then pulled her hair back with combs before turning again to Baptiste. The softness had gone out of her features and when her eyes met his, Baptiste felt dismay; her gaze was on his nakedness, but her thoughts were elsewhere.

"No, Baptiste, nor does he want to take his own life in hand. But if he wants to maintain the economic and social advantages of his position so that he can be free to do his work, then he must expect to fashion a compromise that will satisfy his family. Either that or he must break with Württemberg altogether and make his own way in society. Sadly, his upbringing has prepared him for nothing practical, and his passion for natural history requires significant amounts of money. He will have to choose, and it will be sooner rather than later."

"Paul will have a hard time compromising," Baptiste said.

She flushed. "You would think that making an accommodation with the world in order to preserve your independence were the greatest tragedy." Theresa's eyes narrowed. "Compromising with power to protect their interests is something women do every day of their lives. Never forget that, Baptiste."

As Theresa had foreseen, Paul soon told Baptiste that they would be leaving for his brother's estates in Silesia. He thought of Maura and wondered where she was. Though they had written again as cousins during the summer, he realized that he had forgotten even to look for a response to his last letter. Was she traveling again?

The prospect of being separated from Theresa troubled him more. She was his lover, his go-between, his guide to the peculiar world of Ludwigsburg, his one true friend. The night before he left, he told her he was uneasy about leaving, but her response did not satisfy him.

"You will return to your country before too long, while my life is here. Whatever time we have had together is a gift that life has offered us both. Let us try not to worry about what lies ahead."

So began a nomadic existence as he, Paul, and Schlape traveled around Europe visiting relatives and friends. Baptiste worried that the matter of Paul's debts would soon catch up with them, that he would quickly run out of money and have to return to Ludwigsburg to confront his cousin. But Paul's circumstances did not visibly change: he frequently enjoyed the hospitality of others, but he also spent money in a prodigal fashion when the need arose. The coach and four matched horses they used for travel were splendidly cared for; their meals and lodgings were the most comfortable available on the rare occasions when they were not offered the generous hospitality of rich and titled friends; nor did they forego any diversions or entertainments in the towns and cities they visited. As Theresa had told him, money was not really the issue that set Paul at odds with his family.

In fact, Paul had several sources of income, which made him, by any reasonable standard, a rich man—income from his mother's lands in Silesia, his portion of his father's inheritance, investments in English and French shipping consortia that were regularly profitable, even a sizeable gift from his uncle King Friedrich to his favorite nephew, which Paul referred to simply as "the gold bars" and that he did not draw upon. Baptiste also discovered by happenstance that Paul carried a letter of credit from Theresa, which he frequently used for their travel expenses. But for any future large expenditures, like another expedition to America, he would have to marry and settle down, a contradiction that Paul found intolerable.

Baptiste had often wondered why Paul didn't use his extensive contacts to make a fortune in fur trading. Only gradually did he come to understand that the actual making of money was beneath Paul, something vaguely disreputable and, in any case, unnecessary. Commerce was like a great machine that turned somewhere nearby but unseen, and by Paul's reckoning, it had nothing to do with his life.

First they went to Silesia, a weeklong journey during which they passed through a diminishing number of cities and towns and long stretches of forest and untilled plains. At last they entered Carlsruhe, a rustic village of modest buildings. Slowed by a September storm that had turned the roads to mud, they arrived in the late evening.

"Welcome, welcome!" Paul's brother bellowed over the wind as they hurried inside. Taller than Paul but not as heavyset, he seemed very pleased at their arrival. "This storm is just beginning," he told them. "Tomorrow the roads will be impassable. I'm very glad you got through."

Duke Eugene's castle, though comfortable, was much smaller than the palace at Ludwigsburg, and right away Baptiste sensed a more relaxed atmosphere. It felt like a big family house, and no courtiers were apparent. It stood in the center of the town, a ponderous square building of two stories with rounded corners and a towering central cupola, surrounded by a narrow strip of greenery bounded by a circular dirt road. From this ring extended eight roads symmetrically, like the spokes of a wagon wheel, along which houses and shops were arrayed in a haphazard fashion.

On the third day, after the storm had subsided, Paul took Baptiste for a ride through the ducal forest that surrounded Carlsruhe. It was a vast wooded tract crisscrossed with straight *allées* in patterns that intersected and then continued on through the trees. At intervals they came upon small lakes and little pavilions and houses with artful names—the Swedish Castle, the Doll's House, the Vineyard Pavilion—set against the landscape the way one might place a bauble on a tabletop in a Ludwigsburg salon. It was, Baptiste saw, another version of the pattern he was by now familiar with, in slightly modified form. Paths lined with trimmed trees led through the woods to clearings with fountains, sculpture, and small structures, all made to look welcoming and informal. When he and Paul left the confines of the ducal domain, Baptiste saw that the surrounding terrain was wilder and more remote than anything he had yet seen in Europe. Theresa had told him that bears and wolves were to be found in the far hills. For the first time he was in a region where man did not entirely prevail.

But the still and formal ducal forest, with its cleared understory and eerie quiet, felt like a huge garden—which, indeed, it was. Workers cleared the brush, hauled down wood, and cut the lower branches of trees to achieve the illusion of a wild forest that was pretty to look at. "It makes hunting at a gallop a delight," Paul told him when he mentioned the lack of down wood. Baptiste recalled that the forest of Royaumont outside of Paris was the same, with few impediments for horses. During their ride, they saw no one else in the forest other than workers. Paul saw nothing unusual in this arrangement. "It is Eugene's domain. There is only the occasional poacher, and for that we have wardens."

A miniature temple on a gentle rise, its columns reflected in a placid pool below, reminded Baptiste of the ordered rows of trees receding from the riverbank on the lower Mississippi to frame one of the Creole plantation houses, and of Monsieur Chouteau's big house outside St. Louis, whose walled garden had been hacked from the underbrush. *This is what Europeans do,* he thought, *in Ludwigsburg or Silesia or along the Mississippi, when they are in the woods.*

Paul led him to a cleared rise that commanded a fine sweep of the landscape. Beyond the patterned wheel of streets below, the sun played upon ordered fields, open meadows, and measureless forests that stretched to the far hills.

"Your brother owns all of this, isn't that so?" Baptiste asked.

"Yes," Paul replied.

"You can't go anywhere, as far as the eye can see, that doesn't belong to him, or to another noble."

Paul nodded.

"It is a lot of land for one person to own."

"My friend," he said, "this is not the New World. We hold the land in commonweal for all of society. It has been this way for many centuries."

Baptiste said nothing, but he thought of the endless stretches of land along the Missouri and its tributaries: the Kansas, the Platte, the Knife, and all the other rivers and streams he knew so well. Under the vast sky stretched rolling prairies, wooded river valleys, desolate badlands, mountains and hills rich with game. The different tribes often fought brutally over hunting rights, but not one Oto or Sioux or Pawnee or Mandan would ever consider that he or his tribe owned the land that sustained them all. It would be ridiculous, like owning the air itself. It was a lunatic notion that only the white man was capable of.

From the deck of a boat on the Rhine in October, Baptiste watched the plume of steam emerging from a very tall smokestack near the river's bank. A regular metallic clanging sounded from within the adjacent building, and a jet of pure heat shot from the stack's top, then turned to billowing smoke dancing above a gap distorted by the heat. He had seen other chimneys, even the exhaust pipes on the steamships at Le Havre, but this concentration of energy was greater than anything he had ever known. Paul told him, "It is one of the new iron foundries. But it scares the animals and makes the country folk uneasy. Can you blame them?"

Baptiste laughed at Paul's pronouncement. His eyes shone with wonder. "This just keeps pumping it out, as if all the sulfur springs and smoke holes on the upper Missouri had been harnessed and made to pull the same wagon."

Paul pointed to a line of cliffs off the starboard bow and indicated two castles built on adjacent pinnacles high above the river.

"The nearer one"—he pointed to a mass of fortified towers crowning one of the heights—"is still owned by a collateral branch of my mother's family. In the fourteenth century, holding the higher ground was everything."

"In some places in America, it still is," Baptiste said. "These castles are like the fortified stockades the army is building as more traders move upriver."

Paul said, "From a distance, the white cliffs on the Missouri above Fort Atkinson, with their peaks and crags like battlements, reminded me of these very fortresses."

But Baptiste saw only an unremarkable expanse of an unimpressive river, its shoreline punctuated by drab villages and its surface peppered with boat traffic. "I guess I'd have to see the place you're thinking of," he offered doubtfully.

Often they passed through cities, and Baptiste still wondered at the numbers of people to be found in the streets. In Berlin, they arrived in the midst of a general celebration—a festival honoring the city's founders, Paul told him—and he hung out the window of the coach as it progressed slowly, jostled by the crowd. In Amsterdam, they were on foot during one of the biggest market days of the year, and the press of people slowed their walking to a crawl. The commotion on all sides was exciting, but the inability to move as he wished, hemmed in by the crowd, was deeply unsettling. At last they reached a main canal, where small boats ferried people across the harbor from a crowded pier. Every inch of space was alive with human activity and resonating with the cries of merchants and market-goers.

As they waited for the next ferry, Paul swept his arm wide to take in the scene. "They're all headed for America one day," he said. Baptiste laughed at Paul's joke, but he saw that Paul was serious. "If you lived here, wouldn't you go?" Paul persisted.

"I suppose I would," Baptiste admitted, "but then, I know something about what's there."

"They've heard that America is empty," Paul told him, "and that there is opportunity for every man. What else matters if you are faced with this?"

Of all the seaports they visited, his favorite was Venice. The canals lined with houses and palaces delighted him. An Austrian cousin of Paul's let them use his *palazzo* on the Grand Canal, and from its windows Baptiste watched the boat traffic for hours on end. He thought the gondolas were a precarious and awkward means of water travel, and that the standing rower's way of propelling a boat was inefficient. But as he watched the gondoliers ply passengers and cargo along the main waterway, he came to appreciate how well adapted their craft were for these sheltered waters and how skilled they were at controlling them with a single long oar. This was not the Missouri, with its turbulent currents and unpredictable weather. Once he saw a large, narrow boat with six standing oarsmen come down the canal at a great pace. Their strokes were as rhythmic and fluid as those of Indian braves in the large war canoes he had sometimes seen on the Missouri, and they moved with the same speed, grace, and purpose.

Before they left Venice in early December, Paul took him to see an altarpiece by Titian in an austere brick church called Frari. Baptiste left Paul peering at the image of the Assumption over the main altar, and wandered through the empty church, inspecting the side chapels. Before one of these, near the back of the nave, he stopped in wonder at the sculpture that hung above the altar. At the center of a complicated array of columns and forms floated a life-size crucifix in glowing white marble. The body of Christ was carved with such realism and detail that Baptiste was shaken.

The muscles of the arms, torso, and legs were perfectly formed, the veins and tendons pushing out against the taut skin, the fingers lightly closed over the nails that pierced the hands. The head of Christ hung to one side in the silent surrender of death, though everything about the finely shaped body spoke of youth, power, and life. Baptiste knew what he found so disturbing. The image before him was like that of Jumping Fox and his other friends as they hung overhead after the spirits had left them. Whoever had fashioned this body had observed a young man in the agony of death. The picture of the marble Christ remained in his mind for many days after they left Venice.

During these months, Baptiste was continually impressed by the places he saw and the people he met, but he discovered something about himself that was as true here as it had been in St. Louis: though this was a world whose currents he could navigate, it was not his world. He sometimes felt as if none of the places he had ever visited, either in Europe or North America, would claim him. He lived in between these two worlds in a place that encompassed both yet remained separate. He thought of himself as an in-between person. In St. Louis, there were others like him who moved easily between the white man's civilization in the towns along the Missouri and the network of Indian villages that extended up the river and its many tributaries. Though he met no one quite like himself in Europe, he considered that Theresa had moved to Russia as a young girl and Maura claimed to be both Irish and French without being entirely either. He began to understand how others shared this same capacity to live in two worlds at once.

TWENTY-FIVE

New Year's Day 1825
Stockholm

Dear Captain Clark,

I write to you from Sweden, where for the last couple of weeks we have been visiting friends of Duke Paul. Before we came here we spent time in Saint Petersburg, which is as far north and east as I have been in Europe. The winter in Russia and Sweden is like January in the Mandan villages: blizzards that leave a foot or two of snow in a day, winds so strong you can hardly stand, and air that feels cold enough to bite, if you dared to open your mouth. The furs here are of excellent quality, though the size of the pelts is smaller than what we are used to. I think they take the animals before they are full-grown.

Winter also brings short days this far north. The sun appears only for a few hours, and very low on the horizon. The Swedes drink liquor like no people I have ever seen. I had to slow down after two days of wildness over the Christmas holidays, but our hosts kept at it for the better part of a week, one long party with a kind of brandy that would peel the paint off a parlor. We are the guests of the king, a Frenchman, Bernadotte, who fought under Napoleon and was one of his best generals. I hear about Napoleon everywhere we go; people in Russia talk about him as if he had left yesterday.

In Saint Petersburg we rode in big sleighs pulled by three horses onto a wide lake that was frozen solid, with pinewoods along the shore as far as the eye could see. It was the first time since I have been in Europe that I saw something like the prairie. Not the same trees or terrain, you understand, but a sense of openness that seemed like it went on forever, and a night sky that let me believe I was far up the Kansas or the south fork of the Platte, until I lowered my eyes and it became Russia again. I don't mind telling you that at that moment, and for much of the next day, I thought a lot about home, and was sorry to go back to the city.

In what they call the countryside, it is hard to find any place you or I would call wild. I expect you know this already, but it has come as a discovery to me on my travels. Another difference is that being a "gentleman" here is everything, and you are judged by your family, your friends, the way you dress, the way you talk. There is some of that in St. Louis, I know, but in America how much money you have cuts through everything, while here it is not the most important thing. It has also made me see how free I was when I headed up the river. There it is only your wits and your experience that count, and I miss that.

You may be interested to know that Mr. Chouteau's business associate, Mr. Astor of New York, is known to many of the people Duke Paul and I have visited. He lives now at a big country house in Switzerland overlooking Lake Geneva, and he entertains European aristocrats. They call him "the richest man in America," so perhaps money is more important here than they let on.

Tomorrow we sail down the Baltic Sea to Hamburg. We should be in Paris again within a month.

My thoughts are often with you and those I know in St. Louis. Please be assured I am determined to learn all I can on this great adventure.

Yours affectionately,
Pomp

TWENTY-SIX

DUKE PAUL, FROM HIS PRIVATE JOURNAL
JANUARY 1825
WIED-NEUWIED

I have spent the last three days in the company of Prince Maximilian and his brother, Prince Charles, two pre-eminent collectors I first met in Berlin. Maximilian is a student of Professor Blumenbach at Göttingen and was most insistent on my visiting in order to talk over my findings from North America. He himself spent two years in Brazil, from 1815 to 1817, and he contemplates a similar exploration of the American frontier in the years ahead. After covering the general outline of my trip, then the particular places on my itinerary, I was subjected to the most rigorous questioning about every aspect of my travels: flora, fauna, geography, climate, tribal customs, etc. I answered as completely as I could until, after more than two hours of interrogation, it was apparent to me that the prince intended to cover every step of my way in the same methodical fashion. I cut him off, finally, pleading exhaustion and assuring him that he would have the opportunity to examine my findings in detail when my account is published.

There was something altogether disquieting about his insistence on specifics, and I drew back defensively to protect what I regard as my own hard-won findings, at least until they are in book form, when the world will see my name associated with the work. Are we all but vainglorious schoolboys, obsessed with our own renown? "Esteemed colleague" surely disguises more motives than the pure ideal of a free and full sharing of one's discoveries, though Maximilian and I use this formulation to address each other without a second thought. We are, after all, complicated social beings full of contradictions.

If Prince Maximilian knew of my own financial difficulties in preparing for a study of the works I have collected, he would be well and truly surprised. His immensely rich family supports him and Prince Charles unquestioningly in their pursuit of natural science, whereas I do not have even the means to unpack my tribal objects in suitable surroundings, much less to catalog my collection and write about my discoveries. I must find funds for my projects, and the only hope seems the one urged upon me by my family: a suitable wife.

Maximilian showed me many of the specimens he collected in Brazil, all masterfully displayed in special cabinets that occupy a wing of the building given over to his work. He cannot be faulted as a close observer of animals in the wild—his descriptions are full of surprising details of behavior, which can only have come from painstaking hours of waiting and watching. But one has the feeling that he is entirely consumed by the accretion of detail for its own sake, and takes no time to stand back and assess what he has seen. Moreover, his command of the principles of Linnaean classification is regrettably superficial, and in my cursory visit I found no fewer than three specimens (a small alligator and two members of the rat family) about which I strongly question his attribution of the specimen's genus. I kept this to myself, however, not wishing to question his competence while enjoying his hospitality. When I told him that I had collected an alligator at the mouth of the Mississippi, he asked curtly, "How long does yours measure?" and I discerned a jealous air. That, I fear, is what we are sometimes reduced to in the race to find undiscovered and exceptional members of the animal kingdom.

The prince is anxious to renew his travels in the Americas, and seems keen on visiting the Missouri. For him there is a mystical aspect to confronting the elements under extreme conditions. "Where in Europe can you find independence, danger, unmediated beauty, and an experience of nature unalloyed by metaphor?" he asked me. "In the New World, a lightning strike is still a lightning strike!" Fair enough, but perhaps a bit high-minded.

Maximilian voiced one great disappointment with respect to the material he has published on his exploration of Brazil. He told me he wished he had taken an artist along on the expedition, and he assured me that he would never again make that mistake. I told him that I made my own sketches, and he scoffed. Even von Humboldt had proved unequal to the task, he said. Publication of one's findings increasingly requires drawings with the verisimilitude that only a practiced artist could provide. He told me that Baron Langsdorff is even now exploring the interior of Brazil with two French artists the Russians agreed to pay for when they funded his expedition. Have we truly reached the point where a careful description of a specimen must be accompanied by a faithful image of the subject?

Fortunately, Baptiste and I leave early tomorrow morning for Paris, a timely departure in light of an exchange that has left the atmosphere tense, if not entirely poisoned. It happens that Prince Maximilian purchased a slave when he was in Brazil, a young male member of the Botocudo tribe, whom he brought here to Wied. Baptiste came across the Botocudo native today in the prince's laboratory, where he works as a menial factotum, cleaning display cases, preparing dissection equipment, making sure the lamps have oil, and the like. The prince and I walked in on their conversation, and Maximilian commented that they both seemed to be benefiting from the effects of civilization, as they were conversing in German. Baptiste took this badly, turning on him with a savage look in his eye. "You forget, sir, that we have our New World civilizations, as well. I have as much in common with this gentleman as I do with you."

Maximilian was shocked and offended at this outburst, and things rapidly went from bad to worse. Baptiste demanded to know how he could possibly have bought a human being, and the prince replied that it was only to give him his freedom. "Is this freedom?" Baptiste asked him, to which the prince responded, with perhaps too much self-satisfaction, that his lot was certainly better here compared to what it was in Brazil. "Yes, he has everything but his own people," Baptiste retorted, and so it went, with neither giving ground. "This man is perfectly free, you young fool!" the prince shouted, and left the room.

I am proud of Baptiste—and not a little astonished at how deeply he feels about this matter. I now recall that soon after we met in America, Baptiste was uncomfortable when I discussed with him the fact of black slavery in St. Louis, along the river, and again in New Orleans. His own guardian, General Clark, was a slave owner, and no doubt Baptiste regularly saw Clark's slaves and spent time with them. He told me when we first arrived in France that the slaves' grumbling came to mind when he heard the sullen undercurrent against the king among the poor in the streets of Paris. To be sure, a wall separates master and slave in St. Louis: whites are free; Negroes are slaves. But for those of mixed blood, like Baptiste, the riddle must always come back: "I am not a slave, but neither am I entirely free. What am I?"

Twenty-Seven

Baptiste eased the mare along the roadway at the center of the Pont Neuf as the sky darkened in the west. Shops and stands lined both sides of the bridge. Halfway across, he had an unbroken view down the river, and saw that a storm was coming in fast. Feathery arcs of rain descended from the deep gray clouds on the near horizon and gusts of wind snaked across the river, rippling its narrow surface and shaking the branches of the leafless trees along its banks. *You can never see enough sky here to know what the weather is,* he thought as he rode off the bridge.

Baptiste followed the street up the gradual rise of what the locals called the Montagne Sainte-Geneviève, the "mountain" named for the patron saint of Paris. *We wouldn't even call this a hill at home,* he thought. Paul frequently admonished him that such comparisons were inappropriate. This was a good piece of advice, and Baptiste had gradually overcome his tendency to voice his feeling that the landscape seemed puny.

Sometimes, though, his spirit rebelled. The rain began to fall in torrents, and he leaned into the wind. "Mountain!" he muttered as the mare made her way up the incline of glistening cobblestones.

The towering dome of Sainte-Geneviève rose above the surrounding buildings at the brow of the hill, then was lost to sight as he rode through the narrow, crooked streets. Soon he emerged into the clearing that surrounded the enormous church. Its majestic pillars brought to mind an engraving in his childhood Bible that showed the gates of heaven. He craned his neck to follow the dome up toward the windswept clouds that spit rain down upon him. His cape grew wet and heavy, and he longed for an elk hide rubbed with bear grease to draw about his shoulders. He dismissed Paul's maxim and silently cursed the complication and ineffectiveness of European clothes for dealing with something as straightforward as a rainstorm.

He knew that the street he was looking for lay on the south side of Sainte-Geneviève, and he directed his horse back into the warren of narrow lanes. The downpour had emptied the streets. He threaded his way through the latticework of cobbled alleys without finding it, and approached a young man huddled in a doorway and asked directions.

"At the corner of the rue des Postes, Monsieur, another hundred meters farther on!" he shouted over the din of the rain, motioning toward a wider street that began across the way. Baptiste rode off and a few minutes later he peered through the fading light and found the words he had been looking for etched into the stone of the corner building: *rue du Cheval Vert.*

Above the first doorway he saw a coat of arms with a harp at its center and the inscription *Collège des Irlandais* in gold lettering. Baptiste dismounted, hitched his horse to the iron ring set into the wall, and pounded the large iron knocker on the massive oak door. When there was no response, he hammered again as loudly as possible to be sure his knocking rose above the storm. A small panel in the door slid to one side and an old man's face, lit from below by a lantern, appeared behind four vertical bars. "Yes? What is your business here?"

Baptiste had expected the door to be opened, but he bent down and peered into a pair of coal black eyes. "I am looking for Mademoiselle Maura Hennesy, Monsieur."

"There is no one here by that name," the man responded gruffly, then added, "Monsieur is perhaps not aware that this is a *pensionnat* for young men."

Baptiste was surprised. "I was told that I might find her here nonetheless." Baptiste pulled an envelope from under his cloak and held it up to the small aperture. "Would it be possible to give her this letter?"

The man snatched the envelope and drew it through the grate. The old man's eyes glittered as he saw Prince Franz's coat of arms on the seal. He asked with renewed curiosity, "Who is looking for Mademoiselle Hennesy?"

"Her cousin from America would like to see her," Baptiste replied. He produced a coin from his pocket and passed it through the bars. "Here is something for your trouble, Monsieur."

The man grabbed the coin and the panel slid shut. Baptiste raised his hand to knock again, hesitated as the rain pounded down, then rode away. Obviously he had made a mistake in assuming that the address Maura had given him for a correspondence was where she would be living.

A courier arrived at Prince Franz's the next morning with an envelope that Schlape delivered to Baptiste in the library. "The messenger insisted it was of the utmost urgency," he said. Maura's brief note told him, "Under no circumstances must you present yourself again at the Collège," and she proposed a meeting that afternoon in the Tuileries gardens.

To Paul's inquiries, Baptiste replied that he had personal business to attend to later in the day. After lunch he made his way to the Tuileries on foot. He felt a tremor of anticipation as he remembered Maura's fresh and entrancing features, and her irreverence. *Will she still find me interesting?* he wondered, and quickened his step.

The air was clement for February, a generous sun in a cloudless sky and only a slight chill. Entering the gardens from the broad square at the bottom of the Champs-Elysées, Baptiste felt a sudden twinge as he recalled how startled he had been only a year ago when he first saw this city of carved buildings and ordered plants. Was it possible these surroundings were already ordinary to him?

The gardens were crowded, with knots of strollers along all of the lanes, taking advantage of the sun. Baptiste found Maura sitting on a bench beneath the rows of bare trees at the corner of the garden nearest the Seine. He saw her in profile, reading a book. As if she sensed his approach, she turned and raised her chin in a graceful gesture. When he arrived at her side, she rose, took both his hands in her own, and said, "Why, cousin, how lovely to see you!"

Baptiste smiled, enchanted by the familiar figure standing before him.

"It *is* good to see you," she said. "Let's walk, shall we," and in a lower tone she added, "Then we can talk undisturbed." She gave him her arm and said, "You cannot imagine how many men assume that an unaccompanied woman on a park bench is an invitation to mischief."

They walked arm in arm, and her closeness after the long time apart felt both comfortable and strange, as if they had been together the previous day. "I am very happy to see you again, Maura," Baptiste said.

"I may as well tell you that you complicated things considerably by showing up at the door of the Collège."

Baptiste's cheeks reddened. He told her of Paul's sudden decision to come to Paris earlier than planned, and that he had had no hope of sending a letter ahead of time.

"A man does not call upon a young lady in the evening," Maura said firmly. "Fortunately, Monsieur Dubois thought you were the messenger." She laughed now, a pure, confiding laugh that drew Baptiste in and calmed his fear.

"If you don't live at the Collège, why do you receive my mail there?" Baptiste asked.

"It is a place I can be sure of receiving messages without causing problems for others. Years ago, when my father was young, his family was very generous to the Revolutionary cause through the Collège. Later he was a *pensionnaire* there with Jerome Bonaparte and Eugene de Beauharnais, Napoleon's younger brother and his stepson. He is no friend to the Bourbons and, as you know, his correspondence is closely watched. The Collège allows him to correspond with others by using the names of various teachers and residents who sympathize with his ideas." She looked around quickly, then continued. "There is one thing I must mention. You wrote that you recalled what my father had to say about the Bourbons. That is the sort of language that could cause trouble if the wrong eyes were to see it. You must be more careful."

They walked up and down the *allées,* talking about the months since they had met. Maura told him she had been trying to enroll in the university's medical school. "A few of the professors have allowed me to be present as an auditor, but there is no question of being allowed to sit examinations. One of them suggested I train as a midwife!"

Baptiste could hear the anger in her words; he found her candor stimulating. "What do you do when you are not studying medicine?" he asked.

"I work with my father in the wine business," Maura said. "He has many clients in Paris."

Baptiste was delighted to be hearing English again, especially Maura's, with its engaging lilt. "And are your parents well?"

"They are. My father is busier than ever with his vineyard, and my mother is in Ireland for a visit. When she returns, I'll become her special project again." Maura shook her head slightly.

"What project is that?" he asked.

"She wants to see me married, Baptiste," Maura said with an exasperated look. "Like any mother, she fears the worst. Fortunately, she is not a very persistent matchmaker."

"And your father?"

"It is different with my father," she explained. "I am the one child he has, and in many ways he raised me as he would have raised a son. He trusts me with confidences, he introduces me to clients and political allies, and he teaches me his business. He knows that will end when I marry, and so he is of two minds."

"What does he think of your attempts to study medicine?"

"He sees no reason why I should not become a doctor," Maura responded in a matter-of-fact tone. "But he can do very little to open those doors for me or any other woman."

She held his arm more tightly and Baptiste felt his heart race. For an instant he thought of Theresa, of how they had grown comfortable with each other over time. He felt different now, elated by Maura's enthusiasm and directness.

"Tell me about yourself," she said. "What is the purpose of all these travels?"

"I sometimes wonder!" Baptiste exclaimed. "Paul has relatives and friends everywhere, many of them other specialists in natural history." He mentioned all the places they had visited since August.

"It must sometimes be very tiring," Maura said.

"It is," he agreed. "There are days when I think I would as soon die as sit in a coach." He winced, then continued. "But I've never seen any of it before, and I may never again, so I keep my eyes and ears open and learn what I can."

Maura nodded. "Did you meet anyone of interest?"

"Two or three people," Baptiste told her. "The rest treated me like an unusual new animal."

"That's how I feel in Professor Langlois's anatomy class! I might as well have two heads, for the way they look at me."

They both laughed.

"Did you have any adventures on all your travels across Europe?" Maura asked.

"I almost got myself shot at Paul's brother's castle in Silesia," Baptiste said laconically. He saw Maura's eyes widen expectantly, and he continued. "I took his nephew and two nieces out to play. They had asked me to show them how Indians hunt. We found a wolf's pelt still attached to the head in one of the hunting lodges, and I strapped it to my back and limbs. Then, in the tall grass of a nearby meadow, the children played grazing buffalo and I was the stalking wolf."

"What happened?"

Baptiste shook his head at the memory. "One of the gamekeepers came upon us and mistook me for a real wolf. When I stood up to reassure him, he took a wild shot, then turned and ran. He thought I was what they call a 'werewolf,' some kind of human wolf the peasants in Silesia believe stalks people."

Maura squeezed his hand. "I'm glad the gamekeeper was a bad shot."

Baptiste reddened as he saw that there was more than playfulness in Maura's eyes. Suddenly he mimed the gamekeeper's frantic flight for three or four steps, hands high above his head and face contorted in fear. Together he and Maura exploded in laughter, and only after they sat together on a bench were they able to regain their composure. Looking toward the far side of the gardens, Baptiste could see the river's glint through the gold-tipped iron pickets that enclosed the park. Then the light looked particularly soft, and the trees and footpaths and the distant fountains seemed to glow.

In the days ahead Baptiste could think of nothing but Maura. Beyond her beauty, he was attracted to her practical attitude. Though she was young, like him, she had learned something essential about people in her travels with her father. Her discernment and curiosity pleased him, and her way of thinking for herself reminded him of some of the free spirits he had encountered on the frontier. She was more self-reliant than any of the young women he had met in Europe. Were the Irish all so full of independence? In Maura's company he had experienced a quickening of all his senses, and a near giddiness that he had not known before. She even walked forcefully, with a stride that knew where it wanted to go.

Baptiste considered what Maura had said about her mother's concerns, and he remembered Theresa's thoughts on the importance of a respectable marriage. He understood that for him a marriage in Europe was unimaginable: he was landless, he had no fortune, he was of mixed race, and he was from a far-distant country. No European family would consider him a worthy match for their daughter. *I'm not looking for a wife anyway,* he told himself. That Theresa should take him as a lover and teach him about European ways made sense when he looked at it from a distance. She was nearly twice his age and had no intention of making a life with anyone else. Her wealth and position allowed her to remain entirely independent; she was the only woman he knew who could say that. Their paths clearly would part.

But Maura was genuinely interested in seeing him and knowing him better, and he wondered if there could be any future for them together. He dismissed the thought as he imagined all the reputable young men who would want to propose marriage, and their distinguished mothers hovering nearby, waiting to inspect the merchandise.

Paul and Baptiste stayed in Paris for a week, so Baptiste and Maura were able to see each other once more before he returned to Württemberg. They met in the early afternoon at Maura's godmother's apartment overlooking the Tuileries. After a cup of coffee and some light conversation, Madame Lemonnier excused herself, pleading correspondence that needed her attention.

"I would like to say my goodbyes when Monsieur Charbonneau is preparing to leave," she said, and closed the door on the two of them.

Maura said, "Madame is a free spirit who believes that young people should be trusted. I cannot tell you how unusual that is."

"I have some idea that it is not too common in these parts," Baptiste responded. He was entranced by Maura's presence. Her body had an artless kind of grace, slender without being lean, and for an instant he watched the outline of her breasts rise and subside beneath the dark sheen of her dress. He raised his cup of coffee as if it were wine. "Here is to your free spirit of a godmother." As they drank their eyes met, and neither turned away.

Maura was distressed. "Yesterday I was refused entrance to the medical faculty's operating theater," she told him. " 'Too much blood for a lady,' they claimed." Her eyes were wide with disdain. "So I should return to the Gironde and make my life among vintners," she said with a rueful smile. "Surely the wide world holds more than that!"

"Is there nowhere in France where a woman can become a doctor?"

"Not in all of Europe, Baptiste!" Maura cried. "Is it very different in America? My father's acquaintances say that women there are much more independent." Her voice was hopeful.

All the women Baptiste had known in St. Louis—from William Clark's two wives and the *grandes dames* of the Chouteau and Pratte fur trader clans to the wives of *voyageurs* and tradesmen—were principally responsible for raising children and keeping the household, fancy or modest. "I can't speak for all of America," he said at last, "but I don't know of any women doctors. I suppose you could say that women have to be more self-reliant because they're left for months at a time while the men are upriver. But unless they keep slaves, that just means that they do all the work themselves."

"Are there no other choices?" Maura asked.

"There were some Creole women in New Orleans who ran businesses," Baptiste told her. "And wives of *voyageurs* often keep accounts and trade directly when their husbands are away."

Maura considered his words, then said, "My uncle lives in Philadelphia. He once visited New Orleans and wrote that the Mississippi at its mouth is like the sea. When I was a child, he would read to me from a book called *Atala,* which opens with a description of that river. I am intrigued by that part of America."

Baptiste shook his head. "The rivers I know—the Mississippi and the Missouri, the Kansas and the Platte—are different entirely from what you have in Europe," he told her. "There are no stone embankments or jetties, and they aren't dredged for boat traffic. They're unpredictable and wily, like something alive, full of tree trunks, sand bars, whirlpools, and rapids. When the rains come, you can't even see across them in parts. And the farther you go upstream, the more you leave people behind. Once you get out into it, there is no end to the wild, open land. There is nothing like that here at all."

"Our rivers sound very tame by comparison," Maura said, "but our mountains are certainly wild. In the Alps above Annecy, we saw several chamois on a cliff above the path as we walked around the lake. And there are still wolves in the Alps, and peaks that have never been climbed."

Baptiste looked at her in exasperation. "The Alps are as wild as this drawing room! Every valley has its village and every mountaintop its cross."

Maura wanted to take his hand in hers, but Baptiste looked suddenly distant. She sat down in one of the chairs near the hearth and gestured for him to take the one opposite. The vase of greens on the low round table between them gave her hope—they seemed wild, or at least connected to something that was—and she poured out two glasses of wine from the decanter, placing one in front of him. "The frontier sounds like nothing I have dreamed of, much less known," she said. "Please tell me more."

Baptiste sank slowly into the chair, stretched out his legs before him, and leaned back with his eyes closed, his face a study in concentration. He sat quietly, wondering if he could find the words. What could someone who knew only Europe possibly understand? Even in repose, he conveyed a sort of athletic readiness that made Maura wonder if he would suddenly jump up and dash from the room. She saw again the chiseled fineness of his features, a bony nobility that had led her father, not without a certain respect, to call him a "Tartar" after their first meeting. But the sunlight showed he was a Tartar with the coloring of an Andalusian, a contrast that was at once unexpected and attractive.

The trace of a smile appeared on Baptiste's face and he opened his eyes quickly, determined to tell Maura about his home. He stood and moved his chair back from the center of the room. Crouched lightly on the balls of his feet, he looked into a fathomless distance and swung his arm across a horizon only he could see. Maura thought of someone poised to throw a spear on a long and perfect arc.

"Imagine the Alps seen across a vast plain, from a hundred miles away," Baptiste began, "with nothing between you and them but prairies, rivers, and endless herds. There are deer, antelope, elk, and buffalo as far as you can see, sometimes lost to sight by grass higher than a man's head. The land stretches to the mountains in rolling curves of green and brown, and a steady wind carries the smell of prairie sage." His voice was full of excitement.

"In the wider parts of the rivers, close by, water birds cover the surface so completely that it looks almost like dry land. Only an occasional movement of wings and the noise of the ducks and geese remind you that they are all floating, feeding on the water plants that fill the shallows. From miles away you see what looks like a coil of smoke rising into the air, a strange haze endlessly unraveling upward from the ground until it blocks the sun and begins to move sideways across the plain." He raised his arm to indicate the motion in the distance. "A flock of birds, you realize, undulating for miles on the horizon, expanding and contracting like a dark and porous sheet being borne away in a stiff wind. They make you see the air as surely as if it were something you could touch, and you follow their dance across the sky until they are swallowed up in the clouds."

Maura could see that this vision was more real to him than the chair she was sitting on, or the stone walls of the buildings on the rue de Rivoli, or any part of Paris that stretched below them. Gradually his gaze returned to her, his voice softer now but the intensity undiminished.

"Maura, between where you stand and the mountains, there is no trace of human life—no buildings, no roads, no carriages, no fences or walls. All is open, but that does not mean it is unknown or empty. Each tribe is like a shadow that attaches to the great herds and follows them as the seasons change."

She wanted him to continue before the spell broke. She wanted him to show her what it was like, take her somewhere that only he knew. He told her about hunting buffalo with his Mandan cousins: the long trip toward the herd's feeding ground; the infinite number of animals; the careful attention to staying downwind; the soundless waiting and abrupt explosion of surprise; the chase, with its sudden ration of fear, excitement, and individual exploits. And finally, the celebration, satiety, fatigue, and frequent grief at the injury or death of a friend.

"It is how the tribe feeds itself," Baptiste told her. "If the herd cannot be found, the old, the young, and the weak all drop like autumn leaves."

Maura could hardly find her voice. "My father uses much the same words to describe what happens to the farmers of Europe when the crops fail." She took their wineglasses from the table and handed him a glass as she raised her own.

"To the herds and the crops. May they never fail."

They drank, then Baptiste took her glass and placed it on the mantel. After describing his home to Maura, he felt confident and at ease. He held her hands in his, stepped close to her, and covered her neck with kisses, and her face flushed red. Her body softened and leaned into his and he discovered that her passion equaled his own. Then Maura gently pushed him back, and dimly he saw her shining eyes and the blameless smile on her lips as she whispered, "Not here, Baptiste. Not now."

He drew back slowly and said, "When?"

"I hope it will be soon."

She turned away. As she smoothed her hair she said, "Baptiste, I would like you to have something of mine to remember me by when we are apart. Will you take my handkerchief?"

Her hand went to the pocket of her dress for the square of white linen. She placed it in his hand and Baptiste saw the embroidered letters on one corner: MFH. He smiled in thanks and put the handkerchief in his jacket.

"What shall I have in return?" she asked.

Baptiste thought for a moment, then his features brightened. He undid the top two buttons of his shirt, reached in and pulled over his head a thin rawhide cord from which hung a gleaming crescent of black. "It is an eagle's talon," he explained as he held it before her wondering eyes.

She reached out and touched it. "I can't . . ."

"If you have it, then we will both be protected."

She took it and placed it against her lips. Just then, a commotion of sorts arose in the hall—voices, a door slamming, more voices—and Maura whispered, "It is my godmother's way of telling us our visit is over." She sat in one of the armchairs. A tapping at the door soon followed and the older woman entered.

"Why, you must both be parched; you have hardly drunk any wine at all! Whatever is becoming of young people these days?"

Baptiste made his goodbyes. When the door closed behind him, he put his hand into his coat pocket and stroked the handkerchief until his fingertips found the raised thread that silently said the name that filled his thoughts.

TWENTY-EIGHT

"We have been invited to join the hunt with Monsieur le Comte de Chêneville, a friend of my uncle," Paul told Baptiste. "You will see how Europeans hunt."

They set out for Fontainebleau, a day's ride south of Paris, the next morning. Prince Franz left after breakfast with his new lady friend, an elegant young woman from Milan, in a sparkling green-and-black landau with the roof lowered, pulled by a perfectly matched pair of bay geldings. Paul and Baptiste decided to ride horseback since the weather was clear and not unduly cold for February. The servants brought around a fine chestnut gelding for Baptiste and a tall black stallion for Paul.

They started out at a trot through the streets of Paris, breaking into a gallop only after they had left the old city walls behind. Baptiste was delighted to be in the clear country air and astride a horse again. And what an extraordinary horse! He had narrow withers and his legs were not long (Baptiste guessed he didn't stand above fifteen hands), but what he lacked in stature, he made up for in power, endurance, and an equable disposition. His mouth was responsive without being too sensitive, and it seemed that all Baptiste had to do was point him in the right direction and let him find an effortless gallop. Paul's mount was everything a purebred stallion could be: tall, perfectly formed, temperamental, and fast as an antelope. He demanded far more attention of his rider, but now Baptiste confirmed what he had only sensed on the few occasions when he had seen Paul on horseback in America: he was a superb horseman. Paul could be ungainly and awkward at times, but astride this horse he had a physical grace that was impressive.

That afternoon, they trotted down a long, gentle descent out of the forest and into the placid streets of Fontainebleau. The horses pranced and strained against their bridles, their hooves clattering against the cobblestones and echoing between the high walls that lined the streets in the dying rays of the late-afternoon sun. Paul led them to the house, hidden behind a side gate in the walls of a tiny street. They crossed a gravel expanse that led between flower beds to a fine stone staircase at the rear of the large house. Servants took their horses. They saw the landau on the other side of the garden, its top now raised.

"My uncle is here with his new friend," Paul whispered. "She's singing at the Opéra next week."

Mounted heads of animals jutted from the walls of the main hall: a boar brandished his tusks from on high, several deer and elk gazed from beneath impressive racks of antlers, various goats and antelope displayed their spiral-shaped horns, and a black bear showed its fangs. Guns, swords, daggers, and all kinds of hunting paraphernalia hung beneath the trophies. The polished metal gleamed.

"Come in, come in and make yourselves known!"

Prince Franz had seen them through the door that led to a brightly lighted salon. He drew them into the room and the din immediately subsided. Two dozen guests stood in the *grand salon*, which was comfortably furnished with plush chairs and couches upholstered in wine red velvet or dark green leather. Heavy swags of curtain adorned the windows, and a fire blazed in the black-and-white-veined marble hearth.

"My friends, this is my esteemed nephew, Paul Wilhelm, Duke of Württemberg. Some of you have already had the pleasure of making his acquaintance."

Paul acknowledged the nods and smiles as he and Baptiste accepted glasses of wine.

"His young friend is Monsieur Jean-Baptiste Charbonneau of St. Louis in the Mississippi River Valley of North America." Baptiste inclined his head. Prince Franz continued: "He is also known as Pompy, son of a princess of the Snake Tribe." A gasp escaped the lips of one of the women standing nearby, and a general murmur filtered through the group at this announcement.

Baptiste was fearful that he would be taken for a fraud. Prince Franz's words had nothing to do with how Sacagawea had lived her life, away from the tribe of her birth, and still less with how he had been raised. In all their travels, Paul had rarely mentioned his mother's being an Indian, and never referred to his ancestry as if it were royal. He simply introduced Baptiste as a fur trader from St. Louis.

Paul clinked glasses and said quietly, "To Pompy, Prince of the Shoshone." Then he winked and downed his wine. Baptiste felt the blood rise to his cheeks. Paul said, "No one in this room besides you and me has ever been near the Mississippi or the Missouri, or is likely to go there." A group began to gather around Baptiste.

"How is it that you speak fluent French?" the tall young woman who was Prince Franz's companion asked. She wore a low-cut dress and perfume wafted around her.

"My father is from the region near Montréal," Baptiste responded. "Very many of the traders along the river are French-speaking."

"I see," said the woman, as if such a thing were a wonder. Her voice was rich and her French had a slight accent that Baptiste did not recognize. "What does an Indian prince wear among his people?"

Baptiste smiled, but he forced himself to answer. "There are many kinds of tribal dress, Mademoiselle, depending upon the tribe. Mine is quite simple: a shirt and leggings made from the hide of an elk or an antelope, with some quillwork for decoration. In cold weather, I also wear beaded moccasins and a tanned buffalo hide around my shoulders."

An older man with a huge moustache asked, "Is it true that young men have to scalp their enemies in order to be accepted as adults? Have you scalped anyone?"

Baptiste noticed the singer's hand involuntarily rise to her hair as she listened. "Scalping is practiced by a number of tribes, but only in times of war," he replied. "It is not required for full membership in the tribe."

Everyone, it seemed, men and women alike, wanted to hear about some aspect of Indian life that would shock their sensibilities. Baptiste was polite, listening patiently to their inquiries and trying to provide interesting responses that would please his questioners. It was clear that they had ideas about Indians, and the surest way to satisfy them was to confirm their wild and wrongheaded notions.

Paul's uncle broke through the circle surrounding Baptiste, accompanied by a tall man whose face bore a dramatic wine-colored scar that ran from his right temple to his mouth. "Baptiste, I want you to meet an old friend, Count Arnaud de Ganay. He is an admirer of the Indian."

The man extended his hand and shook Baptiste's with a firm grip. His hazel eyes combined curiosity and humor as they exchanged pleasantries. He and the prince had fought together under Bonaparte at Wagram, he said, and he retained an abiding interest in all forms of battle on horseback.

"One of my cousins contends that the Indians of the North American plains are the greatest light cavalry in the world. Paul tells me that he witnessed prodigious displays of horsemanship when he ascended the Missouri River and visited the tribes in that region." He looked expectantly at Baptiste, waiting for him to elaborate on these propositions.

"For the tribes that follow the herds, Monsieur, the horse is an invaluable ally in hunting."

"And what of warfare?" the count asked. "That is the real proof of the horse's worth, is it not?"

"The assaults among tribes usually take the form of quick raids by a group of warriors, where surprise, speed, and cunning are the most important elements. The ability to ride well and to shoot from horseback are highly prized."

"On the gallop? *That* I should dearly love to see for myself!" The count told him about massed cavalry charges through cannon fire, things far more organized and constrained than the free-ranging methods of tribal warriors.

The prince joined them. "Has Arnaud been telling you about Bonaparte?"

"No, we hadn't gotten to that, I'm afraid," the count said, as if he had shirked a duty.

"Baptiste, you'll never meet anyone with a more direct knowledge of the emperor than the man you're talking to right now." The prince's tone was reverential. He leaned in close to them both and continued. "Louis the Eighteenth and Charles the Tenth have been propped up in gouty splendor these many years, but Napoleon had absolutely *nothing* in common with the Bourbons and their dropsical cousins who cling to the thrones of Europe. No, no, divine right is no longer an adequate pretext for the monarch!" He took a drink of wine and continued. "Say what you will—a Corsican dwarf, a vain and tyrannical man, an *arriviste* with no lands or fortune to justify his name—the one thing the *ancien régime* can never take from him is the quality they all so sorely lack. Napoleon was that rarest of creatures among kings and emperors: an absolute military genius, an unrivaled master of the art of war."

Their adulation and excitement was fervent, immediate, and very personal. In St. Louis, Bonaparte was usually referred to as "a European adventurer" who had come to grief because of his demonic need for absolute power. In Captain Clark's house, this judgment was tempered by the fact that his sale of the Louisiana Territory had made possible the opening of the West to American settlement and had put the Corps of Discovery on the trail. His legacy was mixed for those on the American frontier, yet the distant undertakings and shadowy dispositions had ended favorably for America and badly for France.

The battles these men described and the lands conquered were enormous in scale: twenty, fifty, one hundred thousand men-at-arms, whole countries invaded and conquered, cannon by the hundreds pulled from one end of Europe to the other and deployed with devastating effect. The tension and the excitement were still alive in their stories and reminiscences.

"Friedrich gave his solemn oath! Then he switched sides like a common tradesman when it seemed he could profit. Now the damned English will call the tune in Europe for generations to come!" the count said forcefully.

The prince shook his head sadly. The two men had clearly been over this tale of betrayal many times before, and it grieved them still. They told Baptiste that soon after Napoleon's inglorious retreat from Russia, Württemberg had transferred its allegiance to the coalition that finally prevailed at Waterloo. The specifics hardly mattered, though. The prince's features wore the disappointment that old age made irremediable. Whatever wrong they were talking about could never be made right.

TWENTY-NINE

Dawn was far behind by the time the first group assembled in the courtyard to set out for the forest. Leafless branches stood out starkly against a rapidly brightening sky, and the breath of men and horses streamed into the frigid air in plumes of white vapor. The horses were brought out from the stables, freshly groomed and saddled, and their riders emerged from the house in small groups, descending the wide stone staircase as they laughed and talked in the chill morning air. The other participants in the day's hunt would join them later. The bustle of activity behind the house seemed extraordinary to Baptiste; every hunt he had ever been on had started in near silence, which was maintained throughout the day.

The riders wore special coats of black, brown, or deep blue cloth, with their riding breeches tucked into tall boots. Silk neck scarves and flashy stickpins, low-crowned hats worn at rakish angles, silver-topped riding crops, and supple leather gloves all added to the sense of occasion that prevailed. They looked more like a group of people setting off for a wedding in St. Louis than on a hunt. Nothing suggested that the preparations here had to do with stalking and killing animals. A servant came out from the house with a large tray held high, bearing silver cups, and offered them to those astride their horses. An easy camaraderie prevailed among them, as if a drinking party floated above the gravel expanse.

Baptiste straightened his black coat as he walked to his horse. Though not as well turned out as many of the other riders, he was presentable. The purchase of clothes Paul had urged upon him in Paris was in part for this eventuality. Baptiste resolved to keep a keen eye out for what would be expected of him this morning. He wanted to avoid standing out as a *naïf*. Captain Clark's words came to him: *Lie low and watch those around you.*

A groom held the reins of the gelding he had ridden the day before, its freshly curried coat silken beneath the gleaming oiled tack. Baptiste stroked the horse's mane, then took the reins and mounted. No sooner had he lifted the reins lightly in his right hand than the horse began to balk, fighting the bit and backing up nervously, then rearing and neighing loudly. Baptiste stood in his stirrups and struggled to control the animal, whose front legs flailed the air. He managed to bring him down, and with a deft jump from the saddle, Baptiste descended to the ground, bringing the reins forward over the horse's head. The gelding continued to fight, and Baptiste held him firmly as he reassured him with the low, confident tones he always used with horses. "Hey yo, easy. Hey, hey."

The horse's outburst had cleared a circle among the group, and the other horses and riders still held back, watching. The bridle was far too tight, Baptiste saw, the bit drawn back against the horse's mouth. He loosened it as he cradled the bottom of the horse's head, and noticed a strap passing under the horse's lower jaw. He turned to the groom standing nearby.

"Why has my horse been given a curb bit?" Baptiste asked heatedly.

"Monsieur, most of the gentlemen prefer it for hunting. They find that the mount is more responsive to the rider's lead."

Baptiste handed the reins to the groom. "Please change the harness at once."

"Yes, Monsieur."

Baptiste wiped the sweat from his forehead with a kerchief he kept in his hip pocket. Paul approached on the stallion and smiled down at him.

"Well done, Baptiste! You gave us a show."

"Glad to oblige," he responded testily.

Paul nodded a greeting to those who had begun to fill in the cleared space where the drama had just been acted out. "Everyone is impressed with your horsemanship, I can assure you." He leaned down slightly and, smiling benignly, lowered his voice. "Just one detail. Never say 'please' to a servant."

For the next half hour the group rode through the edge of the forest toward the village where they were to meet the others. They traversed a broad, sloping expanse of open land flanked by trees growing in perfectly straight rows; several large stone basins lay in lower ground nearby, at the center of what had once been a huge garden, now abandoned and covered with the drooping brown stalks of weeds. As they skirted the pattern of overgrown paths and fountains and climbed a gradual rise, they reached a long body of water that was encased in gray stone embedded into the flat ground of a plateau as neatly as a gemstone set into the earth. Baptiste could see the steep roofs and towering chimneys of a majestic stone structure not far off, visible above the long *allées* of bare chestnut trees shaped into a formal hedge. Another hunter drew his horse up alongside.

"Good day to you, Monsieur. I give you the Château of Fontainebleau, and its reflecting pool. Or, as Napoleon preferred to call it, the palace."

Baptiste looked at the rippled surface and saw a wavy approximation of the distant château shimmer slightly and then align itself with the building in the distance as the breeze subsided.

"How ingenious."

They urged their horses into an easy gallop and soon caught up with the others. From the rear, Baptiste could see the rigid bearing of the others in the saddle, their backs straight and legs tensed in the stirrups. He had seen formations of soldiers in Paris riding with the same kind of formality, but never had he seen it on a hunt. He imitated the others, head held high and elbows close against his sides, but he found the posture uncomfortable. He relaxed as they fell in with the group.

Baptiste wondered where the hunting ground was. He saw no indication of game. In fact, the forest looked like an extension of the gardens around the château: not as groomed, but tamed nevertheless. The lower branches of all the trees had been trimmed and the underbrush cleared, as at Ludwigsburg, giving the leaf-covered ground a feeling of great openness and calm.

They reached a clearing where six roads converged, each of them branching into the forest in a straight line. The riders headed down one of these leaf-covered tracks and soon arrived at a small village. A large greensward lay between a stone manor house and a small church. Another twenty-five or thirty riders waited there, already dismounted and talking among themselves while servants held their horses and hurried back and forth to the manor house.

They greeted the newcomers with shouts of recognition, handshakes, and pats on the back. Baptiste quickly understood that many in this assemblage were linked by family and marriage. The introductions began: "I'd like you to meet my cousin." "Christian is my wife's brother." "Prince Franz is our grandfather's nephew. We call him 'Uncle.' "

The day's outing was governed by the knowledge that everything appropriate would be ready when any of these men needed it: their boots and tack were polished in the night, their breakfasts brought to them in their rooms on gleaming trays at the pull of a bell, their horses curried and brushed and led out fully saddled when they strode from the house. The human apparatus that made this possible—the cooks and grooms and butlers and maids—was made to disappear by the simple expedient of acting as if it were invisible.

Baptiste thought of the slaves he had seen in the richly appointed houses where he and Paul had been received in New Orleans. The same nonchalance came across the features of those being waited upon when they turned to one of their servants. The lines were clearer in New Orleans—any person with black skin in a white household was bound to be a servant—but the attitude was the same.

"Baptiste! Baptiste, over here!"

Paul was hailing him from the far side of the lawn. Baptiste approached the small group of men and Paul stepped back, inviting him into the circle.

"Gentlemen, this is Jean-Baptiste Charbonneau, one of the most redoubtable hunters of the Missouri River Basin in America."

Baptiste smiled at the exaggeration, shaking his head as he greeted the others. Clearly in good humor, Paul continued in a spirit of badinage. "Baptiste has stalked the American bison and the grizzly bear, the elk and the Louisiana jaguar. But today will be his first experience of a true *chasse à courre* in the European manner. I hope it will be a fruitful hunt."

The men looked at Baptiste, awaiting his response.

"Duke Paul honors me with his account, but I assure you, gentlemen, my experience is commonplace in America. I am looking forward to the day's hunt."

Small crystal glasses holding the same strong brandy they had tasted at Prince Franz's house were distributed. The prince proposed a toast to their host and the master of the hunt, Monsieur de Chêneville. An older man standing to Paul's left inclined his head to acknowledge the honor, then proposed his own toast to a successful hunt, and added, "My warden tells me that three large bucks have been sighted on our territory. The auspices are favorable!" A murmur of approval passed through the group and they drained their cups.

What kind of a hunt is this? Baptiste wondered. *How do they know those bucks will stay around, especially this late in the morning? Where I come from, it's too early for drinking and too late for hunting.*

The barking of dogs broke through his thoughts. A pack of hounds burst around the far corner of the manor house, tumbling over one another in their eagerness to join the group of men and horses. The dogs were all hounds whose white coats showed large splotches of black and brown. Forty of them trotted among the hunters, barking shallowly with tails wagging, keeping away from the horses' hindquarters, eager for the hunt. Three grooms in bright blue coats and white breeches accompanied them and, with a series of high shouts and feinting gestures, assembled the pack in a rough semblance of order on one side of the green. One of the grooms carried a large black whip coiled over his right shoulder. The dogs' coats had been closely clipped on the right side of their abdomens to make the letters HC, the monogram of Henri de Chêneville, stand out from the slightly longer fur. Baptiste widened his eyes and whistled softly. He had seen designs worked into the hindquarters of horses, but never the coats of dogs.

The hunters stood together in front of the house, facing the church across the grass. A quiet descended upon the group, as if by some hidden sign. The man next to him motioned to Baptiste to remove his hat; he hadn't noticed that the others had already done so. Six men dressed in the same livery as the dog handlers appeared from around the corner of the house and strode onto the grass. Each carried a large brass horn draped diagonally across his chest, and they arrayed themselves in a shallow V at right angles to the group of hunters. The servants had stopped their work and drawn back behind the hunters; a cluster of villagers watched from the far end of the grassy common. The doors of the church opened and a priest emerged wearing a white surplice over a black cassock, a violet biretta on his head. He was attended by two young boys, also in surplices and cassocks, one bearing a small silver bucket filled with water, the other carrying a silver censer that he held low to the ground by a chain and from which a stream of smoke issued forth. Baptiste recognized the accoutrements of a Catholic ceremony from his time among the Jesuits in St. Louis, but he couldn't imagine what they were doing here as the hunt was about to begin. The priest stepped onto the grass, flanked by the two boys, and then faced the hunters.

A blast from the six horns startled Baptiste, and a flock of birds in the surrounding trees noisily took flight. The six men played a kind of fanfare, all striving to hit the same notes yet never quite doing so. The effect was strange, but still Baptiste felt a deep vibration in his gut and delight at the strange beauty of the horns echoing into the forest. The fancy dress of the players and the fierce decorum of the listeners added to the sense of occasion. He thought of the hypnotically loud drumming and full-throated shrieks of the Mandan and of the convulsions they experienced in their dances before a major hunt. A final discordant passage echoed in the dying notes of entreaty.

The priest broke the ensuing silence with a short prayer in Latin, to which his acolytes chanted "Amen." The three approached the hunters and the priest bestowed a blessing in French as he sprinkled holy water on their heads, and the hunters blessed themselves. Baptiste made the sign of the cross in imitation of the rest of the group but noticed that Paul and Prince Franz did not do likewise. Baptiste had the impression that the priest made a particularly vigorous gesture with the holy water as he passed by the visitors from Württemberg. The priest sprinkled the dogs as well, and the boy carrying the censer swung it in a wide arc, dispersing a thick cloud of pungent blue smoke that hung above the pack in the still morning air. Then the incense reached their sensitive noses and they shied at the smell; one of the dogs sneezed three times in rapid succession. The priest moved back toward the center of the green and motioned with his short silver baton to the far side of the square, where grooms held the horses. He mumbled a prayer in their direction, and then he and his assistants returned to the front of the church, where he recited the Pater Noster in a loud and quavering voice.

With one more aspersion of holy water across the grass, it was over. Monsieur de Chêneville briskly crossed to greet the priest; then one of the grooms placed an envelope in the priest's hand and inclined his head respectfully. The master of the hunt strode back toward them and the priest and his attendants disappeared into the church. Monsieur de Chêneville put on his hat and said loudly, *"Messieurs, chassons!"* giving the order for the hunt to begin.

The company of hunters headed for their horses, divided itself into half a dozen smaller groups, and rode off in different directions. Paul invited Baptiste to accompany him and the two rode together with three others. Baptiste was intrigued at their methods, which didn't correspond to anything he knew about tracking animals. He reasoned that the whole group could not pursue the deer together since they were not in open plains, where horses would have a chance of overtaking part of a herd. Nor were they stalking the animal as Baptiste was used to doing in forested terrain; there was certainly no pretense of stealth after the horns had resounded across the landscape and the hunters noisily rode off into the woods. He asked Paul how they proposed to find game under such conditions. Paul laughed.

"We don't need to *find* the game, Baptiste. That's already been done. The only question is, Which of the bucks will be our prey?" Paul gestured toward a group of riders in blue tunics.

"Those men are Monsieur de Chêneville's warden and his assistants, and they've just completed a full circuit of the domain. They know this forest like the inside of their vest pockets and they've been riding all morning. *Batteurs* have been posted on each side of the forest, so we'll soon have an indication of where the deer are."

Baptiste was beginning to understand, though he found it hard to believe that so much effort was being devoted to the taking of a single deer. At home, the rigor of the hunt and the wiliness and luck required to find game included the possibility of returning empty-handed. Today's hunt, he saw, was something else entirely.

Suddenly there came through the trees three sharp blasts of a horn. Paul held up his right hand and the riders stopped abruptly, sitting their horses silently, waiting for something that Baptiste didn't understand. Then there came another report of the horn, followed by three lower tones in rapid succession. Long descending cries from other hunters echoed through the woods, and then they heard the dogs, a deep baying from one or two amid a general tumult of barks.

"They've sighted a buck and he's headed south," Paul told him, whispering, as if their voices could scare off game. The commotion continued, but it was moving away from where they now stood. Over the next couple of hours there ensued a series of similar alarms that gave rise to momentary excitement and short bursts of frenzied activity and, soon after, a disappointed calm as the distant hunt took still another turn. Paul explained that the dogs were pursuing one of the bucks within a large perimeter of Monsieur de Chêneville's property. Only when the pack drew close enough would all hunters be called to the chase. "This is the classic *chasse à courre,*" he told Baptiste.

Occasionally the dogs flushed animals other than the buck, all of which would bolt across the road in their headlong flight. Rabbits by the score crossed the *allée,* and several of the tiny deer they called *chevreuil,* which Baptiste had never before seen. Once, a family of wild boar burst from the forest not more than twenty yards from where they stood, a blur of black bristles, long snouts, and curved tusks. The horses shied at the surprise, but no one raised his gun. "We're not after boar today," Paul said equably.

Eventually the pack again came in their direction. This time the message of the horns was clear to Baptiste. Paul cried, "They're on him now. All hunters join. Let's go!"

They set off into the forest at a gallop and headed over a low rise in the woods toward the others. It was exhilarating to ride through a forest cleared of undergrowth, unconcerned about obstacles. They topped the rise easily and came directly upon a large buck running up the hill from the other side, pursued by the pack of dogs and at least a dozen riders.

"Turn him! Turn him!"

The cry came from the approaching riders, and as Baptiste watched from the crest of the hill, Paul and another rider descended in a mad gallop through the trees, storming down the incline at a diagonal and forcing the buck to turn to the left rather than continue up the hill and through their ranks. Paul pressed his advantage, pursuing the buck at close quarters. Baptiste spurred his horse forward and fell in behind Paul. They continued at full speed with the buck in sight; then they heard horns and cries in front of them. The buck stopped, his head held high, turning nervously in a small clearing. Paul burst from the trees and the buck lowered its head. The animal was winded and was waiting until the last possible moment to bolt. He sprang again into the forest and down a small incline to a stream. Other riders appeared on the high ground opposite the stream and the buck headed down the watercourse, kicking up water and slipping noisily on rocks as he desperately sought refuge.

The stream emptied into a small lake, whose near side was covered in rushes. Half a dozen riders were at the edge of the lake, and the first dogs ran up, feinting and snapping at the buck's hindquarters in the shallow water. He lowered his rack and rolled his head menacingly at the dogs once or twice, then turned toward the lake as if contemplating an escape. The rest of the dogs came on, barking with a demonic intensity as they kept their distance in the shallows. One of the young dogs broke from the pack and lunged at the buck's rear flank, and in a sudden explosion of water, the stag kicked furiously, catching the dog's head on the second kick and sending its lifeless body arcing through the air to land with a splash several yards away. The pack went wild with excitement and the buck eased into the lake and began to swim, followed warily by several of the dogs.

Riders appeared on the far bank of the little lake, no more than a hundred yards across, and three or four of them urged their horses into the water, forcing the buck to turn and then head back to the shore from which he had started. Baptiste watched the animal's labored breathing, and the shallow waves that spread from his chest as he held his head and antlers high above the water. He reached the bank and stood once more in the shallows, his coat dripping and glistening in the feeble sun. The entire hunt had arrived, a good thirty riders assembled on the lake's muddy shore, with four or five others on the opposite bank, closing off all possibility of flight. The buck still occasionally lowered his head and swung his rack of antlers heavily in the direction of the tormenting dogs, but it was clear to Baptiste and to the deer that there was no more to do than stand his ground and await the inevitable.

Monsieur de Chêneville hailed Paul. *"Monsieur le Duc, à vous l'honneur!"* he cried, gesturing with his arm toward the stag at bay.

Paul inclined his head, acknowledging the courtesy, and dismounted. When he asked Baptiste to hold the reins of his mount, he saw the look of profound unease on the young man's features.

"What is it, my friend? I've been given the honor of dispatching our quarry."

Baptiste looked at the stag, which was too run-out to be defiant, then narrowed his eyes and looked away. "Take care of that animal."

Monsieur de Chêneville handed Paul a long, thin dagger whose polished blade flashed in the pallid gray light. Flanked on either side by a uniformed warden bearing a pike, Paul approached the exhausted stag with a resolute step. The animal stood unsteadily, its mouth open wide and its head held low. The wardens braced their pikes forward against the stag's heaving sides. Paul crouched low between them, paused to gauge his mark, then lunged forward with a splash, catching the buck's rack of antlers in his left hand as he thrust the dagger into its neck with his right. The shouting stopped, the horses turned in rigid attention; even the dogs seemed to sense a pause in the frantic activity that had brought all of them to this still point under the wintry midday sun.

The buck staggered once, then its head shook convulsively in Paul's embrace, and the two stood motionless. For a long moment, man and beast were suspended in a breathless arc that connected the hunters to the stag before them. Paul leaned his right arm against the furry coat, the dagger plunged deep within, his back straining mightily. Baptiste wondered whether the wound had been fatal. Then the animal rolled its head to the left, as if listening for a sound it alone could hear. Paul withdrew the dagger and stepped back quickly, and the buck collapsed. A splash rose noisily in the air and a wave broke on the bank. Men and dogs found their voices at the same time: a cheer arose spontaneously and the pack barked with a new frenzy. The water was quickly stained with blood, reddening the dun-brown reeds that covered the shore.

The members of the hunt assembled back at the village. The grooms appeared again and took the horses, and a servant passed among them, offering brandy. The front door of the manor house stood open, and the riders strolled across the grass and into the building, laughing and talking loudly among themselves. Inside the arched door was a large timbered hall, its paneled walls covered with the mounted heads of animals up to the open beams in a more rustic version of Prince Franz's entrance hall. Long tables, draped in dazzling white cloths and laden with platters of food and bottles of wine, were spread around the room. A fire crackled in a mammoth stone hearth. Baptiste blinked to adjust to the dimness, then joined a group that included Paul.

"*Monsieur le Duc,* my congratulations," one of the hunters said with conviction. He turned to the others and extended his glass. "Gentlemen, I give you the health of Paul of Württemberg. He has done honor to our hunt."

They raised their glasses and drank while Paul nodded his thanks with an air of modesty. Baptiste thought he looked like a schoolboy who had done his sums properly. A servant entered the room and announced, "*Messieurs, la curée!*"

The men finished their drinks and filed out boisterously. As they stepped into the wan sunlight, the laughter and conversation died down and the men arrayed themselves along the greensward. The door of the church opposite was closed and locked, its windows shuttered. *What now?* Baptiste wondered.

The horn players stood together as before. At the other end of the lawn, the pack of hounds jostled one another, but none dared cross the invisible line demarcated by the long cracking whip wielded by the master of the hounds. In the middle of the green, the hide of the stag was draped over the bones and flesh that had been its body. The intact head remained attached to it.

The horn players began another unmelodious fanfare and the dogs quieted. As the notes faded in the crisp air, an identical fanfare arose behind Baptiste. Four of the hunters had taken up horns and repeated the phrases that issued from the group on the grass. This call and response continued through four or five iterations, conferring the dignity of ceremony on the proceedings.

Two of the uniformed helpers took up positions on either side of the animal's skin and grasped the top of the rack of antlers. Monsieur de Chêneville strode across the green to this temple of death, followed by Prince Franz, Paul, Baptiste, and the other members of the hunt. The servants gave them each a small sprig of evergreen. One by one, the men stooped before the deer's butchered body and each dipped his twig of pine in the shallow pool of blood that had formed beneath the animal's remains. A few of the hunters touched the bloody bit of evergreen lightly to their lips before fastening it on the lapel of their coats. Prince Franz and Paul placed theirs in the ribbon of their low-brimmed hats, the wet crimson needles glistening among the feathers and tufts of badger fur that already decorated the sides of their headgear. Baptiste bent low before the stag, as if genuflecting in church, then took his place with the others. Monsieur de Chêneville said, "The dogs have deserved their reward today. You may proceed."

The two men holding the deer's antlers picked up the head and swayed it back and forth. Then they pulled the hide back to reveal a glistening mass of pure white bones and violet flesh, laced with pearlescent swathes of ligament and muscle. The dogs unleashed their ·

frustration in a convulsion of howls and barks. The master of the hounds held them back for a few seconds more with savage cracks of the whip and threatening cries, as if to fuel their blood lust. Then he yelled, *"Allez!"* and lowered his whip. The pack exploded, covering the intervening twenty-five yards in an instant and setting upon the remains of their prey. Decorum and reserve had been replaced by the chaos of animals scrambling, jumping, and straining, all fighting to gain access to meat. Paul indicated the deer's head and antlers.

"When next you are here, that head will be on the wall inside. A noble trophy for a noble hunt." He clapped Baptiste on the shoulder and sang out, "Let's eat! I'm famished, and Monsieur de Chêneville's hunt is known for its table."

THIRTY

Dear Baptiste,

How strange to return here and know that you are elsewhere. I have been in the Gironde with my family at their house outside of Bordeaux. The life there is certainly quiet when compared to the city, but the climate is far milder than in the north and the light is almost like that in Italy. Paris seems like a beehive in contrast.

What a traveler you have become! I still savor your descriptions from our visit in February, since they make places I have visited seem fresh, and places I have not sound enticing. I had never dreamed of Stockholm or Saint Petersburg, but your accounts continue to fill my head with wonder.

The way you described Venice makes me want to return there. I agree that it is unlike anywhere else. Who could have imagined it but the Italians? Each time I am there, I feel as if they have rearranged all the buildings at night, so that when I wake, everything looks new. And since I love boats, I am happy merely going from one place to another. I think I would most readily take to one of your canoes.

The Venetians suffered much under Napoleon, and now the Habsburgs are established once again. It is hard to imagine a people less like the Austrians, and yet their rulers sit in Vienna. For how much longer, I wonder.

You will be amused to know that I nearly took flight recently. No, I have not grown wings. Rather, an acquaintance of my father is fascinated with craft held up by great balloons. He spends much of his time—and a great deal of money—building these novelties, like huge market baskets suspended from an enormous silk bubble with netting and ship's rigging. He offered me an "ascent," as he calls it, and I was wild with anticipation. Alas, his craft struck a chimney pot two days before our appointment and he is now encased in plaster from head to toe. But I hope to go up one day. Can you imagine anything more splendid than to survey the world from the height of the clouds? Even as a girl, whenever I looked at paintings of the Virgin rising to heaven, I wondered what she *saw* when she looked down.

I think often of our discussions when you were here. Believe me when I tell you that your thoughts on so many subjects are of interest to me. You are unlike any of my other cousins. I shall think of you as a Venice compared to their predictable array of cities.

I imagine you in Ludwigsburg. Your work with Duke Paul can now begin. I trust that it will hold for you the same fascination you evoke when you describe the places you knew as a boy. Your account of the prairie is still vivid in my mind—I long to see with my own eyes a grassland that resembles the sea.

Last week I accompanied a friend to the Jardin des Plantes. After he inspected the plant specimens he was seeking, we visited the *parc zoologique*. What a melancholy experience. We saw wolves, bears, elephants, even a bison from Poland. But their circumstances are so piteous that I took no pleasure in observing them. Caged in tiny patches of earth, they look horrid, cut off from their birthright. Can it be right to lock up creatures like this in the name of science? Monsieur Meunier advanced all the arguments one can imagine, but my whole being objected in a way that goes deeper than words. I had to leave, so great was my distress at witnessing something so wrongheaded.

Accounts of Mr. Bolívar's most recent exploits in South America have recently reached Paris and caused a stir. They call him "the Liberator," with equal love or hatred, depending on who is talking. Truly, the New World is full of surprises from which we can all learn.

Know, dear cousin, that I wish you well in your endeavors now that your travels have brought you to Württemberg. Nothing would give me greater pleasure than to see you again in Paris and share your news in person. Until that day, I hope to read your letters full of impressions of this *terra incognita* that is Europe.

I send you my most affectionate greetings.

Maura

THIRTY-ONE

DUKE PAUL, FROM HIS PRIVATE JOURNAL
MAY 1825
LUDWIGSBURG

I find myself in the bosom of my family once again. If this is home, then truly I am a nomad at heart. The icy reception accorded me by Wilhelm and his court would have been suitable for a criminal, perhaps, or for an enemy under truce, but never for a family member. How little Wilhelm really knows of the world—despite all his high-minded rhetoric about the responsibilities of the sovereign toward his people. Yesterday we had a most disagreeable meeting in his chambers, during which he scolded me for what he calls my "profligate expenditures" on my expedition to America. I was made to understand that the bills, which will be paid from the treasury, are to be deducted from future revenues from my properties in Stuttgart. I bit my lip, knowing that there was nothing to be gained by arguing, particularly since Wilhelm saw fit to dress me down with two of his courtiers present. It would have been an unimaginable public airing of family matters in my uncle's day. But Wilhelm no longer feels sufficiently royal, it appears, without a pair of his lackeys at hand, and the results are poisonous.

Afterward, we shared a glass of wine. I thought to make a gesture that would mollify his resentment and help him to understand the true nobility of my efforts to study Indian tribes. From a black velvet bag I produced a splendid Blackfoot ceremonial headpiece that I had collected at Robidoux's Post. It is a rounded skullcap covered with ermine and feathers, surmounted by erect horns on either side, each carved to a fine point and trailing a streamer of red-dyed fur. A wide band of red-and-white beading crosses the forehead, and from both temples a tie of six ermine tails falls straight to the wearer's shoulders.

I explained its ceremonial function as a part of the chief's formal regalia, and Wilhelm's interest was aroused. He examined it with care, delicately smoothing the ermine tails and feeling the sharp point of each horn with his index finger. "It is the equivalent of a king's crown," I told him, encouraging him to place it on his head. This he did, allowing me to center it properly so that the horns were symmetrical, just as a Mandan chief would do on an important occasion. I stepped back and beheld the effect, nodding approvingly. Wilhelm had just come from a morning audience, so he wore his court uniform. Grace prevailed in his bearing, and the headpiece perfectly complemented the splendor of his medals, gold braid, and striped trousers. For the first time I saw Wilhelm as truly regal, a king who might have been Wotan's descendant, so powerful was the spell cast by the buffalo headdress. Then one of his accursed bootlickers snickered behind me, attempting in vain to disguise his contemptible mirth as a cough, and the moment passed.

Wilhelm faced the mirror over the hearth. His features changed from surprise to fury, and he wore the same look he had as a young boy when things did not go his way. His eyes caught mine in the mirror and for a few moments the childhood resentments and furtive doubts that separated us when we were young were revived. I read in his look, *My father always preferred you. He wished that you had been his heir. I was never as clever or as strong as you. You are trying to make me look ridiculous once again!* His face was full of controlled anger. Breaking our gaze, he removed the headpiece and placed it on the table. "Your pieces of native costume are most intriguing, my dear cousin," he said coldly as he smoothed his hair and turned away. "But this is a trinket whose price is far too dear. Do you not agree?" I swallowed my bile and declined the provocation, though from his puerile reaction, one would have thought me guilty of *lèse-majesté* rather than a good-faith effort to mend fences.

The truth is that I cannot afford to be at odds with Wilhelm. It is clear that if I am to continue my work in natural history, I must marry. The best hope of making a good match—titled, powerful, and covered in gold—is to exploit fully the rank and prestige of being the king's cousin. The new Paul will have to be affable and cooperative, an intimate in the big happy family that rules Württemberg. So I have returned to Ludwigsburg to conduct my search, with a bit of the Prodigal Son in my demeanor to show that I am accommodating myself to the sovereign's wishes. If need be, I shall put my pride in my pocket and play the acquiescent cousin until my campaign is successful.

Theresa thinks that I shall never be able to endure the months it will require for the negotiations to be undertaken and concluded. "You are not a good-enough actor!" she warns me. Yet who has not made a compromise with his ideals in order to secure a desired end? It surprises me somewhat that Theresa seems not to know that when I truly want something, I can walk on fiery coals if that is what is required.

Baptiste is relieved to be in Ludwigsburg, though perhaps it is more accurate to say that he is relieved to be out of the coach. "Always going," as he says, "and never getting there." On a number of occasions he insisted on riding alongside the carriage, not, I think, to be free of my company, but to be out in the open. He is still uncomfortable having matters taken care of for him, and his conversations among my relatives and friends throughout Europe often lack nuance. But he is a son of the New World, a true American, whose signal feature seems to be the propensity to address any subject at all with direct questions, even to perfect strangers, in order to learn from what he presumes to be their equally direct responses. In this respect he is still made up of rough edges.

For example, he did not appreciate the hunting party in Fontainebleau. He wanted to know if the *chasse à courre* was com-

mon in Europe. When I assured him that it was, he said, "I don't see
the point of going after a deer that has been driven to exhaustion by
forty riders in a closed park." I responded that it was one of the differences between savagery and civilization, and he laughed. I admitted
that where procuring food is the principal concern, stalking an animal
in the wild requires wiliness, courage, and luck peculiar to life on the
frontier. Here, I explained, food is not the point. The hunt is a ceremonial, with a single animal serving as a representative for all the others. "It is what we call a tradition," I told him, but Baptiste was
unsatisfied with my explanation.

His uncomplicated directness is well tolerated by most of my acquaintances, though, partly because they regard him as an exotic who
does not know better, partly because of his youth, and partly because
he has a charm that sets him apart. To be sure, the wonder is not that
he has so many rough edges, but that he has so few. He has fit in almost everywhere we have traveled together, and has never made a
spectacle of himself.

His facility with languages is impressive. He is able to turn an attentive ear to any new language and then faithfully reproduce its
sounds and inflections—if not its sense—soon after. Professor Lebert
tells me he has a faculty similar to some rare individuals for reproduc-
ing music they have heard. How jealous I am! My English, never
more than approximate, has deserted me, as his German improves.
He shows a robust confidence in French that, though lacking in pol-
ish and form, is ever practical and adaptable to the street. Last month
in Paris, I found him trading jokes with Uncle Franz's groomsman in a
vernacular I had trouble following.

His relations with the ladies have met with no great success,
which I attribute to plain ignorance and naïveté. He has had his face
slapped more than once for what he regarded as perfectly acceptable
advances. I despair of his understanding the ways of the salon as concerns the fairer sex. This is one language he does not yet master. The
pleasures of the bordello are always available to him, but the one time
we talked about his experiences—I had given him an address in
Paris—he told me, "It was more like dessert than a real meal." Nothing is said between us about our personal assignations, but he knows

I keep a mistress in Stuttgart. His liaison with Theresa is a mystery to me. I worry that she sees him as a plaything, though they seem to be good friends. His origins are a useful cover for her interest, and both of them are masterfully discreet. In this, Baptiste shows himself to be a patient hunter who is used to covering his tracks.

Yesterday he referred to himself as my "employee" and asked how long this arrangement would continue. When I protested and pointed out that he was my guest, he said, "I learned from Captain Clark that when someone pays you money, you work for him." He is anxious to start work on the book about my travels, and I share his impatience and frustration. How can I begin, though, before I have found a suitable place to examine all my specimens in peace?

THIRTY-TWO

OCTOBER 1825
PALACE OF LUDWIGSBURG

Baptiste didn't slow until he reached the top of the rise. As he watched Paul approach, breathing heavily, he was struck by how much less fit Paul was since they had arrived in Europe almost two years before. Finally Paul joined him on the brow of the hill, a full game bag slung over his shoulder, his rifle alongside. They had been out since dawn, hunting the pheasant that were plentifully stocked in the clearings beyond the forest surrounding La Favorite. Though they had seen numerous other animals, they had taken only the birds.

Paul's breath returned to normal and he motioned to a clearing where the towers of La Favorite were visible above the trees. "Before we return, I want to share with you a little entertainment that used to amuse us cousins when we were younger," he said. "Schlape has made the necessary arrangements."

Paul led him to a solitary oak tree at the edge of the clearing. On it hung a clock. On a small table beside the tree sat an identical one. Baptiste recognized them as the type they called a "cuckoo clock": a painted panel on the front covering the mechanism, two stone weights hanging below, and, above the clock face, a door from which the tiny cuckoo appeared to sound the hours. Paul stopped the pendulum of the clock hanging on the tree, moved the clock's hands to five minutes before three, then gently set the clock in motion again. He walked to the other side of the clearing.

"This is the Ludwigsburg version of that stunt your drunken rivermen in St. Louis delighted in. With the difference, of course," he added laconically over his shoulder, "that no one risks getting killed."

Two *voyageurs* had taken bets on whether one could shoot a glass of whiskey balanced on the head of the other at fifty paces. He and Paul had gone down to the river's edge with half the town, it seemed, to see the shot made. One of the rivermen got his hair doused in whiskey and the two of them were forty dollars richer.

The cuckoo was only one inch tall, and it would be projected out about two inches, three times in rapid succession. Baptiste figured the distance at more than seventy-five paces. He was well acquainted with Paul's extraordinary marksmanship, and he knew how perfectly crafted his rifle was, but, even so, this was a difficult shot. Baptiste stood to one side and watched as Paul raised his rifle and sighted down the barrel.

"Once to get your bearings, twice to aim, three times for the little bird," Paul murmured as he stood poised to shoot. Ten seconds later the cuckoo sounded and the bird appeared, then again, then Paul fired. As the explosion faded in receding echoes, the clock was intact, its profile etched in the spare light of morning. They walked to it together. Paul opened the door and pulled the birdless spring outward. A few splinters lay on the ground, but otherwise nothing remained of the cuckoo. Paul said gleefully, "Now it is your turn."

He replaced the clock with the one from the table, resetting the time as before; then they retraced their steps to the far side of the clearing. When the cuckoo sounded, Baptiste fired. The second syllable of the bird's call was cut off and the clock was blasted from the tree, landing noisily ten yards distant. Baptiste lowered the rifle and turned to Paul.

"I missed."

"Yes, I suppose you did," Paul said. "Anyone can hit the clock, my friend."

But not everyone wants to, Baptiste responded inwardly, handing Paul the rifle.

As they walked back to La Favorite, Paul talked about his plans for the coming week: a short trip to Stuttgart and a round of visits to nearby friends. "Uncle Franz will be here for a few days when I return. He'll see Wilhelm in Stuttgart, then come up here to get away from the court. Monsieur Hennesy will be traveling with him. I gather he'll be bringing his beautiful daughter. They'll continue on to Sicily and Greece when Uncle Franz returns to Paris."

Baptiste's heart leapt at this news. Maura's last letter had come in August, when she had cautioned that travels with her father would likely interrupt their correspondence for a time. Her adventurous image had grown in his mind, and his affection was reinforced by the few letters he had received from his "cousin." Baptiste was encouraged by her curiosity about the frontier, and he mused about showing her all the places that would surprise her. He was very much looking forward to seeing her.

He thought, too, of Theresa. He wondered what she would make of his feelings for Maura. Their physical intimacy had grown since his return to Ludwigsburg, but Theresa let him see that she had other interests. She had recently made a trip to Saint Petersburg, and while she never talked about them, Baptiste understood that Theresa had lovers elsewhere. For her, their meetings were pleasurable way stations rather than a destination, times when she and Baptiste stood apart from life's usual rhythms. So far, their arrangement had seemed to have nothing to do with Maura, but now he asked himself if that would change.

While Paul was away, Baptiste often walked around the town. He had a circuit of taverns and shops and market stalls. Though he was recognized as the duke's friend and *protégé,* he had fashioned his own identity among the townspeople, one that was distinct from Paul and the world behind the gold-tipped fence. In some ways, Baptiste was less exotic to the residents of Ludwigsburg than Paul, once they got used to seeing him regularly and came to accept his efforts at German.

On a clear and cold afternoon the day before Paul was due to return, Baptiste and Theresa met in a salon that looked out on the forest.

"The chambermaids are the least predictable," he told Theresa. "They always twitter like birds, though, so there is plenty of time to lie low. Now that it is growing cold, the wood haulers show up, too, to feed the stoves. But they make more noise than anyone with their sacks of logs, so there is no danger. The only one who can't always be heard is old Suber." Theresa nodded. The ancient major-domo had a kindly face for his masters, but was a tyrant when out of their sight. "He walks with the paws of a cougar and is always ready to strike. If he could move faster, he would be dangerous." Baptiste was by now accepted as a guest of the royal household, but he remained ever watchful when he made his way at night through the servants' corridors to her rooms.

Theresa sat at a round table at the end of the room, playing solitaire, while Baptiste reclined on a *chaise longue*. She turned the cards absentmindedly, listening to what he was saying.

"You told me once, 'Every theater has its wings,' " Baptiste said. "There is a lot to learn from what goes on backstage. Especially," he added, "when nobody knows you're there."

"Ah, there are no mysteries left for you then," Theresa said, flipping a card without looking up.

"There are a few. When you were in Russia, you missed a big court ceremony. The king, the court, and all the ambassadors came up from Stuttgart for the signing of a treaty," Baptiste told her. "Everyone made speeches and bowed a lot, covered in medals and elaborate uniforms. It was an impressive sight, but I wondered when the terms were actually negotiated."

"The real work goes on long beforehand," Theresa said, "when the king's minister sits down with each ambassador and fashions an understanding between their states. They don't wear their plumage for that."

Baptiste nodded. "Captain Clark once called a council in St. Louis for the fur-company owners, the army officers, and six tribal delegations. They were all in their fanciest costumes. One of the old Omaha chiefs said, 'Their clothes are wearing them.' "

Theresa considered the words for a moment. "That's very well put." Then, in a quieter tone, she added, "It is a world I have tried to move away from."

"Is that why you travel?"

"Yes. My mother always said that travel opens the door to chance, and I savor that. You might meet anyone, even"—she gestured toward Baptiste stretched out on the *chaise*—"a young prince from a faraway land." He smiled, and Theresa continued. "It would be indecent to complain about a life of privilege. One needn't look far to see how miserable one's daily existence could be. But if the most that can be said is that things could be worse, there is already a surrender, a long waiting for the end that is the opposite of life, don't you think?"

The conductor in the pit raised his baton, waited for quiet to descend, and then the orchestra began a slow, sinuous melody in the strings, like a river meandering gently through the plains. The three singers onstage joined in, their harmonies intertwining and growing louder or softer as the feeling within the words seemed to demand. Theresa and Baptiste sat in one of the front boxes on the first balcony of the palace's theater. Baptiste had never heard anything so sumptuous or so pure, and he closed his eyes to enjoy the sound. Suddenly a cry came from below and all the beautiful music stopped abruptly.

"Non, non, non! C'est terrible!" The conductor, an Italian, yelled in heavily accented French at two of the singers, and a general confusion enveloped the stage and the orchestra pit.

"It sounded good to me," Baptiste said.

Theresa agreed. "But we do not have Signor Russo's knowledge." Order had been restored and the ensemble prepared to begin again. "A Mozart opera performed before the king must be as near to perfection as possible." In two weeks, Wilhelm would be bringing the court up from Stuttgart for this musical offering.

Baptiste enjoyed sitting in on rehearsals. The satisfaction of seeing and hearing how all the different players assembled the various parts was immense, like watching the secrets of an elaborate puzzle slowly reveal themselves. He particularly appreciated the fiery emotions of the singers: already that afternoon there had been shouting, a fit of laughter, tears, and now this outburst. The conductor had seemed like an excitable tyrant, but Baptiste was beginning to understand how effective his methods were. He managed to soothe strong feelings and channel them back to the performance.

They were singing about the wind, Baptiste realized, *il vento,* in undulating rhythms that soared and gradually subsided. As if to give substance to the word, the candles in the theater flickered. Someone had opened a door that Baptiste now heard close. He saw a small group making its way toward the box where he sat with Theresa. Paul's towering form appeared at the back of the balcony, flanked by Jean-François Hennesy. Between them was Maura.

Baptiste stood as Paul made the introductions. Maura extended her hand to Theresa with a demure smile. Her face caught the candlelight, giving her skin a radiance despite the theater's gloom. When their eyes met, he felt a tenderness fill his heart in a way he had never known. He was captivated by her. Paul said his name and he understood that he was expected to respond. He blushed to the roots of his hair, hoping that the darkness would hide his embarrassment.

"Surely you remember Monsieur Hennesy and his daughter," Paul prompted.

"Yes, of course I do," he managed to say as he shook hands. "We met at Prince Franz's in Paris."

"Our guests arrived an hour ago with Uncle Franz," Paul said. "I am giving them a quick look around."

Theresa turned to Maura. "You must be very tired."

"A little," Maura replied. "We arrived in Stuttgart only yesterday."

Theresa rose. "I suspect you would like some time to freshen up after your journey, before being obliged to be social. Come with me and we shall find a quiet place where you won't be bothered until supper." She put her arm around Maura's waist and said, "Gentlemen, you will excuse us, I am sure," and they left.

Baptiste's delight at seeing Maura gave way to confusion and doubt.

He had not thought about the particulars of these two women meeting.

"Your uncle and I have been up to our usual no good," Mr. Hennesy told Paul. "We must talk about our plans after supper tonight." Beneath Hennesy's bluff demeanor Baptiste caught a glimpse of a calculating mind that could be all business in an instant. He was reminded of Captain Clark.

They were to stay at Ludwigsburg for two days before continuing to Italy and eventually to Palermo. Baptiste had heard Prince Franz tell Paul that the shipment would continue to Greece, "if it was safe to do so," but beyond his general understanding that they were talking about guns as well as wine, he appreciated neither the politics of the matter nor the importance of the outcome.

He saw Maura alone the next morning. At dinner the night before, Theresa had proposed that the three of them take a walk in the forest, but at the last moment she sent word that she could not free herself. Maura and Baptiste set off without her. They would join her for lunch. It felt bold to be walking in the woods with Maura; it had become a private ritual for him and Theresa. The day was cold and clear.

Once the palace was out of sight, Baptiste put his arm around Maura and she leaned her shoulder against his. "Maura, I cannot believe you are here beside me!" he exclaimed.

She returned his smile. "Oh, Baptiste, it is like a dream to me, too. How long it has been since February."

"I wish you could be here longer," he said eagerly, but she shook her head.

"Just the two nights," she said with regret.

They talked then, describing their lives since they had last seen each other. Baptiste's travels with Paul had become less frequent, he told her, and he described the frustration of waiting for Paul to settle down so that they could work together seriously. "Since he has no home of his own, he has unpacked only a few of his things from the tribes," he explained. "The search has begun for a wife who can solve that."

Maura, too, talked of frustration; her attempts to study medicine were fruitless. "I observe autopsies when I can, and I have assisted a remarkable midwife several times, but the doors of the university remain closed. I traveled with my father over the summer, and I was glad to leave Paris this time, too."

"Paul says you may be going to Greece," Baptiste ventured.

"Yes, we may. This whole trip was very sudden. It depends on what news awaits us when we arrive in Palermo."

"Why Greece? Aren't the Greeks and the Turks fighting a war now?"

Maura turned to Baptiste, her cheeks crimson in the autumn air, her blue eyes fixed with concern. "Would it surprise you if I told you that there was more to my father's business than wine?"

"No," he said. "Where I come from, the river traders deal in furs, but guns and whiskey are almost always part of the bargain, though that side of things is usually kept quiet."

"In our case," she said evenly, "you can take away the furs and substitute wine for whiskey. But guns, as you put it, are part of the bargain."

"Isn't it dangerous for you?"

"My father is a very prudent man, Baptiste, with excellent contacts wherever he does business. He is received everywhere and is an extraordinary negotiator whose friends do not forget a favor. And a woman's presence can often ease tensions while an understanding is arrived at." She turned then and took his arm as they continued walking.

"It is more than the loyalty that I owe to my father, though," she told him, "and certainly more than the business. These trips are the only time I am truly alive. Perhaps it is because of the company I've kept, but I find it hard to take seriously the endless concern with respectability. To be *de bonne famille* is everything in this little world." She sighed, then added, "Smugglers have their own sense of what is proper, their own kind of intelligence. You learn the meaning of real trust."

Smugglers. The word surprised him, and then it fit in with the other pieces of the puzzle. He was grateful for her trust.

"What does your mother do while you and your father travel?" He thought of the women at home, left behind when their men went off hunting and trapping.

"She is with Mary now, making yet another pilgrimage. It is terrible of me to say, but much as I care for her, I cannot abide her growing devotion to the Church as she gets older."

The mention of her mother had left Maura looking troubled. He extended his hand to her face, passing his fingers lightly across her eyes until the anxiety vanished. He drew her near, and they kissed passionately as she ran her hands through his hair. He felt her tears against his face before she drew back.

"If only you knew how often I have thought of you since you were last in Paris," she said softly.

Baptiste held both her hands in his. "And I see your eyes, and hear your voice, and feel your touch when I read your letters," he told her. Only the breeze stirring the branches overhead accented the long silence that followed.

"Come with me when I go," Baptiste said impulsively, but with determination in his voice.

She saw in his eyes that he was serious. A wave of warmth passed across her face. She could scarcely breathe.

"There is nothing in this world I should like more, Baptiste," she whispered, raising her hand to his chest. Her eyes glistened.

"Then we will talk about it again," he told her, and she nodded her assent. "I'll have plenty of time to convince you." He took his handkerchief from his pocket and wiped the last of her tears. In that moment, Baptiste wanted to be with Maura more than anything he had ever wanted. The power of the feeling frightened him, but he accepted it with unhesitating sureness. He felt older, changed, ready to shape the life that lay ahead.

Maura and her father were to leave the next day. When Baptiste came down in the morning to say farewell, he saw the two of them out on the terrace, and watched them through the full-length windows. Her father went back inside to see about their luggage, and Maura and Baptiste had a few minutes on their own.

"I want to hold you and kiss you," she told him as they leaned side by side against the balustrade, looking out to the gardens, "but I cannot. You must remember my embraces from yesterday. Will you do that?"

"I will," Baptiste said. "And I will write when you have returned to Paris."

Maura put her hand to her breast, where the eagle talon hung. Baptiste nodded in understanding. As Suber approached to tell them the carriage was ready, she covered Baptiste's hand on the railing with her own, leaned on it for an instant, and turned to go.

Maura's absence affected Baptiste deeply. He turned over in his mind the idea of her going with him to America. His words had not been empty, and he did not regret them. Maura could never be just a dutiful wife whose main purpose was responding to her husband's needs. She wanted to do something for herself; they had that instinct in common. Baptiste did not find this unusual. Sacagawea, he knew, had organized his father's fur trades. In this, too, Maura differed appreciably from the people in Paul's world. It made her even more attractive to him.

Baptiste and Theresa arranged to be together the night after the others had left, and their lovemaking had a new edge, as if each were hungry for something only the other could provide. Late that night they sat talking before the fire in Theresa's salon. Baptiste wanted to tell Theresa about his closeness to Maura, but he was unsure how to begin.

"Paul told me about your adventure with the cuckoo clocks," she said with a mischievous tone. "Surely you aimed at the clock."

Baptiste shrugged.

"What Paul doubtless did not tell you," Theresa continued, "was that when all the cousins played that game as children, Wilhelm could not hit the tree, much less the cuckoo. He is the worst shot you can imagine, and Paul the best. I don't think Wilhelm has ever forgiven him for that."

She rose with her glass in hand to pour herself more brandy. "Your Mademoiselle Hennesy is delightful."

Baptiste's discomfort showed on his face and, mute with confusion, he looked darkly at Theresa. *"Your" Mademoiselle Hennesy, she said. Has she guessed? Did she and Maura talk?*

She took her time filling her glass and returned to her chair. "There's no point in glowering at me," she said.

"No, of course not," Baptiste stammered. "Maura . . ." He paused, then corrected himself. "Mademoiselle Hennesy and I have grown very close."

"Such things are normal," Theresa said without rancor, waving her arm before her in a wide arc, as if she were calming troubled waters. "Let us both acknowledge what should be obvious: she cannot be your lover, and I cannot be your wife."

"I am in love with her," Baptiste said suddenly, as if he were discovering it for himself.

"I am glad to hear it," Theresa said. Then, pouring him more brandy, she continued. "In the spirit of friendship, it may be as well for me to remind you of an essential rule in this part of the world." She clasped her hands and leaned forward in her chair, fixing him with a look of concern. "The two greatest calamities that can befall an unmarried young woman are to become pregnant and, almost as unfortunate, to be discovered in a compromising situation with a man. So always be aware, Baptiste, that no matter how great her passion, no matter how pressing her desire, a single woman must always stifle her feelings unless she is certain of a speedy marriage."

He said, "Maybe Maura and I will marry one day."

"Maybe you will," Theresa said, "but not in Europe."

Thirty–three

Dear Captain Clark,

It has been quite a while since you have heard from me, but I have scarcely sat still these last six months and more. I thought by this spring we were going to settle down in Württemberg. But for many reasons—family problems, court politics, no place to organize all the things he collected from the tribes—Duke Paul decided to keep traveling, with stopovers at his brother's castle in Silesia. If you look at a map of Europe, you'll find a town called Carlsruhe due south from the shore of the Baltic Sea, not far from the Oder River. It is a very long way from here.

We have traveled all over the map of Europe—to Saint Petersburg, Stockholm, Amsterdam, even south to Italy. On every trip we pass through Paris. Duke Paul's uncle puts us up in grand style whenever we like, so it feels like home. Paris is familiar to me now—I never thought I would be saying that!—and France is a place I am always glad to get back to. The people have a way of talking things over that makes you think, and they pay attention when you speak to them.

They can argue all night, so you have to be ready to stand up for what you believe for hours at a time. But the food and wine are very fine; every meal is like a celebration, a combination of serious discussion and entertainment. Duke Paul thinks the temperament of the French is a result of the Revolution, Napoleon, and all the wars and upheavals they have lived through. He says visitors, especially from America, become the center of attention until the French figure out what makes them tick. Duke Paul has similar ideas for what makes the Russians or the Swedes or anyone else the way they are.

You might be interested to know that, ten years after he was beaten, and four since he died in exile, Napoleon is still a presence wherever you go in Europe. It is peculiar to hear Duke Paul's uncle talk about his love for the emperor among friends who served under him. They have a bond with their great leader that I can understand, but when they talk about *"la nation"* and *"la patrie"* and the importance of carrying it beyond their borders, I don't follow. Sometimes they seem to be waiting for another Napoleon. No one here seems to like the current king.

When we first arrived I had trouble making myself understood. My accent stood out. I used a lot of words I learned from the *voyageurs* on the river, but they were unfamiliar here. But I am fluent now. Every court in Europe speaks French, all the discussions of the learned societies are conducted in French, and all the rich and educated people in every country speak it at home. I fit in a lot better than I did at first. My German is decent, too, though not nearly as good as my French. In fact, I hardly ever speak English. It even feels strange to be writing it.

Queen Charlotte, the widow of the former king (Duke Paul's uncle) and stepmother of King Wilhelm (Paul's cousin), lives in a wing of the palace here at Ludwigsburg. When she found out an American was visiting, she invited me to tea so that she could speak English. She is a nice old lady, but sickly. When I introduced myself she asked why I had a French surname. I told her that my father is a French trapper on the Missouri, born near Montréal.

"I am afraid the French have caused no end of mischief in my lifetime," she said. "When I was a girl, they were very wicked in North America, but of course my father was very ill by then." It turns out that she is the daughter of King George III!

I explained that my father had lived among the tribes for many years, rather than in French settlements, and that I had spent time with the Mandan. This lit a spark in her eyes. She asked about Indian ceremonies and wondered if I could give her a sampling of the singing. I hesitated, then explained that it was very different from European music, but she insisted. I told her to imagine thirty or forty braves all drumming and chanting and dancing together, and I cleared away the teacups.

I drummed on the tabletop to begin, then began the Buffalo chant. You know how loud that needs to be: the spirit of the herd is being called! I let loose and whooped and shrieked like a Mandan, pounding all the time on the table. The floor shook and the windows rattled. The color rose to the queen's cheeks, her eyes lit up, and she even moved her head in time with the drumming. But suddenly the door flew open and Suber, the major-domo, burst in, wondering what was happening.

That put an end to the Buffalo chant, and she gave him a look that would freeze fire. Then she looked tired all of a sudden, and old. When I rose to leave, she said she found my American accent pleasing. So Pomp has met a queen. You did warn me that these aristocrats are all related to one another.

Soon it will be two years since I arrived here. But sometimes it feels as if I am just along for the ride, and the ride might end tomorrow or it might go on for years. Meanwhile, I am always Duke Paul's unusual young friend, another one of his finds from his explorations in the New World.

I should warn you about the flood of visitors you may one day find at your doorstep. I cannot count the number of times European noblemen who are planning a trip to "the Indian lands" or "the Mississippi River" (it is the one river they have all heard of) have consulted me for my "expertise." They ask me for letters of introduction to my Indian kinsmen. They think it is like visiting their cousins in Vienna or Paris or Saint Petersburg. They consider Indian chiefs to be "natural aristocrats," and think they have "royal houses," just like in Europe. Every now and again I see these people on the receiving end of a Cheyenne war party. Mostly, though, I just look interested and agree with whatever they are saying, and soon enough they move on to something else.

Duke Paul says it is very stylish these days to talk about visiting the American frontier but that the only one who is likely to go is Prince Maximilian of Wied, a nobleman from a small state on the Rhine who has already been to South America. Do not be surprised if one day he knocks on your door. He seems to know something about several of the tribes.

Duke Paul talks about you as if you were the Great White Father himself. Just recently he was telling me how impressed he was by the way you arbitrated the claims of the Potawatomi tribe when Stream of the Rock and Black Quail parlayed with you in his presence. He says you rule supreme an area that exceeds the size of France many times over. I get the feeling, too, that he is a bit jealous of your collection of Indian objects, since he mentions it frequently.

I have heard that someone in England has come up with a way to string carriages together and pull them along iron rails, like the little ore caddies at the blacksmith's, but big enough to hold people and able to go from city to city. The steam engine would take the place of horses. Duke Paul says it is the way of the future. Long before that day, I will write again to give you my news.

I hope this finds you well, and ask that you remember me kindly to Mrs. Clark, your children, and Mr. Chouteau.

As ever, your affectionate,
Pomp

Part Four

WHAT HE HAD LEFT BEHIND

Thirty-Four

Paul and his bride, Princess Sophie von Thurn und Taxis, had been married a year earlier, in the spring of 1827. The euphoria of the celebrations had been contagious, allowing Paul's entourage to foresee a promising future. The gypsy duke was no more, his family proclaimed, and they were certain Paul finally understood the considerable advantages of joining ranks and helping to administer the lands of Württemberg. His wife was lovely, titled, and rich, but she was also young and unsophisticated. She had imagined starting a family and making an annual round of court visits, an illusion that had been sustained for a time. For his part, Paul saw only a refuge in the form of space for his objects, time to study them properly, and money enough to conduct future expeditions as he wished.

Paul was given Castle Mergentheim as a wedding present, a moated compound at the center of a town that lay a long day's ride to the northeast of Ludwigsburg. It was a nobleman's domain that resembled others Baptiste had visited. Baptiste now saw Paul's determination to make a name for himself in the field of natural history. Everything was secondary to the needs of his book about his travels in North America.

It began with the assembling of the crates in the main courtyard soon after they took up residence. Over the course of two weeks wagons had arrived from warehouses in Stuttgart, friends' houses throughout Baden and Bavaria, even from Silesia, and deposited their contents in the vast space. Baptiste was still astonished at the amount of cargo that had crossed the Atlantic. By mid-July, it was almost possible to cross the wide courtyard without setting foot on the ground.

Princess Sophie could not have had any doubt about what mattered to Paul as she watched the rooms of the castle fill like a private museum that summer. Only one of the five floors was devoted to living quarters, and much of the furniture from her home in Regensburg was banished to storage. Many of the rooms on the second floor were fitted with shelves and long examining tables for dissection.

When the boxes were opened, the contents were sorted by type. Animal specimens were all arrayed along the shelves in a system of Paul's devising. Plants and mineral samples were grouped together on the ground floor in a series of dark rooms that smelled of dirt and mold. In a spacious hall that had once been a ceremonial gathering space for the Knights of the Teutonic Order, Paul stored all the things he had acquired from the Indian tribes.

In the fall following the wedding, Paul and Baptiste had set to work editing Paul's material for publication, combining journals and field notes into a chronological narrative of his journey. As Paul's notes referred to a particular specimen or group of objects, Baptiste searched the storerooms for the pieces on the list. In America, labels had been attached to each object, listing the date it had been collected, the place, and a rough description. Much of Baptiste's time was spent correcting Paul's sometimes vague notions of what tribes he had been in contact with.

Although they worked for nine or ten hours each day, six days a week, the process was painfully slow, and Baptiste despaired of finishing. In six months he had examined less than a quarter of the specimens. Moreover, as the full extent of Paul's obsession with his work became apparent to Paul's wife, she associated Baptiste with his absence from her side, as if Baptiste were the cause rather than the symptom.

Occasionally Baptiste spoke of his desire to go home, but Paul dismissed it. "Yes, yes, of course you shall leave. We will embark together on my next expedition to North America. That has always been my plan." Baptiste held his tongue, willing to see how matters developed. He wanted to finish the project, but he was becoming restless.

Baptiste and Maura exchanged letters regularly, and he sometimes saw her when Paul visited Paris. She was still fascinated by the prospect of going to America, though they had made no specific plans. She understood intuitively that, despite hard work and danger, the New World promised that some essential part of her life would remain in her own hands in a way it never could in Europe. Baptiste's work with Paul had taken far longer than either of them had imagined, but this arrangement seemed to suit her. Perhaps fixing a date for his departure would force her to make a decision about which she still had doubts.

Baptiste carefully arranged the two birds side by side on the examining table and pulled the wings of each fully wide before pinning them to the wooden block. Their feathers still glistened with the water he had used to rinse off the preserving alcohol and he saw that, unlike many of the specimens Paul had collected, this pair was in excellent condition. The darker of the two, blackish brown with a gray metallic sheen to the feather tips, Baptiste knew was the male; the female's coloring was a lighter brown, less showy and more uniform. A small note in Paul's handwriting had been attached to the specimen jar: "Collected 11 August 1823 below Council Bluffs. *Fringilla pecoris?*" Baptiste turned to the copy of Alexander Wilson's study of birds that lay open on the table, checked the Linnaean reference, and satisfied himself that the description corresponded to the specimens before him. He took up his pen and added his comments to the dated entry in Paul's field notes: "Americans call this the cowbird. The Mandan sometimes call him Little Friend of the Buffalo. This is because large flocks follow the herds and these birds eat insects from the backs of the animals."

He turned to the shelves that held the other specimens he intended to catalog before Paul arrived. A russet owl, a green parrot, and a wild turkey floated in large glass containers, their feathers transformed from their formerly brilliant plumage to a flat gray. The owl was sadly decomposed, its head detached from its body, its tissues and bones disintegrating in the preserving alcohol. He generally recognized the birds from his life along the river, and Wilson's book resolved any minor questions he had.

Baptiste knew the appearance and behavior of animals best; their anatomy and bone structure were aspects he had only begun to understand in Paul's laboratory. "This is the summer coat of a rabbit that turns white in the winter," Baptiste would say, or "The feathers of this owl go through a red phase in the male before returning to gray-brown after the mating season." "You do not know how much you know," Paul told him, eagerly recording Baptiste's comments as they worked their way through the collection. Paul often prodded him to look for a feature that would set one of his specimens apart as a new species or subspecies. Baptiste had come to understand that this was the accomplishment Paul craved.

Before moving on to the owl, Baptiste dipped his hands in a basin of water, wiped them on a towel, and walked around to the bank of windows that lay behind his examining table. He could see across the wide main courtyard of the castle. Schloss Mergentheim had been Paul's official residence since his marriage. An extensive lawn dotted with trees spread away to Baptiste's right; to his left stood the main gate to the enclosure, a huge triumphal sally port set in the five-story structure, through which a cobbled road led across an exterior moat to the green calm within. The continuous wall of buildings given over to official functions—a school, a riding academy, administrative offices, a convent, officers' quarters for the garrison—enclosed about three acres of open ground in an irregular oblong that had first been laid out and fortified in the Middle Ages. Within that enclosure, and forming part of the exterior wall, lay the confines of the castle proper.

By crossing the room, Baptiste could look down on the castle's much smaller inner courtyard, an expanse of paving stones surrounded by three-story whitewashed buildings capped by a steep-pitched roof of black tiles. One side of the inner court was dominated by the fanciful curved facade of the castle's tall Baroque chapel, its yellow stucco, carved gray stone, and twin steeples the only relief from the precision of black and white forms that closed the circle.

He walked back to the shelves, picked up the jar that held the dismembered owl, and carried it to the examining table. As he unpinned the two cowbirds and wiped the wooden block clean, he spoke to the owl in regretful tones.

"You, little one, are in a sorry state. Somebody dealt you a rough blow on your long trip from the Missouri to Mergentheim."

"You've come to *Otus asio*. Excellent progress!" Paul's voice resonated from behind him. Baptiste nodded as he removed the owl's head from the jar. "I was hoping to join you earlier," Paul continued, "but instead I've come to take you away to celebrate."

Baptiste turned around. "What is the occasion?"

"I have some momentous news," Paul said, and rose up on the balls of his feet. His tone was ebullient, and a smile spread across his features. "I am going to be a father!"

"Let me be the first to congratulate you," Baptiste said. He wiped his hands clean and grasped Paul's hand in both of his. "May your sons follow the buffalo, vanquish their enemies, and prosper for generations to come." Then he added, "Of course, your wife may be carrying a daughter."

Paul's features clouded. "Say a prayer that it be a son! Once I produce an heir, my duty is accomplished." Then he said, "I have other news that is equally important in its way. Herr Thomm has replied. If I give him the completed text and illustrations by the end of August, he can prepare one hundred copies by November. We can look forward to two births this autumn!"

At the end of the afternoon, Baptiste left the festivities that Paul had organized in one of the summer pavilions in the hills surrounding Mergentheim. Outdoors, light and stillness prevailed, and he breathed deeply. The weather was unseasonably warm for April. He left word with Paul's coachman that he was returning by foot, then set off through the forest.

Quickly the sound of his footsteps through the new growth of bracken came to the fore and transformed the party noises into a faint and distant tinkling that fast receded. Baptiste considered how different he felt when he walked in the woods here. The European countryside did not draw him in as the forests at home did. It did not awaken the place where his spirit bird lived and watched the world through his eyes. Every part of the land he had seen had been changed by man and every place had its owner. Nothing was untouched. Baptiste recalled the one time in Europe he had felt something akin to what he had left behind.

He and Paul had been visiting Naples a few months before Paul's wedding. One of their hosts, a passionate disciple of von Humboldt's theories of geology, took them up the slopes of Mount Vesuvius on a clear February morning. Baptiste had seen prints and drawings of volcanoes in Captain Clark's study in St. Louis, but the experience of walking on the lightly trembling slopes of a mountain had touched something deep and unexpected in him, as if the earth beneath their feet were alive. Fumaroles of steam rose on all sides, whipped across the slopes by a piercing cold wind, and the odor of sulfur was heavy when the smoke blew their way.

They passed several large steam vents and crossed flows of cooled lava. The black trails were rivers turned to stone. Finally they came to a small crater on the side of the mountain that, their host told them, had been the site of eruptions less than six months before. It looked like the spent furnace of an unseen giant, a heap of ash and lava built up in powdery layers of gray, black, and brown. Paul was disappointed that no lava flow could be observed, though he did praise the view of Capri, the bay, and Naples.

Baptiste vividly remembered the sense of delight that he had felt on that February morning in the thin, freezing air. *No one can claim to own this!* he had shouted inwardly. As they made their slow descent, the sere and savage landscape reminded him of what he had been missing. Today he felt that same sense of loss, and it troubled him deeply.

Thirty-five

Dear Maura,

I am relieved to be able to address you in a letter by your given name at last, though I have enjoyed being your cousin these many months. Now that you and your family are in Geneva, I can be sure that your friends will place this directly into your hands.

I did not understand that your father's expulsion from France when he was last in Sicily applied to you and your mother as well. I thought that the two of you would be allowed to return to the Gironde, but your latest letter tells me otherwise, and I worry for you. It must be very hard to have left everything and not know when you can return.

Paul has had word from friends in Stuttgart and elsewhere that the French king is fast losing support, and that he has grown ever more defensive with those he sees as enemies. He says that until he is gone, though, you cannot return to France. Will Geneva be your home now? Or Ireland? I would be sorry to see you go. Geneva is close by and Ireland is very far away. I want to know when we will see each other. Your memory is vivid in my mind, and I had looked forward with the greatest anticipation to seeing you this summer. If there is a way for our paths to cross, please let me know.

Increasingly I think of returning home. These years have taught me many things, and I have absorbed them like a good student. Each day has been a new adventure, where all that was required of me was to pay attention and take in as much as possible. But there comes a time when one wants to stop learning and start doing. Captain Clark often said that the staff officers and personal secretaries who accompanied important visitors in St. Louis "live their lives looking through someone else's eyes, or trying to." It was not a compliment. I have begun to be one of them.

My time here has helped me to think about my life in St. Louis differently. You know how attached I am to my guardian, and that I have always trusted his judgment, and yet consider this: Captain Clark has been a slave owner all his adult life. He even took a slave along as part of the Corps of Discovery, a Negro by the name of York, then kept him in St. Louis as his servant. So, you see, I will not be returning to some perfect place; far from it.

Here the situation is not much different, though it takes other forms. I have seen African servants here in Europe. In some ways they seem to me even more miserable than the slaves of America, since they are so few and regarded as if they were exotic animals. When I arrived in Europe, I was an object of wonder and fascination. Only gradually did I come to realize that this sort of curiosity is rarely accompanied by respect. You will laugh when you read that, but please remember that I was nineteen years old when "civilization" opened its door to me, and now I have reached the ripe and cynical age of twenty-three. I tell myself that if I stay in Europe, I will end up like them, cut off from those who know who I am.

I am beginning to understand the sense of your father's remark that for those of us who live on the edges of different worlds, history has wounded us and love must save us. He was thinking of the Irish, but there are many of us who have more than one home. You and I both know what it is to pass from one world to another, and back again.

Captain Clark tells me that there are more visitors than ever going up the river, and I could find work guiding Europeans on their expeditions. It will be good for me to use my know-how on the frontier, where it is valued. I long for a companion who could make her way there. Will you consider it? You see, Maura, when I am with you, I forget that I am of mixed blood or an American or a Mandan or from the frontier. I am Baptiste, and it is enough.

I have written more a book than a letter, but I hope you will indulge me. I cannot hide my thoughts from you. When I write to you, I think of your voice, your laugh, your eyes, your strong opinions. You are more present in my mind than ever. *What would Maura think of this?* I ask myself many times each day.

Together we will find a way if you are willing. Until then, I am your most affectionate,

Baptiste

P.S. I must add one detail that I know will make you laugh. This *Schloss* is now to be called "Bad" Mergentheim, since "curative springs" have been found in the environs. A local shepherd found two of his sheep in a swampy area containing a salt lick and a few small sulfur pools—the sort of place you see a dozen times in a week in the land I grew up on. The "discovery" has excited Paul. He has taken samples of the water to analyze its mineral content, and has great plans to exploit the healing waters of "Bad Mergentheim" in the name of science.

Thirty-six

This should be a happy time, and yet I find myself in a dark mood day after day. The elation I felt over Sophie's pregnancy has transformed into foreboding. Daily my wife is full of demands on my time, each more pressing and each justified by the approaching birth of our child. I cannot imagine putting up with Sophie's growing needs until October, when the child will come. She talks of going to Regensburg to visit her mother; the day of her departure cannot come soon enough. I suppose her behavior is typical of the caprices of an expectant mother, but she becomes more insistent, more irascible, and more shrill as the weeks pass.

Before now, I have known Sophie to be sweet, a little dull, and inclined to be accommodating toward others. Prospective motherhood has unleashed a dragon whose fiery blasts are directed at me. Increasingly I see that in her mind this baby will turn us into a family with shared responsibilities, ambitions, and activities. I must participate in the deliberations of the Chamber of Nobles in Stuttgart on a regular basis, I must hold a weekly audience for the good citizens of Mergentheim, I must draw closer to my dear cousin the king, I must put away my silly specimens and transform Castle Mergentheim into a home worthy of children: the list is an endless catalog of all the things I am not.

Theresa warned me that Sophie would overlook all that came before the marriage but would see it as her duty to reform my ways. If Theresa is right—and I fear that she is—this ship is headed for a rocky shore.

The prospect of my book's publication fills me with more joyful anticipation than does the birth of my child. Sophie does not yet suspect that Baptiste and I will have to spend even longer hours on it now. How she will complain! But there is nothing for it but to lower my head and attend to my real work.

The thread of my narrative has brought me to my adventure in the wilderness separating the Ponca tribe from the White River. Last night as I fashioned my account of the difficulties on this part of the expedition, I was nevertheless overcome by the strongest sense of longing for those days of discovery, daring, and unsurpassed beauty. Today, Baptiste and I examined *Tetrao phasianellus*, a native grouse that I collected in that region, and its distinctive tail feathers again surprised me.

This afternoon we also visited Herr Kreis, the local taxidermist, to whom I consigned nine of the larger animals I collected. We inspected his handiwork with the wolves and coyotes I had entrusted to his care. The results were superb: Their bared fangs looked truly menacing, and the raised hackles of one specimen gave the impression of imminent attack. While Baptiste is untroubled by the flat pelts of trapped animals, so familiar to him from his work on the frontier, he does not appreciate the illusion of life restored by the taxidermist with the animals' bodies stuffed and their heads still attached.

Baptiste is tiring of the scientific component of our work. He eagerly learned the Linnaean system, always looking for differences that separate one specimen from its apparent twin. But increasingly he questions this process and points out common traits. His own considerable expertise derives, of course, from the close observation of animals in the wild. It is natural that the structural distinctions, not necessarily apparent in an animal's appearance or behavior, should cease to satisfy him after a time. Too, it may be an expression of the degree to which he misses the direct experience of nature that is his birthright. For different reasons, we share a longing to return to the American frontier.

He is traveling on his own to Vienna at month's end, with my knowledge if not my blessing. Theresa is expected there next week at the Palace of Württemberg, and she plans to travel in the environs with friends until July. The rest is easy enough to imagine. If she influences Baptiste to remain with me, how can I object to his absence of two weeks?

Theresa seems to understand Baptiste, while I often have to guess his thoughts. Yet we are not so very different from any two men between whom words are sparse. Still, we share something that only the two of us have experienced. No one else here has been on the frontier, and no one can understand the sacred bond that unites us. In these past several months, that bond has deepened as we have revisited the trip in minute detail. The specimens are a constant reminder of a wild world that stretches beyond the fringes of civilization to the far horizon. General Clark told me he felt the same way in the company of the other members of his Corps of Discovery, who occasionally visited him. "Others think they understand what you have seen when you return," he said, "but they do not; they cannot. Only your fellow expedition member knows what you have experienced." Here at home, I feel that incomprehension keenly.

How am I to describe the solitude and silence of the prairie just before sunrise to someone who has never been there? The horizon appears as a series of feathery lines, defined by the tops of grassy stalks higher than a man's head, stretching in waves to the far distance with the same undulating infinity that one observes at sea. A grouse calls from somewhere in the endless grass, then it is quiet, and then the call is repeated as the stars gradually lose their luster. A long, slow rhythm of awakening ensues as the sun rises above the horizon, first lightening the underside of clouds and finally bursting forth on the living, rolling plain. Accuracy requires that I also mention the hellish swarms of mosquitoes that accompany such visions of heaven on earth, but even they now seem like welcome tokens of a world that I long for.

Among the Indian tribes of the plains, there exists a way of looking at these things that is entirely at odds with our own. I have to thank Baptiste, in these months spent together in the laboratory, for reminding me how everything looks different to a Mandan. More than once he has corrected me when I referred to a distinction between Man and Nature to tell me there is no such separation. To a Mandan, Nature is the world, seamless and true.

One signal example is the Mandan's way of describing things around him from a point of reference that strikes me as demonstrably useful and profound. Mountains are big brothers, nearby hills their little cousins; the Missouri and the Mississippi are great patriarchs of water, their tributary streams lesser kin. Mature trees and saplings, huge granite outcroppings and the scree covering an adjacent hillside, towering thunderclouds and small puffs of cumulus—all are ranked in a cycle of growth, maturity, and death. It has a logic that I find comforting, but I am incapable of applying it to the landscape I encounter in Europe. I need to return to that world to feel the sense of life that resides in things themselves and connects them in mysterious ways.

A letter from Professor Picard tells me that he will visit this fall. How long it seems since I first introduced Baptiste to Picard in Paris and together we examined the first boxload of my treasures from North America. I will present him with a copy of my book, and expect to hear his wisdom on many matters that concern me.

THIRTY-SEVEN

MAY 1828

All morning Baptiste's mind was on Maura. He rode out to the mineral springs just after dawn to look at the work Paul had initiated, and to clear his head. He wondered what her reaction would be to his letter. He mused about the future as he let the dappled gray stallion retrace his steps at a brisk walk along the forest's edge. Would she go with him when he returned to St. Louis? He realized how much depended on her answer, but all he could do was wait.

In the late morning, Baptiste was in a storeroom at Castle Mergentheim with yet another list of objects Paul intended to catalog when he returned from Stuttgart later that day. Baptiste was to search the storerooms for the pieces on the list. *"Kriegsschild mit Hülle, Osagen,"* he read: a war shield with feathers from the Osage tribe. He found it in a corner with the next item on the list, *"Bisonfell mit Quill, Mandan,"* a painted Mandan buffalo robe with quillwork that Paul had acquired from one of the lesser chiefs at Robidoux's Post. The last item he did not recall: *"Puppe mit Menschenhaar,"* a doll with human hair, though they were fashioned by all the Dakota peoples. He set shield and robe aside and began opening the boxes near at hand.

The first contained only pipes, twenty of the long, slender calumets so common along the river and across the plains. Some had beadwork on the bowl, some were carved or inset with shells or lead, others bore feathers and tassels that dangled from the stem. He recognized many of the tribal markings—Crow, Sioux, Oto—though others were unfamiliar to him, and he wondered again at Paul's desire to have so many examples of each tribal piece. Baptiste recalled the gleam he had sometimes seen in fur traders' eyes when they stepped into Mr. Woods's storehouse. After a minute, when their gaze settled on the neat stacks of pelts—beaver, otter, wolf, bear, buffalo—they would nod once with a satisfied look and murmur, "I'll buy everything you've got."

From the next box he removed a pair of fringed leggings, a beaded shirt of yellow-hued antelope, four pairs of moccasins, and four painted parfleches. Finding an item folded separately in its own cloth cover at the bottom of the box, he lifted a woman's buckskin dress with an elaborately beaded top of blue-and-red designs and a skirt with rows of rawhide strips applied with fancy stitching. It was the ceremonial dress of a Sioux woman, doubtless of some status, given the extent and fineness of the handiwork. He let the dress hang full at arm's length, looking at it for a long while as he considered the lives connected to the personal things he was unpacking. As he set them carefully aside, his stomach tightened. They were like the creatures that floated in jars of foul-smelling liquid.

Baptiste shook the image from his head and turned to the last of the small boxes. When he lifted the top, a familiar and pleasing odor rose from it. It carried him to the interior of his parents' lodge in the Mandan village of his earliest memories. It was the smell of buckskin, sweat, and the smoke of endless fires. He carefully lifted the cloth wrapping that concealed the box's contents. A tiny figure stared up at him: two beads for eyes, arms and legs covered by a miniature buckskin dress with beadwork decoration, the feet sheathed in intricately embroidered moccasins, and a lock of human hair attached to the head and draped on either side like a Mandan girl's long tresses. The doll resembled one his mother had made for him. His was a boy; it was one of the few things he still had from his mother. He had left it in the care of Captain Clark.

He held it to his face and inhaled deeply, just as he had done as a child, hoping that the boy spirit of the doll would become his spirit. He breathed in the smell of the lodge that clung to the doll in his urgent need to be there. Tears wetted his cheeks, and he nodded once at the power of the spirit that had been reawakened. He gently placed the doll on a table. A note in Paul's hand was in the box: "A doll with human hair—Dakota Sioux? Collected north of Fort Atkinson—September 11, 1823." A flush of blood rose to his face and he left the room.

Paul returned in the late afternoon in high spirits and full of news from his friends at court and in the city. Paul had visited his mistress, as well. His wife was spending time with her mother in Regensburg, which lightened the mood further. He washed up, changed coats, and went to find Baptiste.

Baptiste was leaning over one of the dissecting tables. "Hard at work, I see!" Paul said as he entered the laboratory. "Professor Tredup feels there may well be a new species among the duck specimens I showed him!" Baptiste turned as Paul's eyes settled on the three long dissecting tables. His features clouded and his smile faded. "What is this?" he asked in a near whisper. The objects were arrayed in neat rows: a tall black boot, an embroidered silk purse, a cavalry saber, a tortoiseshell comb, a set of women's underclothes, various kitchen utensils. On the longest table was displayed a series of children's dolls fashioned after Napoleonic soldiers. Paul was trying to regain his carefree air of moments before, his features a combat between humor and doubt. Looking askance at Baptiste, he thought for an instant he had the key: "Have you been drinking?"

"These are my specimens," Baptiste replied.

"What is the meaning of this?" Paul asked indignantly.

Baptiste responded, "If a natural philosopher from a faraway land, like myself, arrived at Castle Mergentheim, these are the things he might gather for his collection. Isn't that so?" He gestured to the objects. "Tell me," Baptiste continued heatedly, "would you sell your favorite English rifle or the hand-tooled saddle Prince Franz gave you as a wedding present if the price was high enough?"

The two men glared at each other. "Of course not! But that is hardly the point when—"

Baptiste cut him off. "Your idea of success was to collect as many objects as possible, no matter what the cost, no matter what the pieces meant to the people who used them."

Paul was dismissive. "But we can only comprehend the unknown by studying it with scientific rigor," he said.

"Do you care that the beadwork on each pair of moccasins tells a story about its owner, about his tribe and his clan and his life? Do you understand what the pipes and the dolls and the shields and the bows meant to those who used them?"

"Comparing and contrasting similar objects is how we must proceed," Paul said loudly, "assembling facts so that we can think clearly." Then he added with a righteous air, "Even von Humboldt, returning from South America, did not have the range of specimens I have assembled."

"Of course, Paul. You must have more than anyone else." Baptiste's tone was bitter.

"You cannot possibly believe that is the purpose of my collection, you who know it more intimately than anyone but myself," Paul responded. He was growing impatient. "One of the chief reasons for collecting these objects is to preserve a record for posterity."

"They are not dead!" Baptiste shouted.

"Baptiste, your own General Clark told me he is powerless to stop the human tide coming up the river and flowing out onto the prairies. Eventually there will remain little of the Indians' life. Would you rather that I not save the things by which we can know how they lived?"

Baptiste understood Paul's reasoning, but he felt deeply hurt. "You can't understand an entire people, no matter how big your collection, by buying and displaying the things they use."

"That is one thing that you and I can agree on." Paul picked up the cavalry saber from the nearby table, withdrew it from its scabbard, and sighted down the blade before raising his eyes to meet Baptiste's gaze. "This weapon cannot teach you what it is like to be in the army of Württemberg, any more than those cooking implements can tell you how to prepare the food that is consumed here. But they are a start. Can you not see that? The things I have brought back from America are the physical evidence of a way of life that is bound to vanish. They are likely to be all that is left to us eventually."

Baptiste turned away. The truth of Paul's words came to him in a wave. The fur trappers were just the edge of the blade that opens the wound. Already many of the tribes he knew along the lower river had been decimated by the white man's diseases and had bargained away their land. Now, with the army, steamboats, and sheer numbers, white settlers would keep pushing the tribes back until they had nowhere to go. Paul's ignorance of the pieces he collected was painful to consider, but it changed nothing overall. Baptiste looked out the window to the gently swaying branches in the main courtyard, trying to compose himself.

Paul continued in a softer voice. "I beg you to consider how vital it is to educate Europeans about the true nature of the Indian. Europeans describe Indians as violent savages so that they can take advantage of them. Think of the attitudes toward Africans and the endless misery of slavery to see what can befall a race that lies in the path of progress. But progress, alas, is its own sovereign, whose path is strewn with those who profit and those who suffer."

"Those who suffer in the path of progress never seem to be European," Baptiste said, turning slowly from the window. "How will you change anything?"

"There is always the chance that if Europeans know the Indians better, they will not destroy them. After all, public opinion in England has hastened the end of the slave trade in her colonies; that is one result of informing people. If people understand who the tribes of the Great Plains and Missouri and Mississippi basins are, perhaps they won't fall victim to the annihilation suffered by their cousins along the east coast of the continent."

Baptiste looked at the table covered with soldier dolls, their uniforms perfect miniature replicas of Napoleon's Imperial Guard. His spirit bird called him from deep within. He did not belong here.

"Paul, I must go home."

"Of course," Paul replied. "Allow me to propose an arrangement."

He took a step forward, leaning in close to make his case earnestly. "Stay with me until I finish the book and prepare the collection for display. We can return together to the Missouri next year."

"I will help you with the book," Baptiste said, "but I will leave before the end of the year. It is time for me to go."

Paul saw that words would not change Baptiste's mind. "Very well."

That evening, Baptiste walked along the streets of town in the warm and heavy air that followed a late-afternoon storm. Paul probably believed what he had said about using his collection as a tool for understanding, Baptiste reasoned, but his words seemed strangely separated from the way the world actually worked. He had no notion of what it was like to live among the tribes as they watched the white man bring disease, whiskey, and settlements farther up the river every month of every year. Paul saw it as progress, which made sense here in Europe, and his words sounded like those of the missionaries in St. Louis—except that for Paul, "science" was the answer, rather than religion.

Thirty-eight

My Dearest Baptiste,

By the time you read this I shall be on my way to Ireland. We leave tomorrow by way of Amsterdam. My mother is not well, and she wants to be with her family in Cork. My father and I have agreed that I should go with her to see her properly settled there. Beyond that there is no telling, as it will depend on how she fares. Ireland is not where I would choose to be if such matters were in my hands.

What joy your letter gave me, every word of it! I, too, imagine your reaction to things that happen to me or people I meet, and it makes me feel closer to you. I wish you were here by my side at this very moment. Your kisses seem from another lifetime, and I crave them daily. Your touch, your voice, your smell are as present as if you had just left the room. Now I can tell you in writing how deeply you lie in my heart.

The news that you will return to America by year's end was less welcome. I cannot pretend to be surprised. We have talked about this before, and your reasons are sensible. Your world is a place I can only imagine. Your invitation to go with you is ever present in my mind, but I cannot say yet what I will do. Just now my mother needs me most terribly. That will change if her health improves. I must see how she does in the months ahead before I can decide whether to go with you to America. If the decision affected no one but me, my love, I would not hesitate for an instant. Can you understand?

I once told you that I never felt more alive than when I traveled with my father for his business. Now I must amend that: *You* make me feel more alive whenever we are together. I have met no one else who understands so deeply what it means to be from two different places and yet living between them. I long to share that as your companion.

Now I must leave you (for that is how it feels) and ask you to be patient, understanding, and—hardest of all—hopeful. If there is any way under heaven for us to meet before you leave Europe, we shall, and I will give you my answer. If it pleases you, write to me in care of my cousin, whose name and address I shall add as a postscript. She is as trustworthy as the stars, so none of the "American cousin" business is called for.

I think of you daily with the most tender affection. As ever,

Maura

THIRTY-NINE

JUNE 1828
VIENNA

Baptiste watched the troop of mounted soldiers pass, resplendent in green-and-black uniforms with gold piping and wearing tall shakos with raven-black plumes that quivered with the horses' gait. Their mounts were tall and spirited, prancing in a double line as they moved down the boulevard. He thought of the showy display of young Sioux braves after a successful hunt, each astride his best mount in full regalia for the tribe to admire. There was something of that same prideful air here among the cavalry troops on the streets of Vienna; they knew their lordly bearing and striking uniforms made them the envy of others.

He had spent the morning on errands for Paul: delivery of two specimens to the Imperial Leopold Academy, checking on the progress of a new hygrometer with special calibrations, acceptance of a bound copy of a lengthy study on woodpeckers by a professor at the university. He had not hurried as he walked about, taking in the new sights and sounds with a keen sense of discovery. *Vienna is so unlike Paris,* Baptiste thought. The splendid regiments left him indifferent; one saw such things on the streets of Paris, too, if less frequently. But the mix

268

of human beings who crowded the streets of the Austrian capital caught his interest. The empire's geographic and ethnic richness was on display among the passersby. National costumes were worn by many—thick embroidered capes by Hungarian tradesmen, fur-lined silk coats and broad-brimmed hats by Bohemian merchants, tasseled caps and broad pantaloons by Illyrian boatmen. Several times he had come across groups of Romany—the Gypsies he had heard so much about—and in their wariness they resembled the raffish groups of Indians he had seen in New Orleans, with the look of outsiders who did not belong in the city.

He also encountered fair and dark skin, red hair and black, Asiatic features and Nordic. Vienna was the only place where his appearance did not instantly identify him as an exotic. Twice he had been greeted by shopkeepers in Russian. When he explained in German that he was not Russian, the shopkeepers inquired no further, as if a well-dressed young man with coppery skin, chiseled features, and blue-gray eyes walked into their shops every day. The release that came with not standing out was a new sensation for Baptiste, and he savored each day in Vienna.

It felt good to be away from Mergentheim. He was staying at the Württemberg Palace, which served the kingdom as embassy, royal residence, and a showplace of Württemberg's importance. "We are part of the German Confederation," Paul had told him, "so it is very important to have a presence in Vienna. There are also strong ties of blood, money, and politics between the Hapsburg family and our own." Theresa had arrived that morning, and Baptiste was returning there now to meet her.

She was waiting for him in an upstairs sitting room, beneath a section of roof set with glass panes that filled the large parlor with light. Baptiste watched her from the open doorway as she sat reading. She looked younger and more serenely content than he had ever seen her. She was certainly more beautiful than when he had first met her four years before. He was happy to see her, anticipating the pleasure of finding an old friend.

Theresa looked up and laughed. "Sneaking up on me like some wild animal, are you? For shame!"

Baptiste sat beside her and told her about his journey, and of his impressions of Vienna. Before long, their conversation turned to Paul and his problems with his wife. Theresa said, "I fear that he will soon be an outsider again."

Baptiste said, "Theresa, I don't think anything you or I can do is going to change things for Paul." Then he told her about his agreement to help Paul with the book and return to St. Louis afterward. She took his right hand in both of hers.

"I am happy for you, Baptiste, though I would like you to stay here forever." Her eyes were sad, but she still managed a smile and caressed his fingers.

Baptiste had not yet imagined what it would mean to leave behind Theresa and the closeness of their friendship, and now it came to him in a wave of emotion as he felt her touch.

She grasped his hand more firmly. "I shall be spending a few days at a friend's country house," she said. Surprise registered on his face. He had thought they would spend the time together, but Theresa had made other plans. Baptiste felt a pang of jealousy, then realized he had no right to be possessive.

"On Tuesday we will have a musical evening at the Esterhazys'," Theresa continued, "and a night together before you return to Württemberg."

Baptiste was grateful that the music would soon eliminate the need to be social. Theresa introduced him to Count Esterhazy and his wife, a tall woman whose jet-black hair stood out against the shimmering red of her dress. Theresa assumed the role of an old acquaintance, providing the details of his provenance and his connections to Paul's household as he was presented to the other guests.

The air was filled with laughter and shouts and good-natured jokes. The feeling was different from that of other parties he had attended in Paris or Berlin or at court in Ludwigsburg. Though the surroundings were sumptuous, the gathering of fifty had a warm glow that reminded Baptiste of the Chouteaus' big parties in St. Louis. All the guests knew one another well, and much of the talk revolved around music. A grand piano dominated one side of the room. Its fall board was open and the ivory glowed in the candlelight. Baptiste leaned down to read the delicate black lettering inscribed on a white ceramic plaque above the keyboard: *CONRAD GRAF, WIEN.*

A tall, courtly man with dark hair, graying at the temples, approached him.

"It is a beautiful instrument, is it not?" He looked at Baptiste through silver-rimmed spectacles, his face full of enthusiasm. "I am Jacob Warburg of Berlin. Do you play?"

"Yes, I do, though I am out of practice." Baptiste stuck out his hand. "Jean-Baptiste Charbonneau of St. Louis."

Warburg grasped it warmly and talked about the joys of the piano. "I have recently acquired a new piano here in Vienna. Mr. Graf expects to finish the cabinet before I leave for Berlin next week. It's the same model as Esterhazy's"—he inclined his head toward the grand piano gleaming in rich tones of light blond wood—"though done in cherry rather than pear." Warburg sipped his wine and said, "What do you do in St. Louis, Monsieur Charbonneau?"

"I am in the fur business," Baptiste said.

"Then you must know Mr. Astor and his associates."

Baptiste was astonished that this stranger in Vienna knew anyone in St. Louis. "Mr. Astor is very seldom in St. Louis, but his partner in the American Fur Company, Mr. Chouteau, is well known to me."

Warburg spoke knowledgeably about the price of pelts, the difficulties in transportation on the Mississippi, the changes in fashion that influenced the fur trade, and a number of details that would likely be known by only a handful of people, even in St. Louis.

Suddenly a glass was tapped loudly, the room grew quiet, and Count Esterhazy strode to the piano. Warburg turned his head and whispered, "I hope we're about to hear that Schubert will favor us with one of his creations. I hear he has been very unwell, alas."

Esterhazy addressed his guests. "My friends, welcome to you all. It has been too long since this house resonated with such gladness, and far too long since new music was heard within these walls. We shall remedy that tonight. Herr Schubert, a dear and cherished friend, has gracefully consented to share with us the first part of the new piece he has been composing." An excited murmur went around the room, and Esterhazy acknowledged the anticipation and continued. "Even Herr Schubert's genius does not permit him to play music intended for four hands, so he will be joined at the keyboard by Princess Theresa von Württemberg."

There was another round of murmurs and nods, then a hush as Theresa walked to the piano, joined by a young man with a florid complexion. She looked radiant in deep green velvet. The man at her side wore a loose-fitting suit of clothes. He coughed and smiled nervously; a thin line of sweat spread along his brow. Theresa whispered something to him, and he turned to address the gathering, peering over the top of his metal-framed eyeglasses. He had a bashful air, and a flush spread across his face as he spoke.

"Princess Theresa begs me to remind you," he began hesitantly, "that she has only this afternoon laid eyes on this music for the first time. I should point out that we are practically in the same situation, since I only scribbled this piece in the last few days." There was laughter. "I depend upon her extraordinary prowess at the keyboard for this first reading."

He took his place to Theresa's left on the long piano bench and organized the sheets of music on the stand. They sat perfectly still for a long moment, Theresa's earrings flashing in the light of the candelabra that graced both ends of the piano. Then they raised their hands to the keys, looked at each other for an instant and, with a barely perceptible nod from Schubert, began to play. Into the utter stillness of the room came forth the deep-toned rhythm of a burbling stream in the bass, balanced almost immediately by a haunting melody in the treble, a repeated series of six notes. Theresa played the melody, which repeated with minor variations that heightened a deep sense of urgency, as if a horn were sounding a call of entreaty across a great and empty plain. There was something poignant in the dying fall of the notes, as they faded and then sounded again. The music grew more elaborate, with ornaments and variations, but the dark refrain never entirely disappeared. The performance profoundly moved those who listened.

Baptiste watched the two faces, side by side, peering urgently at the sheets of music, with a joy that was almost intimate written on their features. Baptiste was delighted by Theresa's authority and quiet exuberance at the keyboard. Her playing was similar to her manner, he realized—confident, clear, and passionate at once. Theresa could be willful, vain, even unreasonable, but here some deeper current was touched and her intelligent generosity brought the music alive.

After several variations on multiple themes, they reached a great climax. The original melody returned with its haunting insistence as the piece closed in a quiet exchange between high and low notes that sounded like a lamentation. Then it was over, and silence descended upon the room. The listeners were spellbound. Theresa kissed her fingertips and brought them to Schubert's cheeks. *"Egregio Maestro!"* she said loudly. Schubert looked like a cherub smiling down from a church wall, he was so pleased at Theresa's praise. Then the room erupted in applause and friends and well-wishers crowded around the piano.

Baptiste watched the other guests surge forward to congratulate Schubert. Several people looked at the pages of music on the piano. Schubert gathered them in a pile protectively and cried, "No, no! It's only the merest sketch so far." Good-natured groans of disappointment and feigned entreaties arose from those around him, but the composer held his sheaf of pages tightly as he talked to friends and acquaintances. Theresa was surrounded by her own coterie of admirers. Warburg had been among those who approached her when the last notes faded, and now he took her hand in his, a look of rapture on his face. She talked with him for several minutes, unwilling to be interrupted.

As he watched Theresa in the brilliant light of the chandeliers, Baptiste felt the nervous unease in his face and neck spread to his chest. His breathing tightened and he felt a deep resentment for Warburg and the courteous air of respect and devotion he exuded. *How dare he?* he thought angrily. *What makes her smile so much?*

Suddenly Theresa crossed the room and stood at his side. "I want you to make the acquaintance of Herr Schubert." She took him by the arm and gently eased through the crowd to where Schubert stood nearby.

"Franz, let me present my special friend from America, Monsieur Jean-Baptiste Charbonneau."

Baptiste extended his hand.

"Good evening to you, Monsieur. Where do you live in America?"

"In St. Louis, sir." A puzzled look crossed Schubert's face. "It's on the Mississippi River, in the Indian Territories." As always, the name of the river sounded peculiar to Baptiste in a German sentence.

Schubert asked Baptiste to repeat the name of the river.

"What kind of a word is that?" Schubert asked.

"It is from the Ojibwa tribe. It means 'River of Waterfalls.'"

"How perfectly poetic. *Mississippi, River of Waterfalls:* it sounds like an ideal title for an opera, doesn't it, Princess?"

Schubert turned to the keyboard and played a series of rhythmic chords in the lower registers as he intoned in a throaty bass-baritone the four syllables of the name that so captivated him. He repeated it several times, establishing a gentle rolling cadence and changing the chord progressions to add drama. Two or three others standing by joined in the slow incantation of the river's name, adding harmony on the last syllable as Schubert rolled and thundered in the bass notes. Then they laughed together amid a smattering of applause.

Schubert looked at Baptiste and asked, "Is that your River of Waterfalls in any of its moods?"

Baptiste was caught up in the playful mood. "That is what it sounds like before a storm," he said as the other guests drew silent in order to hear his words, "but I hope you will see the river for yourself before you write the opera."

"I should like nothing better, I assure you!" Schubert responded. "How I would love to see the New World!"

Then Schubert was borne off in the direction of an adjacent room, where the Esterhazys were holding forth. Theresa remained at Baptiste's side and they had a few minutes of solitude.

"Tell me what you think of our famous Herr Schubert's new piece."

"I've never heard anything like it," Baptiste said. "I don't think I'll ever forget the very beginning—so much feeling in just a few notes."

Theresa closed her eyes. "I adore four hands when the music has substance. It's like flying."

"Just watching you play was like flying," he told her. She inclined her head very slightly as her fingers, still full of energy, touched his hand.

That night, after he and Theresa had fallen asleep in each other's arms, Baptiste dreamed of something he had witnessed in the wilds above the White River before he had met Paul. The images were clear and connected rather than dreamlike, and the scene unfolded just as he remembered it, as if he were watching it happen all over again.

He had ridden out alone before dawn to check a set of traps he and his father had placed three days before along a wooded stream that drained a shallow valley. "Still some beaver left here," his father had said when they had surveyed the stream, and he had been right. Baptiste collected half a dozen decent animals with their full winter coats that would make fine pelts, then assembled his gear and headed his horse out of the bottomlands. The sun was fully up now and the fast-disappearing rime frost sparkled on the scrub brush that covered the undulating prairie. Only patches of mist remained in the hollows. He sat his horse at the top of a rise, taking in the breadth of the land that was his alone to survey, when his horse spooked. Baptiste reined him in hard, the animal's nostrils flaring and ears erect as his flanks quivered. Baptiste felt more than heard a deep galloping vibration. The buffalo herds were nearby, he knew, but this wasn't a mass of animals. Then there came a frantic bleating, a deep guttural growling, and an insistent lowing. From a fold in the hills on the opposite bank of the stream, less than a hundred yards from where he sat, three animals shot into view.

In the lead ran a spring calf, no more than a month old. It had the short reddish coat and long-legged lope of a young buffalo. Ten yards behind, an adult grizzly pursued him at a full run, his form a mass of muscular agility and his quivering coat showing silver tips in the slanting early-morning light. The calf's mother ran close behind the bear, lowering her head to charge with her horns as she approached its flanks. From right to left across the gentle slope they ran through the low brush. The calf drew ahead, then tried to circle back to its mother, its only hope of safety, but the bear cut it off, then turned to face down the cow. The chase began again. On the third try the frantic calf tried once more to race behind the bear, but the grizzly put on an astonishing burst of speed to intercept it. In a single series of fluid movements, it caught the calf's hindquarters with its right forepaw, broke its neck with its left, and wheeled around to face the charging mother at its full height of eight feet. Its forelegs and claws were outstretched and its guard hairs fully extended as it roared in fury, defending its kill in a menacing rage. The cow stopped short five yards from the bear, lowering her head as if she would renew her charge and calling for her calf. Finally the growling bear dropped down on all fours, seized the calf in its jaws, and dragged it down the slope until it disappeared in another fold of the terrain. The cow lowed for a long while in the silence of the early-morning air.

Baptiste woke silently in the dark. Theresa's regular breathing reassured him and he lay unmoving, wondering at the meaning of what he had just relived. It was more vivid than a dream. The cow had certainly fallen behind the herd in order to drop her calf, he reasoned, and once separated, she had not had the means to find the main herd again. Wolves often preyed on stragglers—he had seen it often enough—but for a grizzly to take on an adult buffalo was rare. And his mind returned again and again to the calf trying to circle back to its mother as he watched from the saddle, knowing the inevitable outcome at the first sight of the three animals. Why this all returned to him now with a sharp edge, he could not tell, but he lay awake for a long while thinking of it.

The next morning, Theresa and Baptiste sat at a table in the drawing room of Theresa's apartment, drinking coffee and eating the breakfast that Marie-Claire had brought to them. Her features had the rosy freshness that he found particularly beautiful.

"You will return to Bad Mergentheim today?" Theresa asked.

"Yes, I leave at noon."

He sensed that she had something more to tell him, and he waited. Theresa put down her fork and lowered her eyes. Her hands trembled, but she raised her chin and looked at him with her usual calm and open look.

"*Mon ami,* I wanted you to know that it is unlikely that we shall see each other again before you leave Europe. I have decided to stay in Vienna until October, and then I shall spend the winter in Naples. I do not anticipate returning to Württemberg."

Baptiste was stunned by her words. "Does this have to do with Warburg?"

Theresa's eyes narrowed. "Herr Warburg is a very close friend, but that is not the point," she said. The ticking of an ornate clock on the mantel underscored the stillness in the room. Theresa's features softened and she said in a low voice, "Baptiste, jealousy makes us all ugly."

"I am not jealous," Baptiste stammered. "That is, I do not mean to be."

Theresa continued with more warmth. "Our paths are turning in different directions, as we knew they would. That does not change the fact that I have loved you as much as I have loved anyone in my life. You shall always have a place in my heart, wherever you may be."

As Baptiste realized the plain truth of her words, he was ashamed of his reaction. *This is truly goodbye.* His eyes filled with tears and his heart pounded.

Theresa reached across the table and put her hand on his. "Partings are not easy when they involve those we truly care for. But life is like that. Come and kiss me, and tell me that you will think of me sometimes with affection."

They both rose and he walked around the table and held her for a long while. " 'Neither knife nor ball shall pierce the flesh of him I hold dear,' " he whispered in her ear. "I will never forget that." Then he caressed her cheek with the back of his fingers, the way she liked him to do, and kissed her deeply, breathing in the smell of her hair, her skin, and her breath for the last time.

He turned away, put on his jacket, and walked to the mantel. "When you think of me, you will remember this, too." He reached to the clock's pendulum and stopped its swing with a deft and rapid movement of his hand, as one might catch a butterfly in flight. When he turned, Theresa's face was streaked with tears, but she was smiling. Baptiste made an awkward bow and left.

FORTY

When Baptiste returned from Vienna in late June, he had found Paul in a state of restless agitation. The book, the book, everything came down to the book. He asked hollow questions about Baptiste's time in Vienna, then returned to his projected work schedule for the months ahead.

So it was that the next morning, just after dawn, Baptiste and Paul were at the laboratory worktable, reading notes and examining specimens at a rapid pace. This had gone on through July and August with scarcely a pause, until Paul finished the narrative of his travels in North America. The last chapter included a terse account of his rendezvous with Baptiste at the mouth of the Kansas five years earlier.

"The hog-nosed snake you collected that day seems to be of more interest to you than our meeting," Baptiste said.

"Nonsense!" Paul protested. "I described our meeting at the Curtis & Woods trading post in June earlier in the text! Besides," he added, "*Heterodon simus* has proved to be one of the most unusual snakes in my collection."

They had spent the last part of August checking a myriad of references about which Paul had voiced a doubt: Was the white plumage of a heron its seasonal phase or the feathers of a young bird? Were the tail feathers attached to a Sauk shield those of a golden eagle? Should he properly attribute the war club he had collected in St. Louis to the Omaha or the Pawnee? The questions were endless. Baptiste gave Paul decisive answers in order to cut short the inquiries. Finally, in the last days of August, Paul announced that he could add no more. Herr Thomm was summoned and together the three men went over the final handwritten version, and drank a toast to the book. Then the printer carefully gathered together two trunkloads of papers, listened politely to Paul's entreaties to keep him informed of any questions that arose, and was gone.

Paul's book ended with a short description of the arduous sea journey from New Orleans to Le Havre, and of all the odd effects that his clinical prose worked on events with which Baptiste was familiar, this was the oddest. The endless weeks caught in North Atlantic storms in the dead of winter were reduced to a few oblique references to heavy weather, numerous latitude and longitude readings, a dispassionate mention of some gear lost overboard, and a summation of conditions in the cabin as "exceedingly unpleasant." The descriptions in Paul's book were very often terse to the point of spareness, a style that Baptiste by now recognized as a convention of the scientific accounts of explorations that Paul so yearned to reproduce. Baptiste shuddered. Once more he would have to cross the endless river, this time in order to find his way home.

"We need to talk about my departure, Paul," Baptiste said. "Arrangements need to be made." They had worked together for only a few hours in the late morning, identifying specimens, before a combination of heat, fatigue, and boredom drove them both from the laboratory.

"Yes, yes, of course. I will be spending a few days in Stuttgart, then visiting my wife in Regensburg as she prepares to give birth. We can talk about all that when I return. Herr Thomm plans to have a first proof ready in six weeks, and your participation in the editing will be indispensable," Paul said. "Professor Picard will be visiting in late October, and he is looking forward to seeing you again."

Baptiste held his tongue. He would have to press Paul when he returned from Stuttgart.

While Paul was away, Baptiste heard from Maura; the letter was distressing. Her mother was still weak and in need of assistance, though there was no certain diagnosis. Increasingly she relied on priests and nuns for companionship, and she was spending money constantly, sponsoring Masses, novenas, and even a side chapel in the local church. Maura was torn about leaving, though her mother had told her not to stay. "I think, somehow, she senses our plans, though I have said nothing," Maura wrote. "She reminded me that she ran off with my father—a mad Frenchman, in the eyes of her family—when she was seventeen." She asked if Baptiste knew when he would be leaving for America, and closed with words that gave him hope: "I want nothing more than to go with you. Please remember that."

Soon word arrived that the baby, a boy, had been born early in September. When Paul came home ten days later, he had left his wife and his son, Maximilian, in Regensburg while Sophie recovered from a difficult delivery. Paul was excited as he told Baptiste about his son. "He has his father's eyes, my friend, and a grip as strong as a hawk's!" He walked about the castle and the town with a broad grin, accepting the congratulations of townspeople and servants alike with genuine pleasure. Two weeks later he received a letter from his wife, who was delaying her return with the baby. His happiness began to fade.

"She finds every reason in the world for not bringing Max home," he railed at lunch, brandishing the letter in his hand, "and not one of them valid!" The trip would be too fatiguing; the heat was still oppressive; her mother wanted more time with her grandson. "I shall have to go to Regensburg myself to bring them back."

He left two days later and returned within the week in a splendid coach that Sophie's family had offered for the occasion. Paul and Sophie were like any other parents with their firstborn, basking in the joy and adulation of all those close to them. The first argument arose over the nursery. Sophie insisted on a series of rooms on the second level, but Paul countered that this would require him to move several thousand plant specimens, when adequate space already existed adjacent to their own suite. This rapidly deteriorated into reproachful looks, angry silences, and emotional outbursts. An impasse reigned.

Herr Thomm delivered one hundred copies of Paul's book in the last week of October. Paul was filled with delight, and proud that his account of the expedition was finally in print. Baptiste shared his relief after all their work on the specimens, but the celebrations also meant that his work with Paul was very nearly finished. He had agreed to read it through for errors, but already he knew that Herr Thomm had done a fine job of printing.

Professor Picard arrived a week after the book. After an initial round of hospitality and visiting, he asked Baptiste to show him the collection.

"This is very fine!" Picard exclaimed, picking up a Shawnee leather bag worked with quill and tufts of hair. He looked closely at the stitching and then, replacing it on the table, said softly, "But surely this is the fourth or fifth example of its type I have seen this morning." Turning from the last of the heavily laden tables, Picard shrugged and shook his head. "Why, it is almost unimaginable that a single person is responsible for all this," he said with a wave of his arm that took in more than the room and its contents.

"There are still some boxes that have not been emptied," Baptiste told him.

"Ah, of that I am sure," Picard shot back. He walked to the window, his hands clasped behind his back. "I am of two very different minds when I consider what Paul has brought to Europe from his American travels." He turned now, and though there was more gray in his hair than the last time they had met, his eyes retained their piercing quality. "The richness and variety of objects will add to our understanding of those tribal peoples. However, the fact that Paul has plans for a museum here in Mergentheim makes me wonder if any of these treasures will enrich more than a handful of visitors. Stuttgart itself would be too small to accommodate this bounty. I proposed Paris, but Paul refuses to consider anyplace but here. He means to make his name with his collection while thumbing his nose at his family in their own back-yard. A fatal error, I fear." He returned to sit across the table from Baptiste.

"Have you seen the book yet?" Baptiste asked.

"Yesterday I spent the afternoon going through it." Picard paused, as if considering what tone to adopt. "Baptiste, I shall speak candidly. Paul's capacity for close observation in the wild is impressive. He is best with plants, since that is his specialty. Unfortunately, though, he has chosen the dreariest form possible for his narrative, the chronological journal. I did this, then I did that. I saw this, then I saw that. Is there a more effective soporific known to mankind?" Baptiste couldn't restrain a smile. "Rather more than most," Picard continued, "he places himself at the center of every scene, just like a duke, and the effect is dull."

"Will anyone want to read it?" Baptiste asked.

"It will find an audience in Paris and Vienna and London. A few dozen members of the learned societies, perhaps, will pore over the text and glean what they may. Personally, I would be more interested in the observations of someone less self-important, an account of the tribes seen from the wings rather than from center stage—that is, what people do when they are not being watched."

Picard picked up a carved pipe that lay before him and ran his hand carefully along the elegant stem as if he were searching for the solution to a puzzle. "Life has played a cruel joke on our friend Paul. He is a player on the wrong stage. He will never fit in here, and yet he cannot bring himself to leave. He can only flee and then return, and I am afraid he is bound to be most unhappy for it."

"He talks of returning to the Missouri next spring."

Picard shrugged. "Tell me about your plans, Baptiste. Paul told me you will help with his museum. Can that be so?"

"No, it cannot," Baptiste replied quickly, his anger rising to the surface. He explained the understanding he had with Paul.

"The important thing is that you have decided to leave for your home before the year is out, and so it shall be. Allow me to tell you how pleased I am to hear it. Europe is no place for a young man of your talents."

"But Professor Picard, when I return to St. Louis the likeliest prospect for me is to become a scout or a trapper, a *voyageur* like my father."

"My point exactly! A go-between to Indian tribes and the European world of commerce. Every kind of human knowledge is called upon daily—skill at languages, tact and diplomacy, the ability to read human nature, ease with animals, mastery of one's moods. That man—an intermediary, vanguard, outrider, call him what you will—is the true lord of the earth, far outstripping the overfed worthies who are driven about Europe in coaches to see one another's palaces." This last, Picard spat out with a merciless sarcasm. "You have enjoyed the benefits of European civilization, considerable to be sure—reading, writing, languages, art, music—and yet you need not be shackled to it. You can go back and forth and survive admirably in both milieus. That is most unusual, Baptiste, and it gives you a passage that is unavailable to all but a very few. It is your birthright, and it is precious not only because it is so rare but also because it is so vital."

Baptiste stared at the pipe that lay between them, considering all Picard had said.

Picard continued. "There is, of course, a price to pay for such godlike behavior. You may never fit in entirely on either side of the divide; you are of both worlds but perpetually between them." Picard rose now and walked again to the window. "When you return to St. Louis, you will certainly be associated with the five years you have spent in Europe, and all you have learned here."

For Baptiste the specifics of his departure were still far from clear, and he voiced his concern. "I have been Paul's guest for five years, but now I must go home. How can I convince Paul to take my departure seriously without offending him?"

"Paul must come down to earth. He can be feckless, but he is an honorable man, and there is no reason for him to take offense. He has given his word and he will keep it. I will talk to him and remind him of his duty."

Later that week, Picard and Paul inspected the frescoes in the castle's elaborately decorated chapel. A student of Baroque architecture,

Picard had long wanted to see the renowned interior. They looked overhead to the painted ceiling, a monumental *trompe-l'oeil* sky with an army of saints and faithful ascending into heaven.

"Very sensitively done," Picard said. "But I am reminded of something Baptiste asked when I first met him. 'Why do you paint the ceilings of your churches and palaces to look like the sky when you can just walk outside?' " Both men laughed. "He tells me he is ready to return to America," Picard added.

"He says so, yes. But I think he still has much to learn here."

"Paul, I must object in the most strenuous terms."

"But he has been indispensable to me in the laboratory," Paul countered.

"Come, come, Paul. You must look at this from Baptiste's point of view." Picard's tone was clipped. "What Europe offers him cannot approach the fulfillment of life on the frontier. It is his home. You should know that better than anyone. Don't condemn him to being a specimen in your collection. Let him go!"

Picard's words resonated beneath the illusion of the soaring heavens, filling the tall space until they died in the abiding stillness.

FORTY-ONE

Duke Paul, from his private journal
February 10, 1829
Bad Mergentheim

It is finally over: Sophie and I were separated last week by formal decree. The negotiations have been so lengthy and rancorous that the only emotion I feel is a deep sense of relief. Since my book appeared in November, she has insisted that I give up my research and, as she put it in one of our many violent exchanges, "clear this house of the stinking animal corpses and Indian trinkets." When before Christmas I announced my intention to return to North America to continue my research, she laid down an ultimatum: my marriage or my travels. So began the vengeful discussions that led us to separate.

Although we will remain married, there will be no contact or obligation between us. I shall keep her dowry as well as a sizeable payment in gold. She will raise Max at Regensburg, and I shall have the right to see him once a year. I can now proceed with my work, unimpeded by domestic duties.

I will return to the Missouri River this spring. This time I hope to travel far above Fort Recovery, where the Arikara forced me to turn back five years ago. Baptiste has agreed to act as my guide and interpreter, after which he will remain in America. Though he is keener than ever to return, he agreed to put off our departure until the dissolution of my marriage was settled. Now that he is to leave Europe, I think again of the ways in which Baptiste sees his surroundings differently from us.

I recall when Picard visited in October how we examined together a splendid specimen of *Ardea cayennensis,* a night heron I had collected on the Mississippi. After looking over my notes listing the bird's dimensions, weight, color of plumage, wing beats, and observed behavior, he said in his matter-of-fact way, "You and I closely record every material element but miss the animal's essence. To know that, you must become the bird: live, hunt, eat, even fly with every part of your self that can follow the heron. That, my friend, is simply not a path available to us. Don't you agree?"

Yes and no. There is most certainly a gut instinct for the ways of animals possessed by the likes of Baptiste, and every tribal hunter I have come across, that defies reason or even clear description. But the accretion of detail from close observation, both in nature and in the laboratory, can yield insights that surprise us, and from those insights come ideas about the underlying order of things. That is our path, but I see no reason why it should be separated from the ways of the true hunter. Picard is, after all, something of a sentimentalist. Perhaps it is fairer to say that Baptiste is in many ways an amalgam of the two ways of seeing things. What amazes us Europeans is that he possesses the one skill that cannot be bought, traded for, quickly learned, or otherwise acquired by force of will: know-how in the wilderness.

Only a tiny number of white men are able to penetrate the barrier separating European from Indian ways and live by their wits from the bounty of a seemingly endless expanse. Baptiste has a network of contacts and friends, based on bonds of trust, which allows him to enter this world where the ancient and shifting claims of aboriginal peoples to hunt and to live off the land's fruits still prevail. This capability and the freedom it affords are, it seems to me, fast going out of the world. After the ordeal of these past several months, I look forward to being on the river, the plains, in the mountains, far from the constraints of society and the judgment of others.

Word arrived today through a courtier that His Majesty is very unhappy with his cousin's disgraceful separation from his wife. Wilhelm can go to the devil, for all I care.

A peculiar local matter came my way last week. The chamberlain informed me that the daughter of the garrison's sergeant major is pregnant and claims Baptiste is the father. She has made a nuisance of herself, carrying on at the guard post and insisting on seeing Baptiste. At the chamberlain's suggestion, I dealt with the situation in the usual way: ten pieces of gold to the girl's father and a clear message that any further complication would imperil his position. I see no reason to tell Baptiste, since it is likely a fabrication. Even if true, it is the only peccadillo that has landed on my account in the five years he has been in Europe. Soon I shall be far away from these hopelessly petty concerns.

I had a most welcome letter from Theresa, who is in Berlin and plans on staying there for some time. She is in the company of the banker, Jacob Warburg, whose family has provided funds for many of the new industrial schemes on the Ruhr. She is happy to be away from court life, and enthuses about the excitement of men who, to read her account, are changing the world, financing huge projects, and building on a scale never before seen. Is this the future?

She sends her most tender greetings to Baptiste, and reproves me for keeping him in Europe. Truly, I believe she loves him and knows she will never see him again, something that cannot be easy for either of them. I see now that both she and Picard are concerned for his well-being.

FORTY–TWO

Dear Captain Clark,

I am coming home. Duke Paul has decided to make another trip up the Missouri, and he wants me to accompany him. He is determined to meet the Arikara and the Sioux this time. We sail to New Orleans in the next month or two, so you can expect to see us by midsummer if all goes well.

I cannot rightly tell you just how happy I am to be returning to St. Louis. I have known for some months that it was time, but an enormous sense of relief came over me once the plans were made. Each time it enters my mind that I will soon see the people I have missed for these five years, I grin like a schoolboy. After all my adventures over here, it is strange to think about going back on the river. I know much will be different, but it feels right to be headed to the place I know best.

I celebrated my twenty-fourth birthday last week. As always, I think of you at Fort Mandan with my parents, helping my mother bring me into the world. This year was noteworthy, since I realize I will see you before I turn twenty-five. I have changed quite a bit, but you will know me. This has been my own Corps of Discovery, and the expedition is headed home! I know you understand what that means, and it makes me look forward even more to seeing you again.

Today I watched a hawk work the winds above the hills outside of Mergentheim. He circled and floated, descended and rose. It took him a long while to get above the ridgeline, but when he got there, the updrafts held him steady. I feel like that bird as I look back at the five years I have been here, taking time to get up high enough to have a look at things and know what I am seeing on both sides of the ridgeline.

I was sorry to hear that Mr. Chouteau is so frail. I would like to see my godfather again before he dies and hear him swear at some of my adventures here. Remember me, please, to my father when you see him next, and to your entire family.

Your affectionate,
Pomp

FORTY-THREE

FEBRUARY 1829

The winter sun shone bright upon Paris, bringing no warmth but flooding the streets with a light that gave the gray stone a golden crispness in the clear morning air. Maura had written to Baptiste to ask him to meet her in Paris, saying it was urgent but giving no details save the essentials. He understood that an element of danger was involved. Without revealing her whereabouts, she told him to ask for a message at the Collège des Irlandais.

He inquired at the small grille in the door for a letter for Monsieur Charbonneau, and the same old man passed the envelope through. Baptiste recognized Maura's hand. He mounted his horse and threaded his way through the streets behind the Collège until he was sure no one was following. He stopped at a tavern close to the little church of Saint-Médard, called for a pitcher of cider, and read Maura's note. He was to meet her the next afternoon at the side entrance to Saint-Sulpice. "Tell no one I am in Paris," he read. "I shall explain when we meet."

He was there early, waiting for the bells to ring five o'clock in the evening. When the carillon finally sounded, Baptiste approached the door on the south side of the church, the entrance that Maura had indicated. An old widow, heavily veiled in black, approached the entrance from the opposite direction, but otherwise no one was there. Baptiste wondered if he had misunderstood the instructions, when the widow spoke to him.

"Give me your arm and let us go for a walk, Baptiste."

Baptiste saw Maura's unmistakable features through the thick layer of tulle as she shook her head quickly to silence his questions. She hunched like an elderly woman and shrilly whined, "Can you not carry your old mother's bag?"

She was laughing now, and from beneath the folds of her black cape she produced a large cloth bag. He took it and was surprised at its weight. He wondered how far Maura had walked with her burden. She was fearful of being followed, so they took a circuitous route toward the river while Baptiste kept an eye out for anyone behind. Once they had made their way along the embankment for some distance and only boatmen and freight handlers were in view, she straightened and pulled back the veil. Her face was a mask of worry. Maura explained that she was in Paris to secure certain family valuables they had been forced to leave behind.

"Does your father know you are here?" Baptiste asked.

"No, he does not. But the things I am taking to Ireland are vital to his future and I am the only one who could pass undetected."

"Is that what is in this bag?"

"Yes. Documents, and a quantity of gold and jewels." Maura told him that the letters of some of her father's clients might prove to be extremely compromising when the political climate changed. Very few were willing to be associated with his business in guns, or with his support for political change. To have such evidence in his possession would strengthen his position considerably. "He says the king won't last the year."

They sat on a stone ledge that protruded from the embankment. Maura explained that her situation in Paris was desperate, doubtless because of an informer. The police had searched her aunt's apartment that morning. She had to leave Paris this very night.

"Can I help in any way?" Baptiste asked, concerned.

"Oh, yes, dear Baptiste. That is why I asked you to come."

She asked Baptiste to meet her at a small street near Saint-Sulpice at ten o'clock that night with two of Prince Franz's horses, and travel with her to Honfleur on the Normandy coast. Before then, he had to secure a Württemberg passport that indicated that the two of them were married.

"It's the only way we can travel together without raising suspicion. But hurry. Prince Franz's secretary will know what is called for. He has done this for my father before."

"What will happen then?"

"We have a house outside the town where we will be safe. My father's boats use a cove nearby. One of them will take me across to Ireland."

"It is getting late. Can you not go with me to Prince Franz's?"

"It is too dangerous. Someone is certainly watching the embassy at all times. Don't leave with a riderless horse. Have a servant ride him to our rendezvous." Maura's manner was serious, then her features softened. "I am sorry for all this, Baptiste. I am afraid it has turned into a bit of an intrigue."

"I like intrigue," he responded, bending down to kiss her. "Be careful."

As he turned to go, she added, "We will talk in Honfleur."

That night they rode out of Paris together. At the city wall they were asked for their papers. The sergeant in the guardhouse, unshaven and smelling of wine, looked at them skeptically.

"Württemberg, eh? Where's that?"

"To the east of France," Maura replied in her flawless French. "My uncle is the ambassador."

"Is that where you're both from?" The soldier eyed Baptiste suspiciously.

"My husband is originally from Andalusia, but he is a citizen of Württemberg."

Baptiste inclined his head, saying a few words in Spanish as if to illustrate the truth of her words.

"Why are you traveling so late at night, and by horseback?"

"My mother is very ill, Monsieur. This is much the quickest way to be at her side." Maura stared him down, appearing indignant before his questioning and anxious to be with her sick parent.

"Very well," the sergeant said at last, and stamped the papers. "Keep an eye open for highwaymen two hours north."

They rode for hours on the road to Le Havre and Honfleur, never far from the Seine. The moon was a slender crescent and waning. They had divided the contents of Maura's bag between them. She carried the jewels in a chambered belt beneath her dress, and two large bags of gold pieces were in her saddlebags. Baptiste had divided the sheaf of documents into two and they rode across his saddle in leather game pouches, together with more of the gold.

After four hours of hard riding, they and the horses needed a rest. They chose a town small enough that no garrison would be nearby, then found an inn with an adjacent stable yard. Baptiste pounded insistently on the bolted wooden door until an old man appeared with a lantern, his face fatigued and irritable. Before he had a chance to complain, Baptiste whispered, "There has been a death in my wife's family." He placed two gold coins in the man's hand. "Please make us as comfortable as possible."

The innkeeper became acquiescent and led them to a room at the back of the ground floor.

Baptiste brought in the saddlebags, carrying them past the dying embers of the inn's main hearth. The ample room had two beds pushed together. They put their cloaks over the valuables, then Baptiste looked around uncertainly.

"Maura, if you would rather, I could . . ."

Her eyes were half-shut with tiredness. "We should do our best to sleep."

Fatigue was in his bones. Maura kissed him lightly. "Good night, now. Let us start before midmorning."

She blew out the candle and, a moment later, pulled the covers close. Baptiste undressed in the dark and lay down beside Maura. He pulled her arm close to his chest and listened briefly to her deep, regular breathing before he, too, fell asleep.

On the outskirts of Honfleur the following evening, Maura indicated a road that led southward from the town. After a few miles they took a narrower track that veered away from the coast. Soon they arrived at a large half-timbered house flanked by a small group of farm buildings. The main house was dark, but across the gravel courtyard stood a cottage whose windows showed light. A thick stream of smoke issued from the chimney and gave the still air the smell of apple wood.

"Wait here," Maura said. "I'll make sure there are no visitors."

Baptiste watched from a stand of leafless trees at the edge of the clearing as Maura was welcomed into the cottage. A few minutes later, when he was becoming alarmed, the door swung open and Maura signaled for him to approach. He was introduced to a stocky older man with a bandage wrapped around his head that covered his left ear, and a young woman who was tending a large iron pot over a well-stoked fire. Michel worked for her father, Maura explained, and Lisette was his niece. Michel invited them to share their supper. When they had all eaten a thick fish stew, the girl excused herself.

"I'll see that the house is ready for you," she said, and left.

Maura described the situation to Michel and he rose to leave.

"I will find Ludovic. He will know what boat is available and arrange a rendezvous." He put on his coat and put a revolver in an inside pocket. "I'll be back by morning. Stay here," he said. "As long as you're not seen on the road, you will be safe."

Lisette had prepared two rooms in the house. After Baptiste had put his things in the second bedroom, Maura called him in to where she lay in a large canopied bed. "I am more tired than last night, if that is possible." She sighed. "But I would like it if you slept beside me again."

Baptiste leaned over and placed his arms on either side of Maura's head so that he seemed to float directly above her as he looked into her eyes. "It feels as if we are safe here," he said gently. He bent down and touched his lips lightly to hers. "Try to put Paris behind you."

"We *are* safe," Maura said, her eyes never wavering from his. "And once we've rested, we'll have time for each other." She drew Baptiste's face to hers and kissed him deeply.

In the morning, Michel told Maura that a boat would meet her on a nearby beach at the high tide after midnight in four days. It would be a moonless night. "If a storm comes up, then two nights later," he explained, "but Ludo thinks it will hold fair."

The certainty of Maura's safe departure changed the mood. Lisette brought them fresh eggs, fish, and cream to add to the house's provisions, which included an abundant supply of Jean-François Hennesy's wine. Maura and Baptiste had only to wait, and make the most of their brief time together.

After lunch, Maura went into the bedroom. Baptiste followed soon after and found her sitting on the bed, where she had emptied the contents of the hidden belt.

"I had no time to look at what I was taking in Paris," she explained. "Now I can see what is here."

He sat on a large wooden chest at the foot of the bed and watched her sort dozens of stones on the linen sheet. When she had made six small piles, she looked up, a glint of guilty pleasure in her eyes.

"The sapphires are my favorite," she said, fingering a mound of deep blue gems that glimmered as she stroked them. "But this is worth all the rest combined." Her hand moved to an immense blue stone. As she held it up to the light, it shot off dazzling sparks. "It is a blue diamond, the rarest of the rare," she said, handing it to him.

"But where—" Baptiste began, but Maura interrupted, shaking her head slowly.

"My father has been paid for his services in almost every way imaginable."

Baptiste nodded and handed the stone back. "Far up the Missouri, there is no money. People barter for everything with beads and pieces of glass and other flashy trinkets."

"I hope to see that river with you soon." She smiled at Baptiste's look of surprise. "I have thought of little else since your letter arrived. To leave my parents would be difficult, though I know my father would understand." She turned away. "But to see you go away forever would be worse."

"Then come with me," Baptiste said softly. He saw her shoulders quiver, and he rose and held her. Excitedly, he outlined his plans. Paul and he had booked passage on a ship leaving Bremen in mid-April. It would stop in Bordeaux approximately one week later, depending on the weather, and she could join him then. Maura assured him that Ludovic would have no difficulty in spiriting her into Bordeaux, where her family's contacts were extensive, and she reminded him that the captain of a ship was empowered to marry passengers. Baptiste inclined his head in assent and pulled her into his embrace.

Tears streaked Maura's cheeks, but her eyes were full of delight. "I must make my farewells at home, then I shall meet you in Bordeaux." She kissed him, and they stood and held each other for a long time, swaying imperceptibly as the rhythm of their breathing became one.

That afternoon they made love with passionate deliberation, as if they had both been holding their breath. Baptiste askéd Maura if she was sure, and she whispered back, "I have been waiting for you." He removed her undergarment and saw that she was wearing his eagle talon around her neck, and he bent and kissed her where it hung between her breasts. As she drew him close, he felt her heart beating rapidly. Baptiste encircled her with his arms and, feeling her body accept his embrace, lifted her onto the bed.

Lying beside her, propped up on his elbow, he caressed each of her breasts in turn as he looked in her eyes. Then he moved his hand slowly down across her belly and, waiting for assent and trust in her regard, continued down between her legs until his touch found warmth. He took the time she needed, and when he entered her, she uttered a little cry of surprise and held him closer, her face balancing on the edge of pain and acceptance and joy. Baptiste savored his role as her teacher, conscious of how he had learned that, in this as in so much else, time was the greatest indulgence.

The next days were filled with an easy rhythm of eating, drinking, talking, and lovemaking. When Maura asked him how he felt about leaving Europe, he said, "I have been standing under a waterfall for five years, and now I am about to step outside the stream." Baptiste explained again to Maura that life on the frontier was very rough. "The weather is either too hot or too cold," he told her, "the work is endless, you're alone most of the time, and whites and Indians still tear one another to pieces when things go wrong."

Maura listened patiently to his account but told him that she was unafraid. "I have seen more perhaps than you imagine in travels with my father. Partisans who trade for guns are no strangers to injury and death, nor to rough living. I know that violence and horror are part of life."

Maura had devised a plan to import wine to New Orleans. "Selling wine is a business I am good at. My father will supply me from our vineyards in the Gironde. The greatest fur trade in the world is concentrated in the Mississippi and Missouri river valleys. All those thirsty mouths could do with some more wine." She described the great number of things she would need to set up as a wholesaler, including a suitable warehouse in New Orleans.

"What about delivering guns?" Baptiste was being playful, but Maura took his words seriously.

"That is something," she said evenly, "I prefer to leave behind."

He told her that living in New Orleans was not what he had in mind, but she brushed away his concern. "Just time enough to get the business under way. The trade is all up the river anyway, and from what you told me, the steamboat traffic was reliable when you left. It could only have grown in five years."

Occasionally during those days full of shared purpose and delight, Baptiste walked by himself around the property, taking care to avoid the road. He considered the little farm, surrounded by scrub pines and swampy clearings, and he thought about returning to St. Louis. He smelled the sea nearby, and that seemed an opening from this contained world of roads and villages, cities and châteaux, tended forests and animals in pens. Even at this watery edge of France, he knew, the system of roads and laws and customs all led back to Paris, and in this regard the rest of Europe was far more similar than it was different. Maura, too, seemed to understand that, and to want something else. *Could anyplace be farther from the frontier?* he wondered.

On the night of Maura's departure, they stood on a lightless beach flanked by a marshy inlet as Michel signaled offshore with a hooded lantern. They saw the signal returned, three lights at brief intervals, and they waited until a boat with two men and two pairs of oars materialized from the invisible deep, gliding with a rasp up onto the gravel shore. The dim outline of a larger craft was visible just beyond the mouth of the inlet. Baptiste's concern was written on his face.

"These are my father's men; that is his ship, the *Sans Peur,* the fastest cutter in the Channel. I'll be safe," she told him.

She asked him for his handkerchief, dabbed at her eyes, then put it back in his pocket. Then she kissed him and let herself be helped into the boat. They shoved off immediately, and the black night swallowed them whole. Only the muffled swish of oars suggested for a few more moments that they had been there at all.

The next morning, Baptiste took his handkerchief from his pocket and something dropped to the floor. Thinking it a stray coin, he bent to retrieve it and found beside the chest of drawers a single perfect sapphire, shimmering in the morning light that filled the room.

FORTY-FOUR

MARCH 1829

When Baptiste returned to Württemberg, only a month remained before he and Paul would leave for Bremen. Paul threw himself into the preparations, equipping himself with the latest instruments, buying three new rifles, even having several suits of clothes tailored to his own design for life in the wild.

For Baptiste, too, this was a time of anticipation, but for different reasons. The prospect of his life with Maura was the focus of all his thoughts. He felt a jubilant shiver of delight when he considered how much he had changed from the young man who had stepped off the boat in Le Havre, curious, naïve, and alone.

He confided in Paul, who widened his eyes slightly when he heard Maura's name but listened to Baptiste's plans with composure. "She is a delightful young woman," Paul said. "If Jean-François Hennesy has given his approval, I will certainly do nothing to stand in your way."

Baptiste thought about the five years he had spent in Europe, and of how France still puzzled him. It was a land of a few haves and of many have-nots, impressively organized and often strangely beautiful for what it had built: cities, churches, roads, bridges, dams.

People talked about how much worse things had been under the *ancien régime* before the Revolution, but Baptiste felt that the privileged few in Paul's world still owned and ran everything of consequence. Change was in the air, he reminded himself; the Bourbons would surely fall. But someone else would replace them and the arrangement of power and privilege would renew its hold over this un-wild continent. He wanted to be where these considerations did not prevail, where his own skills and efforts and ties along the broad reaches of the Missouri would determine his future. Beyond sentiment and the ghosts of memory, he longed for the place where his destiny would take its shape.

Baptiste and Paul arrived in Bordeaux aboard the brig *Thuringia* eight days after they had left Bremen. There had been some difficulty in leaving the estuary due to contrary winds, but once they passed into the North Sea, they made good time. Now they were docking in the evening light.

Paul was wild with joy at having left his castle of problems. Since setting off from Württemberg, he had showed a boyish, frenetic energy. Paul wanted Baptiste to join a dinner party he had organized at the hotel where he was staying until they set sail the next day, but Baptiste declined. He wanted to be alone and hoped that Maura would appear. If she was there, she might have learned of the ship's arrival from the harbormaster, he reasoned, and would come to the dock or send word; they had agreed she would find her way to the ship. Baptiste was not surprised when she did not appear, given the late hour, though his mind began to imagine obstacles that would keep her from him. *What if her mother has died? Or could not reconcile herself to Maura's leaving? What if the* Sans Peur *ran into foul weather in the Channel? What if . . .*

That night, he hardly slept. He thought of her flashing eyes and the set of her jaw, of the intimacies they had shared at the house outside of Honfleur, and he knew that she would not waver in her resolve to join him. The urgent softness of her tongue on his chest came to him then most vividly, and the caress of her hand on his neck, and the way she arched her back at the moment of completion—these and a dozen other sensations washed across him and teased him with longing.

He was up early, and he sat in the bow where he had a view of the docks. He watched the reflection of the gradually lightening sky play on the river's current. An hour after he had come on deck, a movement at the corner of his eye caught his attention and caused him to look up. He saw a woman's figure at the far end of the dock, small in the distance but distinct. Her walk was unmistakable: rapid and purposeful.

Everything that mattered was clear in that instant of recognition. They would be Baptiste and Maura, Maura and Baptiste: here on this dock, on the ship, when they set foot on land again in New Orleans, when they made their way up the river together.

Only when he stood did Baptiste realize that he was breathing heavily, that his heart was pounding. His hand moved to his pocket and found there the piece of etched stone, as if it could shelter him with its wings. He looked up to the sun rising above the city's buildings, brightening the estuary on its way to the sea, and thought of home.

Author's Note

Reliable documents show that Jean-Baptiste Charbonneau and Duke Paul met on the Missouri River in 1823, and that Baptiste accompanied Paul upon his return to Europe in early 1824. The record is also clear that together they went back to St. Louis and the Missouri River in 1829. Beyond these two dates, bracketing their time in Europe, very little is known about the five years they shared in Paul's world of privilege. Because he was a lesser member of an important royal family, we have accounts of many of Paul's activities: his phenomenal collection, his continuing fascination with natural history, his arranged marriage and negotiated separation after the couple's son was born.

Baptiste's five years in Europe remain a mystery. His facility with languages alone commands respect: he conversed readily in several unrelated Indian languages, a capacity we tend to underrate since it was not unique on the frontier. Add to that his use of English, French, Spanish, and German and his circumstances suggest someone with an uncommon ability to flourish at those shifting points where peoples and customs meet, overlap, and sometimes collide. To return to the frontier after five years in Europe was a clear choice, one that proceeded from a direct knowledge of several extremely different ways of life. In Baptiste's case, these included the Mandan tribal villages with their warrior ethos, the river-borne *voyageur* culture of trappers and the fur trade, the strange bubble world of a small court in post-Napoleonic Europe, and the free-form network of European scientists and collectors who gathered facts and artifacts and often shared them avidly.

Baptiste/Pompy was singularly well equipped to fashion an "in-between" path—what the French call an *"entre-deux"*—from among the many he knew early in life. In this he showed a capacity to invent himself that came to be regarded in the nineteenth century as a strikingly American trait. If he captures our imagination—and he has mine—surely it is because he showed himself equal to the extraordinary possibilities that came his way. How and why he did so, we can only guess. I have imagined the other principal characters—Theresa, Maura, Prince Franz, Professor Picard—as composites of those who would have been in Paul's social ambit. While Paul did in fact have an uncle who lived in Paris (inconveniently enough, also named Paul), I have invented the particulars of Prince Franz, who should not be confused with his real counterpart.

So much has been written about Sacagawea—and so much of it is based on pure conjecture—that it is useful to state a few assumptions, even in a work of fiction. Alternate spellings exist for many Indian words; I have opted for "Sacagawea" as the nearest approximation in English of a name about which there can never be certainty. In like manner, I have preferred Clark's own transliteration of what we assume was Baptiste's tribal name—"Pompy"—to the frequently seen alternative, "Pompey." The premise of Sacagawea's death in 1812 is disputed by some, but it remains the prevailing view. I have integrated it as fact and used it as an important element in the story of Baptiste's early years.

Finally, while I have invented the gathering at the Esterhazy home in Vienna at which Schubert plays his new composition with Theresa, there are several accounts of his playing at similar gatherings well into the summer of 1828. One of history's strange secrets is how such a protean talent, already suffering from the illness that would take his life by November, could have remained so active, and prolific, until the end. I had constantly in mind Schubert's extraordinary "Fantasy in F Minor for Four Hands" when I imagined this interval.

Any factual errors or inconsistencies are my responsibility.

Thad Carhart
Paris, September 2009

Acknowledgments

I am most grateful to Marion Abbott Bundy for her wisdom, insight, and good humor as she helped me shape numberless drafts into the story I wanted to tell. My wife, Simo Neri, offered attentive readings, pithy ideas, and unwavering support throughout the process. The manuscript also benefited mightily from Jane Cavolina's meticulous and exacting edit. My agent, Eric Simonoff, patiently suggested changes that always improved matters, and Charlie Conrad, my editor at Doubleday, helped the book take form with both discernment and wit.

My thanks to those who read drafts and gave comments: Lorna Lyons, Lisiane Droal, Bonnie and Judd Carhart, Nicolas Carhart, Joni Beemsterboer, Elise White, Sophie Lambert, and Judy Hooper. Many others offered support and advice along the way: Robert Wallace, Claire Miquel, Richard Dolan and Marilyn Go, Chris Loether, Jürgen Tredup, Mark Illeman, and Stéphane Jardin.

The staff members of many institutions were helpful as I consulted their materials: the Linden-Museum, the Muséum d'Histoire naturelle, the Musée Carnavalet, the Centre Culturel Irlandais (current occupant of the Collège des Irlandais premises), the Bibliothèque Nationale de France, The American Library in Paris, Sterling Memorial

Library at Yale, Schloss Ludwigsburg, and the Deutschordensmuseum at Schloss Mergentheim.

I am indebted to Erica Funkhouser for her gripping and lyrical poem "Birdwoman." It made me see the person buried in the myth of Sacagawea, and gave me courage to imagine my own account.